POOR HARRIET

Marianne knows that the bu
trouble, so she isn't surprised ....,
Irma, asks her to do a little favor for her—take her
diamond bracelet to a man who will give her money for it.
But when she confronts Mr. Moran, he seems a bit shifty
to her. And Moran's wife, Harriet, seems to be an even
odder character. After leaving, Marianne discovers that
one of them stole the bracelet from her, so she returns
and confronts Moran. He takes her to Harriet, and all
seems well when she gets the bracelet back. But Moran
decides that the bracelet should be his after all—he
knows Irma all too well, and figures she owes him a
diamond bracelet at least. Now it's Harriet's mission to
get it back.

THE SILENT COUSIN

Paul—Dr. Potter—has come back to Long Acre, back to his
cousins Millicent and Louise, back to Aunt Cora and
MacDonald. Back to the family estate, where nothing has
changed. But this time, there is a death. Mrs. MacDonald
is found dead on her bedroom floor. And later, Uncle
Humphrey drowns in his fishing pond. Change is in the
air. But is it a change that the cousins can control?
Millicent has some definite ideas about what needs to
happen to the estate, but now they have been "invaded" by
a young outsider, the son of the other half of the family,
who has some ideas of his own. Paul feels the world
shifting about him. Old passions rise back to the surface.
Change may come to Long Acre, but it brings with it—
death.

Elizabeth Fenwick Bibliography (1916-1996)

Mysteries:

The Inconvenient Corpse (1943; as E. P. Fenwick)
Murder in Haste (1944; as E. P. Fenwick)
Two Names For Death (1945; as E. P. Fenwick)
Poor Harriet (1957)
A Long Way Down (1959)
A Night Run (1961)
A Friend of Mary Rose (1961)
The Silent Cousin (1962)
The Make-Believe Man (1963)
The Passenger (1967)
Disturbance on Berry Hill (1968)
Goodbye, Aunt Elva (1968)
Impeccable People (1971)
The Last of Lysandra (1973)

Mainstream Novels:

The Long Wing (1947)
Afterwards (1950)
Days of Plenty (1956)

Children's:

Cockleberry Castle (1963)

POOR HARRIET
THE SILENT COUSIN

Two Novels by
Elizabeth Fenwick

Introduction by Curtis Evans

STARK
HOUSE

Stark House Press • Eureka California

POOR HARRIET / THE SILENT COUSIN

Published by Stark House Press
1315 H Street
Eureka, CA 95501, USA
griffinskye3@sbcglobal.net
www.starkhousepress.com

POOR HARRIET
Originally published by Harper & Brothers, New York, 1957; and
Gollancz, London, 1958; and copyright © 1957 by Elizabeth Fenwick Way.
Copyright renewed November 20, 1985 by Elizabeth Fenwick Way.

THE SILENT COUSIN
Originally published by Gollancz, London, 1962; and Atheneum, New
York, 1966; and copyright © 1962 by Elizabeth Fenwick Way.

"Silence is Terrifying" © 2024 by Curtis Evans

ISBN: 979-8-88601-076-3

Cover design by Jeff Vorzimmer, ¡caliente!design, Austin, Texas
Text design by Mark Shepard, shepgraphics.com
Cover art by Tom Lovell
Proofreading by Bill Kelly

First Stark House Press Edition: February 2024

Silence is Terrifying
Elizabeth Fenwick's *Poor Harriet* and *The Silent Cousin*

• •

By Curtis Evans

In 1950, after several months spent at the Yaddo artists' and writers' colony in upstate New York, Elizabeth Fenwick (1916-1996) published her second mainstream novel, *Afterwards*. Six years would pass before Fenwick produced her next novel, another mainstream work entitled *Days of Plenty*. 1950 had ushered in not only Fenwick's second mainstream novel but also her second marriage, to publisher and printer David Jacques Way, and the birth of her only child, a daughter named Deborah. For Fenwick the next six years, spent with her small family in New York and Connecticut (and back to New York again), would be filled with the challenging dual jobs of child raising and husband managing, David Way proving to be a very difficult man with whom to live. In 1957, however, Fenwick quickly followed *Days of Plenty* with a crime novel, *Poor Harriet*. Published as a "Novel of Suspense" by Harper & Brothers, the book was extremely well-received and, perhaps better yet, actually made some money, with the result that seven more suspense novels would follow from Fenwick's hand over the next eleven years. A writing career finally had been successfully launched by the author, who had now entered her forties.

In a 1960 letter famed author Flannery O'Connor, who had befriended Fenwick at Yaddo, stated that her friend wrote mystery novels to "make money," alternating them with novels written "to suit herself." After the comparative success of *Poor Harriet*, however, Fenwick never again wrote another "straight" novel. It is likely that writing novelistic tales of crime and suspense came to "suit" her too, allowing her to draw therapeutically on difficulties in her own life, and that writing thrillers was not simply about the money.

Certainly *Poor Harriet* suited the critics, who gave the novel one of the warmest embraces ever afforded a criminal fictional "debut." (Aside from Anthony Boucher, they had forgotten about a trio of detective novels Fenwick has published under the sexually ambiguous name "E. P. Fenwick" in the early 1940s.) For example, the great novelist Margaret Millar declared, in a sentence both penetrating and pithy, that Fenwick's debut thriller had "some of the most macabre mood writing since the Gothic tale looked under the bed and found Freud." Prominent male critics of the day agreed with Millar. Anthony Boucher deemed *Poor Harriet* "the work of a highly skilled novelist," while James Sandoe proclaimed it "an astonishing evocation." In Britian, Julian Symons praised the novel's "fine nightmarish quality" that kept the reader on the edge of the chair, while Michael Gilbert declared: "The technique is brilliant." The Book-of-the-Month Club News advanced Fenwick as a literary successor to the late Josephine Tey.

Flannery O'Connor joined in this admiring chorus as well. Writing Fenwick on August 4, 1957, a few days before the novel was officially published, from her isolated country home outside Milledgeville, Georgia, where she resided with her elderly mother, O'Connor wrote praisefully (and amusingly) of *Poor Harriet*: "Well cheers for *Poor Harriet*! I enjoyed her and also my mamma enjoyed her and I must say you are lucky on your [book] jackets.... I have never read anybody else's mystery stories... . My mother read *Poor Harriet* straight through and kept saying, 'Well I just don't see how she figured all this out, I just couldn't do it.'"

What greatly impressed many of the critics about *Poor Harriet* was the novel's sensitive depiction of mental aberration, which is also powerfully captured in the striking cover illustration (by esteemed graphic designers Arline Simon and Marvin Oberman) of the titular, elderly black-cloaked character with her haunted, staring pale blue eyes—surely one of the finest crime fiction covers of the Fifties. The short, gripping novel follows the dire events which occur after Marianne Hinkley, loyal office manager for Bryce Builders, a Connecticut contracting firm owned by likable if haphazard Tom Bryce, embarks on an errand in New York City on behalf of Irma, Bryce's demanding, high-maintenance wife. Having surreptitiously suffered financial reverses on the market, Irma tasks the reluctantly obliging Marianne with selling—to a certain shifty man by the name of Moran—the fabulous diamond bracelet which Tom recently gave her. In New York Marianne encounters not only Mr. Moran, but a woman whom he introduces as his wife: an odd, shyly quiet creature called Harriet. This meeting sets in motion a succession of terrible events which culminate in violent death and other calamities.

Poor Harriet is an excellent fifties suspense novel filled with interesting characters, atmospheric writing and a page turning plot, the sort of work only an exceptionally fine hand can fashion. Flannery O'Connor's mamma got it right. It also movingly depicts—especially for those aware of the physical and mental maltreatment which Fenwick for years endured at the hands of her egocentric, rageful second husband (see my introduction to Stark House's previous Fenwick twofer and forthcoming *Crimereads* article)—the crime of domestic abuse.

■ ■ ■

Elizabeth Fenwick's crime novel *The Silent Cousin* was published five years later in 1962 in the United Kingdom by the author's steadfast British publisher Gollancz. It did not appear in the United States until 1966, after it had been picked up by another, smaller publisher than Harper, Atheneum. Although *The Silent Cousin* was published during the mid-twentieth century, the events in it take place on a grand Hudson Valley, New York estate constructed during the American Gilded Age— a grand setting for a tale which memorably harks back to the old Gothic tradition in Ango-American mystery literature.

There are at least four houses on the estate: the massive Long Acre, where no one actually lives; the Hall, where reside the remnants of the Onderdonk family; the farmhouse, home of Onderdonk estate manager MacDonald and his family; and, lastly, a cottage which serves as the dwelling of an Onderdonk academic demi-relation, Professor Paul Potter, when he visits the estate in the summer, on vacation from his university post in Indiana.

Like a Victorian Gothic novel, *The Silent Cousin* could have used a family tree; and I have appended one below. While reading it, I drew the tree in my copy of the book at the heading of Chapter Five. The starred characters are still alive—for the moment—when the novel opens.

Grandfather Onderdonk, who built Long Acre in the 1890s and with his wife **Millicent I**, had three children:
Millicent 2, the second wife of Paul Potter's father and the stepmother to ***Paul "Polly" Potter** (36), who married
   ***Vinnie**, from whom he is estranged when the novel begins, and produced a daughter ***Cressa** (8), who comes to visit him at the Estate
***Humphrey Onderdonk** who married *Cora and had two daughters, both of whom are unmarried, these being ***Millicent 3, aka Millie** (40) and ***Louisa** (38)
John who moved to Chicago and by *one of his several successive wives fathered a *daughter who married a man named Watson and with him produced ***John Onderdonk Watson** (22), who comes to visit the Estate
And let us not forget the aforementioned estate manager,
   ***MacDonald**, who took a wife and with her produced ***Jenny**, who married ***Pete**.

When the novel opens Paul Potter is staying at the cottage expecting the imminent arrival of his daughter Cressa. There he learns of the sudden demise of Mrs. MacDonald, a death which was unexpected, although the woman had been ailing. Soon another character is found dead in the estate's fishpond (now there is a classic death for you) and we are off to the murder races.

I do not know that I would call *The Silent Cousin* leisurely, as it is, like Fenwick's other crime novels, quite short (about 60,000 words); but it builds subtly to a tremendous climax, like something out of Shakesperean tragedy, giving us a chance to immerse ourselves in the characters, as seen through the eyes of the contemplative not-quite-relation Paul. As her publisher Gollancz insightfully put it: "[Fenwick] creates a deep feeling of suspense, of something unpredictable about to happen, by means of a progression of exactly placed and beautifully judged hints—tiny eddies on the otherwise placid surface, which disturbingly suggest the cross-currents beneath." The central dramatic situation is that the family money is tied up in in a trust which maintains the estate while effectively keeps the remaining Onderdonks wards of that estate. It is rather like the situation in S. S. Van Dine's serial murder classic *The Greene Murder Case*, but the climax may remind you more of Edgar Allan Poe (specifically a short story which shall go unmentioned here).

It seems obvious to me that Fenwick based the Onderdonk estate on Yaddo, the artists' retreat outside Saratoga Springs, New York, where she spent the summer of 1948 working on her second mainstream novel. As mentioned above, this is where she met, and became lifelong friends with, writer Flannery O'Connor, who in her own fiction writing herself could do some mean Gothic. The great mansion at Yaddo was built by Spencer and Katrina Trask, an ill-starred couple who after losing all four of their children at young ages, bequeathed their home to a foundation with the purpose of succoring creative artists.

The name Onderdonk, I would hazard to guess, Fenwick derived from the Onderdonks of Texas, another distinguished artistic family. Julian Onderdonk, known as the father of Texas painting, was a prominent impressionist painter who died in 1922 in San Antonio, where Elizabeth Fenwick would graduate from Jefferson High School a dozen years later. Of course Onderdonk is a grand old Dutch name and there were Onderdonks in New York, the setting of *The Silent Cousin*. (Onderdonks resided at the state's oldest surviving Dutch fieldstone house, now a museum.) However, I feel sure that when Fenwick wrote the novel she thought back to that distinguished Texas branch of the family. Onderdonk paintings graced the walls of the White House when George W. Bush occupied the American presidency.

It was at Jefferson High School, by the by, that Elizabeth Fenwick, then known rather less grandly as Betty Phillips, revealed an early literary bent, winning the state poetry contest two years in a row. In high school she belonged to the Scribblers, the Poetry Club and the Quill and Scroll, the high school honors society for student journalists.

The author's intelligence and sensitivity infuses the Fenwick novels. I have mentioned Van Dine and Poe and I should also mention Shirley Jackson, whose great Gothic novel *We Have Always Lived in the Castle* appeared the same year as *The Silent Cousin* was published in England. Certainly a criminal coincidence, that! Fenwick's Long Acre also could be said to bear resemblance to Jackson's Hill House, the titular haunted dwelling in her most famous novel. There is as well a clever reference to a certain Dorothy L. Sayers detective story, but I shall leave you, dear readers, to spot this for yourselves.

Why Harper passed on *The Silent Cousin* is truly beyond me, unless it was deemed too slow burning for editor Joan Kahn, who was known to be quite cutting in her judgments. Kahn also gave fits to crime writer Patricia Highsmith (another Yaddo guest, incidentally), who eventually left Harper in a huff. As mentioned above, *Cousin* finally appeared four years later in the U. S. with Atheneum, who also published Eric Ambler and P. M. Hubbard, the latter author another great exponent of psychological unease to whom Fenwick bears some resemblance. Personally, I think Joan Kahn's pass on *The Silent Cousin* reflects much more poorly on her than it does on Fenwick. Both it and *Poor Harriet* are among her finest works and, as such, notable contributions to the fine art of mid-century suspense.

—November 2023
Memphis, TN

Curtis Evans received a PhD in American history in 1998. He is the author of *Masters of the "Humdrum" Mystery: Cecil John Charles Street, Freeman Wills Crofts, Alfred Walter Stewart and British Detective Fiction, 1920-1961* (2012), *Clues and Corpses: The Detective Fiction and Mystery Criticism of Todd Downing* (2013), *The Spectrum of English Murder: The Detective Fiction of Henry Lancelot Aubrey-Fletcher and G. D. H. and Margaret Cole* (2015) and editor of the Edgar nominated *Murder in the Closet: Essays on Queer Clues in Crime Fiction Before Stonewall* (2017). He writes about vintage crime fiction at his blog The Passing Tramp and at Crimereads.

POOR HARRIET

Elizabeth Fenwick

CHAPTER ONE

Snow, expensive snow, was falling lavish and free outside the office windows, and Marianne Hinkley (Mrs. Henry) sat and watched it. She was alone. All the rest of the personnel of Bryce Builders were miles away, stopping work, dispersing under the sudden smother of white snow. The part of Bryce Builders that never stopped was here with her: its sad ledgers, mountainous bills, and mysterious invoices.

She was usually alone. The office of Bryce Builders, in a small frame building over Root's Liquor Store on the main street of Willett, Connecticut, had become like the budget worries entirely hers. She had long ago given it curtains and a hotplate in acceptance of that fact. Tom Bryce was in and out (Irma Bryce too, alas, more often than she should be) but this domain of paper records was Marianne's. And the nightmares that went with it.

Tom Bryce had once said to her (he had a reputation for frankness, and never let anything pass without discussion), "If money scared me like it does you, Marianne, I would never have got started. I wouldn't be in business now. And maybe if I sat and kept track like you do, I'd get scared—so that's why I don't do it. Besides, you know that the real story isn't in those books. It's in here," he said, knocking his head, "and out there."

And he pointed out the window, presumably toward Chester Park, that hadn't begun to pay for itself yet, or to the new development going up on the proceeds of Chester Park.

What he said was true, of course; but what Marianne's ledgers told her had equal truth, and he knew that. Sometimes she thought he counted on her worrying, useless though it was. Counted on her worrying, and pitied her for it. Well, that was all right. There were things she pitied him for, areas where he was just as helpless as she with her worrying. About Irma, specifically. But they never spoke of that.

Marianne had times of rebellion. She was having one now, and the snow had begun it—the snow she loved and found too rare as a private person, as Mrs. Henry Hinkley. But the ledgers would say this was the third heavy snow this winter, and February hardly begun, and they had better not have much more of it.

An echo of Tom Bryce (expurgated) went through her mind: "To hell with what the books say!" She allowed the echo to linger, and watched the snow covering Willett. Down in the narrow street, a powder-blue-and-cream hardtop Buick was slashing its way around the big trucks parked for deliveries. That was Irma. Irma, she hoped, passing by.

She watched the blue car's approach, beginning to generate horsepower within herself to make it keep going—don't slow, don't stop. It didn't slow down; but abruptly, finally, and right under her window, it did stop. Well, there was still the grocery store across the street. Presumably

Irma did market, at some time or other.

The blue door opened and a small, furred boot appeared. A mink coat edge fell out upon the snow, was snatched up and brushed hard by a light-gloved hand. The hand impatiently shaken.

"Got her glove dirty," thought Marianne, morose. Six ninety-five a pair, and bought by the dozen. The department store bills came here too.

All at once—because of the department store bills, because of the gloves, because of the snow—Marianne's rebellion rose to bursting point. Why should she care that Irma cost as much as six months of snow? She didn't care. She wouldn't care, any longer.

The downstairs door slammed and Irma's boots tapped up the stairs. Let her come. Let her take away everything there was, or wasn't, to be taken. It wasn't Hinkley money. It wasn't, frankly, money at all.

Yet when Irma appeared and stood looking into the room, Marianne's old impulse rose up strong as always—to bend closer over her books and papers, to conceal, shelter, and protect them.

She did not, of course, do any such thing; but she felt Irma to be perfectly well aware of her impulse. Irma always waited a moment in the doorway, as if to let Marianne get hold of herself. Then she came calmly forward, and took Marianne's visitor chair.

She was just about Marianne's age and size—thirty, small. Not, perhaps, quite so plump. The word for Irma would probably be rounded. There, resemblance ended. It was not just that Irma was dark and self-possessed and Marianne neither of these things. Without quite understanding what the difference was, Marianne had come to think of it in terms of dimples. She had one, too—Henry said so. But Irma had two, deep and steady and entirely under her control. She didn't bother to produce them now, but said only, "Good morning, Marianne."

Everybody else in Willett said, "Mary Ann," but Irma knew better. Also, "Irma" was supposed to be pronounced "Eerma" (Tom Bryce had explained), but luckily she preferred to be called "Mrs. Bryce." There had been a lot of these little things to struggle with in the beginning, but they had soon got past them into solider dislike.

They sat grounded in it now—Marianne less open and therefore less comfortable.

"I'm interrupting you while you save the business, I suppose," said Irma, arranging her coat around her. "No, of course I am—it's a waste of your time and mine for me to have to keep coming here this way. I don't like it any better than you do. Living out of the cash drawer, like a little storekeeper," she said, considering Marianne (Hinkley's Hardware Store).

"Well, he's always done it, Mrs. Bryce. He's usually needed to," said Marianne, calm in the knowledge of three separate Hinkley accounts.

"He hasn't always been married," said Irma sharply. She allowed time for Marianne to finish this in her mind—and better for him, too—before reproving her. "However, that's not really your concern. What I'm here about today, of course, is money. I need some. Rather a lot."

"How much, Mrs. Bryce?"

When Irma replied, "A thousand—in cash," Marianne looked at her almost in gratitude. It wasn't remotely possible. She said so.

"I don't think Mr. Bryce could raise it himself just now—even if I knew where to get hold of him before the banks close. And it's Friday, you know."

"I know," said Irma. "I've thought of these things."

She was quiet, allowing Marianne to think of them too ... who presently, uneasily asked, "Then what is it you want me to do?" At once, Irma opened her bag.

"I think there's only one thing to do," she said. "I'll have to sell some jewelry. This piece."

She put across the desk at careful length a bracelet of clear stones. Marianne knew at once what it was: it was the difference between single- and double-brick facing in Morgantown Acres. She remembered the bill very well, but she had not seen the bracelet before and leaned now, with interest, to examine it.

In snow light the diamonds had cold depth, heaviness. With one fingertip she drew the bracelet under her desk lamp, and that little journey astounded her. Brilliant color exploded all along the moving length, so quick and myriad she could not tell which stones had caused it.

She drew a long breath ... and heard another such breath exhaled. She looked up and saw Irma's eyes fixed on the bracelet. Her expression was private and perfectly genuine, the first of its sort that she had ever shown.

In their first moment of sympathy, Marianne said, "It's very lovely, Mrs. Bryce."

"Yes. I can get a thousand on that, easily."

"But it's worth much more than—"

"I know that," said Irma. "I know it! I also know that if I keep it my husband will find the money for me somewhere, somehow. And you know how much good that would do him, just now."

"Well," said Marianne, "it would have to be some personal loan, I'm afraid."

"Exactly. And since it's perfectly well known how he manages, he might just as well put an ad in the paper that he's come to the end of his rope. Don't you suppose I understand these things?"

Clearly, she did. Marianne understood that she herself was being competently surrounded. She leaned back, away from the bracelet and Irma too.

"If you mean that you want me to help you sell it, I can't. I'm sorry, but I don't know a thing in the world about selling jewelry."

"You don't need to," said Irma. "There's a man in New York who'll buy this in a minute, and give cash. At least as much as I want, probably more. You'd certainly ask more—you can come down if you have to. And

I'll give you fifty per cent of anything over."

She seemed genuinely surprised when Marianne refused. Then she became exasperated.

"Why not? Why on earth shouldn't you? This man won't know or care who you are—you can give any name you like! You're obviously a respectable girl, and the bracelet is obviously worth more than you want. That's all there is to it."

"He sounds like a fence," said Marianne bluntly ... and saw sudden rage in Irma's black eyes.

"He's nothing of the sort. Do you suppose I know such people?" Tart, but controlled, she went on, "A lot of women make foolish mistakes, at some time or other, and if they have jewelry to sell somebody makes a profit from their foolishness. There's no need to be naïve about it. This man's an acquaintance of ours, so I can't go to him myself—it would be just the same as if Tom went out and borrowed the money. But you can go, and earn a nice sum of money for yourself without any trouble, incidentally. There's no reason why you shouldn't."

She was certainly detached about it. The "foolish mistakes" should, from her tone, have been those of another woman—a foolish woman, unlike Irma. Yet she was speaking of herself. What on earth could she have done?

Marianne struggled against curiosity, which seemed ungenerous at the moment. But she would have thought foolishness and Irma to be worlds apart; she could not imagine Irma, so cool, so competent ... And yet, as she thought this, imagination stirred with her; and all at once she *could* imagine the sort of downfall Irma would invite. Not a man. Nothing so warm. No; something to do with greed, with overreaching— and with underestimating those whom she reached across, to take what she wanted. As she underestimated Tom, and made no secret of doing. As, perhaps, she was underestimating Marianne now.

"Well?" said Irma.

Caught, flushing with embarrassment, Marianne replied at random, "I—I don't see what difference it makes, if he knows you. He must have to be discreet, to be in that business."

"Gossip is discreet," said Irma, contemptuous. "And men are gossips— just as much as women. More; because basically they're less serious." And her dark eyes, entirely serious, remained fixed on Marianne's rounded blue ones.

"Listen, Marianne," she said. She sounded almost companionable. "I know how you feel about Tom's finances. It's natural. You've been watching over them for ten years, they probably seem more yours than your husband's. And I know how you feel about the expenses he's had this past year, since we've been married."

"Well, as you say, that's not really my concern," Marianne murmured.

"Oh, of course it is. I admit they've been heavy—which shouldn't matter, if he didn't spread himself out so wide. Actually he spends as much on what he wants as I do—only what Tom spends somehow passes for business. Isn't that right?"

It was one way of putting it. One that Marianne hadn't thought of before.

"Only with two of us, it shows more," Irma added; and Marianne could agree to that. "I know it. And I also know you feel more sympathetic to Tom's extravagance than to mine. All right," she said, "then let's be frank about it. I'm in a hole. If you go down and get this money for me, it's the last large sum I'll be needing until—well, say until Chester Park is sold out. How would that be?"

She was offering a bargain. Tom Bryce's wife was offering to leave Tom Bryce's money alone for a while, in return for … services. Appalled, offended, Marianne stared at her. It was true that both Hinkleys, New England small-town bred, had bargaining in their bones: bargaining leisurely and close, that in the end allowed some advantage to both sides. But what advantage could there be in this for *her* side?

There was none. Yet she cautiously, almost automatically, began to murmur, "Well, selling out Chester Park isn't going to solve a great deal. The new development …"

"All right, then. Set your own time limit—but make it a possible one! None of this until-the-books-balance. They never will, and you know it as well as I do. They never did."

It was perfectly true. And yet—and yet—what a world of relief it would be, to have *only* the business debts piling up. Almost peace, almost solvency.

She was aware of having made no decision until, startlingly, Irma's deep dimples suddenly appeared.

Quite calmly she said, "Good, then", and pushed the bracelet farther from her. "Now, I'll send a telegram making your appointment tonight— that's all you need. And there's the man's address."

Henry was out of the store when Marianne called up, his cousin Morrie answered. Morrie could be counted on to obscure the clearest message, and hers was as vague as she dared make it. The time for Henry to know what she was up to was after she got back. Then she would tell him.

They had never been able to agree about Tom Bryce or her own duties for Bryce Builders—not in the seven years of their engagement nor the one-and-a-half years of their marriage. But Henry was fair in disagreement, as in everything else, and they had been able to discuss it without division for almost the whole nine years.

Henry couldn't really see what she owed Tom Bryce.

"A good girl was hard to get back there in forty-five," he said. "Anybody was, green or not. Specially for an outfit like that. And if he pays you good on paper, what you actually make isn't so special. Not for what you have to do."

"But I've got that stock! And besides, even if that never works out, I've got him too much on my mind to walk out and just not care. It's the way

I'd feel about anybody after ten hard years pulling together, you would yourself, Henry. Maybe it's not reasonable, but there it is."

Henry could see it, and he was a reasonable man.

But there was a limit to Henry's sympathetic vision, and with the new Mrs. Bryce they had just about reached that limit. She hadn't dared to tell Henry everything. She didn't like to think of it herself. Of the desperate times, for instance, when she had been reduced to going through Tom Bryce's desk ... even his pockets ... for bills that would otherwise pile up till he found them himself. There was something about Tom Bryce that made people take that kind of responsibility for him; she wasn't the only one. But she wasn't the only one to be getting a little tired, either.

In those ten years—in less, she and Henry had got the hardware store on its feet, his mother's illness paid for, Marianne's brother through school. But Tom Bryce, as Henry pointed out, was right there in the same muddle he'd always been in.

"It's just bigger," he said. "Maybe that makes it worthwhile for him. I can't see it does much for you, Mary Ann."

Henry was right. She wasn't really disagreeing with him any longer, she just couldn't bring herself to quit. And on the train to New York, staring out through her snowy window on fading wintry light, it occurred to Marianne that perhaps this was what she expected from her side of the bargain: to get free. To snap Henry's patience at last, by this final outrageous service, so he wouldn't *hear* of her going on! Surprised by her own sharpness, a little gratified too, she began to hope she might do as well with Irma's diamond buyer.

CHAPTER TWO

Irma had sent a telegram from the office, making an appointment. Marianne was late to that. Thrift and caution had seized her in Grand Central Station, and she had lost a lot of time wandering around looking for a subway that would take her to the West Seventies.

Even when she managed to find it, and to leave it at approximately the right street, it turned out there was a long way west to walk. In growing discomfort, and some fright, she just about decided to take a taxi all the way back.

It was dark by now, no longer snowing (not here, at least), and bitterly cold. The farther she went down the long blocks, the more darkness and loneliness accrued. House numbers were hard to find. The stone houses were narrow and close-pressed, as if to deny individuality like a guilt. An occasional house number showed itself in occasional street light; twice she had crossed the street pursuing these gleams, and once crept halfway up somebody's steps to peer. At last, almost by touch it seemed to her, she found the numerals she wanted.

Above the sidewalk on a shabby stoop she looked through curtained glass to a hallway that held some light, though not much. Heavy draperies blotted out the windows beside her. The bell she pressed was soundless to her, but it made the draperies twitch. Perhaps she was seen; she saw no one.

Then someone, leisurely, appeared at the back of the hall and came to open the door. There were two doors, enclosing a tiny vestibule, but she wasn't let in even this far.

Through a three-inch opening she had to call to the thick little man who guarded it. She took him to be the janitor.

"Mr. Moran," she said, and he replied, "That's right." The opening stayed the same.

"I have an appointment with him."

"What's your name, eh?"

She told him, and he said again, "That's right." It was a congratulation this time, and the door opened on a full view of his blousy shirt and sliding trousers. "Come on in—I'm waiting for you. Pretty cold, eh?"

"Yes," said Marianne. What she thought was one all-inclusive *No*. It must have shown, but did not affect him.

They stayed squeezed together in the vestibule while he made sure the door behind her was shut, and then she was allowed into the hall itself. It was warm. What she could see looked clean.

"Come on," he said. "We'll go up to my office, nice and private there." Then he suddenly shouted. "Okay—not for you, Mrs. Minchin!" No one was in view; big double doors beside them were tightly closed.

He started to climb the stairs, which were carpeted, the woodwork polished. He talked as he climbed, assuming she would follow. After a minute, she did.

"Very nice old lady on my first floor, she don't like to come out on account of the neuralgia. A doctor's widow, got all her own furniture—been here five years. That's the kind of people I have, all permanent, all nice."

"I don't want a room," said Marianne, stopping. He kept on.

"I know what you want, it's okay. You ask anyone about Moran's house, they all know me. All refined people, never any trouble. Don't worry. Come in here, this is my private office."

They entered the parlor floor, front—a long room heavily furnished and well kept. What made it an office was apparently the great desk of carved wood set in the room's center. Nothing Marianne saw matched the man who stood there watching her.

She turned and looked him in the eye. "You're Mr. Moran?"

"That's right." The question seemed to please him. "I'm Mr. Moran, this is my office. You like it?"

"It's very nice."

"Sit down, be comfortable. Don't worry. Everything here is okay, everybody around here knows Moran. Ask anybody."

He had come from the back of the hall to answer her ring—from the cellar stairs, then. Not from up here. He looked as if he lived in the cellar. And whatever kind of accent he had, it wasn't a brogue. She stood looking at him doubtfully, Moran (if he was) stared back. He was enjoying himself! He sank down in the owner's chair, spread out.

Then, elastic, he popped up again.

"Maybe you'll feel better with a lady in the room—a nice lady like yourself, okay? Wait, stay here—I'll introduce you."

He was gone. Marianne waited in a state of total guard. He had left the door open, and presently from the hall she heard sounds of arrival. She turned, saw with astonished relief the head librarian of her own high school! A little younger (Miss Purdy was in her sixties) and taller, and even more bony, she was Miss Purdy to the life with her graying, washed-at-home hair and patient smile. She was a little breathless, standing there in front of the little man as if she had been propelled down the hall; her smile held puzzlement. But it was still a smile that Marianne at once, gladly, could answer.

The little man was triumphant.

"You see? Only a minute, and why not? This is my wife, Mrs. Moran— an English lady. Shake hands."

The English lady's hand came up at once, a cold and gentle net of bone to receive Marianne's. She said in a voice as clear as her eyes, and as pale, "How do you do, my dear."

The hand went away, the patient smile stayed. Marianne felt emptiness, as though nothing real had happened at all. The little man— Moran, then—bustled between them back to his place and sat down.

"Okay, that's better. All friends, you see? Sit down, be comfortable. My wife's busy, she can't stay."

"I could stay," said the English lady. She spoke to Marianne, and that was real. Moran frowned.

"The lady's on business, Harriet. Come back later, maybe."

"I'd like you to stay, if you can," said Marianne.

Then Miss Purdy's ghost looked at her little husband. He said, hands out, "So—sit down, then. Whatever the ladies want, it's okay with me. I've got no secrets. Whatever people bring me, I'm here to see. Fifteen years in the neighborhood, own my own property. I'm no bank—I could be, too much trouble!"

He laughed genially, alert to Marianne's hands. She had her gloves off and was unwrapping Irma's bracelet from its nest of Kleenex. She put it in front of him, a movement that became dazzling, and he leaned over his desk.

"I understand you buy jewelry," she said, very low. "For cash. I'd like to sell that."

"It's yours?" said Moran, staring up at her.

"No. It belongs to someone I know. She couldn't bring it herself." He put his hand over the bracelet, to retain it perhaps while his attention was away, and smiled at her.

"And your friend knows Moran? What's her name, lady?"

"She knows *of* you," said Marianne; and added, woodenly, "Her name is Smith."

There was silence, in which a third voice spoke, gently encouraging. "What a pretty bracelet, my dear," said Mrs. Moran. "So bright!"

She sat quietly on the window seat at the edge of light, and her thin face kept its offer of friendliness turned upon Marianne. She said suddenly, "Your hat is charming, too."

"Well, thank you," said Marianne. Awkwardness made her explicit. "My sister-in-law gave it to me for Christmas."

"How daring, to give a hat! One wouldn't hope to succeed." And Mrs. Moran smiled in some eager pleasure, perhaps for Marianne's sister-in-law's success.

"How much you want for this?" said Moran. He was bent over the bracelet again. Apparently no more was to be said of Mrs. Smith.

"A thousand dollars. In cash. It's worth much more."

"How much more?" He looked up quickly. "How much did it cost?"

She said, cautious, "I think it's up to you to put your own value on it, Mr. Moran. If you're interested."

"Interested! When Moran doesn't get interested in something beautiful like this, lady, he's dead. This is a fine piece. The best. This is for a lady who's got nothing but the best, everything good. Am I right? Big house, servants ..." He winked at Marianne.

The voice from the window seat spoke again, dreamily.

"My Aunt Eustis made hats for us one winter when we were small, I remember, but we weren't allowed to wear them. She made them of colored string, and they were lined with brocade. We thought them very pretty, but of course they weren't suitable."

"I suppose not," said Marianne politely. She was beginning to feel fatigue, and some obscure anger—whether with Irma or with this little man, or both, she was not sure. Impatience made her ask sharply, "Do you want to buy it, Mr. Moran?"

He looked up, entirely genial again.

"I'll tell you what," he said, a sporting offer, "Right now, I'll give you my check. Moran's personal check, five hundred fifty dollars. Good anywhere, ask anybody. How's that?"

"No. I can't bargain with you, Mr. Moran. I've told you, the bracelet isn't mine. The owner wants a thousand dollars, in cash—she isn't prepared to take anything else."

"That's a lot of cash," said Moran.

"I know it."

"What can I do?" said Moran. His hands went out again. "Sometimes I got this much cash, lots more, right here in my safe. Right now, no. I'm telling you Moran's check is like cash, but if that's no good for you, what can I do?"

"Nothing, I guess," said Marianne. The prospect of failure filled her with relief. In a moment, she would be free to go.

She got up, but she was the only one who did.

"I tell you what," he said again. "Maybe there's something I can do for you. Not for myself—Moran's out. Okay, too bad. But Harriet likes you, I like you, you need some cash right away and maybe I know where you could get it. Nothing in it for me, it's a favor. How's that?"

"You mean for me to go to someone else?"

The idea was entirely unwelcome, she didn't disguise it. Then, startling them both, Mrs. Moran's voice spoke out in reassurance.

"But quite a kind person, Mrs. Hinkley—you needn't be afraid at all!"

Moran, discomfited, said quickly, "What are you talking about, Harriet!" And he got up. "My wife don't know what she's talking about—she's like a child for business, an English lady, she don't know what I mean half the time! Who you think I'm talking about, Harriet, I hardly know it myself yet!" Hard and jolly, he stared her down. His wife's downcast face remained delicately vague. He spoke kindly then, for her. "What Harriet means is, anybody I'm sending you to, that person's okay—and she's right. Anybody you go to from Moran, you got nothing to worry about, she knows that."

"But I don't want to go anywhere else—for one thing, there isn't time."

"You got a train to catch," said Moran, instantly. "What time?

"Okay, never mind," he said, diminishing her refusal, waving away her train. "This person that comes into my mind, he's right around here. In two minutes, if I get hold of him, if he can see you—if he's interested like I think, in two minutes you're walking away with one thousand dollars cash in your pocketbook. Now, is this worth a phone call?"

She supposed that, inescapably, it was … if what he said were true. Hesitating, she allowed herself to become committed.

"One little phone call," Moran repeated, brisk now. "Then I hope I got good news for you. Okay? You go with Harriet a minute, she'll give you some tea—good tea, English. You been to England? A fine place!"

Mrs. Moran, already beside her, eagerly touched her arm. Moran watched them from behind his desk, in some satisfaction she did not understand. Panic came up in her. She said, too loudly, "Give me the bracelet, please!"

For a moment he seemed not to hear her continuing to smile. Then, a flash of light, his hand came up and Marianne saw Irma's bracelet fly toward her, past her, through the air. She gave a cry and turned—but behind her, folding mildly downward like a giraffe, Mrs. Moran was already capturing the prize.

She rose laughing—a breathless, almost soundless burst of laughter—and held the bracelet out upon her palm as she left the room.

CHAPTER THREE

"Let's have our tea in my room," said Mrs. Moran, regretfully watching the bracelet go into Marianne's bag. She had turned it over docilely, once they were in the hall, but as though reluctant to end a jolly game.

She sighed, adding, "It's much cozier, and there are always black beetles downstairs at night."

Moran had got up and shut the door behind them without a word. The house was in quietness.

Marianne, her voice unsteady, asked, "Is there another telephone I can use?"

"But wouldn't you like your tea first, dear?"

"No. I mean, thank you, but this is very important. I must call someone."

Mrs. Moran became resigned, and considered.

"Well, there's a public one downstairs in the hall, you know. But I'm afraid you need money for that."

"I have some change."

"Oh—then that's all right, isn't it? Come along, I'll show you where it is!"

With a return of eagerness, accepting their new plan, she began to descend the carpeted stairs. She went slowly, looking back often with smiles of encouragement. At the bottom she waited for Marianne, and took her arm.

"There it is. You see?"

The wall telephone was plainly visible, at the back of the hall, and Marianne disengaged herself, murmuring, "Thank you."

She walked toward the telephone, Mrs. Moran coming behind her. At the box, becoming at last aware of some hesitation on Marianne's part, she asked, "Are you sure you have some money?"

Marianne opened her bag, pushed past the diamonds, and took out her change purse. There were a quarter and two dimes. Mrs. Moran shook her head.

"It isn't very much money, is it?"

"It's enough—I can call collect."

The problem had become as Mrs. Moran's own, and she stood waiting to see how Marianne would solve it. It was obviously not going to occur to her to go away.

Marianne found herself saying, as if to a child, "Why don't you go and make the tea while I'm calling? I'll come as soon as I can."

"Oh. Well, if you like."

Serious, entirely docile, she turned and went slowly away. Marianne pretended to search her bag until she had gone, a maneuver that shamed her slightly. But a collect call required too many details to be given aloud.

She called Henry. Not in panic anymore—that hadn't lasted; but all the same she was glad to hear his voice. Her own became just as matter-of-fact.

"I'm in New York, Henry," she said. "I expect Morrie told you I had to go."

There was a pause. "Well, he said something like that." Another pause. "Why?" he said, mild.

"Oh—an errand. I'll tell you about it when I get back. I just wanted to tell you not to wait up, because it may be late. I'd rather take the bus anyway, on these kinds of roads. Is it still snowing?"

Time passed, as though Henry had looked out to see.

"No ... it's stopped that. But it's no kind of weather for you to be out all hours in, Mary Ann. I don't see there's any call for you to be running errands to New York this kind of weather."

"I don't myself," she said. "It's the last one, don't worry."

"I think it better be," said Henry. "There's no excuse for you doing things like that, for what you get."

"I'm not going to, anymore."

"I don't think you should. I don't think you should be *asked* to," he said, firm. She knew what was coming, long before he brought it out. "This looks like the end to me, Mary Ann."

"Me too, Henry," she said ... and there it was. Said, and agreed to. But she hung up a little sadly. Now there would be no one between Bryce Builders and Irma. She could pick it to death, and she would.

Talking with Henry had cleared her mind. She got the operator back and put in a call to Irma. At that time of night, Tom Bryce would almost certainly be at home, but Marianne no longer cared. Perhaps because of that, she got Irma.

Irma was not friendly.

"What are you calling me here for?" she demanded. "My husband's home, you know I can't talk to you about it!"

"You don't have to. I just want to tell you that your Mr. Moran doesn't have the money to buy the bracelet. He's calling up somebody else."

"Well, all right! I don't care who buys it!"

"I'm not going to take it anywhere else," said Marianne. "If you want me to I'll get this man's name, and then you can take over yourself. *He* won't know you."

"I never heard anything so ridiculous in my life!" said Irma. She began to sound breathless. "You're down there, you've only to take a taxi to wherever it is, and that's the end of it! How do you suppose I can get away now, with Mr. Bryce here!"

"You'll just have to manage it, Mrs. Bryce. I'm sorry, but I'm not going to any more of these people. I'll be down at the station—I'll wait for you there till midnight, that'll give you plenty of time."

Irma's voice became a rush of frantic sound.

"But you can't behave this way—how dare you waste all this time and then tell me you're finished! You'll ruin everything if you don't go see this other man—why shouldn't you? What difference does another half-hour make! What's the matter with you?"

"Nothing, so far," said Marianne. "Don't forget—the Grand Central Waiting Room. I'll be there till midnight."

For the first time in her life, she hung up without saying goodbye.

Upstairs, the door to Moran's private office stood open but he was not there. She was looking in to see when his voice hailed her from down the hall. She jumped.

"It's okay, I'm right here," said Moran, demonstrating himself. "I'm looking for you, you're looking for me, eh?"

He waited until she came near and added, low, "So what did I tell you? You're all fixed up. No more worrying—in ten minutes you're there, you got your money, you're all fixed up. Don't thank me—it's only a favor, I'm glad to do it."

"And tea is all ready," said his wife, behind him. She sat in her room before a tea service. A Paisley shawl covered her badly knit sweater— she had dressed up in the shawl, and her long hands lay proud and still on its folds. She looked tranquilly into Marianne's face.

"Harriet, not now," said her husband. "The lady will come back. Right now she's got an appointment, she's in a hurry. You come back and see Mrs. Moran sometime," he said kindly. "She likes you, come any time— she's always here."

It seemed probable. Marianne's waiting hostess looked to be, after all, only a tableau, and one that might well be left as it was day after day. Set out for guests who would never come or were, perhaps, not really expected. Were all far away, or dead long ago.

"I'm awfully sorry," Marianne said.

Mrs. Moran remained still. Only her expression had changed, when her husband first spoke; it did not alter again. Marianne saw now that she had spread a yellow lace cloth upon the table, on which was placed delicate, unmatched china. There was a frayed velvet cozy over the teapot. Most touching of all, to Marianne, was the graceful arrangement of crackers on a pink plate. They were just saltines.

The saltines did it. Marianne move forward, passing Moran who leaned against the door. She turned and looked at him.

"Maybe I would just have time for a cup," she said.

Harriet still made no sound. Moran answered, like a shrug, "It's up to you, lady. Like I told you, there's nothing in it for Moran—I only make the appointment for a favor, the rest is up to you."

"I think I would have time for one cup," Marianne repeated to Harriet, who still did not reply.

Moran said, "So show her the spoons, Harriet. They're from England, from my wife's family. Very refined people."

Indulgent, he watched them a minute and then shuffled away. His wife did not move until he was gone, then she got up and shut the door—and came back shining, to turn her full, happy attention upon her guest.

Half an hour later, when Marianne came back into the hall, she found Moran waiting at the top of the stairs. He was sitting there reading a newspaper, in poor light. The door of his office stood open before him, like a view.

He was in no hurry to get up. His head laid back against the wall, he watched her come toward him. His wife had rather strangely shut her door behind Harriet, as though her room were an apartment.

"Well, Mr. Moran," Marianne said, "I'm ready for that address now, if you have it."

She felt more tired than ever, and depressed, too. There seemed to be no limit to the foolishness she could let herself in for—and what good did it do? The quarrel with Irma; and now this poor unbalanced creature with her shabby treasures. She had not made Harriet's world any more real by her visit; Harriet had only succeeded in making her feel slightly like a ghost.

Moran pushed himself up along the wall and stood regarding her. "You had a nice time, eh? Nice tea party?"

"Very nice."

"Harriet showed you her things?"

She nodded. It was unbelievable how much that narrow room had yielded in the way of boxes, and boxes within boxes. Some of the things were interesting, but an awful lot was junk. Harriet seemed satisfied with it all. Marianne didn't want to think about it anymore.

"Have you got the address?" she asked.

"Sure, I got it."

He stood back, as though to let her precede him down the stairs, but there was not much room to get by. Her open coat caught, pulling her arm back, and for one tangled moment she felt her bag pulling at her waist.

"Oops!" he said, friendly. "Two fatties, huh?"

It was a gross lie, so far as she was concerned. She pulled free and went on. Moran came after her.

"Sure, I got the address," he said, resuming their conversation. "But if you still got an appointment, I don't know. He don't see everybody, Mr. Nagy. For me, for a favor, he says you can come—but that's half an hour ago. Now, I don't know."

"If Mr. Nagy is interested in the bracelet at all, I suppose he'll look at it when it gets there," she said coldly. Fatties!

They came to the inner door and Moran took hold of its handle but did not pull it open.

"That little round silver box of Harriet's, now," he said, offhand. "What would you think that was worth? With the little figures on it."

"The button box?" She remembered it—*repoussé*, small, dirty—only because of Harriet's pleasure in it. Certainly it couldn't be worth much. "I don't know. You should be the one who'd know that, Mr. Moran."

He laughed, and opened the door.

"A lady with such a bracelet—that lady knows all about nice things," he said, gallantly burying Mrs. Smith. He crowded into the vestibule with her. "Now, tell me where you're going, eh?"

She told him, rapidly. He was unpleasantly close.

He nodded. "That's right. If you forget, it's all right too—call me up, my name is in the book, I'm always here."

Then he let her go.

When she was gone, Moran went upstairs to his wife's room. The door was locked; he had to search his pockets for a key, and let himself in. Harriet, repacking her treasures, looked up mutely.

He went past her to the table that stood uncleared and pushed at the plates.

"You put this stuff away, now, Harriet," he said. "Come on, right now, clean up. Even for you I'm not having no cockroaches upstairs."

"Oh, of course, I was just—"

"Okay, right now."

He stood to watch her obey, his hands in his pockets.

"You had a nice time with the lady, eh?"

"She was rather sweet," Harriet murmured. "Funny little dear."

"Funny, eh? Well, okay." He went on quietly, "So now I want you to give me Mrs. Minchin's little box, Harriet. Right away, now."

To her busy silence he went on, "You got it. The lady saw it, she told me. I want it now."

"But I haven't cleaned it yet! I only wanted to clean it!"

She looked at him then, her light eyes honest with distress. He ate saltines and watched her. She turned away distractedly, burrowing at random.

"I'm really not quite sure—"

"You can find it. You better."

At last she came and put the button box into his hand. He examined it.

"For a thing like this, you want the police in my house?" he said finally. She gazed past him, as though on passionate visions. He struck hard across her face—back, and across again—saying earnestly, "Don't *do* like that! Don't *do* it—don't *do* it!"

Her little yelps were faint, but redness flamed at once upon her skin. He hesitated, dissatisfied, then put the box in his shirt pocket and went shuffling out. She ran to lock the door behind him.

In the cubicle of a pay toilet, Marianne was going through her bag. She had been through it twice, and now she was taking everything out and piling it up. When she had done that, no more doubt remained.

White-faced, she put it all back, let herself out, and went to find the telephones.

CHAPTER FOUR

As soon as that accursed girl had hung up, Irma knew what she had to do. Now; right away. As soon as her hands stopped shaking, as soon as she could speak to be understood.

Immobile, bent over upon herself in the dark hall, Irma willed herself to call up Moran. The loud poker game in her dining room echoed upon her ears without meaning—a gross noise, a protection, under cover of which she could speak and act in privacy. As she had to act, to speak.

Now.

It was entirely safe. A call to New York would go through with no mention of its origin—she might be calling him from a phone somewhere in New York, for all he would know. And besides, what difference did it make? She was married, protected—he could no longer touch her. He wouldn't dare—he had to behave himself. She held all the cards now, and he had to behave himself.

She straightened, sat quietly a moment, then picked up the receiver. Her own crisp voice speaking restored her further. She was all right now.

The faraway telephone rang and rang. She held on; he was there. Down in the basement, or with Harriet; but he was there. At last, leisurely, she heard his voice.

"Okay, okay," he said. "Hello."

Just the same.

"This is Irma," she said; and with the words, rage sprang up in her and tightened her whole throat. She couldn't say another word.

"So?"

They might have been speaking to each other the day before. He waited; said again, "So, Irma?"

"So," she managed, "I'm just telling you I'm coming there right away. Right now, Moran. That's my bracelet Harriet took, and I want it back. By the time I get there, you have it. I'm starting right now."

She made herself wait through the sound of his breathing, through his eventual, slow reply.

"What foolishness are you talking now, Irma? What bracelet?"

"Moran, don't fool with me. That's my bracelet that came to you tonight. I know she was there, I just talked to her … that stupid cow of a woman!" she cried out, and then checked her voice at once. "Don't try to tell me she wasn't there. She was there!"

"A lot of people come here, Irma. Nobody mentioned you."

"Well, she mentioned you, all right," she said viciously. "She thinks you took it, she wants to call the police. She says you picked her purse! So don't fool around with me, Moran."

"I don't fool around with nobody," he said. He was beginning to get mad. She could hear it; and it calmed her. "Now what's this you want to tell me, Irma? This lady that came here, she was from you? You sent me this lady from Mrs. Smith? That's you?"

"That's my bracelet. And I want it back."

"So ask your friend," he said promptly. But she could hear him breathing, thinking. "Why are you sending me ladies from Mrs. Smith, Irma?"

"Not for Harriet to pick their purses," she said, deadly still. "I'm telling you, she got my bracelet! Go up and look in her room, I'll wait. Go look now!"

But he only went on breathing at her ear.

"I mean it, Moran! I'll call the police if you don't."

"So call the police, Irma. The owner should complain, that's right. Mrs. Smith should complain. Or take a look for your nice lady friend, Mrs. Smith!" His temper was rising. She heard his voice go soft and flat with it; and thought, with satisfaction: Harriet will catch it this time. "You have a little talk with your friend that can't find the bracelet, Irma," he said. "That's my advice for you."

"I'll have a little talk with you," she said, unmoved. "After you have one with Harriet. I'm coming right away, Moran. You better be there when I come. Harriet too."

"Harriet's here, I'm here, all the time," he said, calmer. "Come, sure, come and behave yourself, why not?" And close in her ear, soft, he added, "I'm sorry for your trouble, Irma. It's a nice piece. He gives you nice things."

She hung up without reply, reassured. He was in a mess, and he knew it. Whatever he said, he would go up and look. By the time she got there he would have the bracelet pushed down in the chair where Miss Stupid Cow had been sitting, or it would have fallen behind something on the floor. Yes. She would get it back—he wouldn't dare keep anything so valuable. And when she had it, she would make him take it to Nagy himself. And he could get the money as a loan, while he was at it—she needn't lose the bracelet after all.

Confidence flooded back into her. Why had she been so cautious, after all? She might have gone down herself, in the first place—bypassed that idiotic Marianne person entirely. If only she hadn't, for those few hours, lost her nerve! The call from the broker had shaken her; she had not thought it possible for a commodity to fall so fast. And on top of that shock, the idea of going back to Moran was more than she could face—and where else could she get money in absolute privacy? But she could, now, face the fact that she had briefly lost her nerve. Could face it as coldly as though she were considering some other woman's weakness.

Well, she had her nerve back. She could face anything now—the market loss, that would not, after all, cost her her bracelet. The fact that she was married to a financial idiot who made it necessary for her to take these risks, if she were to have any security at all. Look at him—sitting there in her dining room, in the middle of his creditors! What a host. And what guests—it didn't disguise anything, to call them by first names, to call them 'The Boys'!

They were silent now—The Boys; intent on some new deal. She came silently in on that silence and stood behind her husband's chair, looking steadily down on the top of his head—untidy as a fourteen-year-old boy's. What a husband.

At the other side of the table, one of The Boys noticed her, said like a warning, "Hi, Irma." Instantly her husband swiveled round. "Well, hello, baby! I thought you went to bed."

"Not yet."

"Well," he said, "well, now you're here, stay awhile! Bring me some luck, and give the boys a treat!"

He was bawling like a bull, into total, undeceived silence. Someone cleared his throat, as though in feeble second. Or protest.

She suddenly produced her dimples, smiling steadily all around the table.

"Now, Tom, what are you saying? One woman, in a man's poker game—that would make a nice scandal, wouldn't it?"

No one answered. One impatient male voice said hardily, "Well, good night then, Irma." She ignored it.

"Do you want anything, Tom? Do your guests have everything they need?"

"Sure, we're fine. Thanks, baby."

Now he had collapsed, showed misery. This was his other expression—he had all of two. Without haste, she wished them good night and left the room.

They were quiet for a while, after she left. It wouldn't last. She went upstairs, dressed quickly in her own room, and shut the door when she came out. There was no way to lock it, but no need—Tom would go tiptoeing by, sheepish and drunk, around three or four in the morning. She would be back long before he got himself up.

The house they rented—no development for Irma: Georgian red brick, in its own grounds—lay back from the street; and she had left her car down at the curb. She could have rolled down the street gradient to a start if one of The Boys had not parked in front of her. Another had jammed her in from behind. She let herself go a little, grinding bumpers to get loose, and felt some satisfaction at that release.

But it was a dangerous satisfaction. It started up in her emotions she could not afford—yet. She wanted to go on feeling just as she felt now, when she faced Moran. Cold, contemptuous, in full control of herself.

It was after ten o'clock. The snow had stopped falling long ago, was broken and slushy on private streets and almost gone from the Parkway. Irma made good time, sitting erect in the enclosed warm darkness of her car, passing everything. When she turned out at Seventy-ninth Street and began angling through Manhattan's West Side, she believed herself quite without emotion.

But then she saw the house. And at once, in spite of herself, the fury she lived with woke like a dog sensing destination; and she thought of finding Harriet alone ... Moran gone ... Of how she would tear and strike without a word and hold her bracelet at last: *"Thief! Thief!"*

But Moran would be there. He was always there.

She sat until she was calm again—cold as ice—in the shelter of her car. Then, erect, disdainful, she went down in the areaway and knocked at his door.

He came and let her in after a while.

"Well, you take a long time, Irma," he said. "You don't live in town no more?"

She didn't answer. He shambled off down the dark passage as though he didn't expect her to; and she grimly followed.

He had been asleep. Asleep in his basement den, that he made for himself in every house he ever lived in; and when he turned on the dangling bulb there, she saw the familiar sordidness: the papers on the floor, the wineglass stickily empty, the ashtrays cold and full. The cheap radio that chattered all day long. He had been sleeping dressed on his dirty cot—maybe waiting for her, or maybe it was just one of the nights he didn't bother.

She stood fastidious, after one glance ignoring the litter.

"Have you got it?" she asked.

He sat down behind his table and looked up at her. With slight shock, a stirring of old caution, she saw that he wasn't as placative as she had thought. And his anger was still alive—had deepened, and settled to be an ugly mood.

Well, that was nothing to do with her anymore. She stared back at him.

Negligent, he presently inquired, "So now—what's all this, about Mrs. Smith's bracelet?"

"Did you get—did you find it?"

He put his hands out.

"I don't go crawling around my floors all night for something isn't there, Irma. Go upstairs yourself, look. You're not going to find something. I tell you the lady took it with her—that nice lady. Friend of Mrs. Smith, remember?"

He was really in a rage. And there was nothing he could do about it— except take up her time with nasty digs, try to make her lose her temper too. She hesitated, wary, but not at all afraid. Impatience would do her no good now. With an indifferent air, then, she went over and sat on the cot—there was nowhere else. She sat on the extreme edge, and pulled her mink coat around her like an armor. He watched her do it.

"I don't have to tell you my business," she said. "Why should I? What do you care if I have something to sell?"

"You got nothing to sell now, Irma. You already gave it away, remember? That nice lady. Quick! she says, call up the police! You're not calling up any police, your husband gonna find out all about it—she knows that. She's not so dumb. Maybe it's you that's dumb, got to be so foxy all the time. Mrs. Smith."

"All right, Mrs. Smith. So what? And that girl wouldn't know what to do with a diamond bracelet if somebody gave it to her, so let's stop pretending. She was all right, the bracelet was all right. Why you couldn't simply have passed her on to Nagy—the whole thing wouldn't have taken ten minutes. But no, you had to get Harriet into it."

"Who says Harriet is in something? Harriet lives here, my guest is her guest, she knows how to act like a lady because she is a lady! And you know something, Mrs. Irma Smith? A lady ain't ashamed of who she knows. A cheap little nobody-nothing is ashamed, sure. From Mrs. Smith, she sends. To me, to Nagy! To Nagy, that knows you all your life!"

He needed to make her answer his anger. But he couldn't. Her mind was coolly going over all he said.

"If you think I'll lose that bracelet rather than tell my husband, you can think again, Moran. He paid for it—he knows what it's worth. And he'll see that I get it back."

"So send him to see me, Irma. My son-in-law I would like to know. Send him here, he can meet a real lady—like you'll never be, Irma. Like you don't even know how. You had the chance, I gave you the chance. An English lady you got for your governess when I'm in Soho making nothing. So you can learn how to act right, grow up nice, have some manners. Where?" he said, bitter. "What manners? What lady? A Mrs. Smith, I got."

She said suddenly, "I learned from Harriet, all right. How to get home alone. How to get away fast, when they caught her! My governess! Your—"

"You got a nasty tongue, Irma," he broke in, heavily and slowly. His hands slid down to his waist, and she said sharply: "Just keep your belt on, Moran, I'm not a kid anymore. And I'm not Harriet," she said, in a malice she could not afford, that made him dangerously still. But reckless now, she cried out, "You and your manners! Who do you think you're fooling? You know what that girl thinks about you? She thinks you're a pickpocket—a cheap, dirty dip! And I'll tell you what she thinks about your precious Harriet, too—your English lady! You know what she called her? A poor—"

The old table went over in one great crash, a dozen shattering echoes, and Moran rose from behind it with his thrusting thick arms outstretched still. He came toward her, all bloodshot rage. She was in one instant on her feet.

Neither of them made another sound. The overturned table lay between her and the door. She leaped it and came crumpling down, her descending foot a slide on fallen papers. The hand flung out to brace herself left blood among broken bits of glass. She screamed then, scrambling, sliding always toward the door, the long skirt of her coat dragging behind her. His hand at her back gripped the strong fur that would not yield, that checked her absolutely. She screamed again and flung backward with the bag attached to her wrist—felt it strike, felt the grip loosen—and stumbled ahead. Got her feet beneath her, her legs straightened. Ran.

She ran in narrow darkness. He was behind her, but she could run the fastest—she always could, a skinny, leggy child who flew on fear. Only someone had put grown-up shoes on her, spiky heels—loose slippers she couldn't control. And that smothering long coat! When he caught it again, and she tried to wriggle out of it, he used it like a handle to slam her against the wall and fall upon her there.

She panted against him, "I'll have her put in the loony bin—that's where she belongs! You too! You too! Both of you—"

He didn't answer. All his breath and weight were engaged to hold her there ... and in something else. She twisted, trying to see what he was doing—saw too late, and on her own twisting movement was thrust further forward beyond an open door. That door slammed between them.

She flung herself on it, but it would not move. The dark around her was the remembered dark of old captures, smelling of cellar, mice, coal. She could hear him fastening up the padlock again, panting still, muttering, "Now you'll stay there awhile, maybe next time you'll talk a little nicer...."

He began to shuffle away, and all defense left her. In the old despair, she flung herself uselessly against the door again, crying out, "Papa! Papa! Put on the light ...!"

CHAPTER FIVE

Down in the front hall, Moran was talking at the top of his voice. That meant Mrs. Minchin, she was rather hard of hearing. Harriet leaned, listening, against the upstairs wall.

"... kids trying to get into the basement last night, you heard, eh? Woke you up, maybe?"

There was some sort of quavering reply. Harriet, swaying gently against the wall, made the weave of her heavy sweater scratch between her shoulder blades—rather a nice sensation. Then Moran again.

"Well, that's good. Anyhow just remember you got nothing to worry about in Moran's house. Nobody fools around this property, I'm watching all the time. You got yourself the safest house in New York City, Mrs. Minchin, you know that? Right here!"

More quavering. Oh, get on, Harriet thought. Old bore. She didn't in the least care what they were talking about, she was only waiting there for Moran to go. For he was going out. She had known that since early morning when he came in and woke her up. She saw at once that he had his double-breasted suit on, and she sat up in bed, beginning to laugh, because he looked so funny in it.

He hadn't been in a very good mood.

"Come on, now," he said, in his grumbliest voice. "Get up. Right now, Harriet. You gonna have your breakfast right now, or you're not gonna get any. I mean it, get up. And put your clothes on. Don't come downstairs in no wrapper."

As if she would! It was only in her own dear, cozy room that she liked to wander about in her dressing gown. Possibly, just once or twice, she might have come down for biscuits or something of that sort, to have with her tea, but otherwise she hadn't come downstairs in her dressing gown for years. That was because of Mama being gone. Mama was the one who always defended them, saying, "Poor little dears, let them be happy while they can! Time enough for everyone to start being cross with them when they go off to those awful schools." And then, after all, nobody had gone. Just Papa. So they could stay home after all.

She glanced down the stairs again and saw, with a start, that the hall was empty. What had happened? How could he have gone, without her noticing? Panic pushed her away from the wall, halfway down the steps. Mrs. Minchin's door was shut again, and nobody was there at all! Clutching the banister, she called out thinly, "Moran! Moran!" Then she saw him, coming from the back of the hall. He had only been down there.

She drew back, but he had heard and was peering up at her. Now he had on his overcoat, and that big black hat—rather terrifying. He was frowning.

"What's the matter?" he said. She didn't answer. He began feeling in all his pockets, as if to make sure. "Now listen, Harriet," he said, "I got to go out a little while. You stay in your room. Don't answer no bells, I don't care how much they ring. Just stay in your room. And listen," he said, lowering his voice. "Come down a little." She came down a few steps, and he caught her arm. "Now you stay off the third floor, you hear? Stay away from that new girl's room, I mean it. She's there, anyway—she's home sick today."

That was a lie. She could tell from the way he said it. A shameful, silly lie. Her eyes filled with tears, and she murmured, "Oh, why do you say such dreadful things to me? So humiliating."

He looked surprised, then embarrassed. He gave her arm a pat, and let it go.

"Well, okay," he said. "Just stay in your room, all right? Maybe I'll bring you something."

But she didn't want anything, now that he had made her feel so ashamed. Such a thing to say to her.

When he had gone, she came slowly down the rest of the way and stood with her forehead pressed against the door. The tears were still in her eyes, and the morning light through them made rather lovely patterns. But just the same—for a while, anyway—he had taken away all the pleasure of having the house to herself. She could feel the cold glass of the door through the thin curtain; and presently, blinking, she watched the shadowy forms of people passing on the sidewalk below.

She began to feel better, and to consider which she would rather do first—take out the pretty bracelet (she was going to sew black velvet ribbon on either end, and make a sort of stomacher with it) or go and see what sort of things the new girl had. That was not very tempting, really. She seemed a dreary sort of girl. On the other hand, she might very well leave before Moran went out again, and then Harriet would always wonder.

Someone was coming up the front steps, and Harriet drew back. She could see only a heavily bundled outline—it might have been one of the third-floor girls unexpectedly coming home. But this one had no key. The loud bell rang at the back of the hall, making her start. Go away, she thought, indignant. Tiresome thing! Go away.

The bell rang again. Then, of course, old Mother Minchin had to poke her head out. And of course she saw Harriet, and Harriet had to smile, and speak.

Mrs. Minchin didn't even try to hear her. She simply bawled out, "Where's Mr. Moran—why don't he answer the bell? Somebody's ringing!"

Rude old creature. But that wasn't entirely fair, of course. She really was almost deaf … and yet, she always heard the bell. How? In the interest of this new thought, Harriet considered her. She still smiled politely. Mrs. Minchin grew very agitated.

"Go see who it is, dearie, she might go away! I think it's someone from my daughter—go and see, won't you?"

"It's only a peddler," said Harriet finally, loudly. "You know we don't like them to come here, Mrs. Minchin."

The bell rang a third time, very long, putting the old lady into a dreadful state. She reached out and caught Harriet's arm!

"No, no, it's somebody from my daughter! Now go, there's a dearie, you know I can't go near that wind, with my neuralgia!"

Harriet did not like to have her arm pulled about so much, and she stopped smiling. But gravely, in forced disobedience, she went and pulled open the door to the vestibule.

A terrible shock waited for her there. Not three feet away, straining against the glass that separated them, stood the woman who had been there last night! She saw Harriet, too—her face began to distort itself in some inaudible, urgent speech.

With a whimper, Harriet backed away, let the door fall shut, and fled to the back of the hall. Old Mrs. Minchin wailed at her back.

Around the corner, out of sight, she pressed herself against the door to Moran's cellar. But he was not there! Her heart beating dreadfully, Harriet tried to think what to do. To come back like that—to stand and make those dreadful faces against their glass! *How could she?*

The bell shrilled again, right in her ear now, and with another whimper of fright Harriet opened the cellar door and felt for the light switch. Her hand was trembling, she was so nervous the stairs seemed more difficult than ever. But she got down. And once she was there, safe in the cavey place that was Moran's, she did feel a little better.

She stood still a long while, achieving by patience, by concealment, her escape from the dreadful girl.

Presently she opened her eyes again. What she saw drew her forward at once, in delicate movements of growing interest. All the things he kept upon his table—that she was never allowed to touch—were strewn about on the floor! Why? She had never seen anything so odd!

Fascinated, she was stooping down to explore when a sound at her back made her look round. The woman was standing there. In the house.

It was the most paralyzing of nightmares come true. Moran was gone. *They* could get in at her. They were here. It was all over. She stood like a prize of death, delivered.

The woman moved toward her.

"Don't be frightened, Mrs. Moran, please. I only want to talk to you. The area door wasn't locked."

It wasn't true. The area door was always locked. Harriet smiled faintly and shut her eyes.

The voice went on.

"I don't know what your husband's said to make you afraid of me, but you don't have to be. I'm only here because I need your help—and you need mine, Mrs. Moran. Believe me, you do!"

Harriet's eyes stayed shut. She knew all about people who said they wanted to help you. Next, she would be told to get her coat.

But instead of more words, a queer sound reached her. Then another. She opened her eyes, cautiously, and saw that the woman had begun to cry! She had her handkerchief out, and her face in it! Why?

A tiny, tiny interest stirred in her, and she kept guarded watch.

The woman was stammering, "I'm sorry, I don't know what—I never dreamed you'd be afraid of me ... and I didn't sleep all night ... and I've been sitting out there in the street all morning long...."

Harriet's interest grew, and her fear diminished. Surely that was very odd? Presently, she risked asking, "Why were you sitting in the street?"

"Waiting for you, I thought you might come out to market." The woman was sniffing, folding up her handkerchief. She cleared her throat. "Then when Mr. Moran came out, I decided to come in and see you instead. I thought you would see me."

"Oh," said Harriet. She considered. "I'm so sorry I couldn't let you in. You see, I'm not allowed."

"I understand," said the woman. She came near, and put her hand on Harriet's arm. "Listen, Mrs. Moran, the reason your husband doesn't want you to see me is that he took my bracelet last night. I'm sorry, but it's true. And unless you help me get it back, there's going to be a great deal of trouble. You don't want that to happen, do you?"

Harriet looked at her blankly. The hand on her arm gave it a gentle shake.

"You do remember the bracelet I brought here, don't you? You saw it, you thought it was very pretty."

"Oh, yes," Harriet murmured. "Very pretty." Why *did* people hold on to one so disagreeably?

"Well, it's very valuable, too. And your husband took it from my bag. I suppose I seemed like a very simple person to him, Mrs. Moran, but what I said was true—that bracelet isn't mine. The woman who does own it won't stop at anything to get it back—she's a very, very determined woman."

Harriet did not answer. Another shake (really!) and the voice came closer still.

"You must understand, and try to help! I tell you the police are going to come here, and they may very well arrest your husband! If the bracelet is given back nothing will happen, I promise you. Do you know where it might be? Will you help me find it, now, before your husband comes back?"

Harriet shrank away, pulling her arm free. She said in a trembling voice, "I think you must be mad!"

"I think I pretty nearly am," the woman replied, quite quietly. Then she sank down in Moran's chair, and stayed quiet.

Harriet at once went round to the other side of the table. She watched the woman awhile, and then decided to say, "You really are quite mistaken, you know. The police won't come. There's never any trouble here."

She didn't answer. She didn't seem interested in Harriet at all anymore. Harriet watched her a while longer, and when she continued to do nothing, began to feel rather restless.

"Why don't you go away?" she suggested, at last.

The woman replied at once this time, in the same quiet voice.

"No, I'm going to wait. That taxi driver knows I'm here, and he's not going away till I come out. At least your husband is going to understand that that bracelet belongs to somebody he knows. Or I suppose it does—unless Irma's lying about it."

A rush of terror returned to Harriet's mind—and confusion, too. It was not her fault, she had been paying the closest attention, and yet—whatever could the woman mean, about Irma? Where had Irma come from?

Could Irma be the taxi driver?

No, this was wrong, this was impossible. She only said, sitting in the street. It was Irma who was lying. Could this mean that Irma was in the taxi, and *the woman didn't even know it?*

Despair scattered Harriet's thoughts, and she cried out, "Oh, please go away! Why don't you go away?"

The woman did not move, and said only, "You'd better go upstairs, Mrs. Moran. It's all right, I'll tell your husband I let myself in—he won't blame you."

But nothing could now have persuaded Harriet to go anywhere alone, if Irma was nearby. Waiting, lying in wait, in the taxi. The taxi that would not go away until the woman went away.

Leaning over the table, Harriet whispered, "If I give it you, will you go away?"

The woman stared at her, and Harriet begged, "Oh, shut your eyes!" but she did not. In the end it was Harriet herself who had to turn round, undoing her buttons to search desperately for the little chamois bag caught somewhere inside. She heard the woman getting to her feet behind her, but she herself could not turn—all her buttons undone, the chamois bag between her teeth, her fingers caught in strings, buttonholes, her eyes shut tight and her throat closing up. Helplessness overcame her, and she was still.

The bag was taken. She made no attempt to keep it. A moment later, someone quite gently began putting her to rights, doing up her buttons.

And very close, very low, the voice said, "So he makes you carry it on you ... poor Harriet...."

If she had stayed on for hours, gone on talking all the while, Harriet could neither have looked nor answered. She had done all she could, no more was possible. Either they would all go away—the woman, the taxi, Irma—or it was the end; Harriet could do no more.

They went away. Harriet, continuing to stand in the still darkness she had achieved, heard every sound of the departure. The taxi went away too, she heard it. Still she stood there.

Then, a gratuitous achievement, her eyes opened, her throat gave up one little moan that had been imprisoned there, and it was all right. She had done right, after all. But how tiring it all was!

Listless, Harriet picked up the piece of paper the woman had left on the table for her. She said it was her own name and address, so Harriet would have somewhere to turn, if she ever needed it. Which would have been rather impertinent in someone less strange. Still, it was a real name and address. Harriet was pleased enough to have it, for the little address book she had found on the third floor last year, and had such difficulty filling up. Names out of the directory, no matter how familiar or sympathetic they seemed at the time, became disappointing in the end.

Only what had become of the book? It would be rather a shame to have lost it, just when it was beginning to be so useful! A little anxious, Harriet picked her way through the dreadful muss on Moran's floor and went upstairs to hunt.

CHAPTER SIX

When Marianne came back to the hotel she sat down on the bed and put in a call to Henry. It was disconcerting to have him sound so ordinary. He only asked, dryly, where she was now.

"In a hotel, Henry. I had to stay over. It was too late to call you last night, and I didn't have time this morning. I hope you didn't worry."

He left that to her own conscience, in a pause, and then remarked, "Mr. Bryce was around lookin' for you. He don't seem to know where you are either."

Her heart jumped a little.

"Oh," she said. "Well, I—it wasn't for him I came down, Henry. It's for her—he isn't supposed to know."

Henry sounded as if he had moved up close to the receiver.

"You're down there running errands for *her?*"

"Just this one. The last one. I promise."

"Well, I should mighty well think so," he said. That was all.

"What did he want? Did you tell him where I was?"

"I told him if he didn't know where you were, I sure didn't," said Henry. He let her think of that, before he added, "I don't think he took it in, though. He was over to the house this morning before I'd had my breakfast—said they had some trouble over their way last night, some kind of a car smash. Nobody hurt. I don't know what *that's* got to do with you."

She could hear his exasperation as plainly as if he were in the room. It made her homesick.

"Well, never mind," she said. "I'll be home soon, now."

"I just about had enough of this, Mary Ann."

"I know."

"Well," he said; and she could see him standing there, long-faced, behind the bicycles. "Well, catch your train. You want me to meet you?"

"No, no." She asked, "Mrs. Bryce didn't call, did she?"

"No, she did not," he said, with an emphasis that showed she'd get short change if she did.

For some reason Marianne felt as happy as a bride when she hung up. The bracelet in her bag (in the zipper compartment now, next to her bankbook) weighed nothing on her. She could almost have hung it gaily round her wrist and gone off that way.

She put in her call to Irma, and got Tom Bryce. That was a small shock; he wasn't supposed to be around the house in the daytime. And he instantly recognized her voice.

"Mary Ann! Where are you? Where have you been?"

"In New York," she said, stolid. "Didn't Henry tell you?"

"But why? You—listen," he said, "I've got to talk to you. When will you be back? Irma isn't there with you, is she?"

"No, she's not. Isn't she there?"

"No. Listen," he said again, "what train are you taking? I'll meet you at the station."

She didn't want that at all, and found the firmness to say so.

"No, don't do that, I've got a ride. Why don't you come over after supper?" she said, weakening. "Or come for supper, if Irma isn't back."

When he answered again, he sounded entirely deflated. She knew just how he looked.

"Never mind," he said. "It's all right. Let it go."

"Wait a minute!" He seemed to be fading away entirely. "Tom!"

He was still there. Barely audible.

"You've had enough of my troubles."

"Don't talk like that," she said, automatically. "It'll straighten out, whatever it is. If you see Irma, will you tell her something for me?"

"Tell Irma?"

"Yes. Tell her I found the material, and I'm bringing it back with me."

"You've found—"

"I'm bringing her what she wants," Marianne said, with a sharpness she hadn't meant to show—hadn't known she felt. Nerves, she thought, and cleared her throat. He was silent. "Just tell her that, Tom," she said, calmer, "and we'll look for you to stop by tonight, if you want to."

Far away, she heard him murmur, "Goodbye." He hung up.

She was disconcerted. For a minute she thought she was going to start the inner fidgeting that drove her to work on Tom Bryce's problems (call back; agree to meet at the station; hear all about it) but that didn't happen. All she felt, after her first disconcertion, was relief.

Well, maybe it was finally over—her years of useless bondage. If so, her experience was worth the price.

She wondered a little about Irma, on the way to the station. It was a pity she couldn't know right away that her bracelet was recovered. If she got desperate enough to descend on Moran's house in person (which was unlikely, Marianne thought) that would be hard on Harriet. But then, whatever happened, Harriet was in for trouble.

Marianne tried not to think of her ... nor of the name and address she had left behind in Moran's house. That was a silly impulse. She doubted if Harriet would have the wits to use it ... but somebody else might.

Her discomfort increased, as she considered this. But the fatigue of her sleepless night and agitated morning was increasing, too; and by the time she got to the station, the one had nearly canceled out the other.

Harriet was writing a letter when Moran returned. (She had found her address book, and in it Mary Sidleigh, to whom she had written all her best letters years ago. Mary was real enough ... or had been.) She was absorbed in forming her words without blot or mistake, and did not look up. Moran sank down on her couch.

"Well, Harriet," he said. "I been to see Nagy. It's okay with him we keep it, so that's what we gonna do. Irma don't like it, let's see what *she's* gonna do!"

She frowned, without looking up. Why was everybody talking about Irma this morning?

"Something she owes me, for all those years. That's what I think, that's what Nagy thinks. So now she can pay. I'm right here, I got nothing to hide. I'm not ashamed who I am. Irma's ashamed, so let her keep quiet. She don't make me no trouble, I don't make her no trouble."

Harriet glanced up, uneasy. It made letter-writing terribly difficult, to have to keep shutting out other sounds. She hesitated, then leaned over her paper again.

"Okay," said Moran. "That's the way it's gonna be. You did all right, Harriet. You did good. I ain't ashamed who I am, I can prove everything. Papers I got, passport—everything. Birth certificate, even. Everything regular, picture of my nice little girl on the passport. My nice little girl that looks like Mrs. Smith," he said, and his voice thickened in a way that made Harriet hastily lay down her pen. "From Mrs. Smith, she sends—to me, to me! To Nagy!"

He looked at her now. Harriet sat very still.

"Well, okay," he said again, heavily controlled. "She's got no more papa, I got no more daughter. That's fair, okay? And from those years I'm so crazy," he said, beginning to shake, "those years I keep that dirty kid, I don't throw her out too—now I get something back! Twenty years, I kept her," he shouted suddenly—and like one sighting a sudden adversary, thrust himself forward from the couch, stood spread-legged, wide-armed. "Twenty years! You hear that? Twenty years I put food in her mouth, I put clothes on her back, all the time she's making trouble in my house—why? Because I'm a crazy man!" he yelled. "A crazy man, I don't throw out that dirty kid like her mother!"

Harriet sat frozen, her eyes shut tight. His hand fell heavily on her shoulder, and she yelped faintly. But the sound was lost.

"Now she'll pay back, you hear, Harriet? She'll pay back a little! The bracelet is mine, I keep it! Let the police come to my house, I don't care, I got papers, passports, I can prove! She's ashamed who she is—okay, I'm ashamed of nothing, I prove everything, you hear? That bracelet stays by me, it's mine!"

There was a terrible silence. Harriet, eyes shut tight, began like a rapid prayer, "I haven't *got* it, I haven't *got*—" but he struck her across her mouth, and she was still.

"Shut up. From you I don't need more trouble."

He moved away. He was quiet, except for the way he breathed. Peering, she saw him standing perfectly still, looking at her. More dark silence. Then his voice, altered, spoke again.

"Come on now, Harriet. I ain't mad with you. I know you got it, the lady told me. She don't care either. Nobody's mad—you did right."

She didn't answer.

"Take off the little bag, Harriet. Give it to me, it's okay.

"*Harriet ...*"

Then he came and took it. She sat blind, rifled, flung against the seatback. With a little plop, her recovered address book fell out upon the desk. There was a long silence then.

Calmer, he spoke to her again. But she knew that kind of calm. "Harriet, why you want to play tricks on me? I want you to tell me where the bracelet is, Harriet. Right now. Or you gonna be sorry."

She gave a sudden wail.

"*I don't know—I don't know!*"

He seized hold of her, by the cloth of her unbuttoned clothes.

"You didn't put this down the pipes, Harriet? Answer me, you put it in the pipes? I'm gonna get the plumber and find out, Harriet—you're gonna be sorry!"

"I didn't, I didn't!"

He was quiet so long that she took courage to look. But he was standing there looking down at her. She was caught—her eyelids wide, as though matchsticks held them.

"Harriet," he said, "you look around. I'm tired, I'm gonna go down and take a little rest, and when I come back you'll have it for me. Okay?"

She nodded. He said, "That's right. No more trouble. You look around, take your time, find it for me. Then I'm gonna get something nice for you. All right?"

She nodded again, rapid jerkings of her head. He gave her one dulled glance, and went away.

CHAPTER SEVEN

The waiting room in Grand Central Station contained its Saturday crowd; and Marianne, sunk in the first vacant space she could find, had neighbors close at either flank. One was a woman holding a child, whose restless feet occasionally struck against her. Each time the mother said, "Benny, stop that! Sorry." And Marianne, somnolent, murmured, "It's all right."

She was so tired her bones ached. Luckily, there was a trustworthy alarm built into her mind, and with this firmly set she could allow her eyes to close, her head to fall forward a little. The active little feet at her side meant less than nothing; the part of Marianne that remained on duty had no concern with them.

She was touched again, and the mother's voice spoke.

"Miss ..."

"It's all right."

"No, I think there's somebody here for you."

To that discreet murmur, she woke, saw her neighbor's face, embarrassed, and turned her head. Directly before her, enormously shrouded in old black sealskin, stood Harriet.

She got up at once—a sleepwalker's motion—and Harriet shrank back.

"You looked so—I thought you were asleep."

"What are you doing here, Harriet?" said Marianne.

Harriet did not reply. After a moment, collecting herself, Marianne took her arm. She yielded it docilely, and they walked away together.

Without more urging, Harriet began to speak. "It's dreadfully embarrassing, I hardly know how to tell you. I hope you won't be cross, but there's been a dreadful mistake, and I'm afraid I must have it back. What I gave you, you know."

Just outside the waiting room Marianne stopped. Harriet stopped too, obedient. She smiled, patient.

"How did you know where to find me?"

Harriet said, "It's not Irma's anymore, you see. And she's gone now, anyway. So I'm afraid I'll have to take it back again, I'm so sorry."

Marianne looked around them. There seemed to be no one near, with, or watching Harriet.

She asked again, "How did you know where I was?"

"Oh, well, the Waiting Room, of course—where else would one wait?" said Harriet; and she looked perplexed.

"I mean, here in the station. How did you know?"

"But your home," said Harriet. Her hands moved, making this clear. "Your train, you see—I asked, and it hadn't gone, so you couldn't have gone either, could you?"

"You mean you came down here by yourself, and asked about trains, and found me by yourself?"

"Yes, of course! Because I had to tell you at once, so you could give it me back," said Harriet. "I really am sorry. I did mean you to have it, you know."

Marianne drew a deep breath. She was entirely awake now.

"Listen to me, Harriet," she said. "If you can understand all that, you certainly can understand that I can't give you something that doesn't belong to you or to Mr. Moran! Or to me."

Harriet's gaze had left hers at the first stern word, and was now wandering past her shoulder somewhere. She had begun to frown, as though in concentration.

"Did Mr. Moran send you here? Did you tell him you gave me the bracelet?"

"Oh, no! You mustn't—"

"I haven't any intention of telling him anything. Or of seeing him again as long as I live," said Marianne. "Mr. Moran took that bracelet from me, Harriet. He had no right to give it to you in the first place. But you were right to give it back to me, and I'm going to give it back to the woman who owns it, and that's the end of it."

Harriet gave no sign of hearing any of this. Across the station, the light went on for Marianne's train; and in relief, in pity, she put her hand on Harriet's arm.

"You'll just have to say you lost it," she said. "Throw away your little bag and say you lost the whole thing. I'm surprised it hasn't happened before, anyway. And if he strikes you," she said, reckless, "you go tell the police!"

She waited for some response. Then she said, "Goodbye ... I'm sorry, Harriet," and turned away.

The moment she moved, she was seized. Her bag was grasped so strongly she nearly lost it, and a thin voice screamed in her ear, "Give it me! Give it me! Give it back to me!"

"Let go—stop that!"

People were pausing, staring. Harriet did not care. Her face contorted, her eyes screwed up, she hung on and screamed.

"I hate you, I hate you! Give it back to me, give it back to me—"

Suddenly and hard, Marianne slapped her. The bag was released instantly, the screaming stopped, and Harriet's hands flew to cover her face.

There was an appalling moment when nothing happened, in what Marianne felt to be an arena of interest. Blindly, she got hold of Harriet's arm again and pulled her into motion. No one stopped them, or spoke.

Halfway across the floor Marianne slowed. Her legs were shaking, and Harriet was heavy to drag.

"Harriet, listen. Take your hands down. I'm going to put you in a taxi and send you home, but we'll have to hurry. Please take your hands down, and walk!"

In mounting exasperation, she took hold of Harriet's wrists. They felt as delicate as paper toys, but they didn't yield. She let go of them and turned away.

She meant to go on through the gate. But there, unplanned, her feet swerved aside and turned her round again.

Harriet was gone.

In serious disbelief, she stood looking over the part of the station where she had just been, unable to imagine so rigid a figure springing out of sight. But Harriet was gone. Marianne began to look rather wildly anywhere, in any direction; but the only result of that was black figures, just at the edge of sight, all round. She blinked, and gave it up.

From the train window Marianne stared out on gray air and yesterday's snow, crusty and thinned. They were out of the tunnel at last, and into suburban country. The city—narrowed for her now into Moran's house, the station, the hotel—was left behind; and within two hours she would be home. And there, with Henry, surely she would relax again.

There was no question of relaxing now. Even with her head back and her eyes closed, her hands quiet in her lap, she was still full of inward leaps and tremors. But at least it was over, that nightmare trip.

Someone sat down beside her and was quiet too. No fuss of settlement. Somehow this became, presently, disturbing; and Marianne turned her head and saw Harriet's downcast profile.

The shock that went through her was entire, and kept her speechless.

As if encouraged by this silent reception, Harriet began to speak. "I must ask you to lend me my fare."

Somewhere, she had lost her hat. Her hair was disarranged. She raised her eyes, and they had lost all color—become as inhumanly pale as the snow beyond the train windows.

"It will be sent back to you, of course."

Behind them the conductor was coming down the car. Marianne could just hear his querulous repetitions, the snap of the punch. She turned to see where he was.

On that movement Harriet moved too. Without a sound she was out of her seat and passing forward up the aisle, touching nothing, seeming impervious to the train's movement. She slid through the barest opening in the platform door, and it slowly shut behind her.

Marianne sat and watched her vanish. She could feel her heart's slow, heavy beat throughout her entire body; it replaced thought. When the conductor reached her she was still immobile. He grumbled at her, while she began tardily to fumble with her bag. "Ought to have your ticket ready, lady."

His flat voice, the sane business of finding her ticket and handing it over, ended her isolation. By the time he had her seat stub ready she could speak.

"Conductor, the woman who was just sitting next to me—" She raised her voice, as he bent lower to hear.

"She hasn't any ticket. I'd be willing to pay her fare to the first stop—to Stamford and back, if you could see she gets off there." He stood swaying over her, in impatient attention.

"You want a ticket to Stamford?"

"And return, please. For the woman who was sitting here. She ought to get off there and go back, I think."

He said coldly, "It's up to you to see your friend gets off the right place, lady. I got enough to do."

"She isn't my friend," said Marianne, growing warm. "She asked me to lend her her fare ... and she doesn't look responsible for herself."

He leaned there with the look of a man maddeningly detained, and not in the least willing to get mixed up in this, whatever it was. "She must have been coming down the train ahead of you, conductor. Didn't you notice her?"

He said, grudging, "Tall lady? Black coat?"

"Yes, that's the one."

"She asked you to buy her a ticket?"

"To lend her her fare, yes."

"To Stamford? Return?"

"She didn't *say* where! I suppose you'll just put her off, when you catch her—she ought to be able to get back, at least."

Her face felt red, and probably was. He glanced at it, and began to prepare another ticket. A seat stub was thrust in the chairback next to hers, and the dour voice said: "That'll be two-twenty." She paid, in silence, and was handed another ticket with her change.

"What's this?"

"You wanted return, didn't you?"

"Not for myself—this is for her to go back with!"

But he had got the ticket into her hand, and was moving away.

"I got no idea where your friend is, lady," he said. "If I come across her I'll tell her her ticket's back here."

"But she might lock herself in a lavatory, or—"

He just kept going.

Between anger and guilt, she let him go. Her face felt hot enough to burst.

Presently the woman ahead of her turned round.

"He's an awful old sourpuss, isn't he! I think it was real nice of you to buy her a ticket—seems like the least he could do is give it to her."

"I guess the least he could do is what he did," said Marianne, depressed.

She was operating on minimum standards herself, as much as the conductor—only why had she had to say anything at all? She sat in thoughtless dread, turning Harriet's useless ticket over and over, looking up at each movement, each opening of the door. It was never Harriet.

When they approached Stamford the conductor came through again to take up stubs. With Harriet's in hand he leaned and said, in a faint offer of humanity, "Didn't turn up, eh?" Marianne shook her head. "No sign of her up forward. Didn't think there would be."

He had either a moment to spare or some impulse to justify himself. "I can't go round unlocking lavatories, you know."

"Then what *do* you do?"

He grinned sourly. "She'll turn up. Got to get off sometime. Don't want to buy her another ticket, do you?"

"No. You might as well take this."

But he still wasn't having the return ticket. He went on, and the women in front turned round again.

"Makes you feel silly to pay, doesn't it?" she said.

The train went on, through familiar, wintry country. At Darien, Marianne watched the platform, expecting to see Harriet among the crowd—Harriet trundled along by someone's hand, Harriet wild-eyed, wild-haired, lost. She began to feel a low nausea, that stayed with her like the image of Harriet.

At last she gave up and left her seat, going forward too. There was no way Harriet could have come back unseen. She was in one of the front cars, either bobbing from seat to seat, or locked in a lavatory. Men's or women's, it would make no difference to Harriet, probably. There was a surprising number of cars to go through.

On her way back she abandoned discretion and asked questions, promoting Harriet to a lost friend. Several people had noticed her, but none could say where she had gone. She came on her conductor, who gave her a disgruntled look—the kind of woman, clearly, who would rush home to spout complaints to the railroad; and what did she expect him to do, get out his butterfly net?

They didn't speak.

It occurred to her, as her own station approached, that she might still leave Harriet's name and address with another conductor, or the woman up ahead who had a Boston seat check. But she could hardly do this without giving her own name, and the end of it might well be Harriet delivered on Henry's doorstep. Besides, Harriet herself was not mute, except when she chose to be.

Nevertheless, she was reluctant to leave the train. She stood on the platform, worriedly looking along the windows, and someone gestured to her. It was a stranger, one of those to whom she had spoken, and she could not make out what he meant. She came nearer and saw, in one comprehension, that he was pointing to the seat ahead of his, and that Harriet was occupying it.

As their eyes met, Harriet rose.

Now she would try to get off. And be caught.

Marianne walked toward the steps, and waited there. Nothing happened. The steps went up, the door closed and the train wheels slowly turned; Harriet hadn't got off anywhere, it wasn't possible that she could have.

The train went out, Harriet certainly with it, and someone close to

Marianne said, "Thank God!" Where have you been?"
She turned to find Tom Bryce beside her, looking almost as queer as
Harriet.

CHAPTER EIGHT

It was icy in the old jeep that Tom Bryce clung to, like a favorite toy,
and which he flung along the narrow country roads as if it were one.
Marianne, less than grateful for her ride, thought of the warm and
solid bus and pulled her coat collar closer to her ears.

"I've got to go right home," she said, and he agreed. "I know—that's
where I'm taking you. I just wanted to talk to you a minute on the way."

"What about, Tom?"

Whatever it was, they didn't seem to begin.

Tom gave her a long stare, pulled the jeep back from the edge of a
passing field, and blurted, "Mary Ann, I've got to know what's going on!
Why doesn't anybody tell me things anymore? I've never lived this
way—I can't, it's not the way I'm made! God knows I've got my faults,
they're no secret, they never were—but whatever was going on, at least
it was out in the open, you know that! And now all of a sudden everybody
seems to know more about my affairs than I do, or else they think I
know more than I'm saying—which is it?

"When the police came last night," he said, before she could begin to
answer, "I was sitting there with a bunch of guys I know as well as I
know anybody in this world, and do you know what happened? Right
away, before we even knew what it was about, I could feel like a fence
going up—them on one side and me on the other. Why? What in hell did
they think had happened?"

He was always voluble—a big, fair, rough-faced man, with his tie
generally loosened to the second shirt button and a leather jacket
flapping open all winter long. He was often frantic, too, but he had
seemed, until now, to enjoy his frenzies. He wasn't enjoying this one.

"Well, what did happen?" she asked. He flung up an impatient hand,
from the bucking wheel.

"Nothing—nobody was hurt, the car wasn't even scratched! But I tell
you, Mary Ann, the way those fellows reacted just froze me over. They
couldn't help it, they were trying not to, but it was a thing you couldn't
get past. It broke up the game, at eleven o'clock," he said, in gloomy
anticlimax. "I know it was Irma's fault—well, she must have been sort
of careless, I mean—but it wasn't just that."

"Tom, I don't even know what you're talking about," she said. "Whose
car wasn't scratched, and why was it Irma's fault?"

"Well, not her fault, exactly," he said, backing down, as he always did
when it came to Irma. "I guess they'd jammed her in pretty tight, and
she worked her way out a little too hard, and she couldn't have realized
she'd started Tim Hurley's car to slide. It didn't get damaged—just

went to the foot of the hill and stopped. The only reason it got reported was because it was blocking the turn there. That didn't matter. Why, in the old days, it would have been a joke! Wouldn't it? A joke! We'd have laughed—"

His voice broke. She looked at him with more concern. However incoherent and slight all this might sound to her, to Tom Bryce it was some kind of last straw. Like me, with Irma's gloves, she thought; and she said gently, "Maybe you're imagining how they acted, Tom. Maybe it was just how you felt."

"Well, maybe partly. But I'm not imagining they broke up," he said. "Unless that was my fault too ... but what the hell could I do? They all heard her say she was going to bed. We were sitting there playing, and she came in and said good night, she was going to bed. And then an hour later the police come, and she's gone—her car's gone, how can I act like it's something I know about? I didn't know—I still don't. And where is she now? She's been gone since eleven o'clock last night!"

Their eyes met. The jeep swerved to a stop, and Tom Bryce turned to face her.

"You know where she went, Mary Ann!"

She said, "If she left about eleven, I guess I know *why* she went, Tom. I'd been talking to her from New York, about—some news that wasn't very good. But what she meant to do about it, I don't know."

A look of deathly satisfaction smoothed his face.

"There," he said. "You see? Now it's you. You were calling her up last night from New York, and the whole thing is news to me. For God's say, why? *Why doesn't anybody tell me anything?*"

She said unhappily, "I can tell you, if you want ... but I think it would make less trouble if you'd wait and talk to Irma. It's really her business—and yours, of course. I don't know the whole story. I was just doing an errand."

"What errand?"

"I wish you'd drive on," she said. "Henry'll think I'm lost again."

The strong motor roared and the little car started off again, but more slowly this time. Marianne's teeth had begun to chatter with the cold, making it difficult to sound casual.

"Irma needed some money, Tom, and she didn't want to worry you about it. So she asked me to sell something for her. I wasn't able to. That's all I know."

"Then what was all that about material, I was supposed to tell her?"

She had forgotten their telephone conversation, was embarrassed, now, for her own useless caution.

"I meant I was bringing it back."

"Was it her bracelet? Is that what it was?" He looked sidewise, seeing her nod; then said dully, "I thought so. She wasn't wearing it last night. She always wore it when we had company."

She didn't say any more.

They were going very slowly now. A rising wind seemed constantly to overtake them, crackling the window flaps as it rushed by. The bleak afternoon lay untenanted all around them.

"Tom," she said. "Have you reported her being gone?"

"Reported her?"

"To the police. It's a long time. It's more than twelve hours."

He didn't reply, until the houses of Willett appeared in the distance. Then he said, with apparent irrelevance: "No, it's no use, Mary Ann. It's all finished, I'm standing in a big hole, I'm all through."

"You think she's left you?"

This time he didn't answer at all.

The little pink house that she and Henry shared came into view, up the road. She never saw it without pleasure; but this afternoon what she felt was closer to gratitude, of the humblest. She was home.

The jeep turned up the drive with a sudden hard swing that made the back of the car skid. Marianne scrambled for balance. The jeep's motor died, and country silence fell coldly upon them. Tom kept looking straight ahead.

She said, "Do you want to come in?"—not wanting him to, but touched by his expression.

"I wish you could report it," he said suddenly. "I—I'm ashamed to ..."

"Tom, how can I? There's nothing to be ashamed about. It's something anybody would do, just to be sure, and it was such bad driving last night."

He swung himself out of the car with the sole purpose, she discovered, of helping her out. It wasn't a usual attention, and he looked rather ashamed at that, standing there with his hand out. But he wouldn't come in; he didn't answer, or seem to hear, her goodbye. Before she had her key out, the jeep was well down the road again.

Henry wasn't home.

There was no reason why he should be, at this hour. There was no reason why he should leave the store to Morrie on a Saturday afternoon just to be here when she arrived. Yet she had been thinking of home and Henry as the same thing, and she felt a first, strange loneliness there without him.

It passed, gradually. She called up and talked to him awhile. He said he was coming home for supper (the store stayed open Saturday nights) and she could come back with him, if she wanted. It sounded like an offer of forgiveness, and she accepted it.

She had a cup of tea in her kitchen after that, looking out into their deep wood lot while she drank. She had always liked Henry's choice of ground, and the loneliness hadn't bothered her a bit, but it was true that she hadn't been there much without Henry. She wasn't used to being home in the middle of the afternoon at all, in fact. The house seemed very quiet.

She went upstairs and lay in a hot bath; and there in that soothing warmth the turbulent people who had taken over her thoughts—Tom,

Irma, Moran, and poor Harriet—somehow drained from her mind. She was glad of the respite, without understanding how it could happen so soon. Perhaps it was only that there had been too much—too violently, and all at once—and her mind was shutting them out a while in self-defense.

She crawled at last from the tub, put on her flannel nightgown, and went to bed.

A telephone rang in darkness that had come down while she slept. She went half-asleep through the dark house to answer it.

It was some man she didn't know—a local-sounding voice, but she didn't recognize the name. She said yes, she was Mrs. Hinkley, on the Old Church Road.

"Well, I was bringing a lady over to see you, Mrs. Hinkley, but it seems like I've lost her. Elderly lady, didn't seem real well. I thought I better let you know."

"In a black coat?"

"That's right, sealskin. Don't see many of those anymore. She had your name on a piece of paper, wanted me to bring her over. I don't generally take long rides like that in the winter, but like I say she seemed poorly, couldn't seem to understand about the buses. Anyway, I said I'd oblige. Made her a rate of eight-fifty, she said that was all right. Didn't pay, though," he said.

"Where are you?" said Marianne. "I mean, where did you lose her?"

"Well, it was her lost me, to tell you the truth, Mrs. Hinkley. Said she wanted to phone, and then I guess she forgot about me and wandered off somehow. I don't see how, but I—"

"But where? Where was this?"

"Why, right outside Willett—she'll be all right, she's close enough now. I expect folks know you there, don't they?"

"Yes," said Marianne. "All right, thank you."

"About the fare, would you want me to send you the bill? I have to charge part return fare this time of year, that's why it comes to eight-fifty. Can't get anybody coming back in the winter, you know. The lady said it was all right."

"Yes. Yes, send me the bill."

She turned on the first light she could find, in the renewed—the almost monstrous quiet of her lonely house. The mantel clock, whirring sedately, marked the time at four-thirty—only that! It was as dark as four in the morning, and her mind as fogged as one wakened at that hour, as prone to sourceless fear....

She stood a moment, working one bare foot upon the other, and then picked up the telephone again.

CHAPTER NINE

"You should have called me, Mary Ann," Henry said.

It wasn't a reproach. He was just pointing out what he considered an error in judgment, that Marianne didn't yet see.

She didn't see it at all. To tell the truth, she wasn't trying. What mainly absorbed her attention at that moment was Henry himself, calmly eating up his supper of baked beans and stewed tomatoes. She was having one of those rare discovery-views of her partner that occasionally come to people who live together—seeing, instead of her Henry, an angular, competent, rather intimidating young man. Nice looking, too. The way anybody coming into the hardware store might see him for the first time: Mr. Hinkley.

A little flustered, she fixed a demure gaze on her wedding ring and tried to fish up a sensible answer. (Henry wasn't much on romantic notions. She wasn't herself, usually.)

"Somebody had to go look for her," she pointed out. "Why should you? And Morrie couldn't find water in the sea. Besides, it's Joe Palmer's business—he's paid for it."

Joe Palmer was the town constable. The main, day one.

"That's right," Henry agreed. "Joe's welcome to do all the wanderin' around he wants to, I don't say he's not. But he can't be two places at once. You were alone out here a good hour and a half before I got home— that's foolishness. You know this is the place she's making for."

"I'm not afraid of Harriet! Why, she looks like Miss Purdy, if you can imagine Miss Purdy kind of cracked."

"Miss Purdy still shingles her own roof, and don't you forget it," he replied. "I sold her a power saw fall before last, too. And people that aren't right in the head get mighty strong spells—you remember old Mrs. Leavis. Threw Sam right down the cellar steps, when she was seventy-three."

"Anyway this house was locked up tight as a drum. That was the first thing I did after I called Joe. I wasn't going to let her in."

"You pulled all the curtains, too," he observed. "You were scared all right. Don't tell me."

It was true. Yet it was also true that in any rational, physical sense, she wasn't afraid of Harriet.

"Well, she sort of gives me the creeps, Henry, that's all."

"Shows good common sense. Don't you start talking yourself out of it."

There was a pause, with Henry motionless above his empty plate. Marianne pulled herself together and rose.

"I didn't get any custard made. You want some applesauce?"

He nodded. There weren't even any cookies—Saturday was the day she usually caught up on those. However, Henry was an easy man to feed, and went to work on his bread-and-molasses without comment.

"You coming back in with me?"

"I don't think so. I'm tireder than I thought."

"Then I'm going to send Cousin Morrie in to stay with you," he said. "I'd as soon have him here as there anyway. Put him by the window where a light shines on him—at least he looks big."

She didn't want Morrie. It would mean Parcheesi all evening or else listening to a lot of gossip she knew better than he did.

"I'd rather come in and stay with Catharine," she said. Henry's sister was as sensible as himself, and could always use a hand with the children.

"That's no rest."

"It's better than Morrie."

Henry made no further comment, and she went up to dress.

It was snowing again, a little, when they came out—a thin, icy snow blown by a bitter wind. When Henry had shut them up in the car, she said unhappily, "I hope Harriet's inside someplace."

"She seems to be a pretty smart manager," he replied.

Driving along, Marianne cast him shy glances from time to time. He had that removed look again, as of someone seen fresh, and she was beginning to know why. It was because of all she had told him, and the unshaken way he had received it. Not just his lack of complaint about her carryings-on—they simply meant the end of her job with Bryce Builders, and that was that. But he might have been hearing all his life about the underhanded disposal of jewels, and thieves with mad, ladylike wives, and Irma's shady connections. That was something she hadn't appreciated about Henry—the way he could take in whatever you told him, and digest it, without any need to go back and chew it over in a hundred different phrases.

She herself was less fortunately constructed—more (though not quite so much) along Morrie's lines.

"I keep going over this whole thing in my mind," she confessed, to Henry's profile, "trying to think what I ought to have done that I didn't do. So things wouldn't have ended up in such a mess."

"Besides staying home in the first place?" But he grinned.

"If I hadn't got rattled and just stuck that bracelet in my bag, where anybody could get it out in a minute—"

"Maybe it's lucky you did. If he'd had to hunt, maybe you wouldn't have got away so easily." She shook her head, doubtful, and he added, "No, Mary Ann, it looks to me like the whole mess was there already. You just walked into it. Maybe you were lucky to be able to walk right out!"

"I've still got that bracelet!" she said. "Henry, I forgot to give it back to him."

They thought about that, driving slowly down the main street of Willett in all its Saturday night (comparative) liveliness.

She said, "I'll drive right over, soon as I let you off. I want to see how he is anyway, and if he's heard from her."

"We'll both go," said Henry, firm. "You're not going anywhere alone till things calm down some."

They stopped at the store first and found Morrie happily idle, drifting from one slow browser to the next, full of unanswered remarks. There was always a good crowd in from outlying farms and houses on Saturday night, amusing themselves in this practical way. Most of them would just collect what they wanted, or wait for Henry if they needed help.

There were a few who did; Henry became involved. Presently Marianne took off her coat and went to work too. They could just as well go over after the store closed, at nine.

She was wrapping up a set of Pyrex bowls when Joe Palmer came in. He was off duty by now and wearing his windbreaker and cap, but he wasn't there as a customer. He stood waiting, and she went over to him as soon as she could.

"Any news, Joe?"

"Yeah, I think so. There can't be two of them."

"What do you mean?"

"This is an English lady, right? Looks like Miss Purdy?"

"That's right, Joe."

"Well, here's what I got," he said. "I got a Miss Gaither, or something like it, from God knows where. She's English, and she's got a black sealskin coat, and she's over at Dr. Evans's. You want it?"

Dr. Evans was the Episcopalian minister, a very old and gentle man with a small church. Willett was mostly Baptist and Congregational.

"What's she doing over there?" said Marianne, alarmed. "Is she alone with them?"

"I guess so. Doesn't seem to be any trouble. Dr. Evans just called us and wanted to know if we'd heard of a Miss Gaither staying with anybody local. I asked him about her a little, and it sounded like it was your lady. You want to come over and see?"

"You haven't been over?"

"No, thought I'm come get you, first. *I* don't know what to do with her," he said, grinning.

Henry was downstairs, among the paints. Listening to her hurried whispering, he showed first signs of harassment.

"Well, you'll just have to wait a minute, Mary Ann. Quick as I get through here, I'll go."

"I could go over now, with Joe."

"Joe's a nice guy," said her husband, "but if you go, I go too." He was getting flushed over the cheekbones. Marianne went up and told Joe it would have to be a few minutes.

"Why don't you go ahead, Joe? I hate to leave them alone with her, they're so old. We'll come as soon as we can."

"They sound under control," said Joe, grinning. "Mrs. Evans has got her to bed."

Mrs. Evans was a devoted and implacable sick-nurse, the scourge of both the local doctors. Age didn't seem to wither her, in this respect.

Marianne, a little reassured, settled to wait.

A little after eight-thirty the three of them came up on the Evanses' front porch. The house was lighted upstairs and down, and Dr. Evans came to let them in. He seemed relieved.

"So our poor lady was coming to you, was she?" he said, helping Marianne with her coat.

She couldn't deny this; but Henry, firmer, said, "Not to stay with us, no, sir. Mary Ann thinks she may know who she is, though."

"I see, I see. Well, that's very kind of you. We know who she is, of course, but we can't seem to make out where she was going. I've been here more than forty years, and I've never heard of a Malden House—but all these new people coming in, you know, they change the names of these properties. Impossible to keep up."

His wife came briskly downstairs—a thin little woman not much younger than her husband, but lively with purpose.

"Well, there you are!" she said. "I'd better warn you, you can't have her tonight—she's in no condition to get up again. But you can come up and see her, it'll do her good to see someone she knows."

She shook hands round, with a sharp glance for each, and added, "She should have been met, you know. Wandering round in a strange place in the middle of winter, at her age!"

"How did she come to you, Mrs. Evans?" Marianne asked. "Why, she got lost, poor soul! Some taxi driver, can't have been our Mr. Hooten! let her out goodness knows where—she didn't. Far as I can see she just wandered, till she saw the church. Then, of course, she came right to us. You're calling your place Malden House, are you?" she said, not pleased.

"No, ma'am, we're not," said Henry. "You suppose Mary Ann could take a look at this lady, and see if she's the one that was following her? If it's the same one, then we can tell you as much as we know about her. It's not," he said, cautious, "a whole lot."

"Following you?"

Mrs. Evans turned to Marianne, clearly prepared to defend her patient. Her husband interposed.

"Just take Mrs. Hinkley up, my dear. We'll wait for you in the living room." He led Henry and Joe away, leaving Mrs. Evans no choice but to obey.

Somewhat stern, she took Marianne's arm.

"Well, I think there's some mistake here, but you can come see. We'll just look in—I don't want to disturb her, she's about ready to drop off, and she's had enough upset for one day. You don't really know Miss Gaither, then?"

"Not by that name," Marianne agreed, with Henry's caution.

Mrs. Evans conducted her to the open door of a large bedroom, where one lamp burned softly by an old-fashioned mahogany bed. In this, supine, Harriet lay covered to the chin.

Her eyes were open and turned toward the door with a patient, hopeful expression that did not change when she saw who they were—if she did see.

"Just making sure you're all right, my dear," Mrs. Evans said from the doorway. "Warm, are you?"

"Thank you so much ... so kind ..."

"Harriet," said Marianne. She moved slightly forward. "I'm sorry you've been lost, Harriet ... do you want me to call Mr. Moran, and tell him where you are?"

Some flicker went over Harriet's expression, and she whispered, "Please ring them up, they'll send for me. If you just ask for Malden House—"

"All right, dear, we'll tell them," said Mrs. Evans. She went to make slight adjustments in Harriet's covers, then repassed Marianne and took her firmly in tow. "You go to sleep, now, won't you? I'll be back to look in on you."

This time she shut Harriet's door. But she said nothing further until they were going downstairs again, when she remarked, in slight concession, "Well, I had Dr. Howard take a look at her—nobody could object to that, I suppose. He said shock and exposure, of course, just what I told him! And to keep her in bed, which she was."

"But you can't keep her here, Mrs. Evans!"

"Nonsense, of course we can—why shouldn't we?"

Dr. Evans, when they came into the living room, seemed less certain on that point than his wife. He had been talking to Henry, and turned anxious eyes on them.

"It's the same lady, my dear? This is Mrs. Moran?"

"That's the way I was introduced to her, Dr. Evans. I don't know who we'd call about her except Mr. Moran."

"Then of course we'll call him," said Mrs. Evans, adding firmly, "But whoever she is, she can't be taken out tonight."

"Oh, I think we could wrap her up good and take her over to the hospital," said Joe. "They'll take good care of her. You folks are alone here, and there's no reason for you taking on a sick lady that's not right in her head. Now you know who she belongs to, I mean." There was a pause, in which Dr. Evans looked away from his wife, who was staring at Marianne.

"Miss Gaither seems perfectly sensible to me, considering what she's been through."

"My dear, perhaps if you—"

"You're not suggesting she's violent, are you?"

"It would be a big job to look after her," said Marianne, tactful. "It really would. I think Joe's right."

Mrs. Evans stared at Joe then.

"He doesn't know anything about shock and exposure. You're no doctor, Joe."

"Well, neither are you, my dear," said her husband bravely. "I think perhaps—"

"Why don't we call up Doc Howard," Henry interposed, "and see what he says. You happen to know what her temperature is, Mrs. Evans?"

"I do. It's subnormal—and I'd rather have a good climbing mercury any day. I can tell you exactly what—"

"A most sensible suggestion," said Dr. Evans, hobbling away. "I'll call him myself."

Mrs. Evans went after him.

Half an hour later, the new town-subscribed ambulance came for Harriet—a concession to Mrs. Evans. Willett had no hospital. The drive to the Frampton hospital was one of twenty-two miles, and the driver in prospect a resigned Dr. Howard himself. Joe Palmer and Henry brought down the bundle that was Harriet. She made no protest. Her expression was dreamily vacant still, but she no longer responded even to Mrs. Evans, who kept up a determined monologue with her until she went out the door.

Henry's car followed the ambulance—a concession to Mrs. Hinkley. The doctor would see that Harriet was admitted, and the hospital or the police would notify Moran—as Henry pointed out, it was kind of useless for them to be tagging along this way. But having made his point he followed the ambulance tail lights calmly down the highway, with Marianne huddled up beside him.

CHAPTER TEN

Late Sunday evening, in the February dark, Mr. William Compton returned from New York to his three-acre property within the town line of Willett, Connecticut. He was alone, his wife having two more days to "put in" down in the city (as he later explained), and he got out of his car to open the gate to his driveway. This was part of a high split-paling fence that divided the property from the roadside and the gate was kept latched during the owners' absence. His car's motor and lights were on, and when he pushed the gate back he saw what looked like another car parked up in his turnaround.

This was a shock to him—no car ought to have been there—and his first reaction was one of rage.

"The first thing I thought was, by God, I've got one of them this time! I know they come in here, use the place like a damn' lovers' lane, back all over my grass and shrubs. We have to be down in the city a lot, and a thing like that gets around...."

Mr. Compton got back into his own car and drove up behind the stranger, blocking him off. The car was a pastel hardtop, Connecticut plates, and no heads showed in the glare of his lights. He gave one blast of his horn, then jumped out and strode over to the intruder, yanking open his door.

The sole person lying within did not move. Something slid off the seat and fell on the snow against Mr. Compton's foot. He picked it up and saw that it was a woman's handbag.

Sobered, he leaned in and tried to examine the woman, but she had fallen sideways away from him. She was appallingly rigid to his tentative hand, he didn't try to move her after the first touch. He put the bag carefully on the floor, shut the car door again, and went in to call the State Police.

When the first car arrived he was waiting in the drive, frozen, stammering with cold and nerves. He had touched nothing, he said. His own car's door still hung open and its lights blazed on the strange car. The two troopers had their first version of his story poured over their backs while they made their first, minimal investigation of the woman and her surroundings. Then one led Mr. Compton mercifully indoors while the other called his barracks from the car.

The woman was dead. Had been dead long enough, in that cold, to move all of a piece. She carried identification as Mrs. Irma Bryce of Woods Lane, Willett, twenty-nine years old, five-three. The car was registered in her name, same address. Cause of death was not immediately apparent.

Mr. Compton, when he heard her name, cried, "By God! Irma Bryce!" and then seemed at a loss to explain his recognition, even to himself. No, he didn't exactly know her, didn't even know Tom Bryce, really except to speak to in a store. He was the fellow that was putting up all those hellish developments.

No, he couldn't identify Irma, if that was Irma. They probably understood the way things were nowadays in these small Connecticut towns, fairly near New York. It wasn't a matter of year-rounders and summer people anymore, but rather of two kinds of year-rounders: locals, and New Yorkers (like himself) who were able to live this far out most of the time and preferred it. And then some odds-and-ends of local businessmen who were neither genuine locals nor linked to New York— like Tom Bryce. The result of this kind of populating was that anybody who lived five or six years in Willett (like Mr. Compton) knew an awful lot about all kinds of people he'd never really said six words to. And restored by warmth, whisky, and the arrival of more police, he cried, "Why, if it was my wife in Tom Bryce's drive, I'll bet he could give you chapter and verse about us, but if he saw Betsey on a New York street, he'd have a hard time putting a name to her. My God," he said. "I haven't called my wife about this. Can I?"

Out on the floodlit turnaround, the new snow marked and traveled in the last hour remained comparatively unbroken near the blue car. What marks the car had made on its arrival were covered, were only smooth, slight depressions now. The last fall had ended nearly four hours ago, and had been a scant half-inch. It was the previous fall—Friday's— that must have taken and held the tracks of Irma Bryce's car. It was impossible to tell now who had got down and opened the split-paling fence for it. There was no trace of snow on the high-heeled pumps the dead woman wore.

What examination could be made there, on that stiffly crumpled figure, showed traces of considerable disorder. The dark, uncovered hair was tangled, the face streaked with dirt, one stocking torn. The left hand showed a two-inch cut that had bled, and lacerations. She was wearing a dark woolen dress under a long mink coat; a diamond wedding ring and watch. One light, soiled doeskin glove was thrown on the back seat. Her purse contained forty-odd dollars and two other rings.

"Better get her over to Frampton and thaw her out," said the police doctor. "I can't tell you much more now than you can see for yourself; she's been lying here refrigerating too long."

"How long?" asked the man from State Police. But the doctor could not tell him that.

"She's as dead and as cold as she can get," he said, impatient. "You tell me she's been here since before it snowed—all right, I agree. She could have been here for the last snow, too. It's been freezing right along. Hasn't anybody missed her?"

"If they have, they didn't mention it," said State Police dryly.

Troopers Walsh and Corvi were in Woods Lane, ringing Tom Bryce's bell. The house, the distantly spaced houses of the neighborhood, gave off intense quietness; it was one-thirty Monday morning. The cold, still air ate upon their bared faces.

"Light back there," said Walsh, peering.

"Yeah. Kitchen. Here he comes."

The man who opened the door had not been to bed. He was dressed in plaid wool shirt, slacks. In the hall light, which he put on, he showed unshaven. His vision seemed dulled by fatigue.

"What is it?" he said. He had to clear his throat, repeat the words.

"Mr. Bryce?"

"Yes. What? You're police?"

"State Police. Can we come in?"

He turned, leaving the door wide for them to enter and close behind themselves. He went back through the house ahead of them, in rapid, uncertain progress, perhaps toward the kitchen again. But in the unlighted dining room he turned and waited for them.

"Is it Irma—my wife?"

One of the men flicked the wall switch. Light poured down on a disorder of abandoned cards, poker chips, chairs pushed back at angles. The troopers glanced at this; Tom Bryce seemed unaware of it.

"Your wife isn't here, Mr. Bryce?"

"No—no. What's happened? Where is she?"

"Could you tell us how long she's been gone?"

He stared down at the table then, frowning. His hand turned at his side, as if to indicate what he saw.

"Friday night. We were … She came in, and …" He sat down, in one of the pushed-back chairs. "What is it? Where is she?"

They told him then of the woman in Irma Bryce's car, carrying her identification, who had been found that night.

"She's been there some time, Mr. Bryce. You say Mrs. Bryce left here

Friday night? Could you give us a description of her?"

He said at last, "Dead?"

"Yes, sir."

He got up, and went by them, fast. They moved, stood still again. He was in the living room, fumbling in its shadows. He came back holding a large, framed photograph out to them.

"This is Irma," he said, and watched them.

The dark-haired girl watched them too, steadily smiling a dimpled smile. She looked intensely alive. Trooper Corvi took the photograph, put it gently down.

"She's been taken over to Frampton, Mr. Bryce. If it's Mrs. Bryce, you can identify her there. We'll drive you over. Can you come now?"

He would have gone numbly out of the house without hat or coat if they hadn't reminded him. His windbreaker was flung over one of the chairs in the wildly untidy kitchen; thick-soled boots sprawled nearby. He changed into these, ran his hand through his hair as if in replacement for a hat, and opened the kitchen door. They went out that way.

An old jeep stood nearby and he made for this, became adamant about climbing in, driving himself. The troopers communicated silently; then Corvi went around to the police car and Walsh climbed in the already coughing jeep.

"I'll show you where to go, Mr. Bryce."

"I don't want to talk."

Walsh agreed. "Not much to say till you're sure."

But on the deserted highway, twice checked down to the legal forty-five, he began to talk.

He said abruptly, "What happened—where was she?"

"They don't know cause of death yet. There was no accident. She was in the car, parked, in private grounds. The owners had been away."

"Who?" he demanded; and frowned over the answer. "I know who they are. Irma wasn't—what was she doing there?"

"That's what they'd like to know. It looks like someone was with her when she drove in, Mr. Bryce. Did she leave by herself, Friday night?"

The jeep swerved. Corvi's hand came up, went back. Tom Bryce didn't answer.

In Frampton, they had to wait. In a night-echoing room, harshly lighted, he was given black coffee in a white mug.

"Be a few minutes, Mr. Bryce. Take anything in it?"

He shook his head. They stayed with him, absorbed, low-voiced, in their own concerns. A wall clock audibly moved, minute to minute. In that silence, that alien room and time of waiting, Tom Bryce apparently came to some terms with himself and what was happening. The confusion he had shown at first did not reappear; he no longer looked tired.

He saw Irma without a word, in one long glance. She was not yet an orderly sight, but he gave no indication that this was so. He nodded once, for reply, his mouth tight. Out in the hall tears began to run steadily down his face, but they made no difference in his expression. Later, he talked quietly. Inexhaustibly.

"I don't know exactly what time it was. Probably our local policeman could tell you when he came. It was before eleven, I think. She'd come in around ten and said good night—she had a different dress on, a blue one. No, I wasn't worried. I was surprised. I stayed up because I wanted to ask her what had happened, but she didn't come home."

"No, I didn't report her missing. I didn't want to do that. Because if she meant to go— She must have meant to go. What else would she need the money for?"

He said, "It was her bracelet, she could do whatever she wanted to with it. Or if she'd told me she needed the money ... I don't know where she would have been going, no. Or who with. She'd lived in New York, before we were married. She had an apartment with another girl, but she used to travel a lot. She was a demonstrator for—beauty stuff, cosmetics. And then she was demonstrating for the Tru-Tile people, you know that wall covering, at the Home Show—that was where I met her. I don't know where she would have been going, she didn't have any people. So far as I knew she didn't see anybody except people around here, that we both knew. I guess it was dull for her," he said. "That was what I meant, about her leaving. There wasn't any other reason—I was crazy about her, and she—we got along all right. But it was dull for her. I've been feeling for a long time she—that it was dull for her," he said, a third time, with no change of inflexion.

He showed, when Marianne's name came up, the same stubbornness he had shown about driving his jeep.

"She told me all about it, I can tell you as much as she can. Irma wanted her to sell the bracelet in New York, and she went down and tried. She shouldn't have—I told her that, but she's been with me a long time, she's very loyal—anyway she went down and tried. I don't know just where, does it matter? There's no reason to wake them up in the middle of the night about it, is there?

"She told Irma she couldn't sell it—called her up that night, just before she left. Called up from New York. I didn't know about it then."

He gave, slow and exactly spoken, Marianne's name and address. "But there's nothing more she can tell you. You're not going to bother her about it, are you?"

A kind of breakfast was brought in, and he drank all the coffee he was offered, in scalding gulps that produced no visible effect on him. The Danish pastry lay on his plate.

Before he left, they told him what they could of the cause of Irma's death. She had sustained serious injury to the cervical vertebrae, to an extent not yet determined; but her actual death had resulted from exposure.

He stood trying to understand, his hand groping in imitation toward the back of his own neck. But before any trace of understanding showed he went suddenly down to his knees—then face down, upon the floor.

CHAPTER ELEVEN

Most of the State Police stationed near Willett were known one way or another to Henry Hinkley. He was accustomed to seeing them in town, even in his store, but he hadn't yet had one show up at his front door at eight o'clock in the morning.

Henry wasn't pleased. It had taken all day Sunday to get his wife halfway calmed down, and here they were again. On the other hand, the fellow was only doing his job. Henry let him in.

"What can we do for you?"

"I'd like to talk to Mrs. Hinkley, if she's here."

"She's here. Don't know where else she'd be, at this hour." He said, polite but firm, "This some more about that Mrs. Moran?"

The trooper looked at him, then shook his head.

"No. I'm here about a Mrs. Irma Bryce."

"And what's the matter with *her?*" said Henry.

"She's dead."

"Is that so," said Henry, considerably startled. His annoyance was replaced by concern—a gradual process. "Well, I'm sorry to hear it. How'd it happen?"

"That's what we're trying to find out. Could I see Mrs. Hinkley?"

"Sure," said Henry. "Come on in. I'll get her."

Marianne was rapidly washing breakfast dishes, pale-lipped, but otherwise ready to leave for town. This was the day she was going to give in her notice, and retire to peaceful living.

An inexplicable feeling of pity came over Henry as he said her name. It showed in his voice, and made her turn in surprise. "What?"

"Irma Bryce is dead, Mary Ann. There's a trooper out here, wants to talk to you about her."

"Dead!"

"I know. They're tryin' to find out what happened. Come on." Then he stopped her at the doorway. "You still got that bracelet."

"Oh," she said. It was true. They considered each other's faces.

Then Henry said, "Well, never mind, we got nothing to keep secret. Come on."

But it was funny just the same how nervous a policeman right after breakfast could make you feel. He was standing in the bay window, in front of the crisscross curtains, and he said he was sorry to bother them so early.

"Mr. Bryce tells us you were about the last person to talk with his wife before she left, Friday night. You called her up from New York?"

"Yes," said Marianne. Her throat felt as if it had fingers around it.

Henry said, "No reason why we can't all sit down, is there?" He put himself on the arm of her chair, and they both watched the trooper go down on glazed chintz. "Kind of a shock," said Henry, "hearing somebody's dead that wasn't even sick last time you saw them. I suppose it was an accident?"

"She was found in her car, near the town, Mr. Hinkley. We don't know enough yet to say just what happened. Now about that telephone call—what did Mrs. Bryce say to you?"

"Well ... Tom told you why I went to New York, didn't he? She wanted me to sell a piece of jewelry for her, and she gave me the name of a man she thought would buy it. So I went there."

"If you'll just give me the man's name and address, Mrs. Hinkley."

She gave it; Henry adding helpfully, "His wife's right over in Frampton hospital now—don't know as you'll get much out of her, but she's there."

"Why?" said the trooper. He had stopped writing.

"Well, she wanted the bracelet back," Marianne explained. "Her husband took it from my bag that night—that was what I had to call Irma about, the second time—but in the morning—"

"Just a minute," he said. "Please." He looked at them, one at a time; then, seriously, round the living room. (In the morning light, it looked very nice with its hand-crafted reproductions, all solid wood, no veneers. Marianne was glad she had taken time to dust.) He looked down at his book, then back at them. "There's a little more to this than I'd figured," he said. "Perhaps—"

"There was a little more to it than Mary Ann figured, too," said Henry. The trooper seemed to decide, and got a grip on his pencil again.

"Well, let's just get the facts straight, right through, Mrs. Hinkley. You reported this—this theft to anybody?"

"Just to Irma. Because of publicity, you know, and Tom's credit. His business credit. That was why Irma couldn't go herself, in the first place. I called her just as soon—"

"You said that was the second time you called her. What was the first? Would you mind just going back," he said, "and telling me how things happened from the beginning. I think we'll get along faster that way. Now, Mrs. Bryce gave you her bracelet to take down to this man in New York. Just when was this, and what did Mrs. Bryce tell you?"

They began over. The snowy morning when Irma had come to see her—the tranquil, debt-piled office with its curtains and hotplate, seemed to have sunk into a far time. Not days but events had made this barrier of distance in Marianne's mind, and she found it difficult to go back. She felt like one telling a dream to a stranger ... who had to write it down.

She left out the bargain with Irma; she couldn't bring it up now, even with Irma dead. Especially with Irma dead. What she had agreed to do passed for a favor, and either of the men questioned her doing it.

But there were exacting questions about every word Irma had spoken to her—in the office and over the telephone. She was surprised in going over them to discover just how little real information they contained. It all boiled down to the fact that Irma needed a thousand dollars in cash, right away. That was all.

"I had the impression it was a debt," Marianne said. "Because she said something about having been foolish, or made a mistake." She thought back, and repeated what she could of Irma's little lecture; it added no information, after all.

The telephone calls were less easy to repeat, especially with Henry there (he hadn't been given a word-for-word version).

"Well, what she actually said was, 'You idiot, don't you dare do another thing—you've made enough mess out of this.' Then she said to come right back and keep my mouth shut, she'd handle it."

Henry kept an awful stillness. The trooper, writing, inquired, "Mrs. Bryce had told you this man was a friend of hers?"

"No, she said they knew him, or he knew about them, or something like that. Maybe Tom will be able to tell you."

They came at last to Harriet, and the Saturday afternoon.

"You got in on the 1:41, Mrs. Hinkley—this woman didn't get off with you? You're sure?"

"No, she went on farther, I don't know where to. The taxi man was from Hillyard, and that hasn't got a station on the line."

"And he called you up when? About what time?"

"Four-thirty. He said he was right outside Willett, then—east, I guess, if he was coming down from Hillyard. He didn't say exactly where."

"Then what time did she come to Dr. Evans's?"

"They said it was around suppertime—or Joe Palmer did," said Henry. "You could check with Joe, he'd be on duty now. Ought to be myself," he added.

The trooper acknowledged this, after a moment, by standing up.

"Well, I guess I don't need to keep you any longer. Thanks very much. Will you be here in case we want to reach you today?" he asked Marianne.

Henry answered for her again. "Yes, she will. No point in your going in now, Mary Aim. Tom Bryce won't be coming to work today."

"Is he home?" Marianne asked the trooper.

"I think Mr. Bryce is over in Frampton, ma'am."

"But why?" she asked, making him look at her again. "I mean—isn't he coming back here?"

He didn't know what Mr. Bryce's plans were. Troubled, Marianne trailed him to the door, Henry following.

She said, "And you haven't told us what happened to Irma. What she died of."

"She had a broken neck, Mrs. Hinkley," he replied. He put his wide-brimmed hat on, thanked them again, and left.

When they were alone, had been alone for some minutes, standing side by side, Marianne looked up at Henry. He was rather pale. She took his arm.

"Come on, we're going to have one more cup of coffee before you go. I don't care who wants hardware."

In the kitchen, alarmed by his long silence, she suggested, "Maybe it was a car accident, Henry. You can get a broken neck like that."

"I don't think they'd be asking round this way, for a car accident," he slowly replied. But once begun, he went on as deliberately to say what was in both their minds. "This seems to've been a dangerous business you got mixed up in, Mary Ann. We're lucky nothing happened to you."

Once it was out, she could talk too.

"Henry, that's what I don't understand! What happened was certainly queer enough, and I certainly was scared ... but not *that kind* of scared. Not of somebody—"

"Tryin' to break your neck," he finished for her, calm and dry. They began to drink their coffee, thoughtful.

She said, "That strange little man ... Besides, he was in New York!"

"Well," said Henry, "I guess there's other kinds of accidents besides car accidents. And she seems to have had some mighty queer friends. Acquaintances," he amended, fair. "And if those, then probably there were others you didn't know about."

"Or Tom either ..." she said in a low voice.

In the end she came in to town with him, to Catharine again. Their reason for this decision was that she was too upset to stay alone all day; and Henry had a rather embarrassing telephone conversation with somebody at the State Police barracks, who didn't seem to know who he was. But he managed to leave the hardware store number on record, as the place where Marianne could now be reached, whether they knew what he was talking about or not.

In town, Marianne let him out at the store and drove on down the street toward Catharine's. The weather was gray, unrelentingly cold. It was the time of year when summer seemed irrevocably of the past and future, and hard to imagine in either direction. But she remembered Irma with brown, bare legs, getting out of the blue car into sunshine, on this very stretch of pavement.... Root's Liquor Store, with her closed office above it. Irma wouldn't come there anymore. Neither, presently, would she.

She was too melancholy for Catharine's. Besides, this was no time for her to walk out on Tom's business, when he couldn't take care of it himself. She parked, unlocked the office door, and went upstairs.

The office was bitterly cold, as always after a winter weekend. She turned on the space heater and sat down in her coat, looking over the mail. Everything was just as she had left it long ago last Friday, when she had hurried off to catch the train to New York.

Calls began to come in, looking for Tom. She said what she could, depending on who it was. Even to Tom's foreman she could not bring herself to say more than that Irma had had an accident, and she didn't know how to reach him just now. She would pass on messages as soon as she could.

Tom himself did not call.

At noon she walked over and ate lunch with Henry in the back of the store. They had little to say to each other—partly because of Morrie, partly because there wasn't much to be said—except speculation, for which Henry had little use.

While they were eating, the Frampton police called up for Marianne. They were investigating the woman in Frampton hospital, and would like her to come over and give what information she could about her. They would send a car for her, and when could she come?

"I can come right now," she said, after time out to consult Henry, "and you don't have to bother about a car—my husband can bring me."

Afterward they were both totally silent, until Morrie's feelings became hurt and he went away.

Why were they so secretive about what would soon be all over town? Neither could have explained—except to each other, where there was no need. Part wary, part scrupulous, they put on their coats and hats and went out, leaving Morrie behind them like a sad dog in the store. And about as useful.

CHAPTER TWELVE

The first person Marianne saw in the Frampton police chief's office was Tom Bryce. He stood there immobile, watching her enter. The instant, incredible idea that he had been arrested leaped into her mind, and she stood stock still.

Then the chief—his name was Hovey, he had relatives in Willett— came up and shook her hand.

"You don't mind if Tom sits in, do you?" he said. "This is all news to him too, you know."

She recovered, went over to Tom, made him give her his hand.

"I'm awfully sorry, Tom," she said. "It's just terrible."

"Thanks, Mary Ann."

He cleared his throat, said humbly, "I'd have given anything not to have you mixed up in this. It's all my fault, if I'd only ..."

She could see he hardly knew what he was saying.

Chief Hovey was pushing a chair at the back of her knees, and she sat down. Tom turned away, with his back to them.

"We'd like to know what you can tell us about this lady over in the hospital, Mrs. Hinkley," Chief Hovey said. "She don't seem to have much to say for herself, and we can't get hold of her husband, down in New York. Been trying all weekend."

"You mean he's gone?"

"Seems to be. The hospital tried, and we tried—even had the New York police go by. Caretaker says there's a Mr. Moran, all right, but he's away indefinitely—and he don't seem to know anything about a Mrs. Moran. Or a Miss Gaither. You real sure about this lady?"

All Marianne's first suspicions about the man sprang back to life. She had been right—the real Moran had never been there at all, and the person who had let her in, and had taken Irma's bracelet ...

But then she remembered Harriet's room. The room that could belong to nobody but Harriet, and that must have taken years to create in its mad complexity. And she knew better.

"I'm sure," she said. "And I'm pretty sure there wasn't a caretaker. That was Moran you talked to—it must have been. Pretending he's never heard of Harriet—why, he can't do that! She's lived there a long time, so has he, the people in the house would know! Didn't anybody ask?"

"Well, not yet. Matter of fact, when the New York fellers went by they couldn't raise anybody so you may be right about the caretaker. That was sometime after we called from here. Looks like we're going to have to hunt around for Mr. Moran," he said.

She said, hesitantly, to Tom's back, "But didn't you know him, Tom? Irma said—"

"I never even heard of him," he said, without turning.

Chief Hovey looked slightly embarrassed, and spoke briskly. "Well, now, if you don't mind giving us your story, we'll get it all on the record. Don't mind our stenotype machine—that's just to hurry things up. You just start in like you were telling us about Mrs. Bryce coming round to see you last Friday, and go on from there."

So she began again. It was harder this time, with Tom standing there at the window. Not because he offered any interruption, even of movement or gesture, but because he didn't. The Tom Bryce she knew so long and well could not be this frozen listener. He was all interruption, gesture, movement—you had to talk fast to get anything explained to Tom before he took over, eager and impatient, to finish your sentences for you, explaining to you what you were trying to explain to him.

She went on. Chief Hovey became careful over Harriet's floundering journey and stopped her several times, checking against papers on his desk. She recognized one as a timetable of the railroad.

"You feel pretty sure this Mrs. Moran really didn't know you the last time you saw her?" he said. "Don't think she was faking?"

"Well, I didn't then. No. I still don't."

"Okay. That checks with what they tell me out at the hospital," he said. "Say she's 'completely out of touch with reality,'" he quoted, suddenly grinning. "Guess that means them. But when you saw her on the train, she was all right?"

"Well, not exactly all right, no. She—"

"She knew you, though?"

Did she? Remembering that isolated figure, Marianne discovered doubt. Had she been only one of many beside whom Harriet had sat down, rapidly, privately asking ...?

Chief Hovey, watching her, said, "Let's put it this way: she still seemed to know what she was doing. She could still get around and go after what she wanted. Think so?"

"I think so, yes."

She stared at him; and he became cheerful, explaining.

"Just getting it all straight. Sometime or other, something happened to make the lady's wheels come off, and she can't tell us about it so we have to see who can."

They had both forgotten Tom. His sudden turn into the room brought Chief Hovey's eyes around, and he added more sharply, "All this isn't doing you much good, Tom. You'd be better off to go home and get some sleep. Nobody's over at your place anymore, they tell me. Want somebody to drive you back?"

"No. Listen, Walt. I'd like to see that woman. Could I? Would you go out there with me, Marianne?"

"Why? What's the point?" said Hovey, impatient. "You don't recognize the description, you say you've never heard of these people, and she isn't recognizing anybody, from what they tell me. What good would it do?"

Marianne knew the stubborn look settling over Tom's face ... but she had never seen it mixed with deep bewilderment, as it was now.

In pity, she said, "Mightn't she be a little better today, Mr. Hovey? Or if she saw somebody she knew, over in the hospital, it might show."

"Not from what I hear. Look," he said, getting up, "you go on out. I'll send a feller with you. Then that's the end, there's no more use in your hanging around here, Tom. This—your trouble is a State Police affair, our only angle is the woman out in the hospital, and her husband—if she's got one. Right now they're both a dead end. You go take a look at her, and then that's it. Agreed?"

In the corridor Tom walked silently beside her. She said, "I'll have to leave word for Henry. He's coming to pick me up at two-thirty. He's over at Sears, Roebuck so I can't call him."

"Henry must really hate my guts by now," he muttered ... so strange and private a remark that it refused answer, and she gave none.

Chief Hovey had arranged a car and driver to take them out to the hospital, but out on the street Tom balked at being driven. His jeep was right there, he was going in that. Nobody had to take them, he could take Marianne himself. The policeman was equally obdurate. He was their passport to get in to Harriet, for one thing, and he wasn't going in the jeep. They split up, finally, and Tom sped away furious before them.

The Frampton man, who was young, said in some resentment, "He's really got his own way of doing things, hasn't he?"

"It's a hard time for him," she said; and he replied obliquely, "He's a big guy in the Kiwanis—the chief, too."

After this they did not find much else to say. Tom was standing in the hospital parking lot beside his jeep when they arrived. He seemed to have forgotten the argument, perhaps even the reason for their visit. It crossed Marianne's mind that he wasn't really in a state to drive.

They went across the gravel together and in the back door.

A woman doctor was waiting for them upstairs—pleasant, large, middle-aged. She said to Marianne, "I'm afraid you're going to be disappointed if you expect Harriet to recognize you, Mrs. Hinkley. You're a friend?"

"I knew her," said Marianne. "She knew me."

"Well, come along, we'll see. She doesn't mind visitors, anyway."

Somehow Marianne had pictured Harriet as she last saw her—in bed, alone, her only movement that of patient eyes. It was disconcerting to find her, instead, in hospital robe and slippers, one of a group of quiet women in a large dayroom.

Otherwise she was unchanged. Neither the nurse's voice nor the doctor's—nor Marianne's—made her respond. She did not even seem to hear.

In a sudden movement startling to them all (except Harriet), Tom Bryce turned and left the room. The moment went by in which one of them might have remarked about this. Then the doctor said, "Sit down, my dear. Unless you're in a hurry too."

Marianne sat down at Harriet's side. The young officer stood back, just out of their company. This close, Harriet's expression had a certain air of composure as she sat looking downward—inward—with her long hands in her lap. Her hair had been neatly combed; she was very clean. It was possible to feel that perhaps "they" had come after all (unknown to any but Harriet) and taken her back where she belonged.

"She's in good health," said the doctor. "A few bumps and scratches from that wandering around, but not so much as a sniffle. It's often that way, with them."

Marianne swallowed. She said, "Could I show her something?"

"You can try," said the doctor, smiling.

Irma's diamonds—catalyst to all they did not yet understand—were still in Marianne's bag. She took them from the zipper compartment and held them for Harriet to see. When she would not, Marianne (nervous, a little ashamed) laid them across the folded hands.

Harriet did not care. She must have felt, at least, a coldness and some weight upon her flesh, but she gave no sign.

The doctor leaned and took the bracelet up.

"Well, that's handsome! Is it hers?"

"No. She ... liked it. I thought she might remember."

That was the end of the visit. The doctor, waiting with them at the elevators, said in afterthought to the young policeman, "By the way, someone showed up for Harriet this morning—with a great wad of money, to take her away. I wasn't here, and before one of the other doctors could see him he just disappeared. I suppose he thought we were cash and carry," she said, smiling. "Tell Mr. Hovey for me, will you?"

"That was Moran," said Marianne, when they were in the elevator. The young policeman gave her a harassed look in reply. Down in the entrance hall he said, "You want to wait here a minute, ma'am? I'll bring the car round." She suspected him of wanting to telephone in privacy—useless privacy, she thought—but she agreed.

There was no sign of Tom. She settled to wait inside the plate-glass doors that looked down a long stretch of frozen grounds to the street.

Occasional cars came up the drive, going on round to the parking lot in back, or letting out visitors. One lonely pedestrian struggled up the windy slope, holding his hat: an awkward little figure in a long, flapping coat. She watched him approach, and saw presently that it was Moran.

She looked around the hall, then moved back out of Moran's sight. He gave an occasional short stare ahead, furtive and glum, but otherwise came on head down. Under one arm he carried a gray cardboard box, too large for ease, and he was walking next to the hedge, so close that his passing left a trail of disturbance on the bare twigs.

Peering, she saw that he meant to bypass the steps and go on round the building. She moved then, anxious, and he in instant awareness caught that movement and saw her. He stopped. His glance veered, came back, altered, and fixed upon her. She saw his teeth appear, not in a smile. A moment of that, and he hurried on again.

She left the entrance hall and started quickly toward the back of the hospital, the door to the parking lot. It seemed to her that their routes were parallel, hers and Moran's, and must lead to the same end—and that her way was shorter. She came out at last, breathless, and saw Tom at once. He was there in his jeep, slouched self-intent in the driving seat.

Emboldened by his nearness, she ran toward the corner of the building where Moran ought to appear. But no one was in sight. She hesitated, then went back, calling softly.

"Tom!"

His head jerked up. He saw her, and in one rapid movement climbed out. By that time she reached him.

"Tom, I've seen Moran, just now. He was coming round the sidewalk, over there—"

That was all she had time for. Blank-eyed, an automaton, he went lunging away where she had been pointing. Startled, she called after him; but he kept going, went round the corner and out of her sight.

She had a moment's fearful thought of those two men meeting—Tom the larger, but dazed, and less desperate and wily.... Then the young policeman came out the door, and she ran to him. He listened to her without any enthusiasm at all.

"Where? Both of them?" He started—came back, to say earnestly, "You stay in the car, ma'am. Just stay right there."

"But shouldn't someone tell the hospital people?"

"Just stay there, please," he replied, and went off at a run.

She stayed there. The inclination was very strong to go back into the hospital, raise instant alarm, so that Moran should not ... What? What, after all, could he do? She remembered Harriet far away upstairs, unreachable in herself and guarded too. Between her and that little man struggling up the hospital walk lay the whole ordered, impenetrable world of the hospital. What could he do?

By the time Tom and the young policeman came back (walking a yard apart) she was sitting in the police car as requested, jumpy but resigned.

The young policeman gave her a glance of relief, and came directly to her.

"Mrs. Hinkley, you mind going back into town with Mr. Bryce, here? He'll take you back to headquarters."

She grasped what he meant—which was, to take Tom away—and got out at once.

When she touched Tom's arm, he said angrily, "Must have doubled back. If that damn kid had only gone round the other way when I told him to—"

"Tom." He looked down, and she said, "It's too late. There's too much grounds and building, and not enough of us. Come on. I've got to get back. They know he's here now, they'll be watching for him better than we could. I've got to get back," she repeated. "Henry's waiting."

She had no idea if he were even listening or not. Then, dull-voiced, he said, "All right, Mary Ann. Okay."

They got in the cold jeep, and drove out of the hospital grounds. He drove slowly, this time, and began, frowning, to talk to her.

"That fellow's a crook. A cheap crook. The New York police have got a record on him. Did you know that?"

"I'm not very surprised, Tom."

"His name's Mora, Joe Mora. They've been threatening to deport him for years. How could she know about someone like that?" he demanded. "Why would she send you to him?"

"Tom, nobody knows anything for sure, yet. There's no use in trying to guess. Couldn't you sleep?" she asked, desperate. "Even if you have to take something, you'd—"

"You tell Henry I'm sorry about today, will you?" he interrupted. "I am. It's my fault, I shouldn't have asked you to go out there."

She gave up trying to talk to him. He didn't hear her, seemed scarcely to hear what he himself was saying; and she began to feel as if she were being driven by a trustworthy sleepwalker, given to bursts of confidence and alternate long silence, but essentially not there at all.

Henry was waiting when they got back to police headquarters. So was the State Police trooper who had come to their house that morning; but his interest was now in Tom, and the two of them went away together. So much for Tom's chance to rest.

She read and signed her morning statement, Henry patiently standing by. Then they shared out the Sears, Roebuck packages Henry had acquired and walked down the street to their car, and went home.

CHAPTER THIRTEEN

Mrs. Evans had been calling up the store all afternoon, leaving the same firm message with Morrie every time. He had it almost word-perfect by four o'clock, when they returned.

"Mary Ann, you call up Mrs. Evans right away, please," he said. "It's important." And he offered her the top half of the telephone, apparently on a share-alike basis.

"I'll go over," she said, making his face fall. "Henry, you pick me up there if I don't get back in time."

She was glad to go out again—too restless to settle in store or office for what was left of the day. It wasn't much. The shoveled, hard-packed snow was gray in darkening air, and already lamps burned in the houses that she passed, as she walked the few village blocks to the Evanses' house.

Mrs. Evans was pleased by her arrival in person—a Congregationalist attention she clearly hadn't expected. She offered tea in return, and took Marianne back to the kitchen with her while she made it.

"Now what's all this asking round about poor Miss Gaither?" she demanded, there. "I can't get any sense out of that hospital—waste of time, calling hospitals. We ought to have gone over there today."

"Well, I did," said Marianne. "I just happened to be in Frampton anyway, so I went. It wasn't any use—she doesn't know anybody at all."

"Feverish?"

"No, the doctor said she's perfectly well. She just doesn't notice. It's her mind," she said; and got (as she expected) a sharp, steady glance.

"Then she's gone downhill in that hospital," said Mrs. Evans. She went on abruptly, "That man was a policeman, you know. The one that came here."

"I know."

"I mean a real policeman, not Joe. What business is it of theirs? Unless he was after that disgraceful taxi driver."

"No, I think it's something about Irma Bryce, Mrs. Evans. They want to know where everybody was when Irma was lost, and if anyone saw her. If Harriet did, I don't believe they'll ever find it out," she said.

"Maybe that's what's troubling the poor soul," said Mrs. Evans, yielding a little. "Auto accident, wasn't it? That would be a shocking thing to come across on a strange, lonely road."

The news about Irma was still partial—due to the fact that the Comptons were not really "local" and to the discretion of the Hinkleys, who were. Not much more was known than what the Monday paper carried.

Mrs. Evans went on to the subject of Irma. She hadn't known her, except by sight, but her tragedy inspired Mrs. Evans to some rather surprising reminiscences about Tom.

"Indeed I'm sure," she said. "Right down there on the Hillyard Road, not so far from the junction, you know. The house may still be there, though I doubt it. It didn't look as though it would last many more winters then, and that was 1917 or '18. Many's the time I went out there and spent the night with the poor woman, when that dreadful flu was going round. She couldn't seem to get her strength back, and there was nobody to look after her but the boy, and he was only nine or ten. So far as anybody knew, the man was just gone for good. I think he was supposed to have come back, later, and packed them up and taken them off somewhere—that was the story, and it may well be true. Somebody must have taken them—she didn't have the spirit left to take herself off, by then. Anyway, they were gone, and the house as bare as a bone next time I went out. Not that there'd been much in it before. I often wondered about poor Mrs. Bryce. But by the time Tom came back here, he only said she'd been dead many years, poor soul."

It was a sad—and to Marianne, a shocking tale—one which she wasn't sure she ought to know. Tom Bryce, with his lack of interest in yesterdays, might simply have pushed it back in his mind but she had known him very well for ten years. It seemed strange she should not even know he had been a local boy.

She was thoughtful when Henry came by for her, and inclined to be quiet on the ride home. But so was Henry. When they got home, inside the warm pink house, he left his paper unopened and came out to sit in the kitchen with her.

There, he remarked, "Tom Bryce came by, looking for you. I told him where you were."

"But I just saw him, in Frampton! Why?"

"He didn't say."

"He didn't come by the Evanses'." She wondered if he were unwilling to see her in company with Mrs. Evans, who knew and would speak of his boyhood. "Well," she said, "I expect it was something about the office that could wait."

"He seemed pretty upset."

"Well, that's natural, Henry."

"It's not so natural," said Henry steadily, "for him to keep thinkin' you ought to do something about it."

In the circumstances, this was adamant—even from Henry. His wife, fresh from Mrs. Evans, looked at him reproachfully.

"Why, I don't see that. In a way, it's like what Mrs. Evans says—that there's more trouble in this world than any of us suspects, unless we look round—and it's our duty to look."

"Well, Mrs. Evans is a nice old lady," he replied, "but she's got what you might call professional ideas about it. That's natural. I must say I don't see Tom Bryce lookin' round much, though. Except maybe to see who's looking out for him."

She was astonished. After all these years, for Henry to come out like this in open dislike—and at such a time! She said without thinking the strongest thing that came into her mind.

"Henry, that's not fair!"

"Well, fair works two ways, Mary Ann. It seems to me a mighty thin chance that it's Tom Bryce's wife over there with her neck broke instead of my wife. That's about as close as I want to come, bein' fair."

He looked up then, showing a distress as real as hers.

"Maybe we don't realize how lucky you were, you just saw that lady in the station, and on the train, where there was people all around. Maybe if you'd been alone in your car like Irma was in hers, you wouldn't have got home safe with that bracelet. That dang bracelet," he said, bursting out.

"Henry, who have you been talking to?"

"Nobody," he said. "I don't need to. I know that crazy woman was wandering round here two, three hours, nobody knows where, last Saturday. They found Irma late Sunday night, didn't they? And she wasn't one to be taking any stranger in to ride with her. She says she knew those people. I know that that Harriet must have gone somewhere pretty quick when she ducked her taxi, and the quickest place I can think of is some other car—with somebody in it she knew, maybe sitting there getting gas or something. And you told her you were going to give Irma her bracelet back as quick as you got home."

"And she wouldn't believe that Irma didn't have it...."

Up to that point, her thoughts were absorbed in following Henry's. There, they revolted. "No. No, Henry. The most Harriet would have done was to have a tantrum and try to pull Irma's bag away from her, like she did mine. And the minute I slapped her, she stopped."

"*Then*," he said significantly. "She might have been a little more desperate, time she caught up with Irma. Besides, Joe and I carried her down the Evanses' stairs, and she's a good hundred-forty pounds, whatever she looks like. A hundred-forty-pound tantrum could do a lot of damage, if it got out of hand."

She was quiet, remembering Harriet as she had last seen her—inert, enclosed upon whatever experience, or combination of experiences, had finally broken her thin link with the present.

At last she sighed. "I don't know, Henry. I just don't know."

"Well, I don't know myself," he said, impartial again. "But it's something to think about. Course, that doesn't say where Irma was all Friday night and Saturday morning."

"Are you going to tell the police about this?" she asked.

"No," he said, surprised. "Why should I? They know everything we do. I expect they can think for themselves."

That evening Trooper Corvi, whom Henry knew a little, came round to see them. He had some snapshots he wanted Marianne to see. Tom Bryce had found them in the house.

She spread them out under the bridge lamp, leaning over them in deep interest. There were four. They were old, and showed what seemed to be a small family group with the pallor and odd clothing of another decade. From the woman's clothes, this might have been the thirties.

She saw that the woman was Harriet. An incredible, almost sleek Harriet, with a contained, contented smile, her eyes cast secretly down.

"Why," she said, "she looks almost pretty!"

"You recognize her?"

"Yes, it's Harriet—and Moran!" she exclaimed, her wonder deepening at this second discovery. She bent again to examine the smiling woman's dapper companion. Yes, a Moran much less chubby, or at any rate carefully dressed to conceal fat, but Moran. His smile was open and enormous, and he was staring eagerly into the camera, holding Harriet's arm. In front of them, like a small figure that had wandered in unobserved, stood an impassive little girl.

"How about the child?" said Trooper Covi, over her shoulder. "Recognize her?"

She temporized, glancing up at him in disbelief.

"Does—did Tom recognize her?" He smiled, and she said, "But she looks so much more like Moran, here, than like—like herself." Trooper Covi reached over her shoulder and turned one snapshot over. A male hand had written lavishly on its back: "Brighton—my girls—1932."

"Poor Irma," she said. For the first time.

Trooper Corvi, pleased, took up his snapshots again.

"The New York report on Mora mentioned a daughter, but nothing recent on her. Whereabouts unknown."

"Like papa," said Henry; and Corvi grinned at him.

"Well, we know one place he isn't, anymore," he said. "That's Frampton Hospital—building or grounds. Too bad you didn't tackle him, Mrs. Hinkley."

"I think Mary Ann's tackled about her share," Henry replied gravely. She scarcely heard him.

"But what was her name, before they were married? Didn't you ask Tom?"

"I bet it wasn't Mora," said Henry. "Or Moran either."

"No, it was Moreau. Close enough. She wasn't a citizen, you know — that was one reason she dropped out of sight. By the way, Constable Palmer thinks you people ought to have some protection out here until Moran is picked up. You talk to him about it?" He took his answer from their expressions; and went on, "Maybe you'd better, if you're at all nervous. I'm afraid it would have to be a town deal, Mr. Hinkley—we just don't have the men, and Moran doesn't rate the 'desperate and armed' treatment, from what we get on him."

"Goodness, I should think not," said Marianne. "Whatever is Joe thinking of?"

She could see that Henry intended to find out, and was reserving judgment until he did. As soon as Trooper Corvi had left he was at the telephone, calling the Palmer's house—Joe would be off duty. His wife said he wasn't there. He was over at Mr. Bryce's, they could call him there.

"What's he doing over there?" asked Henry. But she couldn't say. He hung up and sat thoughtful, not calling again.

"Well, it'll keep till morning," he said.

Joe Palmer didn't appear to think so. He arrived at their door past ten-thirty that night, serious on the trail of what he considered to be his duty.

Luckily, they were still dressed and downstairs.

"I'm not trying to persuade anybody of anything, Henry," he said. "It's up to you what you want to do, but I figure you ought to know how things stand and what you got a right to. This fellow had gang connections down in New York. Maybe you didn't know that."

"I don't know anything about him at all," Henry replied. "Except the way he treated Mary Ann. That's enough."

"Well, he's what they call a known associate," said Joe earnestly. "Walt Hovey has a report from the New York police. They know all about him down there."

"Did you see the report, Joe?" Marianne asked.

He looked down, dignified.

"Well, I heard enough to think we better be ready for him if he decides to come over this way. And that's a thing he might do, with both you and Tom Bryce here in Willett."

Between the State and the Frampton police, Joe was evidently feeling left out of things.

He went on, "You're entitled to a special constable out here till they pick this guy up. Or till we do, ourselves. The town isn't going to grudge a little expense on you folks—not after what happened to Irma Bryce."

"You putting a special constable on Tom Bryce?" Henry inquired.

"Well, he feels it's different for him—he hasn't got his wife there."

Marianne saw in Henry's expression the end of Joe's hopes.

"When my wife is here, I'm here," said Henry. "She won't be alone. You save the money, Joe. Looks like we'll be needing some more snow removal before long. I'm obliged," he said, ending it.

But he was thoughtful after Joe left. Later, he took his hunting rifle out of the storage closet, looked it over carefully, and loaded it. When he came up to bed he laid it across the bureau top, and said to his wife, "Now, Mary Ann, don't you touch that, no matter what happens."

She just looked at him. He didn't even notice.

CHAPTER FOURTEEN

By Tuesday the complete news about Irma was all over town; and Marianne became so besieged by telephone calls—and even by shameless visitors climbing her office stairs—that she closed up at eleven o'clock and went over to the hardware store. It was an ordeal just to get through to the back room.

There, indignant and bewildered, she said to Henry, "What's everybody so sympathetic about? Irma wasn't any relation to us!"

"I expect it's because they can't get hold of Tom Bryce, and you're the next best thing," said Henry. He looked at her thoughtfully. "You heard from him this morning?"

"No, I haven't. I wanted to call him and ask if I could help about the funeral. I suppose there'll *be* a funeral, sometime," she said. "But that office is just like a county fair! It's a disgrace."

"Well, I got it here, too. Like you see." He paused. "Couple of people asked me if the police weren't holding him, over there. Seems nobody's seen him around."

She looked at him in total attention.

He went on casually, "Mack Varney says he don't blame him a bit—says if he caught his wife out, he'd break her neck too. I asked him who she was supposed to been caught out with—he don't know. Says, don't tell him she didn't have some New York feller. I didn't."

Marianne went on looking at him, but he said nothing more. She buttoned up her coat again.

"I'm going right back to the office, and lock the door, and call round till I find him," she said.

Henry offered no objection. She wouldn't have been there to listen if he had.

The worst thing about what Henry had told her, she realized when she was back at her desk, was that it hadn't struck her as a new idea. It was more as if some thought-privacy of her own had been suddenly published. Yet not once had she consciously considered that Tom himself might be to blame.

She sat a moment, facing down the idea. The fear of the idea. It did go down, of course. The telephone rang, intermittently, while she sat there. In a moment of quiet she dialed Tom's number.

He didn't answer.

Thoughtful still, she got up and began to make coffee on the hotplate. The telephone rang twice more before she came back. With a steaming cup on her desk, she found the courage to put in a call to Captain Hovey over in Frampton. He wasn't there either.

She was sitting there in thought, with her hand on the telephone, when it rang again. She absent-mindedly answered; and it was Tom. The gladness in her voice strengthened his, so that it became almost audible.

"I'm home, Mary Ann—I've just not answered the phone. Everybody in town's taken to calling up this morning, and I couldn't stand any more of it. Look, I'd like to talk to you ..."

"Well, I've got the downstairs door locked," she said. "If you can get out of the car and inside the hall without collecting a crowd, there's nobody here."

He said he would be right over.

She watched at the window and when she saw the jeep coming, ran down to let him in, to save him fumbling for his key. Her first sight of him shocked her, so much so that she could find nothing to say on the trip upstairs. He, noticing her look, was silent too. But up in their familiar office, Marianne pulled herself together.

"Sit down, and I'll get you some coffee," she said. "It's just fresh." And having begun, she could add, "You look so *thin*, Tom."

That was only part of it. What he had—incongruous in so un-feline a man—was the wild, thinned look of a lost cat brought into a strange house. Almost as if that locked door downstairs were to keep him in instead of other folks out.

Far from comfortable with these queer notions in her head, Marianne made herself sit down with a second cup. Their accustomed behavior, in their old places, helped a little—not much.

"I wanted to ask if I could help about Irma's funeral," she said. "Have you made any plans?"

"Oh, that's all arranged for—Bill Cooley's taking care of it at his place, over in Frampton. It's tomorrow, by the way. Private," he added with fierceness on the last word. Her widened eyes brought his voice down at once. "I don't mean you, Mary Ann, of course. Or Henry, if he's willing to come. But I'll be damned if I'll have a procession of local ghouls parading through there."

He got up, and began walking the floor over Mr. Root's head (that would be noticed, Marianne could not help thinking).

"Neither Irma nor I belong here," he was saying. "Once I thought maybe we could ... but it didn't turn out that way, and it wasn't Irma's fault any more than it was mine. We're just not—local types, and I was a fool to think we could be, I guess. But I'm not fool enough to go on pretending anymore," he said. "Not now."

Did he know what people were saying? There was no way to ask. She said, "Why, I guess almost anybody would want a private funeral in the circumstances, Tom. Nobody'll hold it against you."

He shook his head.

"No. Don't try to smooth it over. I know what I'm doing, and what'll be said about it, and I don't care. It's the way it's going to be done. This is the end of me, here, and I know that. The town might as well know that I do."

He sat down again, to her relief.

"And yet I was born here, Mary Ann—just as much as you. Lived here the first ten years of my life. You didn't know that, did you?"

It was not a rhetorical question, but she tried to treat it as one. He was too raw from gossip—or the idea of it—to bring in even old Mrs. Evans. She didn't get away with her attempt at tact.

He gave an awkward laugh, and said roughly, "Of course you knew, and of course you wouldn't mention it till I did. Well, it's true—my mother and I lived here ten years, a lot of the time with town help, because we needed it. It's no secret, I never meant it to be. In fact, one of my ideas in coming back here was that maybe I could pay the town back for some of that help. And by God, I have," he said. "I've brought a lot of money here! Spent a lot, too. Haven't I?"

This one was rhetorical; but she murmured agreement anyway. And added, "There's no reason for you to talk about being finished here, Tom. Of course you aren't, and nobody thinks you are."

"Well, I say I am, and that's the deciding vote," he answered, making a smile. "Bryce Builders is liquidating, Mary Ann—that's what I wanted to talk to you about."

"But you *can't*, Tom! Not now, right in the middle of—"

"Yes, now, right in the middle of," he said. "Look, I know Henry wants you out of here. In fact, I called you at home this morning first, because I didn't expect you to be here. I'm surprised he let you come. All right, you don't have to say anything, I understand. And I appreciate your coming. Now, what I want to ask you is whether you'd be willing to stretch it a little further—you and Henry—and stick by it till you can go over the whole affair with me and a CPA. Wind it up. I'll push it through just as fast as I can, I promise you. And if you want me to, I'll talk to Henry about it."

"Why, you don't have to do that," she said quickly. "Of course I'll stay, if you're really determined to do this. But I don't see how you can! You couldn't have picked a worse time ..." She flushed, remembering that he hadn't exactly picked it, and then said desperately, "I just don't think you *can* liquidate, the way things are now!"

"Don't you worry about that. I've had tougher problems than this one, and got out with all my back teeth. This kind of thing I understand," he said. "It's got no scare for me. But a jinx I don't understand, and that's what this town is to me—always has been. A jinx. Maybe that's what I came back to break, I don't know. For a while, I guess it looked like I had it licked. But the thing about a jinx," he said, low, "the reason you can't win—that you're crazy to try—is that you never know what direction it's going to hit you from. No man's got his guard up every minute, all directions—he can't have. But that's the only way you can live with a jinx ... and even then, someday, you lose. You lose, and you don't know why. You just lose."

He fell silent; and she, impressed against her will, felt a small shudder go down her spine. Then she had to protest.

"Tom, that's just a lot of depressed talking. You're in no state to be deciding things now—you couldn't be. I think you ought to wait a while, really I do." He shook his head, an absent gesture. "Besides, if there was a—a jinx, it seems more like Irma's, doesn't it? And those people in New York—"

His attention came back to her then.

"You know what she wanted that money for, Mary Ann? A broker! She'd been playing the commodities market, poor kid. He thinks he's going to get it out of me, now—says he's covered the account as long as he can, and the whole thing's going down the drain unless I cover some kind of a drop." His voice was steady, equable. "I told him to go ahead and pull the plug. Down the drain! He should know what we know about drains, right?"

She couldn't bear much more of this luxury of destruction he was proposing; and suddenly flushing, she said shortly, "Tom, stop it. Don't go on like this! I don't know about Irma's commodities, whatever they are—perhaps they're a loss and perhaps they're not, but you could at least look into it! You've still got the bracelet to use, the way Irma meant to. But the business, you—"

"By God, that bracelet!" he said. "Look, that's yours, Mary Ann. I mean it. It'll make up to you for your stock, at least. There's no reason why you should lose out in this mess, and you're not going to—I won't have it! The receipt's around here someplace, isn't it? You'll have no trouble selling the thing, and it'll bring you in a good piece of change. I mean it—the bracelet's yours."

She didn't try to argue. It was a hopeless suggestion. Neither Henry nor she herself could consider taking over that—well, that jinxed bracelet of a dead woman in payment for sober services. But she saw that the notion gave Tom Bryce some animation back, and she let him talk.

She was beginning to see, too, what his need was, and why it was useless for her to go on protesting. Bryce Builders was going down the drain, all right—she didn't doubt that he would do what he said. Because he *had* to be doing something, making some tremendous reply to all that had happened, even if that reply was to wreck everything he (and she) had worked for years to try and build.

Well ... goodbye, Bryce Builders. Yes, she would stay—would sit through the sad sessions with some appalled CPA, and as long after that as necessary. And then that would be that. Ten years.

When Tom finally went away, it was too late to join Henry at the store for lunch. She was hungry, anyway. Instead she walked down to the bank—the small local branch where Bryce Builders kept its account— and there deposited Irma's bracelet in the bank safe, to the firm's name. Now it was just an asset, impersonal, lying there awaiting whatever creditor got to it first. And Tom could leave town believing she had the value of her stock, or else was wearing a blaze of diamonds to the Congregationalist jumble sale—whatever he liked to believe.

If he ever thought of it again.

"I'm blue, Henry," she said, confessing long after the fact had become apparent.

They had finished dinner and were just sitting there in the kitchen together, in spite of fish plates that should be washed at once.

Henry acknowledged this by a rather shy look. It wasn't the kind of remark he knew how to answer.

"Well, that's reasonable," he said, after a pause.

He looked sort of blue himself, now that she noticed. Her conscience moved her, and she put a hand over his.

"I'm awfully sorry about all this," she said.

This time he answered right away.

"Why, you couldn't help it, Mary Ann. The one thing keeps leading on to the next, how can you help it?"

"But you worry about it. I wish you wouldn't. All the police are working on what's happened—even Joe!"

He nodded, to her attempted joke, but remained grave.

"I know that. The trouble is," he said, "it's getting so I can hardly see what it's all *about*, anymore. I never was mixed up in anything so piecemeal and spread-around before, and it doesn't seem like it ought to be that way. I keep feeling like too many people are scribbling all over the same piece of paper, and whatever was on it to start with is just getting buried right down ..."

For Henry, this was almost pure poetry—and like poetry, it gave Marianne a sudden clear view of her own feelings.

"Why, I know just what you mean," she said. "There's so *much*..."

"Well, now, there isn't so much, if you come to think of it," said Henry, recovering. "I mean *facts*. Now, Irma's dead, and she didn't die natural. That's a fact, for certain. And just about the last thing anybody knows she did, she sent you off down to New York to sell her bracelet. To her own father," he said, wavering slightly. "Or *probably* her own father." He considered. "I'd call that a probable fact."

"But she did send me, Henry."

"I know, I know. That part's fact. All right, that bracelet got took off you in this feller's house—that's another fact. You couldn't have dropped it, you're real sure, I suppose?" he asked.

"I'm positive," she said warmly. "And *that's* a fact, Henry."

He indicated that he would accept this, after one view of her face.

"All right," he said. "So far we got good, solid facts. And there's more. You got that bracelet back from this Harriet, and she followed you home on account of it. Or anyway, she did follow you home."

"Why, of course she followed me home on account of it! What else—"

"Now, just a minute, Mary Ann," he said. "She never said so. She wanted the bracelet, sure, but you made it pretty darned clear she couldn't have it. So how do we know why she tagged along? How do we know she wasn't coming up here to see Irma, hey?"

She gave this suggestion time, but no enthusiasm at all. Then she remembered.

"Why, because Irma's already been down there, don't you remember? How she said she'd handle it herself, and went right out and—"

"Wait a minute. Now wait right there a minute," said Henry. She did. "We're getting off the track, Mary Ann."

"I'm sorry," she said. "But what track, Henry? I thought—"

"We don't know where Irma went," he said, emphatic. "We know what she said to you, and that's all. And not much. We don't even know she went *anywhere*."

"Yes, we do! Don't you remember her car was—"

He got up suddenly, startling her considerably.

"I'll tell you what I'm going to do," he said. "I'm going to start and write down every single fact we know about what happened. Right from the beginning, I don't care what it is. Then when I've got it all listed down, we'll start a little sorting of our own, and see if we can't figure out just what's been happening around here!"

He strode out of the room, and was back almost at once with paper and pencils. Marianne got up and hastily cleared space for him. Before she got all the dishes off the table, he was beginning to write.

He didn't say a word more. Whenever she glanced his way, however, he looked busy and determined, so she supposed it was all right. It was, at least, a reasonable reaction to all the pressures and confusions that were beginning to surround them. More reasonable, she thought, than Tom's—he had to be "doing something" too!

When the kitchen was in order she left it—and Henry—and went in to turn on the television, low. But her mind, untidy and dissatisfied, refused all entertainment. She was more aware of the tiniest occasional sound from the kitchen than of fusillades of shots, hysterical screams, from the throttled plays. Nevertheless, she made herself stay where she was.

Ten o'clock came round at last, and she was just going out to rouse up Henry with some hot milk when the front door chimes sounded. She peeked out and saw the top light on the car in front of the house, and went to let Joe Palmer in. It wasn't Joe, however, but the night constable, and he had someone behind him. They didn't want to come in.

"Just want to introduce you to Special Constable Ed Moag, Mrs. Hinkley. Guess you know him anyway. He'll be watching your house till further notice, so tell Henry not to shoot if he hears anything."

Ed Moag was dressed up as if he were going hunting. She looked at them helplessly.

"But Henry told Joe—"

"I know, but that crazy lady got out today from the hospital. Joe says it's got to be this way till they catch her, and the fellow too."

"Harriet got out! You mean she escaped?"

"Yes, ma'am. Don't worry, Ed won't make no noise. He won't bother you, he'll just be here all night."

They made saluting gestures, and turned away. She shut the door and rushed out to the kitchen.

"Henry, Harriet escaped from the hospital! They don't know where she is, and Joe Palmer's sent Ed Moag over to guard the house!"

He gazed up at her. His expression was that of a man being slowly drowned. His lips moved; a hoarse voice said, low, "Don't tell me anything else yet...."

Then, of course, he pulled himself together—wanted to know all about it, went out to talk to Ed Moag himself. Marianne saw that the paper he had been crouching over was perfectly blank; all the written-on pieces were crumpled on the floor.

CHAPTER FIFTEEN

In milder air than the week (or the month) had yet shown, he had come plodding up the long hospital hill again. This time his hat stayed on his head without being held there, and his long coat no longer flapped in hard wind. He didn't notice. Indifferent to discomfort by now, he was equally indifferent to the lack of it. Clutching his big box, head mostly down, he had stayed close to the winter-dead hedge and followed it by touch.

It turned off at the big, plate-glass entrance to the hospital, and so did he—both of them continuing along the walk that rounded the building. Halfway, man and walk parted company. With one cold glance round he had stepped from the main walk to a short stretch of concrete between bare bushes—what would be forsythia and spiraea in later months, though he neither knew nor cared about that. Harriet was the one for flowers and fancy names, that belonged to the part of their life he left to her. Or had left.

Expressionless still, he had put down his box and stood close to the locked, knobless door, employing both hands—he looked rather like a man relieving himself. Then the door opened slightly, he held it so with one hand and thrust something back in his pocket with the other. He picked up the box again. Without any glance round—it made no difference who saw him now—he went inside.

Unhesitant, unhurried, he went down a short flight of fireproof stairs, along a deserted subterranean passage and through double swing doors to another stair. This was also of concrete and steel, but on a wider scale, and went from floor to floor round a large well. It was deserted.

He began to mount—a dogged, head-down climbing that made little sound, even in that echo-prone enclosure. Two interns, or residents, passed him between the first and second floors without interrupting their discussion. A nurse, alone, gave him a sharp glance as they passed on the next landing but did not speak. He paid no attention to any of them, but plodded on in the tired, surly manner of a man tied to old labors, expecting nothing from them.

At the sixth landing he looked—a confirming gesture—at the watch he managed to extract from an inner pocket; muttered; pushed through another pair of doors into another corridor. This one was quieter; he met no one. Past numbered doors—a few standing open or half-open— he kept on his way. He had no need to watch numbers, or to examine his surroundings. Like one obeying an old habit he came up to one closed door, opened it and entered, and shut it behind him.

He was in a narrow, light room of absolute silence. The woman in bed made no sound to break it, nor did he. She was awake—her eyes were turned upon him, or upon that part of the room which he occupied, but neither spoke. On the bare dresser top where flowers might have stood he put down his big box and untied the string. That done, he made his first hesitant move.

Turning to the woman in bed, he said in a low, pleading voice, "Harriet … Harriet, you hear me?"

If she did, there was no sign of it. He sighed, and took from the box what appeared to be an enormous floral offering, somehow dead. She saw that. He let her look at it a moment, then laid it carefully just out of her reach at the foot of the bed.

There was a moment of nothing happening, in which sweat appeared on his heavy face. Then the woman's hand came up, her eyes fixed on the flowers still, and a small yearning sound escaped her.

He took in air, then said, grumbling, "That's right, your own hat—you gonna have it. Be good."

He turned back to his box and took out shoes and stockings, and brought these to the bed. She ignored him—ignored the sudden loss of her covers, the awkward struggle he made to dress her feet. But when once his shoulder obscured her view of the hat, she slid sideways a little to see it again. He noticed that.

When her feet were dressed he lowered them to the floor. Her head wavered, to keep the hat in sight. He took sudden hold beneath her arms and pulled her upright, and for a moment they seemed to struggle like drunken dancers. Then when she stood in some kind of balance he reached out—breathing hard—and pulled a long velvet garment from the box. Empty, the box dragged to the floor, and he gave it a kick away.

Then luck happened. He had sudden luck. While he was trying to get the cloak around her, to fasten it over her short hospital gown, she raised her hands and began a soft, absorbed stroking of the dark velvet. She watched as she stroked—there seemed almost to be expression upon her face.

Sweating, panting, he burst into low, excited speech.

"That's right! You know, eh? You gonna be okay now, you get out of this crazy place! Come on, take the hat—you take the hat now. Put on your hat, Harriet—you can have it!"

But she was too long over her dream of touching velvet. He could not wait. He took up the hat himself, jammed it over her hair. Then, forced to patience, he tried to see Harriet in the hat as strangers might—saw that it would not do. It was a big, soft thing of velvet, a kind of beret strewn with cloth roses. She was beginning, groping, to put her hands up to it; but now he struck these down and, in desperation, pushed and tugged the floppy thing—stuck hair out of sight beneath it, pulled it back, whatever he did, her thin face looked lost and paper-white beneath it.

At last, with a little snarl of defeat, he took her arm and pulled her toward the door with him. She came like one coming unstuck—a forward stumble, then more stumbling steps. He stopped again, at the end of his endurance, whispering like a malediction:

"Walk better! *Walk better!*"

Her bare look told him it was no use; he got a grip on himself again, another, firmer, on her arm. Through the door—shut the door—down the hall. Very slowly; it had to be that way; no help for it. And now came the last, the riskiest part—and no help for that either, Harriet couldn't walk all the way down. They stood together by the little elevator door where the dirty hospital linen disappeared in its canvas baskets. The elevator came. Its silent door opened on emptiness, and he pushed Harriet in. He put his shaking finger on the "B" button and held it there, and they went slowly down together.

They were outside. But the loose stones of the parking lot were more than her weak ankles could manage. Three times she nearly went down; and then—nearly at the end—she stood like a dog in defeat and would not move. Rage overcame him, and he seized the hat from her head. The damp, chilly air moved her tumbled hair softly; she was not aware of it. He began to weep, lost all care. Seizing her limp arms he turned, drew her over his back, and staggered away with that long, limp burden trailing behind him, toward the covering trees.

By the time they got on the bus he was calm again—sullen, resigned. She was unchanged. He left the hat off—with her hair smoothed, it looked better that way, and she kept those blank pale eyes upon it as it lay in her lap. That made her look better too. They sat side by side, Harriet next the window.

The bus went out through streets of little houses, developments, "garden court" apartments, until there was more empty land than building, and almost no passengers were left in the bus with them. He rang to get off, and began the furtive process of getting Harriet out of her seat, down the aisle.

The driver was in no hurry now. His bus drawn up at the roadside, the door open, he waited for Harriet to negotiate the narrow steps down. He got out of his seat. Moran looked up in snarling panic, but he only took Harriet's other arm, helping her down.

Moran stammered, "Thanks, you a nice fellow, thanks!" and the driver patted Harriet's shoulder, said "Okay, ma", went back to his seat and drove away.

They went along the highway to a side road, unpaved, and started down that. At their own pace, now. Nobody around. On the level ground at the roadside, Harriet kept her footing and went along steadily to his pull. His spirits suddenly zoomed upward, and he began to chuckle ... then to laugh out loud, in high, spasmodic gusts to which Harriet paid no attention whatever. His performance, half hysterical, began to offend his own dignity, however; he forced himself to stop. Frowned. Frowned at Harriet, who would not see.

They went on. A little farther along the road the car was drawn up to the side, waiting. It was old enough to explain its own presence, abandoned there. Obviously something had broken down, and the harassed owner had gone for help. But nothing was broken, it ran perfectly well. Moran regarded it as he might have looked at treasure, and he had, in fact, hunted for it as if it were. Of all the cars left out at night, on miles of city streets, this was the only model he knew how to start without a key. Unfortunately, it was a noticeable model nowadays. He hadn't dared to leave it any nearer than this to the hospital, nor would he be able to keep it long.

Well, that was all right. Suddenly exasperated, he pushed and shoved Harriet inside and shut the door on her tumbled arrival there. Then he went round. His mood had changed again—plummeted. All very well to talk about luck now, when they were done for. Nagy would have nothing more to do with him, nobody would. The house—his house—that he daren't go near. That bitch Irma—that bitch!

He began to growl aloud, a relief. Just to be able to say it all out loud once more! because Harriet was there again, beside him; listening or not, she was there. He grumbled all the way, sitting high in the old car and steering carefully with both hands. Harriet tumbled over on him once, and he shoved her back in a burst of furor, relieving rage.

They came nearer the sea, left the main road and jounced over rutted, clayey soil. Ahead lay the summer cottage, deserted and solitary. He drove behind it and parked, leaned back, and examined the place with an eye already proprietary.

"Okay, we get out," he said with renewed kindness to Harriet. She didn't move. He shrugged, got out himself, and went round for her.

On the desolate small porch he felt gravely in his pocket, selecting the metal shaft that served as his key. He used it like a householder, and once inside gestured proudly round the room. It had a fieldstone fireplace, a great deal of wicker, shabby maple, grass matting.

"Not so bad, eh? I got everything—blankets, something to eat, everything. You gonna be fine."

Harriet had turned rather blue. It occurred to him that the cotton hospital gown and velvet cloak were not, after all, much protection against the February seaside weather, even on a fairly mild day.

He said briskly, "Come on, I'm gonna make a fire."

She didn't move.

He flared out at her.

"Come on! What's the matter with you? You're out, you don't have to act like that no more! Don't do it," he said, warning; and his hand came up, automatic to the words. She didn't notice it. After a moment he took her arm instead, and led her over to the daybed by the fireplace. Pushed her down on it.

"Now sit here," he said. "I'm making you a nice fire to get warm, okay? You're gonna be all right, you'll see. You don't have to act like that no more, Harriet."

Uneasy, he watched her a moment. Then, in sudden decision, left her and went out back of the little house. Firewood was there, gathered and stacked by the back door in the hard-thinking hours he had spent here alone. Driftwood, dead branches, twigs, and brush —they made an awkward armload, but he managed it.

When he returned, clutching as much as he could carry, she was sitting as he had left her. She seemed as unaware of his return as she had been of his leaving. For the first time, nothing occurred to him to say; and in a bustle of queer embarrassment he knelt to build the fire.

The silence between them grew long ... longer. He was aware of every second of it, but no longer glanced behind him. The fire burst upward at last, fine and bright; and as it did so there was a small sound, like an echo, from the daybed.

He turned quickly round, saw Harriet's face altered, as though brought to life, by the lively flames. He burst into triumphant chuckles. "There! What you think of that, eh? Pretty good? You feel it?"

She certainly saw it, saw it with entire and mindless attention, even raised her long hands and held them gropingly forward. He pushed himself up and stood watching them alternately for a while, Harriet and the fire, in restored good humor.

Then, leaning, he nipped the hat from her lap and tossed it across the room.

"There. You want that back, you gonna ask me, Harriet," he said; and grinning down at her, he began to take off his coat.

CHAPTER SIXTEEN

The house in New York had settled into chilly desertion. Four heatless winter days had drained it of oil stored warmth; and Moran's next-door neighbor complained that her own heating problems were being aggravated by those clammy walls. She had no idea what was going on—knew nothing about him, and didn't want to.

One last occupant remained. A Mr. Harvey Freid, third floor rear, doggedly continued to live in his room, and he was more than willing to let the police into the house.

"Connecticut cops, eh?" he said, as if hopeful of bad news. "They tell me the local guys were round before. What's next—FBI? What's he done?"

He took them up to Moran's office, offering it as an exhibit of some interest.

"Quite a layout, no? I used to wonder what kind of a racket he had, and then I decided he didn't have any—just delusions of grandeur. You ever see his wife?"

He was lonely, curious, hard to get rid of. One of the Connecticut men went upstairs with him, leaving his lieutenant and the man from Manhattan homicide to themselves. There was a chance Mr. Freid might have something to say; and eventually it appeared that he had. Moran had been back to the house.

"Sure it was him. By that time there wasn't anybody else. The old lady downstairs was gone the first day the heat went off—her daughter came and took her away. Says she's an invalid, and she's going to sue Moran for endangering her health. And there never was anybody on the second floor but the two of them. Besides, the door was locked—that office door. I came down a couple of times because I was damn sure I heard someone, and I could see light through the keyhole, too. He wouldn't answer, though."

That had been Monday evening. Freid was alone in the house—the other roomers had taken to staying out as late as possible before coming back to their frigid rooms and beds. That was when they were still coming back, he said—now they had given up, were staying with friends, or in hotels. One had gone for good.

He didn't know what time Moran had left. At first he had meant to wait and challenge him when he came out, but the cold drove him back upstairs—Moran took too long. He went back at last to his electric fire—the only one in the place—and left his door open a little. He admitted he dozed off a little. When he woke and came down again, about ten-thirty, the keyholes were dark and the office door opened when he tried it. He thought he had first noticed sound on the floor below around eight o'clock.

"In the hall," he explained. "I think he was going back and forth between the rooms, you know."

Harriet's room bore the signs of his visit, where his own did not. There, he had had to hunt—and had hunted with abandon, tipping out drawers and boxes, gutting closets. A trunk in one corner had been stripped of its rug covering and searched and left open. The clutter was unbelievable. The men stood appraising what they could see without attempting to delve into it.

The Manhattan detective, more accustomed to one-room hoarders, turned away first.

"String-saver type," he said.

The rest of the house was in order, or seemed to be. The drawers of the great desk in Moran's office had a look of old untidiness, but contained only receipts and records, endless and unfiled. Gaps indicated that whatever was of value to Moran had been taken away with him. It began to seem clear that he wasn't coming back.

Down in the basement they came on Moran's snuggery. The bare table with its smashed contents lying scattered all around drew their eyes. The shabby blanket was half-drawn from the cot and trailed on the floor, as though dragged by someone in haste.

"Looks like a roughhouse," said the Manhattan man, cheered.

The Connecticut lieutenant was down on one knee, picking through the litter. He held up one glove—a woman's glove in pale, soft leather, smeared with dirt.

"This could be the mate to the one we've got," he said.

Wandering, wary-eyed, the men began a separate inspection of the cellar, noting any other trace of disorder. There were many—some obviously of years' standing. Moran's house pride had not applied, down here.

From the narrow corridor to the area door, one of them called out, "Come and take a look at this."

He indicated the door of the furnace room—a flimsy board door, part of a cheap partitioning job. It had been fitted with a double hasp and padlock, all of which now hung together, the lock closed, on the door itself. The marks where it had worked free of its fastening on the partition board were still new.

"Somebody wanted out—or in."

"Got it, too."

There were stains on the wood, dark stains. They stood examining these without touching them, although it was not a surface for fingerprints.

Then the Manhattan man said, "I think we could use some lab on this. Want me to call?"

"It's yours," said Connecticut. "We can give you blood group on her, if that's any good. She didn't die of wounds. Broken neck, and then exposure—they found her out in her car, a couple of days after she left home. Looks like she might have come down here. She could have been driven back up. No way to tell exactly when she did die. Or where."

"That makes it nice," said Manhattan. "This sounds like one you can keep."

Moran, explicitly described—even to the clothing in which Marianne had last seen him—proved memorable to anyone who had come in contact with him. By evening a kind of trail had emerged, that crossed and recrossed itself and led nowhere.

He had bought blankets and two pillows at a neighborhood dry goods store in Frampton, across town from the hospital. The clerk had wanted to help him carry them out, assuming a car waited somewhere; but Moran refused. He looked pretty funny with his load, the clerk said, reminiscent.

He had bought a box of groceries at a general store on the road to Willett but no gas, although there were gas pumps outside. A nurse had passed him on the fire stairs in Frampton Hospital—he was going up, carrying a large box. She said he looked like a delivery man who had got lost and was mad about it, but he didn't ask for help and she didn't offer it.

At last, someone saw the car he must have had, although none was registered to him in New York. Around noon he had arrived at a Frampton suburban station carrying a can, explaining that he had run out of gas just a couple of streets away. The man remembered that the can was new, and that he had made some joke about it—Moran laughed too. Later, driving home for his lunch in a nearby street, the gas station attendant had passed the little guy struggling to refuel an old Ford— real comical, that hat and all. Like something out of the old-time movies. He had tapped his horn, but Moran didn't look up. He'd say it was a Model A, '32 or '33, maybe—himself having obviously been in grammar school in those years. He hadn't noticed the license, which meant it was probably Connecticut.

No such car had been reported missing. It was probably one of the ones that stood on the streets for weeks, objects of intermittent police attention. The hunt for it began, as discreetly as possible; but after that one ludicrous appearance with his pre-empted car Moran seemed to have taken it to ground.

Either he and Harriet had fled at once, miraculously unobserved anywhere, or else they were still lying low in the vicinity of Frampton.

The pillows and blankets, the groceries, pointed that way. And on this assumption the state and local police went intensively to work.

CHAPTER SEVENTEEN

The Hinkleys did not after all go to Irma's funeral. There wasn't any. Tom Bryce, in that remorseless state of apology in which he constantly addressed Marianne these days, made a furtive visit to the office to explain.

"They aren't releasing her till tomorrow—that's what they call it, releasing her. She'll be—it'll be a closed coffin. And with the only family she's got hiding out from the police—I don't know, it seems like a farce to try and do what—what people ordinarily would do."

He was just going on over by himself, with Bill Cooley from the funeral parlor. He didn't, honestly, want anyone else. Not even Marianne—and Henry, of course.

Marianne said she understood. It was true. She couldn't at this date, and with Tom standing there bedraggled before her, imagine how to make Irma's leave-taking in any way usual.

She said, "Well, will you come and eat supper with us tomorrow? We'd be glad to have you, Tom." She didn't want to think of him just going back to that big house alone afterward.

"I don't think I will, Mary Anne, thanks. I know how Henry feels about all this, and he's right, of course. It's not your mess and you should never have been mixed up in it in the first place. Wouldn't have been, if you hadn't been mixed up with me."

"Oh, for goodness sake, Tom!"

She controlled her impatience, but could feel it still simmering inside. He went on standing there with the dejected, stubborn air of a man who knows he is making things worse and has no flexibility left to stop it.

In the end he did agree to come, making it clear that he could appear only as an acknowledged and offensive burden to Henry, if not to her. She took his acceptance on these terms, as matter-of-factly as possible, and then seized on his being there to ask for help in the muddle of her accounts.

"Couldn't you just tell me what kind of an agreement you did make with Tim Hurley, about those plumbing fixtures? We got them all right, but the invoices weren't a bit like specifications, and I don't understand the bill at all. Look at the—"

"Oh, don't worry about that," he mumbled, already turning away. "I fixed that up with old Tim, it's all right."

"I know, but if that accountant's coming tomorrow ..." Tomorrow. The day of Irma's non-funeral. She was checked, and lost out—he got away. She sighed, and put the Hurley papers in a growing file of Matters to Be Gone Over with Mr. Bryce Personally. She didn't look forward to her dinner party any more than Henry would.

Henry, in fact, heard about his prospective guest without a murmur. In the first place, he thought it was the Right Thing to Do, which would have been enough in itself. But he showed too much willingness, she thought, for duty to be all of it.

Tentatively she said, "I hope you won't go asking him about your list, Henry."

"Lists," he corrected.

There were now two—necessarily two. After that first, unproductive evening (when, Henry later explained, he had just been clearing his mind), he had spent an abstracted day at the store making notes on a pocket pad; and that night he had got down to work and covered pages. The first list concerned Henry's own firsthand knowledge. A second list had grown from rejects from the first, with a code notation for degrees of probable verity; and now he was contemplating a third, in several different colors of pencil, to correlate the two.

She accepted the correction.

"Lists," she said, placative. He was silent; and she went on, "I was wondering if I oughtn't to ask somebody else. Maybe the Evanses, if they could come. Mrs. Evans knew his mother."

"I don't see the connection," said Henry.

He didn't like the idea. She didn't feel able to defend it, and gave it up.

She might have known better, however, than to worry about how Henry would behave. He behaved as he always did—like himself; which was more, Marianne acknowledged, than could be said for her. Or Tom.

Tom arrived with painful punctuality, wearing a pressed dark suit she had never seen, white shirt, and dark tie. He sat where Henry put him and was gloomily silent over his drink. Marianne said all she could think of to say, and Henry courteously backed her up. There wasn't much of that. It began to look like a long, silent evening.

But later, from the kitchen, she was astonished to hear an animated conversation begin. Both voices. She couldn't make out what they were saying, and became convinced that Henry had whipped out his lists … but this no longer seemed so dreadful. At least Tom had found his tongue.

When she came in to call them to the table, no papers were visible. And it was Tom, flushed, who was doing all the talking.

"Why *should* she have had a police guard on her?" he was demanding. "At that point she was just a patient! The only concern Walt had with her was to try and help the hospital track down her husband. Which he did, right away! He did his job all right. If he'd done any more then, they'd have said he was trying to horn in on them. Isn't that a fact?"

"Mr. Bryce is kind of sore at the State Police," said Henry. "Seems like they been riding Chief Hovey about that crazy lady getting out."

"Well, not exactly riding him," said Tom quickly. With Marianne in the room, he lost his volubility. "They could hardly do that. But Walt's a guy that feels things—he doesn't need a brick wall to fall on him. And he did what he was supposed to do, all anybody could have expected him to do."

"Oh, I'm sure they don't blame Mr. Hovey about Harriet," she said. "How could anybody expect a thing like that to happen?"

She moved them in to the table, where Tom fell back into silence.

Then Henry said, "Well, anyhow, they got all hands out looking for those people now, I hear."

"And there's another thing," Tom said sharply. "Sure they want all the facilities Walt can give them but whatever *they're* doing is still their own private business! Why, they were down in New York yesterday, going through that guy's house, and the first Walt knew of it was when it was all over and they got back here with one of Irma's gloves! Probably he wouldn't even have known about that if they hadn't had to get in touch with him about this area search. It seems to me," he said, flushed, "that they think they're a little too special—kind of above ordinary kinds of police! And just about as far apart from ordinary taxpayers as a bunch of Martians. Those extra-fancy uniforms, and the way they're always careful to keep on their side of the fence, and make sure you keep on your side—why, what's the point of it? Don't we pay for them, just the same as any other kind of public servants? How are they so different from the fellows over in Frampton? Or Joe Palmer, for that matter! If all those guys can do their jobs and find time to talk to you like a human being, then what's with these State guys? It seems to me they think they're some kind of elite guard," he said bitterly. "Don't have to answer to anybody but themselves. That's next door to a damn Gestapo, in my opinion. We got no place for that kind of police in our country, that I can see!"

Marianne, embarrassed, did not know how to reply. Henry looked thoughtful too. But he remarked, in the first pause, "You say they found Mrs. Bryce's glove down there in New York? Just the one?"

Tom nodded, glum.

"That's right. She had the other one with her, when they found her. This one was down in that guy's cellar."

A shudder went through Marianne, so rapid she could not disguise it. Tom did not notice but Henry did.

He said matter-of-factly, "Then I expect she must have been down there right after you, Mary Ann."

It was an observation, offered with restraint. Marianne saw that he was no more inclined than herself to begin speculating about Irma's last trip, with her husband sitting there.

Tom, however, raised his head and said impatiently, "How could there be any doubt about it now? Why, she as good as told Mary Ann she'd go down and handle it herself—they ought to have been after that end of it days ago! Somebody around that neighborhood might have noticed something, or heard something. It's a rooming house—they could at least have questioned the people that lived there!"

"They say folks don't pay much attention to what their neighbors do, down in the city," Henry said, good-humored. But Tom wouldn't accept any lighter tone.

"That's a lot of baloney. People notice something out-of-the-way anywhere. They just don't rush around and volunteer information about it, like they do out here. But those fancy police aren't paid to sit around waiting for volunteers. They ought to have been down there digging, right away."

An idea came into Marianne's head, and popped right out.

"Have they been bothering you, Tom?"

"Who? Those State boys? They don't bother me." Then, as quickly, he burst out, "Yes, damn it! I'm sick of the way they work! God knows, I wanted to help them every way I could. I've done whatever they wanted, turned the house over to them. I even turned over things they were too dumb to find—"

"That's those snapshots, you mean?" Henry murmured. He wanted to keep things straight as they went along.

"Well, yes, that was a pretty important find, wasn't it? I turned them right over to them, not to Walt, though he's got just as much right to them. To them. I took it out to the barracks myself," he said. "I bet I was there all of ten minutes—and as far as they were concerned, that was about five minutes too long! Anybody'd think it was *their* family pictures I'd found, and they didn't want strangers horning in. We'll get in touch when we need you, that's all, brother," he said, in bitter mimicry. "But just let *them* have one jackass question they want answered, any time! If they want me to know they're keeping tabs on me, okay, I know it. I get it! But what's the point? I've told them everything I know, and they're not interested in what I think. They've made that pretty clear, God knows!"

Suddenly tears came into his eyes. Nobody spoke. Marianne looked at Henry, but he was considering his embroidered linen napkin as if he had never seen it before—which he certainly had.

She stammered, "Well, I—I know it's been an awful strain on you, but they've got to do it, I suppose."

"It's not what they have to do, it's the way they do it," he replied, sullen. "They don't have to be so different from everybody else."

As the evening dragged on, Marianne (and even Henry) gave up being embarrassed for him. It was a waste of time. He was almost unaware of them, in his exhaustion and obsession, except as an audience to whom he could at last express aloud the angry complaints that filled his mind.

She had wondered, in these last days, what he was doing with himself in so much solitude. Now she knew. Hours and days wouldn't be too much to let this stream run dry—this torrent of introspection, that must have kept him silently engrossed in his empty house.

Or perhaps, not silently. Perhaps he talked aloud there in the same way, not missing a response any more than he missed one here.

Unable to bear any more, she broke in. "Tom. Tom! Come on, let's go have our coffee by the fire. You go in with Henry, and I'll bring the tray right in."

She heard him start off again while she was hastily gathering cups, and came in on the full flood.

"But what else can they think? How else could that glove have got left there, if she wasn't attacked right down there in New York, in that man's cellar? Him, or that mad woman of his—whichever one it was, it must have been there! Hell, why else would he run out like he's done—ditch everything he's got? That's what he's done!"

"Well, I been thinking about his coming up here," Henry broke in. "The funny way he's acted, I mean. Now when he first came up to get her out of the hospital, he maybe wasn't sure just what—"

"Not sure!" Tom exclaimed. "Listen, who else could have driven Irma all the way back up here, if he didn't? He—"

"Just a minute," said Henry. "Please." He leaned forward, enforcing this request, intent on what he had been about to say. Then, with a glance at Tom, he seemed to think better of it.

"Well, that's all guessing," he said, leaning back. "After all, we don't know—"

"Certainly we know! We know that Irma's glove—the mate to the one she was found with, mind you—"

Marianne broke in this time.

"I think what Henry means is that Moran couldn't have been sure what Harriet had been up to *up here*, Tom, by herself. Perhaps he's had trouble with her before, it seems awfully likely. He certainly didn't want to talk to anybody at the hospital, when he first came there. Then when the local papers came out with the news about Irma—that would be enough to make him panicky, whatever. Don't you think, Henry?"

"I don't know," he said. That was all.

Her evening-long restraint broke a little, in the only permissible direction.

"Well, I don't mean they're *facts*, Henry," she said. "I don't mean you'd put it on your list. Lists!"

Henry didn't reply. Tom looked vaguely from one to the other of them, as if he sensed that a tactful remark would be in order but couldn't produce it.

Finally he said, "What lists are those, Henry?"

Henry courteously explained, ignoring his wife.

"Why, just a few things about what's happened, Mr. Bryce. Seemed to be so much rumor and mix-up going around, I thought it wouldn't hurt to jot down a few facts. Hope you don't mind. I figured it might sort of clear my mind, but I can't say it has, so far."

Tom was polite too. He said it sounded like a good idea.

"Long as it's come up, though," said Henry, "I wonder if you might recollect what time it was, that morning you came by here, lookin' for Mary Ann." This was a tactful way of saying, the morning after Irma disappeared; but Tom didn't seem to get it. He just looked at Henry, dull-eyed. All his animation had dissolved.

"When she was down to New York," Henry helped him. "I remember I was buttoning up my shirt when I looked out the upstairs window and saw you walkin' up the drive—ordinarily, that'd be about seven-fifteen. But with Mary Ann away I get a little off the track, it might have been as late as eight o'clock, I guess, but I wouldn't think it could be much later. You have any idea?"

Tom's stare began to acquire a drugged quality. Marianne decided she had let Henry go on long enough.

"Does it matter very much?" she asked, in a hinting voice.

He answered her soberly, "Why, yes, it does. It's on my certain knowledge list, of course—no place else it could be—and I'm not certain. Not about the time, that is. Of course, whatever time you do judge it was, Mr. Bryce, I'd have to put in like a footnote. Corroborative," he added. "You can see that."

Now Tom was looking like a sleepwalker who has suddenly come to in the waiting room of a dog hospital, or a busy beauty parlor. He got to his feet.

"Why, no, Henry," he said calmly. "I'm sorry, I can't tell you."

Henry replied generously, "It doesn't matter." He got up too. "Just thought you might happen to recall."

Tom Bryce turned to Marianne. Apology was coming over him again.

"I'm afraid I got talking about my troubles and forgot the time. I'm keeping you up, and you've got that CPA to meet, haven't you?"

He left with surprising collectedness, behaving almost like himself again. He said twice, once for each of them, that the evening had been a real oasis.

"A real oasis, Mary Ann. I know I'm a rotten guest just now—never was much of a one."

When the jeep had backed precipitately down to the road and vanished, she turned out the porch light and put the chain on. Then she went in to Henry, who stood with a full ashtray in each hand, thinking.

"Leave those, Henry," she said. "I'll clean up in the morning."

"Now that's something I never thought about till now," he replied. "Why in time did he *walk* up here, that morning? He did—I recollect that very clearly—he was walking up the drive. Don't suppose he walked all the way out here, do you?"

"He probably got a ride from somebody," she said, and took the ashtrays away from him. "Henry, I'm sorry I said—"

"But why would he do that? That jeep hasn't been laid up for repairs since before Thanksgiving."

"I don't know. He was probably upset, and didn't realize."

"Didn't realize what?" said Henry, slowly trailing her. "A man don't have to realize anything, to come out the door and get in his car standing right there."

"Henry—" she said, and turned. "Henry, I just don't want to talk about this anymore, if you don't mind. This whole evening—this whole *awful* evening—"

"Why, that's all right, Mary Ann," he said ... and, after a moment, "Now that's all right, don't you fret. There, there ..."

CHAPTER EIGHTEEN

There was nothing to do but talk, and sleep, and keep up the fire; and that was how Moran passed his time ... with Harriet. Already they had fallen into a routine, in the way that two people entirely used to each other will do, no matter where. After a while it didn't make so much difference that Harriet no longer said anything. He had stopped listening to what she did say years ago.

The main thing was that with Harriet there, recovered, beside him, he could talk once more. He thought by talking, and he needed very much to think, to come to some decision. They couldn't stay there forever, as he told Harriet a dozen times an hour. Did she think they could? Did she think they could just live in this shack forever?

Harriet, attentive to the fire, offered no opinion. Her expression never changed. If, in a rage of nerves, he struck or shook her, she simply fell to one side and stayed there; he had to put her back himself, and that did upset him a little. Afterward he would have to go out, grumbling, and find some small chore to restore himself. Hunt more wood, or fix something to eat, or go to that stinking, icy pond for water. Water was his minor torture. Who could imagine such a wilderness, that the taps gave only silence, nothing?

Sometimes he would come back melancholy enough to cry, and would sit down on the hearth with his head against Harriet's knees. That had made her jumpy in the old days; but she didn't mind now. In a mournful, self-comforting voice, he would begin to accuse her.

"What do you care what I got to do, all the trouble you make me and then you don't pay no attention—what do you care? Moran's always gonna fix it, that's what you think, you don't even know how, you don't even care. All right, now you done something I can't fix—nobody can fix it, the police gonna get you this time for sure. I know you hit Irma. You're not fooling me, Harriet, I know what you did. How you think I'm gonna fix something like that? Nobody could fix it. Not even Nagy, even if he wants to. And he don't want to."

At this point, despair would caution him to silence. Because what he was saying was true. The pleasure of his triumph over the hospital had faded; and no new plans, no new contriving, had occurred to him to occupy his mind. He had done a good job—had planned and persevered and succeeded in getting Harriet out; that was the kind of job he did well, and could be depended upon to do. But afterward, what? After his "little jobs" there had always been somebody else to take over, to praise and instruct him about what came next. But that somebody now wanted nothing more to do with him. With him and his "loony girlfriend."

That hurt. That was too bitter to think about ... and so, instead, he talked with bitterness of Nagy. Nagy, to whom class in a woman meant nothing, who didn't care who was in his bed so long as she didn't give him trouble. Nagy, who had been making cracks about Harriet from long ago—from the beginning; who hadn't even wanted to let Moran bring her over from England with him.

"That's trouble," he had said (as if Harriet was some horse or dog Moran wanted to bring with him). "Trouble we can always get, we don't have to carry it around with us. Leave the lady there."

But he hadn't. Harriet comes or I don't come, he had said. Said now, aloud, again, in this room where no one remained to hear but himself … and Harriet. She gave no sign of hearing.

He pushed himself away from her and got up, in sour discontent. But it was no relief to give her a smack, when he would only have to pick her up again himself—or see her lying there crooked until he gave in. He gave her, instead, a long and thoughtful stare, which did not in the least intrude upon her preoccupations. Then he turned away, uneasy again.

What was it that had happened? She had followed Irma, somehow? But why, how? Or had Irma, that bitch, fixed something up that night in New York, before she left his house? In the morning he had found only the torn-away lock where she got out—and since he had slept through that, maybe he had slept through Irma creeping by him, going upstairs. Finding Harriet—waking her up, and saying what?

That part was unimaginable; he never got past it. Yet he knew that something just as incredible had really happened: Harriet had left his house by herself. And had turned up here, miles away, in a hospital. About Irma he knew only—like everybody—what the papers in that town had told him: that she was dead "of undetermined causes"; that "police were investigating." He knew it was Irma from the picture—there was no mistake. Besides, it sounded like something that would happen to Irma.

But how was Harriet mixed up in it? He didn't dare ask, didn't dare wait and see. All he could do was to get her out, and then lie low until things cooled down. Until he got word from Nagy they could come back.

Now that word wouldn't come. Nagy wanted no part of his troubles— had, in fact, forbidden him to get in touch with him again. Nagy, to whom he had been like a hand, an arm, a little brother, for half their lives! And in savage sorrow he cursed himself, once again, for his fatal frankness with Nagy. Telling him everything, like that, because he was Nagy.

I should have come back first, he said. (To Harriet; to the room.) I should have said nothing, brought her back.

And then what? Police in his house, Nagy cold and disclaiming, Harriet acting so queer he couldn't hope to hide it.

"What you keep on acting like that for?" he shouted down at her; and her pale, unanswering stare enraged him so that he struck and rebalanced her in almost the same movement. She was a shocking doll, treated so; and all at once his rage—fed by thoughts of Nagy—became entirely for her.

"Sure, sure—do nothing, say nothing!" he screamed. "First you make all the trouble, then you just sit! You think that's a lady? You think a lady does like that? I'll tell you something, Harriet—you're no lady! Nagy was right—what you are, you're only trouble! I should have listened—I should have left you there so you can make trouble for your fine family, not for me. You know what he said? Long time ago, Harriet, when you looked nice, acted so fine, impressed everybody. Not Nagy! That's no lady, he said. No lady would go with you, Joe."

His voice died, struck silent by that hurtful echo from long ago. Why had he remembered it ... repeated it, at last?

Helpless, he looked down at Harriet. She gave him no help.

"I should have stayed by Nagy," he said. "Not you."

And to take back all that he could, now that it was too late, he pulled from under her hands the hat he had put there in some coaxing earlier moment. A hat! A craziness, to make people laugh. Like Harriet ...

With one great sob, he threw the crazy hat to the fire. She never stirred. He no longer cared if she did or not, but turned and threw himself on the daybed and lay face down, with one sullen eye staring steadily at Harriet.

After a time, the eye closed. His breathing grew heavy and choked; Moran slept.

The hat was lying beside the fire. Almost in it. For a long time, smoke had been secretly rising from it. As though a little secret fire were burning away beneath the hat.

Harriet began to lean forward, very slowly, as she watched. She leaned with long pauses, imperceptibly. She never looked toward Moran. Finally she sat doubled forward like a woman in pain—her body speaking of pain, but her face expressing nothing except a vacant, steady attention to the hat.

Her hand came out and fell upon the hat. Then hand and hat came slowly up together. There was no fire beneath. Nothing. But the secret smoke rose in clouds. Harriet watched, in patient contemplation.

A cloth rose burst into flame. A rose of flame burned upon the hat! Harriet hesitated, then threw the hat away.

On the floor it continued to burn. It lay now by the daybed, and presently another rose—one printed upon the daybed's cretonne skirt—ignited too. Little runs of flame went up the cloth, and Harriet watched these. Soon, very soon, flame seemed to spring up everywhere. Moran lay still, in a growing frame of fire.

Harriet rose. She made several low sounds, addressed to no one, to nothing. She began to back away, slowly.

She had reached the middle of the room when the air was shaken by one terrible yell. At once, Harriet turned and walked toward the door, head down. There was a loud crash, and Harriet stopped. She did not turn until the noise had ended; then, in shy, slow movement, she turned her head and looked backward at Moran.

He was not following, He lay quite still, but on the floor now. Fire ran upon him, a race of blazes. His eyes stared after her, but he did not speak.

Harriet walked outside and shut the door. The fire was all inside now. Outside it was night, and cold. Through the windows she could still see the leaping of the fire.

She stayed there, on the porch, until the house no longer contained the fire and the heat became too intense. Then she went down the steps. She stayed near the house. Whenever a heavy piece of burning stuff fell near her she moved away, or back; but she stayed as near as she could.

Wild wailing began to echo in the far night, making her raise her head. A shriller screaming began, and persevered. It came nearer to where she was.

When the screaming thing was almost upon her she began to walk away, leaving the brightness and warmth behind her.

The missing Model A Ford had been found.

It was undamaged; but the cottage which had hidden it was no more than a fiery black framework. An on-shore wind carried the flames away from the car and there it stood, intact, its registration plates on view at last. The uncomplaining owner could be traced through them now, but not Moran. There was no need; that hunt was over.

He had apparently died beside the daybed he had been lying on—had gotten as far as the floor, in one convulsive roll, and stayed there. What was left of the iron daybed stood in the corner next to the fireplace—or what was left of the fireplace. The chimney still stood, precarious—a danger point that the firefighters kept clear of, once Moran's body had been taken out.

There was not much that could be done about the cottage. The new Hillyard equipment boasted chemical tanks, but it was a waste of time (and chemical) to try to save the cottage now. Mostly, the men from the towns were ditching, beating, spraying, to keep the fire from going inland; for the wind that had protected the Ford was blowing destruction among the inland pine and scrub.

The little side road that led only to the cottage was jammed with trucks and cars; a police blockade cut it off from the main road. Just in view from the burning cottage was the useless expanse of Long Island Sound.

The land formed a point, and was privately owned. The area search for Moran and Harriet had been within hours of reaching it. Now, with the point as a base, a new search would have to begin—for Harriet.

As soon as it became clear that Moran had died alone, that no woman was wandering nearby, a concentration of police took over the vicinity. Roadblocks were set up at the nearest junctions in either direction;

Harriet's description was broadcast at fifteen-minute intervals until the area station shut down, and then on the later New York and Boston programs. It seemed a thin chance that any motorist or householder should acquire so strange a refugee without reporting her; but Harriet had proved herself a person of too many surprises to be narrowly estimated.

Chief Walter Hovey of the Frampton Police, roused and aggressively active, called the hospital and demanded authority. He got, eventually, a tired woman's voice that said yes, she had seen Harriet on her admission and several times afterward. What did he want to know?

"Well, now look, Doc, I want the straight dope—you people tell us she's out of con ... con ... out of commission. What the hell does that mean? She's just burned up a house with her boyfriend in it and got clean away. What else is she likely to do? According to you folks, she couldn't do anything—well, what do you call nothing? What else is she going to do? I got to know what I'm up against, here!"

He was hard to talk to—irate, defensive, too nervous to listen well.

"Why, I would have had a man on her right along, if you people hadn't told me ... And now lord knows where she's got to, out there on the roads passing herself off for anybody!"

The tired voice said, sharpening, "Harriet isn't passing herself off as a normal person—that's quite impossible. Anybody who comes across her is going to find exactly the same woman we did. If he likes to consider that normal, that's another matter. I can't answer for every night driver in Connecticut, Mr. Hovey."

He backed down a little.

"No, no, I understand that, Doc. All I want to know is—"

"As for Harriet setting a fire, she's exactly as capable of it as any young child left alone with matches. If you have visions of her soaking rags or pouring on kerosene, you'd better forget it. And may I also point out that Harriet did not leave this hospital by herself—that she was not and is not capable of any such performance. She doesn't plan, and she's entirely passive and irresponsible. Is that what you want to know?"

It wasn't; but it was all he was going to get, so he took it. And sat glum, listening to spot announcements on the radio that rubbed him on the raw. What he really wanted was to put the blame for that nut squarely on ... somebody. But there wasn't anybody else there. He went out, aggressive, to look for somebody.

It seemed to Henry Hinkley that he had barely got his wife to sleep, after that crying spell, when the fire alarm hooter woke them up. They lay automatically counting the hoots, and then relaxed. It wasn't near them; and this was Henry's year off duty as a volunteer.

The Hillyard hooter began; they could hear that, too.

"Big one," said Henry sleepily. Then he slid suddenly out of bed. "Ed Moag's a volunteer," he said, to his startled wife.

She watched him push up the window, struggle with the storm

window's catch, and then let freezing air into the room. He stuck his head out, calling, and Ed Moag answered right away.

"You go on," Henry yelled down at him. "That's a district alarm, you better get going!"

"Well, I guess I better, Henry. I'll be right back soon as I can—or send somebody—" Ed's distracted voice yelled faintly back. She lay in a daze of sleepiness, watching Henry latch up the window again and race back to bed. He felt icy all over, already, as he curled himself round her warmth. In a moment, they were back asleep.

CHAPTER NINETEEN

At some dark hour of the night, the fire alarm hooter had wakened Mrs. Evans. Her hearing was still keen, and long years of night nursing had made her a light sleeper; she woke quietly, at once, and lay counting the long, lonely blares of sound that told of the fire's location. One-two; one-two-three. One-two; one-two-three. Twenty-three. That meant outside the town, to the east. If it were far enough east, the Hillyard hooter would come in too.

She lay listening, and soon had the satisfaction of hearing the fainter, farther blasts of warning begin.

"District alarm," she murmured aloud, although no one could hear her. (Dr. Evans wore a hearing aid, which he naturally removed at night. It was one of the major dissatisfactions of Mrs. Evans's advancing years that she could no longer communicate with her husband by night.)

Now the volunteers' cars were starting up all around her in the sleeping town, the exciting sound of racing motors came from every direction—some quite near (the Varneys, the Leighs), others in the distance. The fire apparatus went screaming by, audible in decrescendo as it left town.

She heard it all; and when the succeeding quiet gathered round her once more she stirred restlessly, sighed. If her husband had been awake too … If they had been a little younger, and could have gone out after the men to offer help, coffee, shelter … But he would not wake; and if he did, they no longer drove themselves. No longer even kept a car.

She sighed again, wishing back her sleep, since there was nothing else to wish for. But sleep would not come. Nowadays she woke more easily than she slept again; it seemed to be just the other way round for her husband.

She knew where the fire, the men, the excitement would be—knew, too, almost every building of consequence in the vicinity. That the fire was a real one and not just some chimney or trash pile blaze was becoming clearer every minute. For something minor, they wouldn't stay so long.

Mrs. Evans got out of bed, put on her woolly slippers, and wound herself up in her padded robe. Then she went across the hall to the bedroom that faced east and peered hopefully from its windows. Nothing, of course. It was too far. She had known it would be.

She sighed once more—this time with a tinge of exasperation—and turned back into the room. It was the one in which she had, so briefly, kept poor Miss Gaither; and she gave the tidy big bed a regretful glance in passing.

Out in the hall, she went resolutely downstairs, making her way surely through the dark house. In the kitchen she turned on the light and put large quantities of water to boil on the stove. Then, fortified by these preparations, she sat down at the telephone and called Mack Varney's number.

As a volunteer's wife, Tessie should certainly be up and waiting for her man to return. That she had probably not got out of bed in the first place, Mrs. Evans chose to ignore; she let the phone go on ringing insistently until it was answered. The minute she heard Tessie's faint hello, her own voice came out crisp with authority.

"Tessie, those men have been gone more than half an hour—that means it's a real one. We've got to get out there with coffee for them. Are you dressed?"

"I—what? Oh ... Mrs. Evans ...?"

Her voice became hopeless at once—the voice of one who, after forty years, had still not got the Nicene Creed by heart. She made one feeble attempt at defense.

"Why, Mrs. Evans dear, what are you doing out of bed this time of night? You—"

"I'm making the coffee, naturally," Mrs. Evans replied. "By the time you get here I'll have everything ready, you needn't bring a thing. But don't waste time—those poor men must be exhausted. And chilled to the bone," she added firmly, drowning some feeble voice-sound from Tessie's end.

It took a few more minutes—every one of which Mrs. Evans begrudged—but by the time they hung up it was (of course) settled: they were going to the fire. Mrs. Evans moved briskly then. When her unhappy driver arrived, she was not only warmly dressed and provided with two large cans of coffee, but had set out the handsome cake a parishioner had just brought them, and of which Dr. Evans had not yet had one bite. She was just pinning a note to the empty pillow beside him, in case he woke (GONE TO FIRE), when the car drove up. Mrs. Evans skipped downstairs like a girl.

"Now, Tessie, if you'll get those cans out, like a good girl, I'll bring—let's see, paper cups, cake, knife, napkins ..."

"I only hope they'll let us through the line," said Tessie, in one last murmur of rebellion. But she knew—they both knew—that the line didn't exist through which Mrs. Evans couldn't bully her way.

It turned out to be the Frazier place on Quonaquah Point—most satisfactory, since it would be both deserted and fully covered by insurance. Probably the young Fraziers would be glad of a chance to rebuild anyway. And they managed to arrive at just the right time—when it was nearly under control and the men were milling or standing about, and yet hadn't begun to disperse. They had to leave the car, but were allowed—helped, in fact—to a position equivalent to fifth row center, where Mrs. Evans went cheerfully into action.

"Wiring, I suppose? Woodchucks, or rabbits? (Milk? Black?) What a blessing no one was there! No, but how could there be? Oh, how dreadful, the poor soul!" She turned to Mack Varney, coming up in pleased surprise to greet his wife. "Mack, they tell me some poor creature lost his life here, but whoever can it have been? Surely not one of the Fraziers?"

"No, no, Mrs. Evans. It was that fellow the police were looking for, you remember, the one they put out the broadcast on? With your—"

"Tessie, they *both* have sugar—for energy, you know. This one's black ... Oh, but how dreadful, all the same! A fugitive, you say?"

Just then the belated ambulance arrived, and police activity superseded that of the firefighters. The townspeople drew back—had a tendency to draw together, depending upon which town they came from—and Mrs. Evans did brisk business. And listened, more and more thoughtfully.

She was a woman of ready understanding, not in the least dimmed by her years; she very soon grasped who it was that had died in the fire ... and who had not. But her years had made her less and less inclined to accept the world's opinions as her own. Harriet might be, to the community, "that crazy woman that escaped from the hospital"; to Mrs. Evans she remained Miss Gaither, whom she had encountered and weighed for herself. A helpless and childlike woman, certainly, but also one of undoubted good breeding and pathetic gratitude—and, almost certainly, one of their flock. People were very quick to put sad labels on those who differed from themselves—and who, perhaps increasingly confused by their difference, did nothing to assert themselves. Mrs. Evans understood this, and did not condemn. But neither was she intimidated. She said nothing—it was not the time—but she considered. She considered along the lines of the man who had lost his cow and thought where he would go if he were a cow. It was not, of course, that simple; but she meant to try.

Accordingly, to the surprise of Tessie, who had rather begun to enjoy herself, she presently said, "All right, dear, that's all. We've done what we can, and we mustn't hang about and get in people's way. I think you could bring the car down this far now that things are clearing up a bit—it would make packing so much simpler. Will you try?"

Tessie went to try; and since their position was now semi-official, she succeeded. When the car was packed, and themselves in it, Mrs. Evans said, "Now, Tessie, there's no use in our going back through all that roadblock nonsense when there's a perfectly simple little road over there a way. Just keep driving forward, and your headlights will pick it up. On the right."

It seemed to Tessie not simple at all, since she was forced to drive over plain bumpy ground for quite a distance. Coincidentally (or was it?) the Hillyard fire trucks were leaving, and all attention centered on these, so that nobody checked their awkward meandering. Tessie, losing her temper slightly, wanted to know just how long it was since Mrs. Evans had been over this simple little road. Mrs. Evans said serenely that they had always used it in Margaret Frazier's time; it was the existing road then, and so much more convenient. At that point the headlights did pick up a kind of track and Tessie, regretting her sharpness, started down it. When it was too late to get out, she gathered that Margaret Frazier's time could not have been recent.

She said with restraint, "What we need for this road is a bulldozer"; and Mrs. Evans sadly agreed that it had not been well kept up at all. The main trouble was that branches had been allowed to grow long, which obscured the view ahead and whacked them constantly as they passed; but the road itself, as Mrs. Evans pointed out, was still quite passable. Tessie, gripping the wheel, forbore to answer.

"Somewhere along here," Mrs. Evans said presently, "Margaret had her little studio. She painted quite well, you know—I think you've seen her flower studies in my hall? Yes, just past this lovely old pine, I remember very clearly. If you will just stop the car a moment, I think I will get out."

"Get out!" said Tessie. "Here, in these woods? Whatever for?"

"Just for a moment, dear. Just stop here."

Tessie stopped the car, but only in order to give her full attention to her passenger.

"Mrs. Evans, what are you up to?" she demanded. "Are you looking for that woman—that *crazy* woman? You are, I know it! Do you really think I'm going to let you go wandering around in these woods at night, looking for a—a—"

"A fellow being, my dear," said Mrs. Evans, in a new, stern voice. "A lost, lonely, and frightened woman, who has no one to—"

"No!" said Tessie. "If you think she's hiding there, then let's tell the men—they can come look for her. I'm not going to—"

Her voice died. The gear she was changing stuck and groaned horribly before it slid back into place. Then there was silence. And in that silence, before them, at the edge of the headlights' path, a figure stood motionless.

Mrs. Evans rolled down her window.

"Miss Gaither? Harriet, it's Mrs. Evans. Come here, my dear."

"No," Tessie whispered. "No, no, no ..."

"Tessie, will you be quiet! Come along, Harriet, it's quite all right, I'm going to take you home with me again."

For a space of seconds none of them moved or spoke. Then, before Tessie could act to interfere, Mrs. Evans had opened her door and stepped out.

In the pale, branch-shadowed light ahead of her, Tessie watched the small figure advance toward the larger one that did not move at all. In a moment, something would happen. Whatever it was, Tessie knew herself as incapable of acting as a witness in a dream.

The two figures came together and stood so. Over the running motor, Mrs. Evans's voice could be heard in the night silence persuasive, wordless. Then both figures moved, one leading the other back toward her; light reached upon them as they came near and Tessie saw a gaunt, blank-faced woman, coatless, in shapeless pullover and skirt, stumbling toward the car in Mrs. Evans's wake. Tessie changed gears violently, and began to pray.

"Tessie, this is my friend Miss Gaither who is coming back to stay with us—I think perhaps we'll sit together here in the back seat, if you don't mind. Now, Harriet, just get in, dear. *Get in*," said Mrs. Evans, with a first, pardonable tremor in her voice.

Tessie did not attempt to answer or look round. She just waited—through crashing sounds, that somehow involved the empty coffee cans—until she heard the back seat door close. Then she sent the car lunging violently ahead.

Afterward she felt quite sure that they had parted company with the "simple little road" at that point. *No* road could have produced the rocking and leaping they underwent, and in any case she was only steering by trees—or by spaces between them. It was a wonder, she said afterward, that they hadn't just gone round in circles in that wood all night.

The highway, when they burst out on it, looked utterly strange. For a time, she could not even think which direction to take. Mrs. Evans, directing her from the otherwise silent back seat, seemed surprised to find how close they were to town.

"I don't believe we've come out quite right, Tessie," she said. "But it's all right, dear. You did very well."

It was at that point, Tessie said, that she felt herself begin to go to pieces. Otherwise, she said later, she would certainly have driven straight back toward all the police cars, Mrs. Evans or no Mrs. Evans. As it was, she had to admit that she had done nothing of the kind. She didn't even remember that last part of their journey ... remembered only, as an incredible release, sitting limp behind the wheel and watching those two incongruous figures slowly progress up the Evanses' front walk ... up the steps ... in the door.

When the door shut, cutting off Mrs. Evans's hypnotic voice, the silence roused Tessie to independent action. Not, she confessed, of a very useful kind. She couldn't even face driving the car an inch farther but simply left it standing there, doors open, and staggered off on foot toward home and—she prayed—husband.

CHAPTER TWENTY

She was really rather glad to find Dr. Evans up, and waiting for her to come home. (An empty other-half of the bed would wake either one of them, by now.) And to see that he had built a nice fire to wait beside; she had got colder than she realized. Colder, and more tired. Harriet, of course, must be even colder. She realized this with compunction, seeing their guest make her first voluntary movement, toward the bright flames.

And toward Dr. Evans, who just remained, half-risen from his chair, doing nothing to receive them.

A little irritable with fatigue, she said, "You remember Miss Gaither, of course. It was—she was staying in the house that burned, so I've brought her here."

Did he have his hearing aid on? She could not quite see, and said, a little louder, "Miss Gaither—Harriet, you know."

"My dear!"

She placed Harriet in one chair and then allowed herself to sink down in the other—an exquisite relief. But when she opened her eyes again he was still standing there. Looking alarmed. He did have the hearing aid on, though; so she murmured kindly, "I'm quite all right, dear— don't be worried. But if you could bring me a little wine? And Harriet too, of course ..."

He turned at once—she was sorry to upset him, but he really shouldn't *let* himself be upset so easily—and there was a short interval of peaceful nothingness. Then a glass was being put to her lips....

She opened her eyes again, and took hold of the trembling hand that held it.

"Thank you, dear. Please don't worry, I'm just resting. You sit down."

But there was nowhere for him to sit. Reminded, she looked over at Harriet, who was quietly watching the fire.

She said, "But you've brought none for Harriet."

"My dear," he said (in such a voice that she looked back at him, attentive), "what have you done? Don't you realize that the—the authorities are searching for this poor woman?"

Equally low, she replied, "Please don't discuss it now."

"But she is completely unaware of us—surely you can see that!" They both regarded Harriet, who continued to regard the fire. Then Mrs. Evans sighed.

"That dreadful hospital! If only they had let me keep her. You remember how pleasant she was, when she was here before ... and quite content. It was very damaging to take her away so roughly—it shouldn't have been done."

"My dear, you cannot keep her."

He sat down, carefully, on the arm of her chair, and took tight hold of her hand. She said wistfully, "If we were only younger ..."

"We are as we are, my dear, and Harriet is as she is. There are things that cannot be altered. We must send Harriet where she belongs now."

She did not protest, but looked back at Harriet again. She had leaned forward somewhat, as though she were considering holding out her hands to the fire, but the process was taking a long time. Mrs. Evans sighed again, yielding.

"Well," she said, "at least I've saved her from being hunted through those woods by a lot of strange men. Caught by people who would be afraid of her, and rough."

"Yes. That's a great deal. But now we must—"

"Now we must decide," she said more firmly, "on the kindest possible way to take her to—to her new home. I wish we could do it ourselves. Where's Tessie?" she asked, looking round. "Didn't Tessie come in with us?"

"No one came in with you, my dear. And you've been out quite enough tonight. I think myself that we had best call Dr. Howard, and—"

"No," she said. "It should be someone she knows, and trusts. I still feel sure that that makes a difference to her, even though she can't let us know. Now, what about that nice little Mrs. Hinkley? You remember, she said she had met Harriet in New York, and Harriet seemed quite willing to speak to her the night she came here. And they do have some responsibility for her coming here in the first place, as I understand it. If we were to call them first thing in the morning—"

"Not in the morning," he said, with equal firmness. "No. Whomever we call, it must be tonight. Now. We are not equal to the responsibility of Harriet, my dear, and it's useless to pretend that we are."

"Then I suppose you had better call them now," she said, yielding once more. (Really, she was so tired. So much more tired than she had known. And the drive had been such a strain, poor Harriet really so changed...)

"I believe I had better call the hospital too, to let them know that Harriet will be coming back. So they will be prepared to receive her."

"Yes. Yes, do that, dear."

He went out of the room, purposeful and relieved, to the telephone in his study. She was glad that he should be relieved—glad, to tell the truth, that he had made her acknowledge the limitations in her strength that she herself did not always recognize. But she turned toward Harriet with regret still, and compassion.

Harriet's nose was running. She did not even sniff, as a child would have done. Mrs. Evans leaned forward and took a paper tissue from the box on the table between them and gently wiped Harriet clean. She threw the tissue on the fire and, in a gesture of courtesy, placed a clean tissue in Harriet's hands. Then she leaned her head back and closed her eyes.

The smell made her open them. Then she acted quickly, without quite understanding what had happened—only that a bit of the fire, a burning something, had been in Harriet's hand. Harriet herself did not seem to know that she had it, or when it was taken from her. But she was leaning forward still more—and stayed so.

Mrs. Evans rose and took gentle hold of Harriet's shoulders.

"Sit back, dear, there's no need to come so close! And you mustn't touch the fire, you know. It will harm you."

Somehow, although Harriet looked so limp, her position could not be altered. Mrs. Evans then tried to move the chair back, but this was quite beyond her strength. She sat down at last, but kept a watchful eye upon Harriet this time. She was puzzled, still breathing quickly, ready to act again if necessary.

Yet what happened was so strange that she was really not quite prepared after all. Harriet in some clumsy manner—without even looking round—managed to knock the tissue box onto the floor. Once it was there she paid it no attention; but Mrs. Evans, after a doubtful moment, bent to pick it up.

She could not. Harriet's hand, like an inanimate thing, fell upon it before hers and could not be dislodged.

"Oh, dear," said Mrs. Evans under her breath. She was not frightened—not of poor Harriet!—but a sadness like total fatigue fell upon her, acknowledging alike her own inadequacy and the difficulty of Harriet.

Rather ridiculously, they remained as they were—both leaning forward, with Mrs. Evans giving little tugs at the box and Harriet passively holding on. Then, yielding the box for the moment, Mrs. Evans simply took hold of the tissues within it and removed them.

She said steadily, "Now, Harriet, I see you have learned a naughty trick, but you must not practice it anymore. Give me the box, or I will have to be severe with you."

As if this were what she had been waiting for, Harriet pushed the empty box forward until it touched flame.

Perhaps it was a growing confusion, rather than fatigue, that made Mrs. Evans clumsy. Her mind was certainly divided—half on Dr. Evans, who ought at any moment to reappear (the hearing aid was not very useful from room to room), half on the urgency of that box, which had begun to smoke. Or perhaps it was not clumsiness at all but some outer force—some contact that made her lose balance.

All she knew clearly was that she was half-risen, leaning forward, with a good grasp upon the box ... and then that she was falling ... falling against, or fallen against, she could not tell ... But her balance was gone and the world become rough, askew, darkening ... and dark.

Mack Varney was in a rage, shouting down at his weeping wife.

"You mean you just left them there alone with that crazy woman, Tess? You just been sitting here, waiting for me to come back?"

"But Mack, what could I *do?* You just don't *know* what it was like—and everybody's gone to the fire. I did try to call Joe Palmer, I did—I did! And that terrible ride in the woods, and Mrs. Evans wouldn't listen to a word I said—and that—that *creature*, right there behind me all the way back!"

"You could have called State Police, couldn't you? There's always somebody there!"

But he spoke more quietly, seeing that Tessie was really getting hysterical. A little more of that, and she'd be in a state where he couldn't leave her. He hesitated—a grimy, booted, and jacketed heavy figure—

and then put his hand on her shoulder, patting.

"All right, never mind," he said. "I guess you did the best you could. All right, now, Tess! Pull yourself together, and I'll get over there and straighten it out. You better call up the State Police right away, though, will you do that? Tessie!"

He waited, impatiently patient, until she was able to look up at him and nod. Then he gave her one last, heavy pat and left the house—went striding through the deserted and frozen village night, making for the just-visible parsonage on the next street over.

"This time of night?" said Henry, incredulous.

Even half-asleep, however, he was a careful listener, and respectful of the cloth. He couldn't, without a little more time to pull himself together, decide whether Dr. Evans's request was reasonable or not; but it seemed like one of the few times when a man might agree first and think it over afterward. He agreed, deliberately, and went back upstairs.

"Mary Ann," he said, sitting down on the edge of the bed.

The room was cold. Just her eyes peeked out at him, in the light he had turned on.

"I guess you better get up. That was Dr. Evans, he says they got Harriet again. Wants us to come get her, and take her over to the hospital."

"Wants us to take her to the hospital?" Then she sat up. "Harriet! You mean she's there—in their house?"

"Put your robe on," he said, and reached for it. "That's right. Mrs. Evans found her, out at the fire. Seems that's where she was, and it burned down, and Mrs. Evans brought her home. He says they feel like she'd be better off in the hospital, but they don't want her scared anymore, so will we please come and drive her over to Frampton because she knows us."

She sat staring at him, with the icy robe round her shoulders. Their room had the deadened stillness of country night; the lamplight looked anemic.

"Something doesn't sound right, Henry," she said at last. "Where's Moran? And how *could* Mrs. Evans have found her? That fire was away over—"

"I know," he said, "but I think we better go on over just the same, and figure it out later. Main thing is, they got her there, and they're alone with her."

After that, they were quick and silent. In less than ten minutes Henry was nosing the car down their steep driveway into the main road. He paused to let another car sweep by, in a blaze of headlight, and then they both heard the passing car brake sharply. Henry went on, coming up level with Tom Bryce's jeep.

Tom was leaning out, waving them down. Their own lights showed, briefly, a man disheveled, untidy, excited.

"Where you going?" he yelled. "It's all over! Did you hear? It was—"

Marianne got her own window down.

"We can't stop now, Tom. We're on our way over to Dr. Evans's, they have Harriet! I'll see you tomorrow," she added, as Henry pulled away, cutting her short.

It hadn't been a comfortable encounter. That gesticulating figure, too excited, stayed in their minds.

Marianne said presently, "I expect he was out at the fire. He certainly is getting more and more wound up. I wish ..."

She didn't complete her wish, and Henry didn't inquire for it. He was concentrating on driving, fast. They had the dark, winter-rough roads to themselves, now.

CHAPTER TWENTY-ONE

It was not a question, Dr. Evans thought, of fear or bravery or any of those temporal qualities by which we attempt to understand our lives. The question was quite simply one of life itself; and in the face of that great simplification he had no doubts.

True, on first coming into the room he had not quite grasped what was going on: had paused to say, admonitorily, "Harriet!" Then she had thrown the bright piece of fire—that was what it seemed to be—and he had seen that further strange brightness, and where it burned: near, too near, to his wife's body lying upon their hearth.

After that he simply went forward and knelt down. Harriet was standing there—he no longer thought of her, or saw her; he saw only the flames that had begun at his wife's skirt, and his own hands beating upon them. Then the hastily taken, the providentially near pillow from his chair, with its larger, heavier surface for beating. He heard himself begin to cough ... and his wife's stillness ... and felt her weight all along his arms and back, an impossible weight, one that he could not—and must not—move. She, who was so light and little! Whom he had easily caught down from so many heights: carriages, steps, even ladders. But not in these years ... and a live, descending weight was different from this dead weight that must be dragged ... and dragged.

Dead weight. The words were in his mind, an unexamined despair. He did not stop for them, did not stop at all until he had her out into the room and away from hazard (of fire? of Harriet?) and could bend over her, to touch her with his hurt hands, to see and implore.

Yes, he'd entirely forgotten Harriet. Not even that strange burst of blazing from the window corner, where no fire ought to be, reminded him of her presence. It said to him only: Farther. Take her farther. Out of here.

And that was what he had done. What he had almost done, when his front door crashed open and an enormous loud shape came and put hands on them. Even then he had struggled on—to take her out, to defend her—not, for a long time, comprehending the sense of what he heard.

"... me have her, for God's sake, man! It's me, it's Mack Varney! Give her to me, and come on—you've got a fire in here!"

He had let go, stood back enough to see her raised up and carried away (like the light, little thing she was) but had never been more than an arm's reach behind—stumbling after Mack, and struck by sudden, icy cold air as she must have been.

And as soon a Mack had put her down, along the seat of the car that stood with gaping doors at the curb, he said clearly, "She must have cover. She must have cover, or she will die."

He saw Mack strip off his heavy jacket, and was fumbling at his own, lighter one when Mack turned back, caught at his hands.

"No, Doc! Leave that on—you've got to stay out here with her, hear? Stay with her, she's alive. I can still get to your phone—"

She was alive. Of course she was alive, he had never doubted it. Had never *allowed* himself to doubt. Crouching beside her in the narrow space he told her so, told her more than once—told the first person who looked in upon them there.

"She is alive, my dear, don't be afraid. She is alive."

It was a woman. Behind the woman was, briefly, a man. He knew them both, of course, as he knew everyone roundabout ... yet for the moment ... and then they were gone, the man running toward the house. The woman came back, giving to him—helping him to spread over his wife's body—a warm, inexpressibly beautiful carriage robe. He almost wept with gratitude to see it.

After that, the night became pandemonium. Sirens, cars, faces strange and known—he no longer attempted to keep up with it. What was most important was still clear in his mind, and he spoke it clearly to Dr. Howard as soon as he appeared. Rising (with a little help), holding his burned hands out, he told his tidings with great joy: "She is alive ..."

That was the night when hardly anybody slept.

By the time the disheveled fire apparatus got there, Mack Varney and Henry Hinkley—old hands at firefighting together—needed help only in clearing up. It was the curtains and draperies of one window that had gone up in that luckily visible blaze: there wasn't much left of them. The wallpaper and woodwork round them were ruined, and some fiery fragments had fallen on the sofa which, scorched and then drenched, would need a lot of fixing. Otherwise, everybody agreed, the Evanses had been lucky. An old wooden house like that in ten minutes more would have gone up past saving. If Mack Varney hadn't seen that curtain burning, and come running ...

Then there were all the State Police cars, something you wouldn't ordinarily expect for a town fire. The watchers who stayed on in the street speculated, uninformed for some time, about the reasons for that; those of their neighbors who could have told them why were no longer there.

Marianne had left first, with Dr. Howard and the Evanses. Henry would deduce where she had gone: she fully expected to have to ride over to Frampton in the back of the ambulance while Dr. Howard drove. But there was no ambulance ride. Mrs. Evans, already feebly conscious, was put to bed at the Howards' and tended there, for leg burns, for possible slight concussion. Almost the first thing she whispered was, "No hospital, now ..."

"At her age, I'm not going to cross her," Dr. Howard told Marianne. "In fact, I think she's better off to stay right here, all things considered. God knows, it's certainly her turn to get some nursing."

Dr. Evans, his hands greatly swathed, was allowed to lie in the twin bed adjoining his wife's. It was a situation he found of interest, since he confided that they had sometimes wondered how it would seem to have twin beds. He could see that there were times when it was a most useful arrangement.

He was by now entirely reassured. His wife was perfectly all right—she had told him so herself. Poor Harriet, whom he had forgotten, had not perished in his burning house, because his house had not burned. He hoped they would not be hard on the unhappy creature for what she had done.

He was assured that they would not. This was the stage at which everyone, except the harassed police, believed that someone else had taken care of Harriet, and knew where she was. Surprisingly, in the circumstance, no one thought much about her at all.

Dr. Howard's daughter drove Marianne home. The Hinkley car was not in front of the Evans's house, and she assumed that Henry had gone on home, assuming that *she* had gone to Frampton. So Rose Howard, a beginning and enthusiastic driver, gladly offered to take Marianne the whole way.

It was an adventure that Rose enjoyed but Marianne did not. When they came wavering up to the steep Hinkley driveway she said, "Please don't try to go up, Rose. I always stall, and I've driven longer than you. Just let me out, and you'd better not try to turn round, either. Go on up to Field Road and circle back that way."

She stood by the roadside to watch the red tail lights weave away, then mounted the driveway.

The total quiet in which she moved struck her, at first, as a relief. The house was dark—Henry not there, or in bed?—and nothing obscured the vast reach of night sky upon her vision. The winter constellations were clear and bright. She stood still a moment, in spite of the cold, and tilted her head back to see. That overhead view, so pleasant with Henry, was oddly disquieting alone. It made her feel unprotected, vulnerable. There was too much night and silence out here for one lonely woman.

She went on, unconsciously avoiding making sound, and stood hunting her key at the front door. But when her hand first touched the door it yielded—pushed inward. She thought in surprise, Did I leave it that way? It was possible—they had left in such a rush. Yet it was automatic with both Henry and herself to close a door at least, even though they might forget to lock it.

With this dissatisfaction in her mind, she entered her house doubtfully. The air was warm and still. She went into the living room and turned on a lamp, stood looking round in its soft light. The room was itself, said nothing in particular—she wished now she had gone round by the garage and found out in advance whether Henry were here or not.

But this was silly. She had only to go and see—or even to call out. It was an effort to raise her voice, against that doubtful emptiness.

She said presently, in the subdued voice of one among sleepers. "Harriet ...?"

That shook her badly. *Why?* Why should she have Harriet's name in her mind now—believe her to be here? How could she be here?

Marianne, in the mental cadences of Henry, told herself she was not being reasonable. And that it was necessary to move. The longer she stood here, immobile, the more courage it would take to move again.

She went back into the hall, pressed the light switch, looked up. It was like an appointment, kept. Tom Bryce stood waiting on the stairs above her.

CHAPTER TWENTY-TWO

As soon as she saw him he came down the rest of the way. There were papers in his hands—papers held and crushed as though to make them disappear. But they were very evident.

She said in wonder, "Tom! What—"

Then she saw his eyes, his expression, and stopped.

He came on, beginning to speak in a toneless soft voice.

"Why are you back so soon, Mary Ann? I don't like for you to be mixed up in this, you know that. It's not the kind of thing for you to be mixed up in."

She whispered back, because that was all the voice she could find. "Those are Henry's lists...."

He said, "It's not Henry's business, either. What's he doing this for—writing all this down? Have you seen them, read them?"

She shook her head. He went on earnestly looking at her, and she made herself say, "He doesn't want anybody to see them. Or know about them. They're just for himself."

"But he talked to me about them."

"Only because I mentioned them, and he wanted to know why you walked over—"

She stopped, aware of her mistake. That wasn't what he had asked Tom. It was only what he had been asking himself, when Tom was gone.

But he pounced on her words, in terrible eagerness. "Walked over? Here, you mean—that morning? But I didn't walk over here! Why does

Henry think so? What did he say?"

She could only shake her head again. To be afraid—afraid like this, of someone you knew, belonged to childhood: to the perils and exaggerations of a child's mind. No part of her understood how to be herself, her grown and married self, and to be so afraid.

He moved nearer to her.

"Mary Ann, listen, it's not true! I didn't walk over, I drove—I left the car down by the road, that's all. Henry saw me walking up the drive and he made a mistake. I drove, and I left the car down by the road!"

Her treacherous mind instantly presented her with the word: *Why?* She pressed her lips together, terrified that it would escape in sound.

And as if he suspected this, he went on frowning down at her. He said, "Why is Henry doing this? Why does he *want me to know* that he's doing it? What's his idea?"

He was looking directly at her now, but he wasn't seeing her. Not anymore.

"I know Henry doesn't like me," he went on, arguing it out. "I know he resents me—he always has. But is it my fault? Does it give him the right to hound me, and spread hints about me this way?"

"Tom ... he's done no such thing!"

"He's told you. And you believe him. You believe him against me."

She wanted to say, *I don't believe anybody against you*. But it was no longer true. He saw that it was no longer true—past any protest she might have made, if she could have made one.

Very slowly, his big, powerful workman's hands began to destroy Henry's lists. She watched them go, falling in twisted shreds to her floor. And said, in a voice dredged up somehow from their common past—a calm voice, familiar to them both, "You oughtn't to do that, Tom. There's no need."

"I've got to do it," he replied, as calm.

"Then don't stay here. I'll get rid of those pieces. I won't tell him."

His hands empty at last, he looked at her without any belief.

"He's got a small mind, Mary Ann," he said then. "All he can see are the little, niggling things that don't matter. That aren't true. Any big, whole, simple truth about a man doesn't matter to him. I would never try to hurt Irma—any woman. She got her own death, right where everybody but Henry knows she got it—from those people that brought her up. If she hadn't gone down there that night, nothing would have happened to her. I swear that, Mary Ann. Nothing would ever have happened to her."

There was silence between them, intent on his part. His eyes flickered in some change, he came closer to her. Her back, pressed to the wall, was becoming a pattern of pain—yet she could not change one muscle to relieve it. Nor could she look away from him, so long as he stared down at her.

"All right," he said. "Henry was right about one thing—one small thing. She was in the car, that's why I left it down by the road. But why do you think I was coming here, Mary Ann? What would I have brought her here for, if I wasn't trying to get help—to help her? I wanted to help her! If I hadn't wanted that, why would I have carried her out of my house and brought her all the way over here? I was bringing her to you," he said, earnest, "and then you weren't here! You weren't even here—and that was her fault too, she did that too!"

He put his hands over his face suddenly—a man beleaguered past endurance, fighting bewilderment. Then as quickly his hands came down, his voice was low again, rapid.

"Listen, if I hadn't wanted to help her, I only had to leave her where she was and say it was an accident. Don't you see that? That she fell and hit herself on—on a chair. I only had to tell them the way she came back, that night—like a crazy woman, Mary Ann, like a woman so full of hate she wanted to destroy the whole world—everybody, me, herself! You never saw Irma the way she was when she got back that night, you can't imagine how she was. No man could have taken it," he said. "To sit there all those hours, alone, waiting, trying to figure it out, and then have her come in like that—like a crazy woman! Yelling and screaming at me just because I was there, because I was trying to understand what it was all about. I only wanted her to tell me what it was, what she'd done. But she wouldn't, she wouldn't ..."

Marianne drew a long breath.

"Tom," she said, "I'm sorry. I— But why didn't you call Dr. Howard? When you knew she was still alive—"

"That's a lie," he said—sharp, quick, a voice like a blow that struck out her breath. And his eyes came up to hers—stranger's eyes again, watchful and dangerous. *"Why do they keep saying she was alive?* She was dead! She was dead when I left her there, that's why I left her! She was dead when I got back to the car, from this house—and if Henry says she wasn't, then he's a liar too! Is that what he says? Is that what he's hinting about?"

Her wrist was caught in a grip that sent pain like fire up to her shoulder. She screamed, felt herself free, and turned in a desperate, unplanned attempt at flight.

Almost as soon as she moved, she was caught.

"What's the matter with you, Mary Ann?"

The voice at her ear was subdued, dazed. Had no connection with the brutal hands that held and hurt her.

"Let me go—let me go!"

She fought to be free, to dart past him—but the unleashed, terrified strength of her body only served to release in him an overwhelming answer, of greater strength. Before she had begun to fight, she was finished—locked in a vise that might have been iron rather than bone about her neck.

Knowledge in a cold flood brought her still. The knowledge of death ... her own ... Irma's. *This was how it happened.*

He was as still as she, yet kept his tense and painful hold. She could hear his breath above her own—louder, harsher. She made herself stay absolutely still—as Irma, already maddened by rage and terror, could not have done ...

Then he spoke—a sobbing, almost incoherent rush of sound.

"You too? *My God, you too?*"

It was as though he did not know how to let go. Did not dare to let go.

A sharp rapping sounded nearby, and a muffled voice inquired, "You all right in there?"

She knew by his checked breath that he heard too. For a moment nothing happened. Then the arm upon her throat tightened ... tightened ... and was gone. Before she could cry out, move, she was flung down— had one blurred view of his moving legs, and then was alone.

By the time Joe Palmer got in she was sitting up in the middle of the hall floor, with her hand at her throat. Frantically she waved him away—past her, toward the back of the house.

She managed to croak, "Tom Bryce—" but Joe wouldn't listen. He was bent over her, urging her up with easy lifts under the arms. His face was set, closed.

Tom's jeep roared alive, somewhere down by the road; and she saw then by the bursting of Joe's expression—into agonized regret—that he knew. Knew, and wouldn't leave her.

She pushed at him, croaking, "Go on—go on!" but he shook his head. "He's not going anywhere—not now. It's all right, Mary Ann."

When he had put her down on her couch he went at once to the telephone. She saw sweat gathering on his face while he got the State Police barracks; talked; but his voice remained careful and even. He didn't miss any details, he even knew the number of Tom's jeep. And when he hung up he said to her, without any pause, "Now what doctor do you want me to call for you?"

She shook her head, but he was firm about it; when she wouldn't say he decided for her, "Doc Howard, then."

Henry came up the drive while Joe was getting that number—came up fast, not even running the car back to the garage. The slam of the car door and the front door seemed almost simultaneous, and then he was in the room, wild-haired and furious.

"Where in *thunder* did you go, Mary Ann! I been—"

He saw Joe, stopped. Joe, just putting up the receiver, nodded to him.

He said, "You got any objection to old Doc Henry? Seems like Doc Howard's already busy."

"I *didn't* know it was him," said Joe. "I thought it was Henry, come back after he took you wherever you had to go in such a hurry. And left the car down by the road to go get you again, that was what I figured. He just walked up and in the front door, like he lived here. He have a key?"

"Not that I know of," Henry replied. They both looked at Marianne, lying there doped to the gills and still wide-eyed. This was after Dr. Haney, after the State Police and the statement she had insisted she could make. But she wasn't supposed to talk anymore. She shook her head now.

"Then you must have left the door unlocked," said Joe. This time neither one of them looked at Marianne. "Wonder what he'd have done if you hadn't?"

"Break and enter, probably," Henry decided. "He was certainly bound to get my lists." He said this carefully, without pride.

"Mary Ann, I never heard her at all," Joe said then. "You came up awful quiet," he told her, dissatisfied. "I heard that car, sort of moseying, and then what I took to be some ladies talking about where they ought to turn round, or something. But I never heard you come up. First I heard was a sort of scream. I *thought*. I wasn't real sure, then ..."

"... if it was a private fight?" said Henry dryly. "I'm glad you give me the benefit, Joe. Real glad."

Joe said sturdily, "Well, I figured if it *was* a scream, then something was wrong. If it had been Tom Bryce's house, now ..."

They considered that, in silence. Henry said, "What I still can't understand is him bringing her over here to Mary Ann, with her neck broken. What in time did he think Mary Ann could do about *that?*"

"I don't think he was bringing her to Mary Ann, Henry. If he'd been, he'd have brought the car right up to the house. He had something in his mind about an alibi, I'll bet you anything. Going to stop by and go on record he was out looking for his wife, and all the time he was driving round looking for a good place to leave the whole mess. Course he didn't want you to see he had Irma's car, instead of his own jeep. He thought she was dead, all right. That much I'll believe him. Not," he added, "that it'll do him much good. Probably make the difference between manslaughter and first-degree, leaving her out to die like that."

There was a croaking sound from the couch, and both men turned.

"Write it, Mary Ann, write it," Henry told her. She had a small pad and pencil beside her, which had already begun to slip away. So Henry thought, had she. He gave Joe a look, and both men rose to their feet.

"Come on, let's get you upstairs," Henry said to her. "Joe and I aren't going to talk anymore—there's nothing to talk about, till we know what's going to happen. And Harriet'll be all right, whenever they find her. They got your statement, they know she didn't kill Irma. There's nothing more going to happen tonight."

"I sure hope not," said Joe. "I never heard so many whistles and sirens around this town before in one night! That poor lady may not have killed Irma, but she sure made a lot of other things happen."

"Irma too," said Marianne, suddenly clear. They allowed her this, in a pause; then Henry put his arm around her waist to support her upstairs. She stood still, mutely held out her hand to Joe. He took it before he noticed the tears coming down her cheeks, and then was frozen, unable to let go.

Henry tried to help.

"She feels bad about making that statement," he explained. "I mean, about having to be the one that gets Tom in trouble."

"Got himself in trouble," she said, with hoarse firmness. She took her hand back and turned away, starting upstairs by herself, still crying steadily.

The men looked past each other. They murmured, shook hands; Joe let himself out. He looked relieved to be the one that was going, instead of the one that had to stay and figure it out.

Tom was taken at once, with no difficulty.

He had simply gone home. There, in manly embarrassment, he admitted to a violent loss of temper at the Hinkley's. He hoped he hadn't upset Mary Ann; she knew how it was with him—his nerves "shot," all to pieces. He was surprised to find she had reported their Misunderstanding. Supposed it was her husband—well, that was natural, he guessed. But he couldn't believe that she herself would want to make charges against him.

Or if she did—okay, he could understand that too. He was willing to take what was coming to him, for blowing his top that way.

On the subject of Irma he was blank. He had already told all he knew about that, long ago. There was certainly some notion Hinkley had got in his head, about the morning after Irma's disappearance; that was what he, Tom, had lost his temper about. But whatever it was, he was sure they could straighten it out.

Later, confronted by Marianne's statement, he grew silent. White, ugly, and silent. That lasted for some hours.

Later still, just before morning, he changed his mind and began the first in his series of endless explanations—of how Irma had happened to die, or not die, under his hands.

CHAPTER TWENTY-THREE

That morning Harriet turned up.

She was in a henhouse, sitting crouched in its far corner. The woman who had opened the door on her, and then fled into her house, came back on the heels of the two State policemen. She had just run off and left the henhouse door open—who wouldn't? Maybe the poor crazy creature was miles away by now.

But Harriet hadn't gone anywhere. She still sat in her corner, her sweater and skirt a streaky mess of raw egg. She had another egg in her hand and held it to her when they came in—looking up at them, or at the movement of their entrance.

"Why, she's hungry!" the peering woman said, touched by awe. "She's trying to suck an egg, and she don't know how."

When they stood her up, the egg she was clutching fell and broke. She made no fuss about it, once it was gone. Nor was she concerned about her dangling, sticky hands, her ruined clothing.

Before he could put her in the car, the trooper had to take out his own handkerchief and mop her up as best he could. She stood submissive to this attention, staring past his head. He had never seen anybody go so long without blinking.

THE END

THE SILENT COUSIN

Elizabeth Fenwick

CHAPTER ONE

By a quarter to six on summer mornings, Dr. Potter liked to have his coffee dripping in the big aluminum pot and his bacon beginning to sizzle in the pan: major and joyous sounds, in that deep country quiet, and emphasizing it, like the rackety bird calls all round him.

He knew just how they felt, those early birds, and was in entire agreement with them. Short of whistling or singing, neither of which he did well, he liked to add his own accompaniment. So the coffee loudly dripped, the bacon rose to a sputter, and the screen door gave one emphatic summery slam when he took out the skunk's milk.

That slam stopped the birds—only for a moment, though; they were on to his game with them by now, by August. Next year they—or possibly their fledglings?—would have forgotten him and his screen door entirely. Unlike the skunk, who took up her routine with frowsy fidelity each June, just where it had broken off the last September.

She wasn't visible yet. He cleared his throat, said "Puss, puss," and put the saucer down—just as a barn swallow practically dive-bombed him in passing. He turned in surprise—a big man, too slow to see where the bird was going with such authority. He hadn't thought he had a barn swallow nest this year, with the car shed closed and locked on emptiness.

That reminded him of Cressa, and the train which he must arrange to meet this afternoon. He went back indoors and turned his bacon thoughtfully, wondering what was the best way to get a car. If he asked Millie or Aunt Cora they would expect to come too, naturally. Yet it was an awkward day to approach MacDonald about the Ford or station wagon, with the old lady so ill. He ought to walk up to the home farm and inquire about her this morning, too. That was something else he mustn't forget.

Uneasily, with a sense of obligation beginning to crowd his lovely, empty morning, he tried the ritual comfort of frying eggs. Not a successful escape. He had, unfortunately, the kind of duty-memory which kept a faithful sense of oppression, but no details. He never forgot that he was supposed to do something—only what it was; and lost the notes he wrote to remind himself; and wore himself out doing wrong things in hopes that one of them might be right.

He suddenly put down his spatula and took up one of the ballpoint pens, blessedly cheap, which lay all over the house, and wrote on the wall over the stove: CRESSA 2:35 TRAIN. It didn't come out very clearly because of frying spatters, but he would certainly notice something up there when he made lunch.

Partly reassured (and why only partly? Something else?) he took his perfect eggs from the pan and was laying bacon round them when he heard the sound of a car, quite near. As if it were coming down his lane.

Nothing could be more unlikely. Perhaps it was some acoustical trick of a car passing along the main road of the estate. Although that wasn't likely either, at this hour. He set down his plate and went to peer through the screen, just as the home farm Ford jolted into his clearing. MacDonald was driving.

He went out at once. In passing, with a sinking heart, he saw his skunk in plain view beside her milk. Too tame to disappear, she stood there making a half-hearted sidle at the stranger—as if that would save her, poor idiot creature. MacDonald was a man who might put down anything, even racoons. Even chipmunks.

For once, however, he didn't seem to notice. He got out and put a heavy hand on Dr. Potter's shoulder, and said directly: "Paul, I'll ask you to come up to the farm with me right now. You'll bring your little case with you, please. Have you got it handy?"

"Yes, of course."

He turned—and turned back.

"Is she worse?"

"She's worse," said MacDonald.

Dr. Potter hurried back indoors without another word. His doctorate was in Letters; but long ago, when his medico-missionary father still lived, he had got far enough into medical studies to learn the simple art of giving injections. Shortly afterwards his father had died; and Dr. Potter, aware even then of his tricky memory, had changed with relief to a less lethal field—or one where everyone whom he would examine was dead anyway. But historian, medievalist though he might be, he still gave a superb injection. On the isolated estate, with their elderly physician living ten miles away, his knack had become a useful accomplishment. Ampoules and directions were left for him (with someone else, of course) but Dr. Potter kept his own syringe, cared for it scrupulously himself, and never mislaid it. Perhaps he might have made a medical doctor after all. Aunt Cora still thought so. But it was not she who had faced the possibility of becoming a murderer.

He was back again by the time MacDonald had the car round and they shot away, leaving the skunk in surly possession. His breakfast he abandoned to cold death; and ashamed even to think of this at such a time, Dr. Potter turned to MacDonald.

"What happened?" he asked.

MacDonald said something between his teeth which sounded like: "*She wullna stay doon.*" Then, with an effort, and in his ordinary almost-American, he began an inquiry.

"When you were in the medical school, Paul. Back then."

"Yes?" said Dr. Potter, helpful.

"Did you ever hear them say, now, about wandering near the end? It's what the women call it," said MacDonald, huge and despairing. "I don't know how they'd call it in the medical school, or if there's really such a thing at all. Did you hear of it?"

"The mind wandering, you mean?" said Dr. Potter, cautious.

"The mind! I'm speaking about the body, man, the body! Walking about the place when they're too sick to be out of their beds, even! Did you never hear of it?"

"No," said Dr. Potter. "Not officially. But of course I wasn't there very long. I've come across it in old wives' tales," he added, without thinking, and went on quickly: "But whether there's any medical basis for the idea, I don't know any more than you. Why?" he asked, as the big man remained grim. "She hasn't been out on the road again, has she?"

"The road. She can't even make the door of her room," said MacDonald, bleak. "Jenny found her halfway. Trying."

Gradually, superimposed on the morning beauty of pasture and wood rushing past them, the one word evoked a portrait of old Mrs. MacDonald too uncomfortable to keep. Her spare, straight body grotesque upon the floor, full length and writhing. The thin, composed face with its sharp grey glance a mindless mask, distorted in impossible effort. *Trying*.

They fled past the turnoff to Long Acre, that closed museum of eighteen-nineties splendor. All the ghosts of its empty rooms, so terrible to the boy Paul, could not compare with this sudden offer of a real Mrs. MacDonald such as he had never seen, and did not want to imagine.

"She must *want* something, MacDonald," he said at last.

"Then tell me what it is!" MacDonald roared out, staring ahead. "There's nothing we wouldn't fetch for her—me, or Jen, or even that boy of Jen's! She knows that, she knows she's only to say! If it's not the wandering, then *what is it the woman wants?*"

The cords on his neck stood out, as in rage, and the heavy arms and crushing hands upon the wheel were like great engines of destruction capable of ripping the Ford apart piece by piece. MacDonald's rages, rare and legendary, belonged to boyhood memory too: never turned upon the children, evoked only by some stupid offence to the land or its equipment, nevertheless they remained among the children's most thrilling memories. Perhaps because they were the only sight of human passion ever offered to the little Onderdonk girls, the little Potter boy.

Yet to Dr. Potter, now, this powerful rush and swell of blood and sinew said, not rage, but pain. Unbearable brute pain. It took him a moment to surpass memory and realize this was so, and then the realization left him quite helpless. Beyond doubt, some part of MacDonald would die with the death of his old wife—and already, uncomprehending and restive, MacDonald felt the wound.

There was nothing to say. Dr. Potter could only pray (and surprised himself by doing so) that there would still be something he could do.

The Ford swung up to the long, low, fieldstone farmhouse—an Onderdonk version of some Scottish croft—and MacDonald's daughter came out of the door. She had her father's big, sturdy frame, no look of her mother at all, and a distracted sullenness all her own. Perhaps two parents so strong in their different ways had been too much for her. She had been a late child, very pretty, but a whiner. Now at thirty the prettiness was gone.

MacDonald said, "Well, Jenny?" But she came up to Dr. Potter and caught his arm.

"Oh, Mr. Paul—she's very low …"

He went in, she still clinging to him, and MacDonald lurked behind with his gaze on the bedroom door.

"Did you call Dr. Kennedy?"

"Oh, yes, and he's coming, but you're to give it right away!" And she thrust into his hand one of the familiar little boxes. "In the—in the— oh, God, where did I write it down?"

"Never mind," he said. "I know."

Neither of them followed him into the darkened bedroom. It was a small room, or the great bed made it seem so, and small-windowed. Tidiness was paramount, even in the bed itself with its smoothly drawn quilt. Even in the small figure under the quilt. He stood looking down, for a moment, at the still face turned up to the ceiling—could hear his own breath, no other sound, as he gently turned the quilt back at one side—just enough to find and clasp the little bone wrist of Mrs. MacDonald. He slid his hand free again, and gentle, inexpert, lifted one of those closed eyelids.

Jenny stood in the doorway, her father a motionless bulk behind her. When he looked their way she gave, at once, a low cry. And fled. MacDonald didn't move.

Even at that moment Dr. Potter remembered his syringe case. He came away from the bed holding it carefully, a failed magic, but carefully reserved. The doubt in his mind made it difficult to speak.

MacDonald saw that.

"Well, what is it, boy?" he said stolidly. "You think she's gone?"

"Yes," said Dr. Potter. There was no doubt in his mind of that. "Dear MacDonald … I'm so sorry …"

MacDonald brushed heavily past and kept going. So did Dr. Potter— through the empty sitting room to the kitchen that lay behind. Jenny was there. She had the look of having gone as far as she could go, within walls.

"Jenny, I'm going over to the Hall now, and get Mrs. Onderdonk to come," he said. "Will you be all right? Is your husband here with you?" She nodded, once. He said, diffident, "Perhaps you would—the two of you would stay here near your father until we come back. He will probably be in the bedroom—if you and Pete will just stay in the house, here?"

"Are you real sure, Mr. Paul?" she blurted then. He looked at her in surprise.

"Oh, yes, Jenny. I'm afraid—anyone would be." The kitchen door stood a little ajar, and he decided to leave that way; there was more chance of coming on Pete at the back of the house. But leaving, he hesitated.

"Was it you who put her back to bed so nicely, Jenny?"

She began, at last, to cry.

"Pete helped you, I suppose?"

She did not seem to hear that at all. Dr. Potter went out into the yard. No one was in view. Even the dog was invisible, who generally hung round the nearest human being. In the henhouse yard the chickens were mutedly busy; someone had fed them. Walking as quickly as he could in his leather house sandals, Dr. Potter went round to where they had left the Ford—but the keys were not in it. He did not like to disturb MacDonald to get them, nor to explain this grief over the centrally placed telephone. So, with a sigh, he set off down the road. The half-hour or so of privacy, before they could return, might be the best thing for MacDonald. Dr. Potter did not think it was he who had closed his wife's eyes.

CHAPTER TWO

For years everyone (except Onderdonks) had speculated on what would become of the Onderdonk Estate if anything should happen to MacDonald. Who else could be found with the strength, the dedication, and most of all the honesty, to administer so enormous a toy? The original idea, of course, had been that MacDonald would bring over and train to succeed him another young Scot, as he himself had been imported, a raw farmer, by Grandfather Onderdonk. And young Scots did come, from time to time. A couple of them were crofters there still and good crofters—but no more. The trouble—and MacDonald's one apparent flaw—was that no young man with MacDonald's potentialities would put up with MacDonald himself, for the necessary years before he could be succeeded.

If there had been a MacDonald son, perhaps that might have done it. (Again—thinking of Jenny—perhaps not.) But not even Onderdonks thought to wish there had been an Onderdonk son. Or grandson, rather, since there had been two male Onderdonks of MacDonald's generation, and neither of them the slightest use for their father's beloved plan. Nor, either of them, the slightest threat to MacDonald himself. It was true that they had not had much incentive to take over, with the queer way the estate had been left (to itself, so to speak); but long before Grandfather Onderdonk's canny decision to tie up his land and the funds to maintain it, John had been out in the world and gone, and Humphrey shut up at the Hall in fretful dignity, already completely dependent on MacDonald.

No, MacDonald was unique. No one disputed or even thought to resent the fact. He was unique to the point that none of those dependent on his strength even feared that it would fail. There had always been MacDonald, there would always be MacDonald—at least, to last Our Time.

But to Dr. Potter, sweating his hurried way from home farm to Hall in the already gathering Hudson River Valley heat, a new wonder occurred: what would become of MacDonald now that Mrs. MacDonald was gone?

No one had ever considered that. If he had not witnessed that outburst in the Ford, Dr. Potter might not have considered it either. But he realized, as MacDonald himself might not yet realize, that some indispensable part of their indispensable MacDonald was gone. The breakup had begun.

She was such a quiet woman! Hardly anyone ever saw her, except by coming to the home farm itself. Even then, even when he and the girls were children, Dr. Potter remembered her as always the same. Always there, always composed and briskly ready to receive them, and always with some fine treat to serve. And thinking back, Dr. Potter wondered if what they had not enjoyed, as much as the treat itself, was their own perfect behavior in receiving it. Behavior was never a problem at Mrs. MacDonald's. She knew exactly how they should behave at any age— and so, with her, did they. It seemed a mutual recognition, with no need at all to be enforced.

(*How* to explain Jenny?)

Panting up the drive at last, Dr. Potter thought that might be MacDonald's deepest loss: something like the moral consciousness, given in tastes to her visitors, which MacDonald's wife had steadily supplied to him. Besides, of course, the ties one must feel for one's wife of over forty years. About that, Dr. Potter could only surmise.

He spotted at this point his Uncle Humphrey already out beside the fishpond, stretched out in the rattan lounge with his hat pulled forward, for an after-coffee, pre-breakfast nap. Dr. Potter did not disturb him. It was enough of a prospect to break news (any news) to Uncle Humphrey, without expecting his help. No; this was something for Aunt Cora, after she had pre-digested it herself.

He found his aunt where he expected her to be; in the enormous, old-fashioned kitchen getting breakfast. His cousin Millicent would with equal dependability be upstairs doing bedrooms. There was no help except a once-a-week (most weeks) woman for heavy cleaning; yet many of the nearly thirty rooms were kept open, and the house was comfortably run. Aunt Cora and Millie were hard-working women.

The moment she saw him, his aunt began to smile, which confused him.

He said, uncertain, "Aunt Cora, you—"

"I know, I know! I've got it on my calendar. But you remembered too, didn't you, dear?"

She kissed him proudly, and he said: "Oh." And then, "Yes, but this is—"

"And Millie remembered too, of course. The first thing she said this morning was, Polly is going to need the car today. So you needn't have rushed up here and got yourself all—hot—"

She saw the syringe case, which he was still clutching.

"What's that for, dear?"

He told her. She had her apron off before he had finished, and was turning the stove's switches to OFF.

"All right," she said, in an entirely different voice. "Don't be too upset, dear. It's not entirely unexpected, you know. Just run up and get Millie, will you? She can finish her father's breakfast while you drive me over."

He left her rapidly filling a basket (with what?) and went back through the wide hall, up the great staircase. The confounded leather sandals slapped as he ran; perhaps it was this sound which drew his cousin out of her father's room. She was standing with a pillowslip in her hands, looking towards him as he appeared. The light from the open door made a lovely profile down her full face, like a kind of Picasso. Even making beds at seven in the morning, Millie reminded you of painting.

"Goodness, Polly," she said. "What are you doing up here so early?"

He told Millie too. As prompt as her mother, but without seeming to be so, Millie got rid of the pillowslip, closed her father's door, and started downstairs. She did not say anything. In the hall, finding and handing him the car keys, she dutifully reminded him about the faulty clutch. Her voice, her long blue eyes, were equally abstracted. It occurred to him that Millie was one person, besides himself now, who might grasp all that Mrs. MacDonald's death could mean to them.

Aunt Cora came out of the kitchen door as he got the car to it. Millie was with her.

"Just tell your father where I've gone," his aunt was saying. "Not why, though—I'll tell him when I come back. He's perfectly used to me running over there, with the poor soul ill so long."

In the car, effortlessly retracing the painful mile he had just trotted, Dr. Potter gave his aunt a fuller account. "Apparently she left her bed, and collapsed trying to leave the bedroom—Jenny found her there, MacDonald says. He is probably going to ask you about 'wandering', in people who are near death, so you had better think of an answer."

"He ought to have the answer himself," said Aunt Cora. "Undoubtedly the poor woman was trying to get to the bathroom. I can't imagine anyone less likely to submit to a bedpan than Mrs. MacDonald, Polly."

"She wasn't trying to get to the bathroom yesterday," he said, "when they found her out on the road."

"No," his aunt admitted. "No, she wasn't ... My own idea about that— I don't want you to repeat this—is that she wanted to come to me. We have been closer than we seemed, for many, many years now. Mrs. MacDonald was a reserved woman, but her feelings were strong, I know. And I was the only person—the only other woman—she had to turn to."

His aunt's voice faltered; she put a hand to her eyes. Dr. Potter covered the other with a comforting palm. Just the same, he could not help thinking that any such womanly yearnings were more likely to come to his aunt's mind than to Mrs. MacDonald's.

Dr. Kennedy's car was already in front of the farmhouse, he was glad to see. But his aunt did not want him to come in.

"No, you go back now dear," she said firmly. "We're quite enough for the moment. I'm holding you in reserve, you and Millie," she added, to comfort him.

Not comforted, Dr. Potter drove back to the hall. He meant only to leave the car and return to his own house on foot; and not to go pumping his faulty clutch up the drive, in his uncle's hearing, he took again the back turning by which they had left. It was a little longer round, and narrow. Halfway, he nearly ran head on into a yellow car. In automatic reflex Dr. Potter swung over; and the yellow car, without any friendly pause, shot on. There was a brief glimpse of the dark, handsome face of Jenny's husband—in profile, since no attempt at greeting was made. Irritated, though not surprised (Pete had no use for the estate, nor for any Onderdonk), Dr. Potter finished his errand. Then he decided just to look in on Millie.

She wasn't in the kitchen, and the oatmeal was still turned off; but she came hurrying back into the room before he could leave.

"Oh," she said, turning switches. "What is it? Did mother forget something?"

"No, just didn't want me. You and I, Millie, are the reserves."

"As usual." She smiled at him, her lovely, small smile. "Well, I want you, Polly. Father's awake and fussing—he smells something, and it isn't oatmeal."

"All the traffic, maybe. What did Pete want?"

"Pete?"

"Yes, I nearly ran into him, in the back lane of all places."

"Eggs, I suppose," she said, indifferent and busy.

"*Eggs?* Today?"

She looked at him then.

"Oh. Well, I don't know, then," she said, rapidly setting a tray, "and I care less. Polly, I'm going to give father a tray out by the pond—it's so much simpler than setting up the breakfast room, and there's going to be no extra time today. Take it out, will you? He won't argue with you."

"Oh, yes, he will," he said; but received the tray none the less, and took it outdoors and round the house. He saw that his uncle was indeed up, and pottering round his fishpond—the new trinket wrested from estate funds, with MacDonald's approval. His very tall, paunchy figure did not look restless, but when he turned Dr. Potter saw that this was not his usual petulant restlessness but some more lively mood.

"Well, Paul, there you are," he said, receiving Dr. Potter and the tray with equal amiability. "The great day at last, eh?"

They were all practiced in changing step to match Uncle Humphrey's mood, since he was eerily adept in never matching theirs. Dr. Potter said now, after only a tiny pause:

"That's right, uncle. The two-thirty-five today."

"Vinnie not coming with her, I suppose?" his uncle went on, cheerfully making his yearly blunder.

"No," said Dr. Potter.

"She works too hard," said his uncle, sitting down with interest to his tray. "All the wives seem to, nowadays. I'm not really in favor of it, you

know, Paul—though I don't say anything. It's dispiriting to the men."
Since Aunt Cora was not there, Dr. Potter allowed himself to reply.
"Perhaps they work hard because they have to, uncle. Times change."
"Well, people don't, my boy. The female isn't made to stand the kind of
life that's natural to a male, and it's unnatural for her to try. Look at the
MacDonalds," he said, lavishly pouring cream. "They're in my mind
just now, of course. Poor woman—they've matched each other in hard
work all these years, and what's the outcome? MacDonald a fine,
strapping fellow, thriving on life, and his wife a worn-out old woman.
Finished. You see the women go down first every time, in that walk of
life, Paul. The widows come from our group. Nature knows. She can't be
fooled. Where's *your* breakfast?" he added, looking up, less friendly. "I
didn't understand that I was to breakfast entirely alone."

"I've eaten," said Dr. Potter, with no conscious deception. By this time
he usually had. He stood with one rather sore, sandaled foot on the
pond rim, and looked down into the elaborate little piece of water. His
uncle ate in offended silence.

"You didn't see Pete just now, did you, uncle?"

"Pete! No, certainly not. Why should I?"

Uncle Humphrey was fortunately distractible. His expression began
to alter.

"I did hear a *very* noisy car, on our back road. Do you mean to tell me
that boy has taken to racing wherever he pleases on the estate? Is that
who it was?"

"He delivers the farm things. I suppose there's no reason he shouldn't
come that way," said Dr. Potter vaguely. He started off, to pick up his
syringe and go home.

"Certainly there's reason; he's not to do it!" said his uncle's following
voice. "And I *know* he swims in Lake Millicent, without any permission
from me, that I'm aware of. And I doubt that your aunt would—Paul?
Paul?"

"Yes, uncle. We'll see you this afternoon, as soon as Cressa comes," he
said absently, and flapped away.

Round the corner of the big stone house he had already caught sight
of his cousin Millie, and thought at first that she was waiting for him—
until he came closer, and saw that she was not.

"What is it?" he said, when she saw him.

She shook her head, turning to go in with him.

"I don't know—one of those funny blank moments. Because there's so
much to do, I suppose, and none of it beginning yet … I'd better go
finish those beds while I can," she said, gaining decision.

"Don't," he said. "Let's eat up the oatmeal. I got hungry watching
uncle, and you will be. Sit down, I'll get it."

But she was too deeply trained to sit idle in that kitchen; and it was
Dr. Potter who was seated, with Millie serving him, when their old
doctor opened the screen door and came quietly in.

CHAPTER THREE

"Goodness, Dr. Kennedy—I didn't hear your car at all," Millie said— no more flustered than when her cousin had surprised her upstairs.

"Didn't mean you to. Or your father, rather." He sat down, tiredly—an old man, when he was not being a doctor. "Got more of that?"

"Yes, of course. Mother's staying on? Is MacDonald all right?"

He didn't answer. He had, they knew, got to the years when he simply turned his attention off when it was not needed. With no constraint, Millie served him too and they all began to eat. Unlike most women, even her admirable mother, Millie allowed unlimited silence.

Dr. Potter, to his own surprise, broke it.

"How long do you think she's been dead, Dr. Kennedy?"

He got a sharp look, but no reply for a time. The old man—and Millie— ate oatmeal.

Then he said, "Dead when you got there, wasn't she?"

"Yes. And laid out. Her eyelids closed, by someone."

Millie's long eyes were on him now, but seemed only thoughtful.

He went on, "I don't suppose MacDonald slept in there, while she was so ill. I was wondering when Jenny found her—and if she mightn't have been dead some time before."

"Quite possible." Dr. Kennedy pushed his empty dish away. "No thank you, Millie—no more. I'll take some coffee, if you have it. Jenny was terrified to tell her father, of course, and sent him haring off for you. Best thing she could have done."

"I didn't understand that her heart was that bad. And she seemed to be round the bend with that pneumonia. Even in spite of yesterday."

He was aware of trespassing; but Dr. Kennedy, fed, now regarded him with tolerance.

"Never sure which bend they're around till they're all the way round it, Paul. You know that much."

"No. I don't really know anything about it. I have just got—a layman's surprise, that's all."

Dr. Kennedy's tolerance acquired a faint amusement. Far from being alienated by Dr. Potter's defection from medicine, he seemed to have taken an increased interest in him from those days.

"Layman-schlmayman," he said, unexpectedly. "Why do you keep thinking you're so different, boy? Or that we are."

"You weren't surprised?"

"No," said Dr. Kennedy, "I wasn't. I didn't like that business of her getting up all the time, for no reason. You get an X factor like that coming in, something's going wrong somewhere—no matter how pretty it looks. Remember that."

These little 'tips', which Dr. Kennedy still continued to give him, depressed Dr. Potter. But he said only, "MacDonald called it 'wandering'.

Sort of a sign of approaching death."

"Something in that. Sign something's wrong, anyway. I'd have put a nurse in there with anybody else," he said. "She wouldn't have stood it, though. Finished her right off. I thought you were going over last night, Millie?"

"So did I. Jenny came round and said they didn't need me. I had an impression the message was from you," said Millie, without inflection.

"Well, it wasn't. I don't know what's the matter with that girl. And I think that the sooner that husband of hers takes her away now, the better it will be for MacDonald. She'll drive him wild."

"Oh, I don't think they'll go," said Millie quietly.

"Why not? Pete's been fussing for years to get out of here, hasn't he? Get down in the village again with the rest of his buddies. Well, there's nothing to keep her now. Nothing to keep me, either," said Dr. Kennedy, and pushed himself up. "Thank you, my dear. Give you a lift, Paul?"

At the kitchen door Millie gave her cousin an unexpected hand.

"Don't worry, Polly dear—I won't forget about the train. Have a nap, and I'll come by for you in plenty of time."

"What's that about?" said Dr. Kennedy, in his car. "You're not leaving so soon?"

"No, no—the baby's coming today. Cressa, I should say."

"Yes. Shoot up, don't they? Let's see, now—eight, isn't it?" Dr. Potter, after brief thought, agreed. "And more trouble with that ear?" He liked to astonish in these small ways, remembering what no one expected him to: the ear infection was from several summers ago. Dr. Potter said the ear was fine now, and that he would bring his daughter in for a visit while she was there.

"Do that. We'll give her a good looking over, never hurts. A month, is it, she stays?" When Dr. Potter agreed to this too, he gave a sudden shake of his head, a "chk-chk", and pulled the car over to stop by Dr. Potter's road. "You give things up too easily, Paul. Underestimate yourself. It's a mistake, you know. I blame your aunt a bit for it."

"Why not? She never minds." On his slight rise of anger, he found himself adding: "Are you going to have an autopsy?"

"I am not. What would be the purpose?"

"Well," said Dr. Potter, "you might find out what that X factor was."

But Dr. Kennedy acknowledged no jokes but his own. He said flatly, "The purpose of a postmortem is to determine cause of death. The cause of Mrs. MacDonald's death was the failure of her heart under prolonged strain of illness. As for the X factor," he said, with his sudden fierce grin, "I'm more likely to discover that by cutting open Jenny. Or Pete."

"Then you didn't consider her deranged at all? You think that whatever her purpose was, in wandering like that, it was quite reasonable?"

"Paul," said the old man, patient. "The body affects the mind. You get a weakened body with a strong mind, and perfectly ordinary problems turn into anxieties. An anxiety is a problem you can't cope with, for some reason. Mrs. MacDonald's reason was physical. She couldn't get out of bed and cope with that rackety bunch of hers, and the weaker she got, the more it worried her. If you want to argue the point of where anxiety becomes a derangement, let's do it another day. Mrs. MacDonald hadn't got to that point."

"I don't think she had either. And MacDonald was there—he keeps a pretty firm thumb on those two."

"And who's to keep the thumb on MacDonald?" Dr. Kennedy demanded. He had his teasing look, which disappeared when Dr. Potter said, slowly, "If you mean the ladies, I don't think he was up to anything like that while she was ill."

He saw that the old doctor was rather taken aback—perhaps that 'the children' should know such things about their elders. In any case, he seemed to lose both interest in and patience with what they were saying.

"Oh, get out," he said. "Go home and find yourself a real problem, you and your anxieties. And mind you bring the girl in this time—you missed last year, you know."

Dr. Potter walked slowly down his road, as silence succeeded the sound of the doctor's departing car. It was a deep, midmorning silence by now, the birds quieted, the leaves no longer rustling. Another good, hot day ahead, in the place he knew best in all the world. Perhaps that was his whole trouble—that change, any change, should suddenly happen, where no change ever came.

In any case, Cressa was coming, and he wanted to get things ready for her. There mustn't be any shadow of disappointment for her when she came, he would have to manage that, even if they stayed down here by themselves for a few days. There must, mainly, be no shadows in himself.

He picked up the skunk's saucer, went indoors, and carefully put away his syringe. Then he dumped his cold breakfast into the raccoon's garbage and set to work cleaning house.

The house was a small one, soundly built in stone like all of Grandfather Onderdonk's buildings. Its original purpose Dr. Potter did not know, though undoubtedly MacDonald would; ever since he could remember it had been the cozy little retreat which the second Millicent Onderdonk had made of it for her new husband, the first Dr. Potter. His Study in the Woods. Since everything had still been done on the grand scale in those days (before 1929), the Study in the Woods had also a very pleasant bedroom, kitchen and bath, full electrification, excellent plumbing and a telephone line which the present Dr. Potter did not use. The present Dr. Potter had no legal right to any of this. Although his Aunt Millicent (they had settled on this title as best, for a little boy who still remembered his own mother) had left him all she had to leave, the Study was not part of it. Nevertheless he was the only person on the estate to whom this scruple would have occurred.

It occurred to him more and more often, as the summers of his full maturity came round each year. "Your little house is waiting for you,

Polly," his aunt would write, "and, oh, so are we!" It was not his little house. Yet he had missed only one summer of return—and that summer a haunted one, although their letters had contained no reproaches, unless the detailing of their empty days were somehow a reproach to him. They were not meant to be; that was the heartbreaking part.

No; if this were Nobody's House, then he was that Nobody—by inescapable obligation, perhaps, to the loving 'aunts' to whom his widowed father had turned him over, and the young 'cousins' who had taken him like a small brother into their lives. Or perhaps he was that Nobody simply by default—of all the 'somebodies' who had gone away, or never come at all. He didn't know; he gave up questioning; he just showed up.

And at least Cressa adored the place.

In his butcher's apron, trudging into the kitchen in search of something for the bathtub ring, he became aware of someone standing against the light of the screen door. Before he could rouse and focus himself, for recognition, the voice of Jenny's husband said, persuasive:

"Why don't you get that telephone connected up, Doc? This is a heck of a place to be without one."

The yellow car was outside. Dr. Potter hadn't heard a thing. He said, not welcoming: "What is it, Pete?"

"Well, I'm supposed to tell you to forget about the train—your cousin's going to drive up for the funeral and she's bringing the kid with her."

Pete never said 'Mrs.' or 'Miss' anybody—to the point where it was sometimes hard to understand him. But why 'the kid'?

"All right," he said. "Thanks. My daughter's name is Cressa, by the way."

"Well, sure—I know that." But he understood the correction, and lingered to bury it. "You really need that phone, Doc. If it's the bucks, I could connect you up kind of quiet. You know—no bills."

"No, thanks. I don't want a telephone."

"Yeah, but you need one. Like this morning, for instance. That was really bad."

Sudden anger brought Pete wholly to his attention.

"Nonsense," he said sharply. "Radar wouldn't have helped, and you know it. Why did you send MacDonald down here, anyway?"

"Me? I don't send my dear father-in-law any place," said Pete. And grinned—his movie-star grin, entirely attractive. "Not that I wouldn't like to. No, that was just old Jen, losing her head as per usual. But I still think she lost it smart this time. I mean, she had time to pull herself together and get the old lady straightened up, and then you were there to break it to him. He'd take it better like that. Everything that goes wrong around there, it's always Jen's fault—I wouldn't even put it past him to jump on her about her own mother dying," said Pete, no longer grinning. "We couldn't *tie* her in the damn bed, could we?"

"You could have had help," said Dr. Potter. "That night and day business was too much for Jenny. Why didn't you let Miss Onderdonk take over last night, for instance?"

"Let her! We were perfectly willing. She just never showed up, and Jen wouldn't call up and remind her. That wouldn't be nice, or something." There was a short silence, and he added: "Sure Jen was tired—and I'm tired, after a full day at the garage, on top of all those damn farm chores my dear father-in-law lays out for me. Maybe we did drop off when we shouldn't. But by God, we did a hell of a lot more than anybody else did for her—all we could and more, and anybody that says we didn't, he's a liar. He *or* she," said Pete, breathing hard.

"Well, nobody does," said Dr. Potter—but irritably. Anger was catching, on top of so much confusion.

"Yeah," said Pete. "Well, they better not, that's all."

"All right, they don't. Go on, Pete," he said, tired of it. "And don't be so damn paranoid."

"Yeah," said Pete, and blindly turned away. "Well, okay. You too, Doc," he added, to show no personal hard feelings.

The door slammed behind him, and then the yellow car shot round and out of the clearing. Whoever owned that one was going to need some alignment work.

Dr. Potter, going at once to wash the train information from his wall, felt himself standing still instead. Like one of Millie's 'blank' moments ... which came, of course, from an overloaded mind momentarily rebelling.

He had meant to ask Pete about being on the back road behind the Hall. But that wasn't the main thing.

On second thoughts, he had better leave the wall alone to remind him of the new arrangement, and go get the bathtub clean before he forgot; the main thing now was the bathtub.

But it was odd the way that anger still clung to him, from that senseless exchange. Except that he didn't much like the business of saying Millie wouldn't come—Millie, who went out of her way to take on chores. Another of Jenny's ball-ups, no doubt, of which Pete probably knew nothing. But just the same, he didn't like it at all.

CHAPTER FOUR

About the time that Cressa's non-train was coming in, Dr. Potter allowed himself a small rest before cleaning up. Unshaven, unwashed and unfed, he then slept the rest of the afternoon away. The house looked fine.

He woke in late sunlight with his daughter lying across him in loud delight and his cousin Louisa standing beside the bed. It was exactly like waking from a good dream, to find some essential part of it true; and only Louisa's doubtful expression suggested any flaw.

The flaw, of course, was himself.

"Oh, Lord," he muttered, and struggled up—as far as he could.

"Ladies—children—excuse me. I was cleaning the house and I forgot about cleaning me. Let me up, Cressa. Now, please."

"But you look all right," she said, crushingly. "You look fine, daddy, except why are you wearing a dress?"

He sloughed her, and the butcher's apron too. Lou silently took it. "Go out in the study," he said, desperate. "Or the kitchen, just for a minute. See how—how nice and clean it is. *Lou*—?"

But this cry for help, which Millie would not even have needed, only inspired her sister to a grasp of Cressa's arm—which she naturally resisted. In the end he simply ducked into the bathroom and slammed the door.

When he came out again, feeling manhandled by his own haste, but clean, Louisa was making coffee and his daughter eagerly unpacking lots of little hampers, baskets, and even paper bags. The kitchen was already a mess; but Cressa herself still looked charming. He could see that Vinnie had taken great pains with her straight dark hair—like his—and got it back somehow to show her high forehead and round dark eyes—like his—and the lovely smile that was Vinnie's. Or would be, when those teeth came into scale. The essential part of her, though, was all Vinnie—that lively sureness he had never had, and never tired of, and encountered each time with a new shock of pleasure.

Louisa had found one of his books to read and was standing at the stove, waiting for the coffee to drip. He kissed her first, in case he forgot later; and she looked flabbergasted, and then smiled with relief.

"Oh ... Polly. Coffee coming."

"Yes, fine," he said; and cleared himself a chair. "Is any of that alive?" he asked gravely.

"Yes—look. Vin rosé! Six bottles. I couldn't have brought it on the train, so isn't it nice Aunt Lou brought me? That's why we're late, because there were so many more things I could bring in the car. First we spent the whole morning taking things out, and then we spent the whole afternoon nearly putting them back in. We're ridiculous," she said, proudly. "Do you like the wine?"

"Yes," he said, and gently touched one of the long bottles. This was Vinnie's gift—as always, something he had forgotten that he loved.

"That's from mother, and love, and this time she's *really* coming for Labor Day. And this is from me, and I made it. Only do you want to read it now, or go swimming first?" she asked, suddenly finished. "It was very hot in the car."

The coffee had finished dripping, but Louisa read on. He got up and took down cups, a glass for ginger ale.

"I think we should have a little something, and then go swimming," he said; and heard his voice rise with the joy those calm words released. The visit had begun.

Louisa heard it too—or heard something, and looked up.

"I haven't been up to the house yet," she said, frowning. "I expect I'd better go along now, Polly. You're bringing Cressa for dinner, aren't you?"

"Yes. If we can come in our bathing suits."

"Oh, *daddy*—do I have to wear a bathing suit this year?"

"For dinner, yes. Don't you want coffee, Lou?"

"No. I made it for you. I'd like to take this along, though, if I may—I'll take good care of it."

He had no doubt of that. Louisa, thrown into the sea with a book in her hand, would come up clutching it. Probably with a finger marking her place.

"Take it," he said. "Keep it. Wear it in good health."

In complete understanding, she smiled and went out. Ordinary sounds often went by Louisa's ear, but not many of real consequence.

Later, in swimming suits and sandals, Dr. Potter and his daughter walked up the quiet road to Lake Millicent. The shadows were long now, and the air lightly alive with breeze, but the calm heat of the day lasted still, and would last, well into the night. Dr. Potter carried a small case containing Cressa's dress and his own slacks and shirt, so they would not have to walk back down to their house again.

"I'm sorry the car's gone this year, puss," he said. "It just wouldn't go anymore."

"Couldn't Pete fix it?"

"Not anymore. No one could."

This summer she didn't say, "Not even God?"—though he waited. She was practicing a complicated skipping maneuver, holding heavily to his arm.

"Never mind," she said. "Cars can be anywhere—but this is the only place in the whole world you can walk anywhere and it's safe."

He looked down at her helplessly, and let it pass. But there was one piece of serious business that had to be got out of the way.

"You know about Mrs. MacDonald, don't you, Cressida?" he asked, using her full name for weight. She stopped bobbing and looked up at him.

"Yes. Aunt Louisa told us."

"Well, if everybody seems a little heavy tonight, that will be why. It won't be about you."

"You mean they're all sad?"

She sounded incredulous. It threw him out of stride. "Well, it's a rather sad thing, isn't it?"

"When somebody dies, you mean. Yes, I know."

He was both dissatisfied and curious, but let this pass, too. They had come in sight of the little lake, lying quiet in its ring of old trees, and she left him and ran crying like some little seabird to the water. He let her go. She was, as she had said, quite safe here. Queer about Mrs. MacDonald, though. Cressa had made the same visits as he and Millie and Lou had once made, and had hung around the farm in the same way. Alone, too—and she wouldn't have gone back alone if she hadn't been well received. He began to wonder, anxious, if the difference were in his child.

But when he arrived to find her, skinny and disarming, shuddering her way into the water, her defense rose up unasked for in his mind: a civil reception was one thing, affection another. And Cressa had not grown up to the lesson of 'dear old Mrs. MacDonald'—like children who belonged to the estate. If it were MacDonald who had died, he thought, she would care.

He picked up her little suit and laid it over the bench, sat down to pull off his sandals. She was looking back at him, in a luxury of woe.

"Go on—get in! Swim hard."

"It's co-o-old!"

"Of course it's cold, it always is. That's the springs."

But she was indignant to be told something she knew perfectly well—like a stranger!—and flung herself on the lake with a claiming gesture, and splashed away.

The splashes, the echoes of their voices, rang muted in quiet air—held in to them by the guardian trees and the solitude. It was an intimate little lake, this water named for the first of the Millicents, Grandmother O. He was glad no one else was there, and felt some momentary sympathy with Uncle Humphrey in the matter of Pete. The trouble was, of course, that Pete had taken to inviting buddies, and the buddies their girls; and Dr. Potter, often turning back from what sounded like the beach at Coney Island, had wondered how MacDonald could not know. Apparently he did know, now, for there were no more swimming parties, no more barbecues, no more buddies and girls. But Pete and Jenny still came (respectively defiant and apologetic in a meeting) as of course they should come: there was no place else for them to swim. It amused Dr. Potter to think of the Trustees considering a recommendation for an Employees' Swimming Pool (or a Lake MacDonald?)—certainly a more useful expenditure than, say, Uncle Humphrey's new fishpond. It would never happen, though. MacDonald would be scandalized by the idea.

They had the lake to themselves for a long, peaceful hour and then, Cressa being the proper shade of blue, he toweled and buttoned her up, dressed himself, and they started off for the Hall. Vinnie's hairdo had collapsed and he could not restore it, which depressed him. Just once, he wished Millie could receive Cressa when she was not in need of attention.

But that was a selfish wish. He recognized it as one, when he saw his cousin's long hands come to the little girl's hair: hesitant, then lingering and assured. If he had brought her an orderly Cressa, she would have had no excuse for that rapt intimacy. Aunt Cora, of course, needed none; and even Uncle Humphrey (who had found his own daughters terribly irritating) insisted on drawing Cressa down upon his lap—a babyish position which rather embarrassed her. As every year, Dr. Potter's watchfulness was half touched and half doubtful. So much absorption in a little girl who was not even theirs, not an Onderdonk at all—only

Polly's child, by the wife who wouldn't live with him. He felt almost as if he were offering his daughter for some sacrifice—another little human being, to help bear this terrible weight of land! Nonsense, of course; but how starved they were, all of them. Even Uncle Humphrey. Starved for something that Cressa brought and would take away again. Queerly, he didn't feel that this was love.

Louisa made a pleasant exception. His eye fell upon her with relief, where she sat watching too—without a book, but looking as if she knew just where to find an excellent one, and presently would go and get it. He saw that Millie had lent her black (Lord. It hadn't occurred to him.) and done what she could to make it fit, but Louisa's honest big bones declared themselves everywhere. It was surprising, really, that she could wear Millie's clothes at all, she looked so much larger. Once, very briefly, they had all hoped that Louisa might marry: a rare book dealer, hopefully (and vainly) casing the estate, had clearly admired what many larger men found appalling, that great girl-structure. And since she had been equally pleased to find someone willing to spend hours in the libraries (of the Hall and Long Acre) her usual barrier of taciturnity never went up. At luncheon, when she referred to a lettuce as 'foxed', her conquest seemed complete; no one was surprised when the rare book dealer came back, and back. But whether he altered his intentions or only pursued an original one, the offer he finally made to Louisa was the chance to learn his business, and come and work for him. That was the end of him, so far as Uncle Humphrey was concerned; but Louisa went. And stayed, and seemed entirely content. No one knew or inquired what her relations with her employer might be; they were clearly amiable. There was a long stiffness between Louisa and her father, because her father had said angrily to her: "He only wants you for prestige—a Hired Onderdonk!" But she came home regularly just the same, and the stiffness wore off.

Apparently she hadn't questioned the fact that she must rush up here for Mrs. MacDonald.

With Cressa's indifference, or whatever it was, still in the back of his mind, Dr. Potter found himself wondering what the rest of them really did feel. Besides, of course, shock. Once the excitement of receiving Cressa had worn off, he could perceive a real sadness in his aunt, and an unaccustomed thoughtfulness in his uncle. But what his cousins felt was more important to him, and less clear: Millie was always reserved, and Louisa always remote. (It was no use trying to examine himself; he had given that up long ago.)

He decided to stay with the girls after dinner, instead of going out by the fishpond in their new ritual. His uncle and aunt would have Cressa tonight; he was not needed. Since his cousins were only staying in to clear up, they seemed a little surprised by his choice—but mildly pleased by it.

"There's no reason why the men should always loaf around here," he said, to explain himself. Millie was amused, but didn't comment; Louisa didn't seem to hear. He ended up, of course, having more coffee at the kitchen table.

"Well, did it surprise you, Lou?" he asked her presently.

"No," she said; and then turned. "What?"

"Mrs. MacD.," said her sister.

"Oh. Well, no. She was quite sick, wasn't she?"

"But mending, we all thought."

No one commented; and he went on to Millie: "Pete swears they were expecting you last night, and you didn't come. And Jenny wouldn't take the liberty of reminding you."

A faint color came up in her beautiful skin, and her lips tightened. But it was Louisa, unexpectedly, who said: "Really, they are so awful, those two. I don't know which of them is worse. Jenny isn't mean, but then Pete isn't stupid. Perhaps there's a whole person somewhere between them," she said, with interest. "Perhaps that's why they got married."

Remorse began to invade Dr. Potter.

"I'm sorry, Millie. I shouldn't have repeated that to you. There was no point in it."

She suddenly burst out, "You are quite wrong, Louisa—they are *both* mean, and they are *both* stupid, and I don't want to talk about them another minute!"

She then made five unsuccessful tries to take down a dish towel.

By the time Dr. Potter had got to his feet (it was all he could think of to do; Louisa apparently couldn't think of anything) Millie had recovered.

"I'm sorry," she said, and turned round. "But I do wish we could get through one evening without talking about awful Pete and poor Jenny. And wonderful MacDonald. It's really such a *limited* subject."

"Yes, it is," said the other two, together.

Then they were all silent.

"Besides, there's something I really do want to talk about, now that you're here, Lou," Millie went on, leading them back to normalcy. "But I'd like to wait till we really can talk. Polly, could you and Cressa stay up here tonight? Then you wouldn't have to take her down to bed and come back—and you wouldn't want to leave her alone there, anyway."

"Yes," he said, after a little thought, "I guess we could stay. She'll have to have something to wash her teeth with ..."

For some reason, this began to strike them all as very funny—even before Louisa, gravely holding up the sink brush, inquired: "This do?" Each of them, beginning to smile, looked away and then back ... the smiles grew. It was really very silly.

Millie suddenly gasped, "That marvelous new thing father's got for the fishpond—" and then both women were lost, bursting out, bending over—but still able to dive for and hold up, in aching silence, every unlikely object the kitchen held.

Dr. Potter, laughing heartily too, got a sudden glimpse of his cousin Millicent's face that sobered him. He blinked, looked again, and fell quiet, his smile like a faint rictus upon his face. But this distortion was nothing compared to poor Millie's. Her skin stretched to the skull, her eyes squeezed shut and pouring tears, her mouth wide in silence— deadly pale, she looked a mask of agony, rather than just a woman laughing.

Another moment, and he knew that the mask was true; she was in agony, an agony of laughter, and could not help herself. Louisa saw it too, her own laughter was choking away ... but it was Dr. Potter, leaning quickly forward, who had to raise his hand and bring it stinging down across his cousin's face.

CHAPTER FIVE

They met in Millie's room later that night—as they had always done for conclaves, back in the years when his father and Aunt Millicent had been stationed in South Africa, and he had been left to grow up on the healthy estate under Aunt Cora's loving care. But since those days Millie had taken a different room, the big one under the turret; and in winter carried coal up and ashes down to earn her privacy.

It was a very pleasant room, almost a little world; and Dr. Potter looked round him, there, with an increased respect for his cousin's power to survive. Then he came over to her bed, where she had stayed after the little attack of hysteria in the kitchen. Officially, she had her migraine.

"Well, how do you feel?" he asked.

But to look at her was an answer. Her delicate beauty was more than restored; the long blue eyes shone up at him in soft lamplight as she sat relaxed among her pillows; and she smiled.

"Marvelous. Isn't that disgusting?"

"No. Nothing like busting loose now and then, I find."

"You find," said Louisa, with affectionate scorn. "Where—in some book?"

"Pot," he said; and she, happily, "Kettle"—the magic squabble-ending words of childhood, which Millie had made them say. Louisa had changed least, he thought, looking down at her where she lay curled against the foot of Millie's bed in an old mud-colored dressing gown: a good and happy child of thirty-eight. His own ancient place on the other side of Millie's feet was left vacant for him; but he pulled round an armchair instead and dropped down in that, stretching his legs out long.

"Pipe?" he asked Millie; and she nodded her permission.

"Lovely. Lovely, lovely, to have you both again," she said softly, and he saw her eyes faintly misted as she spoke. So she was not so completely recovered as they all wished to think; Millie had no easy tears.

"We always come back, Millie."

"But you're gone so much, too. I miss you so in the winter, Polly—and they're such long winters ... And I miss you all the time, Lou. Always."

She was openly, quietly, crying now.

Louisa, in an agony of stillness, muttered at last: "You know I had to go, Millie. I would have got so ... queer, just staying home and ... reading ..."

Dr. Potter didn't speak. There was nothing left to say on this subject between Millie and himself. She would not come with him, to spend a winter with Vinnie and himself, or to keep house for him now that he was alone, or even to visit and meet the bachelor professors, the youngish widowers, he still marked in his mind for his lovely cousin. Millie was no visitor. She belonged where she was rooted; and whoever loved or wished to love her must come and find her there.

And then after all he said: "Wouldn't like to try the winter in Indiana, would you?"

She didn't even answer that, except to wipe her eyes. "Or maybe you could wangle another trip out of the Funds," said Louisa, looking up. "Millie—really, why not?"

Millicent's one trip abroad had been achieved as a kind of errand, at the expense of the estate: to inspect new Scots families applying to come there. It had, surprisingly, been Mrs. MacDonald's idea, at a time when Aunt Cora had been worried about her beautiful, restless daughter; and Dr. Potter's impression had been that Millie went reluctantly even then. And came back gladly.

She certainly didn't seem anxious to go again.

Her expression tightened. She said, "That's another topic I'm rather tired of—wangling the Funds."

"Well, there you are, then," said Louisa, discomfited but blunt. "You're just sick of everything around here, Millie. You need to get away for a while—you really do."

She had lost her sister's attention and knew it. Dr. Potter cleared his throat and asked, "What is it you have in mind, Millie?"

"I have in mind that we should change what's wrong in our home, instead of running away from it," she said directly. "It's quite possible, if we can all agree."

"You mean trying to end the trust, I suppose," said Dr. Potter.

"Of course, I mean ending it."

"But I thought they tried that a long time ago," said Louisa. "I know they did, Millie. After all the other money went."

"No, that's quite wrong, Lou. I know we've always thought of it that way, but it was quite different. Uncle John tried, and father opposed him. And he was quite right, then. But Uncle John," she said, "has been dead for a long time."

Dr. Potter felt cold despair beginning inside him. Here was his cousin, sitting up in her false calm and innocent reason, and starting down the last long avenue of frustration that was open to her. And he didn't know how to stop her.

He cleared his throat again.

"I think, Millie," he began, "your answer is right there. Uncle John has certainly been dead a long time. Nearly twenty years, isn't it? If he were the only objection your father had to ending that trust, he would have started action long ago."

She surprised him with a smile—not big, but real.

"Polly, how long has father been talking about putting in that fishpond?" she said gently. "How long have we been complaining about our 1890 furnace, and saying we really must ask for another one? And father complaining the most, mind you!"

"And it's still there," said obliging Louisa.

"And it's still there. And father hasn't said a word about it yet. Not officially."

"Well, I suppose he doesn't like to wangle either. But—"

"It isn't that at all, Polly. He feels he has a perfect right to those things—and he has. Do you know what it is?" she asked, sitting up straighter, clasping her knees. "Father has got a *habit* of caution! He doesn't like to change anything at all. He really can't bring himself to do it! I can understand how he feels, because I can understand what a terrible shock it must have been for him when all his money disappeared—and Uncle John's, and Aunt Millicent's!—and there was absolutely nothing left that was worth mentioning except—the estate. The land, and the funds to keep it up. Nothing else in the whole world for him. It must have seemed like a strong raft in the middle of a terrible ocean to him. I can understand very well how he must have felt."

"And then Uncle John trying to break his raft up and push him into the ocean," said Louisa, whose mind enjoyed this kind of metaphor. "With just pieces of it."

"Exactly. And Aunt Millicent too, you know. She wasn't coming back here, and she needed money for ... I'm sorry, Polly, but for your father's work, and for you."

"Yes, I know."

"Well, he had to fight them both, and you know they were both much more ... vigorous than he was. And he was *right*. At that time, you know, the land and the fund together wouldn't have brought anything. Not nearly enough to split three ways and make anybody secure. They must all have realized it. But I suppose Aunt Millicent didn't need much, and Uncle John wasn't a prudent man at all. Any cash probably looked better to him than no cash—and he hated Long Acre anyway. He wouldn't have lived there if he'd been starving."

Dr. Potter cleared his throat again. Louisa was getting little red patches of excitement over her cheekbones, and Millie's eyes were shining. He didn't know how to stop them.

"I think you're forgetting," he said. "That 1890 furnace."

"No, I'm not, Polly."

"Have you said anything to him at all?"

"Of course not. You don't think he'd listen to his own child, do you? A *woman?* The ideal person would be MacDonald, of course," she added thoughtfully. "If MacDonald told him to do it, he would do it. That's the only reason he has his fishpond at last, because MacDonald coaxed him into it. MacDonald approves of gentlemen's fancies," she said lightly. "He doesn't approve of central heating at all, of course. Not with all this fireplace wood on the estate, and coal fires so healthy."

Dr. Potter said moderately, "I don't think you can expect MacDonald to embrace this idea either."

"I wouldn't dream of asking him."

"Mother?" said Louisa suddenly.

"No. She's another woman. And his wife."

"I mean, have you asked her about this?"

"Lou, what for? She won't make up her mind until father tells her to, and there's no use burdening her with a secret. That's all it would amount to."

"Yes, I suppose so."

There was a pause, in which Dr. Potter started to clean out his pipe and then didn't.

"It's really not very fair to you, is it, Polly?" said Millicent at last. "I'm not even sure any of it would come to you. And it's no use saying that what we have, you have—you even fuss about using that miserable little house of yours. It would just have to be pure philanthropy on your part, I'm afraid—if you could bring yourself to do it."

"Why wouldn't Polly have a share?" Louisa demanded; but neither of them answered.

In his agitation, Dr. Potter did knock out his pipe, and shattered a tiny ashtray.

"Oh, I could bring myself to do it, all right," he said. "I would gladly dance the fandango on Uncle Humphrey's tummy, if it would help. But I'm afraid I haven't any more status with Uncle than you have. As an ex-child. And a failed M.D."

"Polly, you really are so exasperating! Father is terribly impressed with you, don't you realize that? A scholar and a gentleman, darling—with a university press publishing your books!"

"I am not in favor of this unless Polly shares," said Louisa abruptly. "If he's left out somehow, then he will have to be put in. Legally."

She was still ignored.

Dr. Potter said, "I'm not the one, Millie. If I failed, that would be the end of it for you—and I don't have the slightest confidence that I would succeed in talking Uncle off his raft."

Millicent did not reply.

"It does seem to me," he went on, "that you may have a point here. And I think there might be two ways of going at it. One is to get a contemporary of Uncle's—a male contemporary, whose advice he is accustomed to take—to put it up to him. Dr. Kennedy, say. Or that man who handles Aunt Cora's money—what's his name?"

"Mr. Leach, you mean," said Louisa.

"Yes. Another way would be to approach the trustees yourself, which you have every right to do. See if you can't get the suggestion to come from them."

"It's just a bank, now," said Louisa. "It has been, for a long time."

"Why don't you talk to a lawyer about it first? If the idea is as reasonable as it seems, then that might give you the confidence to put it to the bank. I'll do that part for you, if you like."

"I have talked to a lawyer."

"Oh," he said. "Mr. Leach?"

"No. A man in New York."

"Well—what did he say?" her sister demanded. "And when were you *there?* You didn't even tell me!"

"He thought it was ridiculous for all this land and money to be tied up for nobody's benefit. After all, Louisa and I aren't likely to have children," she said steadily. "And—I have to keep saying this, Polly—legally you don't count."

"No. But didn't one of Uncle John's wives have a little girl?" he asked. "Or did she have it when he married her?"

"It was his. They were Chicago people, and I think quite rich—that's all mother knows about it. She tried to keep up, on account of the little girl, but that particular wife seemed rather bitter about Onderdonks."

"All Uncle John's wives were rich," said Louisa dreamily. "I suppose he really made his living that way, didn't he? It can't have been very easy, though—I remember him just before he died, and he looked older then than father does now. Do you suppose he came back to have another whack at getting the funds, Millie? I bet he did!"

Her sister did not even seem to hear. The return of health and spirits she had shown them must have come from a very small stock, which seemed depleted now. Apathy was rapidly claiming her, and Dr. Potter did not like the look of it, nor its suddenness.

He pulled himself up, and stuffed his pipe in his pocket.

"I think we've talked enough about this tonight," he said. "Let's break up, and think about it. Lou, shouldn't Millie have some milk, or something?"

But it was Louisa's turn not to hear now. She was looking thoughtfully at her sister.

"Millie," she said, "would it mean the end of the estate?"

"I don't know. We can't know, until we know how much the funds amount to now. Isn't it absurd, that we shouldn't even know a thing like that? About our own money!"

Louisa said shyly, "It would be nice if the land could stay as it is and we could just get the funds loose. Wouldn't it? We know there must be enough to keep the estate in very good condition—and just out of income! MacDonald seems to have every possible sort of machine. Perhaps we could just divert a little more of the income to us, and a little less to the cows. Or we could even spend capital! Why not?"

Her sister regarded her quietly.

"I think you will have to understand this a little better before you can say that you agree, Lou," she said. "Whatever amount is—got loose, will have to be shared with Uncle John's descendants. It's not likely that there are none."

"And with Polly!"

"I'll get mine, Lou," he said, impatient. "Now stop it, and let's hear about this. You mean that if your two-thirds isn't enough to continue running the estate, then the land would have to be sold. And to pay off the value of a third of it, to Chicago," he added, thoughtful.

"One-half, Polly. Father and Uncle John would share equally, since Aunt Millicent had no legal descendants. But what if we did have to sell a great deal of the estate?" she said, passionate. "At least what was left would be really ours—and so would our lives be!" She checked herself, to add: "But I want Lou to understand how it might be, before she agrees."

She was growing whiter, it seemed to Dr. Potter, every moment, and her voice fainter. But it continued.

"Try to think how much your home means to you, Louisa. It may mean more than you realize."

But almost in panic, her sister protested: "It doesn't mean more to me than you! It doesn't—I don't care about it at all, Millie—really! I agree absolutely."

She made no reply. Nor could Dr. Potter speak. In spite of himself, he found that he had begun to listen with the ears of Uncle Humphrey— and to what was no more than a plan to hack his raft in two, and give half of it away to strangers. What could he gain, compared to what he would almost certainly lose? The estate would have to go, of course, to pay off half its value, and his whole identity would go with it. MacDonald, perhaps the person whom he most trusted in the world, would go too— at least as Uncle Humphrey's caretaker. He would be left, perhaps, with his house (besieged on every side) and an increased income for which he had no use whatsoever. And he would have lost his trustees, who decided everything.

She hadn't a chance. Not while her father lived.

He had never felt so sorry for his cousin in his life, as when he leaned to wish her goodnight—running his hand over the pale hair which already shone with silver. With a lot of silver, in this close view.

"Millie," he said, his heart aching for her, "you are rich, you know, whatever comes of this. You have got two whole slaves, who love you dearly—hardly anybody has got those anymore."

She shook her head, not smiling. Her voice was barely audible.

"I don't want to have slaves ... or to be one. Besides, you belong to Cressa now, and Lou has got her life ... But if you were my slave, Polly, then I would make you talk to father. I would. You're the one."

Oddly enough, he had begun to feel that she might be right. No reasonable male contemporary would ever get this proposition across— or even be willing to try, probably. Some sort of family legerdemain was the only hope. Somebody close to him emotionally would have to— to panic the old bastard! he thought. Put it to him that Millie was on the point of cracking up! (He would never credit that for an instant. Dr. Potter would only get himself suspected of instability.) All right, then— a proposed highway. Cutting right through the heart of the estate! Forced sale, rock-bottom prices, secret advance information—act now!

All at once, in the tomb-like upper hallway, Dr. Potter began to chuckle. It wasn't a happy chuckle, not entirely under his control. Lou came up to him leaning there against the wall, and gave him a very doubtful look.

"What's funny, Polly?"

He shook his head.

"Is it us?" she asked simply.

That was *his* slap in the face. It worked beautifully.

"No," he said, with a deep breath. "Not us, Lou. The world that made us, maybe, but never, never us. Perish the thought. Goodnight, pot," he added. "Let's all go sleep on our hopeless hopes."

She didn't answer, but stood to watch him down the hall and into the room.

CHAPTER SIX

Incredibly, it was not yet midnight.

In the deepened night beneath the old tulip tree, the water lily pads lay dark upon black water, their closed buds without color. Coming out of the dim house again, Dr. Potter's night vision cleared almost at once and he saw the old man lying as he had left him, supine and flat beside his sleeping fishpond. He seemed also to sleep.

Dr. Potter's knees shook badly now. He started to lower himself to the edge of the rattan lounge, but found he could not bear to sit in the presence of this death. Closer, Uncle Humphrey's sparse, wet hair could be seen trailing on his brow and eyes, and all illusion of a sleeper vanished. Dr. Potter looked away again.

He stayed where he was, standing and trembling. After a long time he heard the car coming from the home farm. He heard it stop at the foot of the drive and then nothing more until the two men, running silent upon grass, came into view. He moved to meet them, his guardianship over.

Pete's breath was the more audible, and he did not say a word—stood behind his father-in-law, taut and wary. MacDonald looked enormous. His chest was bare. He said very low, "Where is he, Paul? By the wee pond?"

When Dr. Potter nodded he strode past, and into the tulip tree's pool of shadow. When they came up he was kneeling, with great gentle hands upon the old man's shoulders.

But he heard them, and looked up sharply.

"He's all wet, boy!"

"Yes. His head was in the water when I found him. And his arms and shoulders."

On the rim of the pond lay the tangled long roots which had come out with the old man's body, clutching the arms still. MacDonald began to tear them away.

"Aye. There'd be no help in them things. And it was me that got them for him!" He stopped and rose to his feet, very close to Dr. Potter, so that their faces almost touched. "The two of them, Paul—the two of them, that ought to have had years in them yet! And no reason for it! Only the Lord's wull," he said in desperate restraint. *"The Lord's wull."*

None of them spoke, until MacDonald spoke again. "Well, take up his feet, boy," he said like a sigh. "He'll go in to his bed now."

"I think we had better leave him here until Dr. Kennedy comes, MacDonald."

"No, we'll not. He'll lie in his own bed."

It was no disagreement, but a mandate. Pete, swiftly leaning, was struck back hard. But MacDonald's voice remained quiet.

"This is for Paul and me to do, Pete. You'll go ahead, and open the doors."

The old man was heavy ... and the ankles in Dr. Potter's grasp were hard bone within silk, no life remaining to the touch.

The great staircase seemed to suck silence from the empty rooms below it. One light burned in the lower hall, and one in the upper, for Uncle Humphrey to find his way to bed. Sometimes that would not be until three or four in the morning, for on hot summer nights he liked to lie outdoors and doze, and sometimes sleep.

His study-bedroom, which he had taken years ago for insomniac privacy, was at the head of the stairs; they did not need to pass any other door first in their slow, hard-breathing shuffle. Pete had the light on and the covers flung back on the bed when they came in; and MacDonald, with a sharp backward glance, disapproved.

"I didna tell you to unmake his bed," he grumbled. And then: "No, leave it be now."

Dr. Potter, straining to the final lifting, still caught—and was startled by—Pete's familiar shrug of ironic submission. His unusual silence was clearly one of discretion only, and a lively interest. To Dr. Potter's next glance he grimaced, purposeful.

MacDonald saw none of it.

"Did you tell the doctor the same—not to drive his car up to the house?" he demanded. When Dr. Potter nodded, he said: "Good boy. I'm afraid for her, Paul. The two in a day, and she's no' so young."

"Perhaps Pete will wait on the lawn, and tell Dr. Kennedy where we are."

"Aye, do that, Pete," MacDonald agreed; and watched his son-in-law's vanishing, sprightly back without expression. "I'm thinking it's Millie we'd better wake first," he said when they were alone.

Dr. Potter shook his head.

"She's been ill this evening. It'll be enough for her to hear about it in the morning. I'll tell my aunt," he said, "and I think I had better tell her now."

"Aye. She's too close to sleep through much more of this marching and muttering. And you're as much a child to her as any other, Paul, you're all the son she has."

It seemed a mournful verdict, in the dead quiet of his uncle's room, and sent Dr. Potter sadly into action. He knew what a blow he had to deal. Whatever the world might think of Humphrey Onderdonk's end, if it thought anything, he knew that for Aunt Cora a Titanic had gone down in those several gallons of water.

He opened her door softly and went in—and had the shock of finding her erect in bed, staring towards him.

"Polly!" she whispered at once. "Whatever is your uncle doing? Isn't that MacDonald I hear?"

He came and sat on the bed to answer; and then, beginning to speak, took his aunt in his arms and found himself at last gently rocking her, like some plump and bewildered child.

She was so quiet. As if, above all things, they must not wake the children.

When Dr. Kennedy was heard at last—not his arrival, but some recognized murmur of his voice—his aunt pushed herself free.

"We must go in, Polly. Go ahead. I'll come."

In the next room MacDonald stood mute at the doctor's side, with the glazed look of expanding shock, now that no more action was required of him.

To the old doctor's bent head, Dr. Potter said: "Aunt Cora's coming, Dr. Kennedy"; and to MacDonald: "Come on. Come downstairs with me."

Docile as a lamb—or as a pole-axed steer—MacDonald stumbled away at his heels. When they reached the dining room Dr. Potter turned on the light, found the sour mash whisky that was MacDonald's choice (and kept here for him) and poured him out half a glass of it. Just watching, MacDonald found his tongue.

"How can it be this way, Paul?" he burst out. "The two in a day! The two in a day!"

"I don't know," said Dr. Potter. "Sit down and drink that, MacDonald."

But Pete had appeared in the doorway, drawn from somewhere by the light or the clink of glass. MacDonald exploded at him: "Get on home with you, Pete!" But he came forward instead, as Dr. Potter silently poured and handed him a glass too. For a minute Dr. Potter thought MacDonald would hit him. Instead, something appeared to hit MacDonald—a mighty blow. He fell into a chair, and turned from both of them. Pete jerked his head in a significant gesture, and Dr. Potter said coldly:

"I think you'd better get back to Jenny. I'll bring your father-in-law home later. Thank you for coming so quickly."

"Any time, Doc." He swallowed his whisky, grimaced. "Well, okay. Sorry for your trouble."

When they were alone Dr. Potter sat down too, and put the bottle between them. They were there some time before Dr. Kennedy appeared.

He said at once, "MacDonald, go up and see Mrs. Onderdonk a minute—she wants you. Be quiet, and don't wake the ch—the girls," he said, vexed.

MacDonald got up without a word.

"There is a child here, you know," said Dr. Potter. "Cressa and I stayed the night. Luckily, we're up in the old nursery—Aunt Cora thought Cressa would like the pictures."

He got out the doctor's Irish whiskey, as he spoke, and the old man received it impassively.

"You found him?"

"Yes."

"Your shirt's still wet," he said suddenly. It was.

"I had to lean pretty far in to get a grasp on him. His whole head and shoulders were in. His knees were bent, to one side—I thought perhaps the one with the bad cartilage had torn again, when he was leaning over, and he lost his balance—and there wouldn't be anything to catch hold of in the water."

Except those long, trailing roots ...

"Poking the frog," the doctor grunted. "I've seen him do that many a time."

"Yes." Perverse, he added: "Even so, it must be that he lost his head. From shock, or pain, or something. He ought to have been able to scramble back somehow."

Dr. Kennedy put his glass down and rose.

"Come out and show me," he said.

What the doctor had in mind, Dr. Potter discovered outside, was that he should get down and emulate his uncle's position. He stood by the fishpond, looking incredulously from it to Dr. Kennedy.

"What—down in?"

"Down in. Go on, go on—I'm here to haul you back if need be."

Once past distaste, Dr. Potter discovered some curiosity in himself. Feeling rather furtive, he got down and arranged his legs as he remembered his uncle's to have been. Then, with a deep breath, he leaned upon his elbows and lowered his head and shoulders, then his arms, into the water. The gentle water and cold entangling weeds received him; he felt entirely in control of his situation, but repelled by it. He kept his body down, however, until he felt the water's touch upon his upper spine at the point where he judged it to have been upon his uncle's. To rise then, he had thought only to inch back until his elbows could become levers upon the edge again; the bottom was out of reach. But some lack of success occurred, and he was aware of splashing, and lily roots, and of a hand hauling at his belt before he got his elbows where he wanted them.

"Sorry ..." he spluttered. "Did that wrong ..."

Dr. Kennedy's laconic voice replied, "Go dry yourself off and come back to the dining room. And take off that shirt!"

The doctor was pouring himself some more Irish when Dr. Potter returned from the downstairs lavatory (courtesy of the funds, c. 1935) and he looked at him grimly.

"Now I want to hear how long you were away from him," he said.

"Away from him when?"

"When he fell in, of course."

"I hadn't been with him at all—no one had. We were all upstairs. You know how he sat out there at night."

"Then how long had he been sitting out there alone?"

"Why, two or three hours, at least. We all went up pretty early—Aunt Cora and I to get Cressa to bed, and then I went along to Millie's room. Lou and I were meeting her there for a conclave."

"What—still? I never liked those conclaves, Paul," he said severely.

"I know. We held that against you, for a while. Then we found out that secret conclaves were even better, and we forgave you again."

"Millie didn't," said the old doctor. "She never liked anything she had to hide. Too proud."

As in any conversation here, the obscuring past was creeping in upon the present: even upon this present. And the doctor's tone, just then, brought back another memory: of the rumor that he had loved Millie once, and even come to court her, in the early days of his widowhood. He in his fifties then, and she in her twenties. Well; it was probably true, and not so very awful—though Dr. Potter had been indignant at the time and refused to believe his aunt. Nor had he had the courage to challenge Millie herself. Nothing had come of it, of course. But it was probably true. Almost everyone was in love with Millie at some point; you had it like measles, and it ran its not-dangerous course and was forgotten.

But he looked with faint curiosity at Dr. Kennedy, and missed what he was saying.

"I'm sorry, what—?"

"I said, you found him when?"

"Just before I called you. Just before, around eleven-thirty. I came down again," he said—paused, and went on: "I wanted to talk to him, and when I saw the downstairs light on and realized he was still out, it seemed like a good time."

"You being where?"

"In bed. We all were, by then. I got up to have a cigarette—the smell wakes Cressa—and saw the light on."

"You got up and dressed and came down to talk to your uncle, Paul? Why ? What went on around here this evening?"

Total fatigue was beginning to make him dull, Dr. Potter realized. The whisky did not bring its usual enlivenment; he was past any more response to stimulation. But a dull perseverance burned in him still, like a kind of hall light.

He sighed, and answered.

"Nothing that involved Uncle Humphrey, of course. What ever did? No, it was just something Millie wanted me to speak to him about, and I said I wouldn't ... and then I decided I might as well, just to put an end to it. She's got an idea in her head about attacking the trust again ... a plan, rather; I don't mean to sound disparaging. A perfectly reasonable plan. But with one slight obstacle. Which now seems to be removed."

Dr. Kennedy sat turning his glass upon the polished table.

He said presently, "You're out on your feet, Paul. Go on up now."

"No. Not yet. I don't know how to allow for the effect of partial immersion in cool water," he said, "or much about old, arthritic joints. But it seemed to me that uncle had been dead a long time when I found him. Hours. Maybe years."

Dr. Kennedy pushed his glass away and got up.

"Come on, while you can," he said. "How much of that whisky have you had?"

"Quite a lot. I want to tell you something about Uncle Humphrey's last evening, before I go. It was very pleasant. He and Aunt Cora sat by the fishpond with Cressa after dinner—you can imagine how they enjoyed that, a real child. When I came down to get Cressa I noticed that my uncle did not have his head in the fishpond. This was around eight-thirty. At this time my cousins were up in Millicent's room where they had gone directly from cleaning up the kitchen, because of a slight attack of hysteria Millie had. But that didn't interfere with my uncle's evening, because he didn't know about it. Between eight-thirty and ten, or so, all of us except my uncle and the frog were upstairs and in each other's company. Millie and Lou were in the turret room and Aunt Cora and I were in the nursery. Then I was with Millie and Lou in the turret room and Aunt Cora was with Cressa. After ten o'clock nobody but Cressa and I was in anybody's company, but I suspect by that time my uncle had already made his peace with the lily roots and possibly even with the frog. What is your opinion, doctor?"

Dr. Kennedy, steadily receiving all this, said from the doorway: "My opinion is that you are either drunk or in a state of shock. Let me see your hands."

"I've dissected a hand," said Dr. Potter, getting up. "I've also dissected a frog. Do you intend to dissect Uncle Humphrey, Dr. Kennedy?"

"Can you walk?" said the doctor. "Let go of that chair." He came back across the room. As soon as they were close enough, Dr. Potter let go of the chair and seized the doctor.

"Now you've sat this out for thirty or forty years, Dr. Kennedy," he said, "and you're a good observer. I think by now you must know pretty well all you care to know about my uncle's lungs and stomach and heart, and even his knees. Not to mention the fact that he had his life, and a good slice of everybody else's. So why are you still so curious? *What is it you want to know?*"

Dr. Kennedy did not reply. In the silence between them Dr. Potter became aware of the shoulders beneath his hands: an old man's shoulders, delicate and bony; they felt like his uncle's. He let his hands drop.

"I beg your pardon," he said.

"Yes," said. Dr. Kennedy, almost absently. He went on "I suppose I ought to ask yours. I go on speaking to you all without bothering to explain, as if you were still children, and I've no right to do it. Let me explain to you now, Paul, that I wanted you to help me understand how your uncle might have had his accident, and how he came to be alone so long that early in the evening, with all of you here. Now I understand. Do you understand me?"

"I don't know," said Dr. Potter. "Probably not. I seem to be turning into an expert at confusion."

"You are a little confused now because you are a little drunk, and very upset," said Dr. Kennedy. "Why don't you go out and make a big pot of coffee for all of us? We need it."

He added, from the door, "I will want to see Millie before she is told. I don't like the sound of that hysteria business."

Then he left Dr. Potter alone in the big, lighted room with its debauched table and empty, awry chairs.

CHAPTER SEVEN

"We think he leaned over to poke the frog," said Aunt Cora, "and lost his balance. You know he had a badly injured knee. It was never reliable after he tore the cartilage." She was saying this to Jenny, who not only knew these facts but had heard them from Aunt Cora herself several times before. But even Jenny knew by now that the importance of this message lay in the way in which Aunt Cora was able to deliver it—with increasing firmness, each time. Perhaps Aunt Cora herself knew this. She rather seemed, by now, to be estimating her words than speaking them; and Dr. Potter did not quite like it.

So he broke in on Jenny's murmur, saying: "Well, if you're ready, Jenny, I'll take you back to the farm."

"Yes, go along, and don't feel you must come tomorrow unless you want to. You've been very kind to come all week, Jenny, with your own loss so new."

"I'll come, Mrs. Onderdonk. I'm glad to come."

It was probably true. The farm with only her father around during the day must be an uneasy place, for one of Jenny's uneasy temperament. The Hall, on the contrary, seemed eerily normal. Louisa had gone back to town until the weekend, and Aunt Cora and Millie were back at their never-ending chores again. He had to force himself to realize, now and again, that Uncle Humphrey was not out by the fishpond, or walking one of the roads at his careful gait, or reading upstairs. He had lived so separate a life that what Dr. Potter most noticed now was how little he noticed his absence.

But about Cressa's continuing presence in this eerie normalcy he still had doubts. He had called Vinnie before the funerals, and the verdict seemed to be that she might stay if she liked; about his aunt's and cousins' wishes he hadn't needed to ask. But the day after his uncle's death he had called Vinnie—going all the way in to Cold Spring to do it, and shutting himself up in a drugstore booth. There was furtiveness for you. The only one in on the plan was Cressa herself, who kept coming and knocking on the glass of the booth in case the decision might be going against her.

Sweating with heat and shyness, frowning and shaking his head—and trying not to sound as if he were doing so—Dr. Potter did his best to be fair.

"They want her—of course they want her. It's just that I'm not sure they ought to have her, just now. For her sake, I mean."

"Oh," said Vinnie. She sounded uncertain too. Perhaps she did not have an office to herself, he did not know how to visualize her at all where she sat, presumably, making fabric designs all day long.

"Well, what does Cressa say?" Vinnie wanted to know. He could hear her getting impatient at how badly they were doing, and answered briskly.

"Oh, she's all for it, of course. Staying, that is."

"Well, then ... why ought she not to? I mean, why do you *feel* she ought not to, Paul?"

"Well, I don't know that I do. I just want to be sure it's all right with you—the funeral, and so on. Even if she doesn't go."

"Oh, you'd better let her go—if she's not in anybody's way ... It would probably be much more trouble to keep her from going—she'll want to see what a funeral's like, and I suppose she might as well. It's not as if it were anybody very close to her ... Well," said Vinnie's voice, beginning to sound excited, "I don't mean exactly *that* ..."

"But it's quite true."

"No, I mean I don't want to sound so calm about something that—that must be very sad for all of you. I am truly sorry, Paul, and ... Oh, perhaps you had better send her home!"

"No, no," he said, "listen, Vinnie—there's nothing here that she ought not to be *around*, I don't want to give you that impression. It's a shock, of course, but nobody's prostrated ..."

Appalled at himself, he shut up. Vinnie heard every bit of that.

"Oh, you don't know *what* you feel about it, any of you!" she cried out. "Except Millie—and she won't say! That's all I mind for Cressa to be around, it's all I've ever minded! That terrible confusion—and *dishonesty!* I won't have her—*You send her right back here this* ..."

She had begun to cry, and hung up.

He would not tolerate such an ending. Groping, constricted, running with sweat, he somehow swept his change off the shelf on to the floor;

and while he was struggling to recover it Cressa knocked the door in upon his head.

"Get out of here ..."

"But what did she say, daddy?"

"We are still talking, we were cut off—and if you will please let me find that quarter, I'll—" He gave up, and pushed the door wider. "Can you see it? Right down there somewhere."

"Here's a dime."

"All right, now see if you can find the quarter ..."

The telephone before him rang. He took down the receiver and heard Vinnie's voice, stiff with control, saying: "Is that you? Paul, I will not let this subject go on defeating us every time."

"That's precisely what I was about to tell you, Vinnie—but the damn money fell down." Cressa offered him the quarter. He pushed her out with it and shut the door again. "Vinnie, I think we—"

"And you see I know where you are. In Morton's Drugstore! You're sitting in that drugstore telephone booth to call me. *Who has to die before you'll call me from the house?*"

"Oh, Vinnie—please, dear—!"

But she was crying, and hung up again.

This time he did not have any impulse to call back. What was the use, he would only make it worse—by now she was furious with them both, because she kept crying. He knew how to visualize that. The excitement of anger was what made Vinnie cry—with real sorrow she became pale, with big, dry eyes.

The door tentatively opened; he let it.

"Can I stay, daddy?"

"Yes," he said. "I guess so."

"If what?"

"If you're good and don't bother people. Come on."

"Can I have the quarter?"

Then she wanted to stay and spend it. While he stood waiting a terrible hope came up in him that Vinnie would call again; he knew he could not. Neither, apparently, could she.

Yet driving home on the faulty clutch, doggedly thinking it over, he told himself that this business about the family was only peripheral, always had been. Only part of the outer tangle they could never get through to arrive at the real trouble. Which was that basically they seemed to be going in different directions. He knew that Vinnie's New York friends, to whom she had eagerly returned (no doubt) from Indiana, must think her well rid of a man who kept burrowing away backward from his own time. And it was true that many of his friends and colleagues frankly implied that he was better off without a human soufflé like Vinnie. But he knew better. For him, the parting was all loss.

Back at the house he quite simply sat down in the hall and called her office again, and she quite simply received the call, and they had a short, sensible exchange and settled the matter. It left him feeling very empty.

So here was Cressa now, gravely hearing Aunt Cora explain to Jenny for the fifth or sixth time how Uncle Humphrey had leaned over to poke the frog and lost his balance—and seeming no more tired of it than Aunt Cora herself.

He said with controlled impatience, "Do you want to come, Cressa, or stay here?"

"Oh, come to the farm, lovey," said Jenny, coaxing. "There's the new chicks, and I'm going to bake ..."

"Oh, I'd love to, Jenny—but Aunt Millie's waiting for me, we're going up in the attic and find me a costume! Maybe I'll come later, and show you?"

It would be a wowser of a costume, too. In spite of those boxes to the Missions, the attic seemed to contain clothing left from all their lives, in case they ever wanted to live them over. He knew for a fact his own school uniform was there: Cressa had come down wearing it.

"Well, don't keep your aunt up there all day," he said; and she assured him that Aunt Millie *liked* it, which was probably true. Or true enough.

But he didn't like it. Didn't somehow like the thought of the long, musty quiet that would enclose his little girl and his lovely, sad cousin, perhaps all afternoon. He felt a little like Aunt Cora, with her constant urging to 'go out in the fresh air', and smiled. But he still didn't like it. He wasn't liking anything much, these days, including himself.

CHAPTER EIGHT

In the car he said to Jenny, who never initiated a conversation: "Well, I suppose Pete will be taking you away to the village now, won't he?"

"Oh, Mr. Paul—who told you that?"

He looked at her in surprise.

"Nobody 'told' me. Is it some kind of secret? He's always wanted to go, hasn't he?"

"But I can't go now," said Jenny, retreating. "I can't leave my dad."

He gave her another doubtful look, but left it alone. He had thought the subject an old (and rather tiresome) one; but it seemed to have taken new life.

Beside him, Jenny gave off an impression of hovering. "What put it into your head, though, Mr. Paul? Did Pete say something? Or Miss Millie?"

"I don't think so."

She didn't believe him.

"They never say anything to me anymore. I wish you'd tell me what they said. Do you think it's true? Can they do it?"

"Do what?" he replied—but more in caution than in genuine inquiry. Perhaps caution returned to Jenny too, at this point, for she dried up.

But he could feel her resentful stare.

He said finally, "I don't really see what Pete has to do with it, you know."

"Then it was Miss Millie told you," said Jenny, with the rapidity any hunted mind can show. "Please don't tell Pete I said anything!"

"Why should I? And you haven't said anything. But why don't you like the idea, Jenny?"

"Oh, it'll kill my dad, really it will!" Jenny cried. "When he had mother it didn't seem so bad, I could imagine them going home to Scotland like they talked about sometimes. But he wouldn't go alone—and what would he do? I think it's *wicked*, Mr. Paul—the whole thing! What *good* will it do?"

What good indeed, so far as Pete was concerned? Aside from the simple pleasure of wrecking his father-in-law's life, Dr. Potter couldn't see any. Not for a practical man like Pete.

Drawn up in front of the farmhouse, Dr. Potter turned and looked at Jenny curiously. He had a feeling her outburst was genuine, but shallow over depths. She was "playing" Jenny, as he had known her to do before. But her distress was real.

He said, to that, "Well, don't worry about your father, Jenny—that's no use. Pete's your concern. Maybe you'd better take a stronger stand with him." Useless, every word of it. He leaned and pushed open the door for her. "Besides, it's just an idea, it may never happen at all."

"Oh but it *will*, Mr. Paul! Pete said when the old m—"

She sat there and lost all her healthy color, every drop of it. And it took Dr. Potter a minute to swallow his rise of rage.

"Pete," he said finally, "isn't God, Jenny. Whatever he thinks. Just tell that idea over to yourself a few times every day. And when you get used to it, tell it to Pete."

Any anger terrified her. She scrambled out of the car without a word, and ducked indoors.

Back at the Hall, he took the first wide, shallow flight of stairs three at a time and strode along the upstairs hall to the back stairs. Not a sound, not a soul to see him go by. All these rooms, and nobody. Only the two women who served them. Up again; and then the last stairs, where the door stood open and there was, at last, the sound of one small voice: his daughter's.

His temples felt as if they might burst, as he stood on these steps and said: "Millie." Just that.

They both came—Cressa running, getting there first, alive with invitation and delight.

"Not now, baby. Millie, will you come down a minute?"

She came at once—a few low words, and Cressa stayed behind. No fuss. She followed him down the narrow hall and into the old nursery. He shut the door behind her and stayed against it.

"Millie, what interest has Pete got in this thing you're trying to do? *What's in it for him?*"

Her first concern changed. Diminished. She began to look, simply, vexed.

"Oh, Polly. I thought at least you were ... Well," she said. "Goodness. What a face!"

He kept it.

"Don't tell me he's been nagging at you, Polly!" she said then. He saw her vexation growing—her color coming up a little, too. It wasn't much, but it was something. He left the door and went over to sit on his bed.

"No, he hasn't mentioned it to me and I don't think he will. If he does, I'm not going to discuss it with him." He asked, "Why did you?"

"Well," said Millie, and paused. She began to look uncertain, but her color was going down again. "You make it sound so shabby, dear!"

He didn't comment.

"And I suppose it is. Things about money seem to be, sooner or later."

She sat down on Cressa's bed and looked across at him—her usual thoughtful, even somber gaze.

"Well, it was his idea. I know I didn't tell you that, or Lou, so I suppose I was ashamed. That we hadn't the sense, any of us, to think of it for ourselves. It's humiliating to be so impractical, Polly. It is to me. And then," she added, "It was he who gave me the lawyer's name in New York, in case I wanted to ask. You know I did."

"But why would he suggest it, Millie? And to you! How did you come to listen to him, at all?"

She made a small gesture, of the long hands lying in her lap. A curiously helpless gesture, for Millie.

"Polly—you're away so much, you forget—I know you forget how many days there are, here, and how much time for things to happen ... and so little that really happens ..."

She was making some sort of beginning; and he waited.

"I suppose Pete was curious about us even before he came here. The way everybody is. Only more, because that's the way Pete is. And I suppose he very soon got out of Jenny what she must know perfectly well—that none of us had any money, only the land had it. Then he must have gone on picking up bits, perhaps even from poor father—it's possible. Father didn't dislike Pete, when he first came. Well, he's been here six years now, Polly—do you realize that? And it was only last winter he began trying to mention it to me. That's very slow, for Pete."

"He certainly had a clearer idea of our situation than I did," she admitted. "And perhaps of me. At any rate, who else could he have spoken to? It's hard to explain this, Polly, but really, he was almost funny, at first. So indignant—almost *frantic*, at the idea of all that lovely money locked up, and such a creaky old lock! And nobody doing anything about it."

She said, like an afterthought, "He wants enough money to buy out that garage for himself. Like a finder's fee, he said."

She made it very clear. He could see those two, moving parallel through the slow days of the estate, slowly converging under Pete's long determination. He could even see Millie thinking it funny, since she offered him this chance: could see her small amused smile at the exasperated Pete, blurting it out at last.

And then the idea that stayed with her. Pete's "nagging"—Millie herself had used the word of him.

But what of all the days *afterwards?* And that furtive visit to Pete's lawyer friend?

"Millie, why didn't you talk to us about this long ago?" he said. "You know Lou and I want what you want, we always have."

"You weren't here, Polly."

"But lord, you could have written! For anything so important to you, I would have got loose and come here, if you wanted me to. And so would Lou. You aren't," he said, "driven to the point where there's nobody but—a Pete."

She looked right at him, but her look was absent. And she said with a genuine if faint amusement: "Well, it's been complicated. What a shock poor Pete had when he heard about Uncle John's daughter! I didn't remember—didn't take it into account, I mean, until I had been down to see the lawyer. Pete kept saying, 'That's done it, that finishes it!'—as if he could see his garage sinking right down into the river, before his eyes!"

"And what changed his mind, Millie?" he asked.

He knew her too well to accept her unchanging, reminiscent expression, as she continued faintly to smile past him. She heard. He had hold of it now.

"He had another idea, apparently. Was it me? Did he say, 'You've got to get Doc to talk him into it'? Or Polly, perhaps. Surely he knows us that well by now." He made an effort at control, but it wasn't good enough. "So it's thanks to Pete that Lou and I finally heard about it. I'm much obliged to him, Millie. Much obliged."

Her long eyes had long ago come back to meet his.

"You have every right to judge me," she said. "I gave you that right, when I asked you for your help. I'm sorry for both those mistakes."

"You should have taken Jenny in too," he said, unable to stop. "She's got the real dope. She could tell you how it's bound to go through now that the old man's dead. *Or could you have told her?*"

He might have been bouncing pebbles off rock—except for the sudden sharp, staggering thrust of pain within himself.

"Oh, Millie ... Millie, *why?*"

She was only waiting for him to move away from the door. Waiting with the composure, the experience, of all her years of waiting. She didn't even glance his way as she left the room.

It was several minutes before he realized she hadn't gone back to the attic, either. His daughter reminded him by appearing on the stairs, in a tangle of long skirts.

"Where is everybody?" she inquired.

It was a good question.

He came and took her hand—seized it, almost.

"Come on," he said. "Come on and—help me get a picnic ready, we're going to have a picnic supper up at the lake. With the vin rosé," he said, hoisting her, for speed, "and—and hot dogs."

And nobody but themselves. But he would be able to explain that somehow, when the time came.

CHAPTER NINE

About nine the next morning Dr. Potter was able to ambush his aunt alone in the sewing room. His cousin and Jenny were apparently doing something vigorous and distant with the vacuum cleaner, and Cressa was off on her own.

Aunt Cora turned with her usual pleasure, which bordered on delight, to receive him—but he had time to see her private face, first. The way she must look, these days, when no one was with her. It didn't make his errand any easier.

"I need a little confab, auntie."

"Yes, dear. I thought something was wrong, yesterday. Don't be upset about it—you know Millie just needs time to think things out, by herself, and then she'll be all right again."

She didn't ask what it was, probably taking it for granted that he didn't know, since this was often the way.

"No," he said, "I don't think we can leave this one to Millie. Not any longer."

He sat down, drawing one of the rickety sewing room chairs close to hers. She pulled aside the sheet she was mending to make room for him.

"You know Millie's going to be forty this autumn, auntie," he began; and she nodded.

"Yes, dear. And Lou thirty-eight last spring, and you just thirty-six. I don't even dare think how old we are ... I am," she corrected herself sadly.

"Sixty-three, you fraud, and the baby of the family."

Tears sprang into her eyes; but they were of nervous pleasure, and she bent to hide them, murmuring: "I think Millie is turning into a very handsome woman, don't you? But then, every age seems to become her—I don't remember her ever to have gone through an awkward stage."

"She's in one now," he said firmly. "That's why I'm here—you and I have got to help her, and she won't like it."

"Oh, I don't think we—"

"On her own terms, auntie. That's the only way Millie can be helped. I don't know why it's taken me so long to realize that."

He was up again, too restless to be still, and she made no attempt to interrupt him.

"All these years we've been urging her to do our sort of thing," he went on. "Lou trying to get her down to New York, and me trying to make a visiting cousin out of her. Even that trip abroad. Of course she wasn't interested in any of it! She's had her own purpose all the time, auntie—and oddly enough, I think it's exactly the one Grandfather Onderdonk must have had in mind when he tied this place up. To wait for somebody like Millie. Only she was a girl; and there was already MacDonald."

"I'm sure Millie has always had a strong sense of purpose, dear—and she did enjoy her trip, you know. I don't know why she says she didn't, after all this time!"

He saw that he had lost his aunt somewhere.

"Well, never mind," he said, "all that's past. All of it. Even if we could sweep MacDonald out tomorrow, the place stinks of him—it's his. She's turned against it. She looked a long time for what ought to have been her life—ought to have been here; but it didn't work out for her. Maybe she went about it wrong, or maybe she was wrong to begin with—but whatever it is, she's had all she can take, auntie. We've got to get her out of it."

Aunt Cora knew when to be quiet, whether she understood or not. She was quiet now. He sat down again and took her hands.

"It seems very soon to be asking you to go against uncle's wishes," he said. "It is very soon. But I know—believe me, dear—it can't be too soon for Millie. And I don't know that it actually is against his wishes, you know. He had got into a certain habit of living, and it lasted as long as he needed it—but it isn't necessary to him or to anyone any longer."

"Is it about the funds?" said Aunt Cora at this point.

He looked at her with relief.

"Yes."

"But that's going to be all right, dear! I thought Millie would have told you—she said you knew …?" She went on hastily, "We heard from Mr. Leach yesterday, and he's got hold of Uncle John's little girl—only she isn't a little girl now, of course. Polly, it was her *son* who answered—isn't that incredible?"

He was incapable of a word.

"You did frighten me," she said then, softening to his expression. "I couldn't make out at first what you meant, except that you must be against it—Millie being so angry, you know—and I just couldn't think what to do. You *aren't* against it, are you?"

"No, dear."

"I'm so glad. It is sad about your little house, Polly—I just don't understand why it never occurred to any of us that your Aunt Millicent ought to adopt you legally. I suppose you seemed so much ours already … But we're going to keep this house, you know—Millie promised me that—and this is your real home, of course. Always, dear."

"When did Millie ask you, Aunt Cora?"

"Why it just came up, I think. One night when Millie and I were talking about—how our life would be changed, now. And about how there was really no one left, for all this ..."

"I wanted to ask for our money a long time ago," she said presently. "Did you know that, Polly? After Uncle John died, and the girls were at a rather restless time of their lives. Out of school, you know, and needing to get out and do things, like other girls. And then the town boys used to always be round the estate in those days—swimming, and picnicking, and so on, and your uncle didn't like it at all, but they were the only boys there were ... But your uncle was always so level-headed. Even then he realized it was just a phase, and that it would be wrong to destroy the girls' real security just for a passing phase. And of course he was right—Louisa went off to her books, and Millie had her trip and settled down very nicely when she came home, and we were so glad we hadn't done anything foolish.

"Darling, you are sad about this," she said; and touched his hair. "Confess—I can see you are. I'll tell you a secret, so am I. Just a little. It has been our dear home for such a long time, hasn't it?"

"Yes. A long time."

"I'm glad Cressa is old enough to remember. Do you think she will?"

"Oh, Cressa remembers everything, don't worry."

"Yes—she's so intelligent. Just the way you were, dear. And she's like you in another way, she has your loving heart. No, now don't go away, Polly—you never let me say anything, but I think you might—just today, when we're saying everything!"

Her spirits were rising, perhaps only because she had been able to confess to being "a little sad," and he was touched by his aunt's simplicity of spirit. It was true that it might have been better for them all if she were not, always, so easily persuaded and made content—but it was hardly his place to think so, who had disappointed her only two hopes for him: that he should finish his medical training, and marry Millie.

He managed to answer her coaxing smile.

"We couldn't begin to say 'everything' in a day. Or a month of days."

"No, we really couldn't. But I'll tell you something else, that's just come to me. Not to talk about, you know. But I don't believe Millie is angry with us at all! I think she feels just as badly as we do, about the estate, you know—but she feels she ought to do it, and she will. She's like her father that way—they never could speak out the way we do, poor dears."

"What does Millie plan to do afterwards?" he asked. "Do you have any idea? Has she said anything to you?"

But his aunt had no idea, and no real concern. Whatever Millie decided to do would be the right thing.

He ran into his cousin later, on the stairs; and while she said "Hello, Polly," in a normal voice he was aware that, for any real approach, he might as well have been back in Indiana. This was Phase Two of Millie's anger, and could last indefinitely.

"Are you looking for me?" she said, pausing.

"Well, yes, in a way. Would you take Jenny home today? I'd like to go on down to my place."

"Jenny's not here."

"Oh," he said. "But I thought I saw her."

"Well, you may have—she came by to say she wasn't coming. I suppose she thought that was more polite than calling up."

"Nothing wrong at the farm?"

"She didn't say so," said Millie, going on upward.

He walked home. The road was hot in mid-morning sun, its shade-border already too narrow to be of use. MacDonald's men were haying in the long field which bordered the State road; and he realized that the sound had been pleasantly in his head all morning without reaching a level of consciousness. So much of living here—the whole routine, in fact—was made of these mild recognitions: a series of them, changing with the changing year and then coming round to begin over again. Ideally, he supposed, this ought to leave the mind quieted and free for larger thought; and perhaps this had been Grandfather Onderdonk's hope in establishing (not to say enforcing) the life of the estate. But it seemed that only birds, and skunks and raccoons, knew how to profit from sanctuary. Human beings turned restless and went away, or stayed and turned ... fretful, at least.

Perhaps that was what was the matter with him. Just turning into a nag in his old age. He found the idea oddly comforting, as a rest from the underlying uneasiness he lived with these days—and a way of acknowledging it, too. It was further comfort to come into his clearing and find Cressa cleaning up the last of the raccoon's mess.

She gave him a stare of conscious virtue, and he allowed that. But when she added severely, "You didn't clean up the kitchen, either," he slapped her rump.

"You do it. I'm going swimming."

He caught his suit off the line and strode away again, at a pace that would allow her to catch up, panting, about halfway to the road.

CHAPTER TEN

Mr. Leach, Aunt Cora's lawyer, came over to see them the following week. He was an elderly man from Aunt Cora's home town, farther up the Hudson, who had handled her small inheritance ever since she received it and sent her the modest dividends on which, to a great extent, their household economy depended. He seemed pleased, even gravely stimulated, by the possible upheaval ahead; but Dr. Potter suspected that without Millie (or without Pete, to be exact) it would no more have occurred to him than to themselves to defy Uncle Humphrey. At least, not so quickly.

Certainly there was no real reason for him to come in person this time, except for the pleasure of giving importance to his message: which was just that Uncle John's grandson, entirely friendly, wanted to come and see them.

Aunt Cora made an occasion of Mr. Leach's visit—using the dining room for luncheon, summoning Lou home a day early, sending Cressa over to Jenny for a while. ("Children are upset by talk about changes, you know, dear".) Both she and Mr. Leach glowed with solemn pleasure, as if they had planned and would carry out great maneuvers—for an indifferent Lou, and a tired Millie.

Mr. Leach liked to go over and over his ground, and embellish it.

"Now I gather that this young man feels a little doubtful, about whether or not he would be entirely welcome here. You understand he doesn't actually say this—but in writing to me, and putting it to me to put it to you, I think he's showing a very nice tact. Just in case he might not be entirely welcome, you know."

"But he is!" Aunt Cora cried; and a little flush came up in her face. "He's more than welcome, Mr. Leach, and you must tell him so! Surely he knows there isn't any quarrel—there isn't even any reserve about Uncle John's family, not on our side!"

"They were the ones who didn't answer," Louisa remarked.

"Yes, exactly," said Mr. Leach. "And I think that is where he is showing such nice tact, you see. In case any offence—any quite justifiable offence had been taken. Here, you know. Because of his family's failure to respond."

"Oh, what nonsense, Mr. Leach! I'm going to write to him," said Aunt Cora, looking as if she meant to go and do it at once. "You can enclose it in your letter. I'll tell him myself that we're *longing* to see him—then he won't wonder about it!"

"Mr. Leach," said Millie. Still smiling, he turned to her; she waited until he did. "Are you sure that he does quite understand what we want to do?"

"Why, he seems to, Millie. In fact he seems to have a very good general grasp of—investment principle in general. I meant to read his letter to you, but I'm afraid I've left it behind. I think I did look through my briefcase, in the other room, just before we—?"

"Yes, you did," said Louisa, rather coldly. "Millie helped you."

"I have the gist of it in my head, of course, but it was a very good letter, I thought. Very well expressed for so young a man. He is still in college, you know. In fact, he says that it is only this year that he has become empowered to deal with these affairs—which probably means that he has just turned twenty-one, you know—but he makes it clear that he has been trained, actively trained for many years, in handling his own and his mother's affairs. Trained by his grandmother, he says. That would be the former Mrs. John Onderdonk, of course. Perhaps you remember her, Cora."

"Oh, so well! And I remember being so very sorry when that one didn't work out either, because she came to see Long Acre, and she seemed to like it. It would have been so pleasant, all these years, to have had John's family there," she said wistfully.

"Well, well, perhaps you will yet," said Mr. Leach comfortingly.

"I should have liked so much to see the letter," said Millie, smiling. "Perhaps you wouldn't mind sending it to us? Would it be a great bother for you to send us copies of all the letters that go back and forth between you, Mr. Leach? We get so confused when you aren't here to help us," she said charmingly, "and you can't be coming all this way very often."

Dr. Potter suddenly cleared his throat, and Louisa looked at him; but he had no message for her. Mr. Leach, pleased, was saying that on the contrary he considered it a pleasure as well as a duty to come to clients who were such old friends, and especially when they found themselves on the brink of such a long and serious undertaking. Aunt Cora, still thoughtful, reclaimed him then by saying:

"I don't think she can have been so very angry with poor Johnny, if she has got her boy wearing the same name. Do you? And that O. must be for Onderdonk. Don't you think so?"

"Well, that will be one of the things you will be able to ask the young man, if he should come. Or perhaps the good lady herself, who knows?"

"I wish you would send us the letters," said Louisa suddenly. "The copies, I mean. I'm not here much, and I'd like to see them."

There was a pause, not awkward. Anyone used to the house was accustomed to Louisa's habit of entering anywhere into conversations; it was something allowed to her, on account of her shyness. Mr. Leach said kindly, "Then you shall have them, Louisa"; and she said, "All of them? The back ones, too?" and he agreed, as to a child, "The back ones too, most certainly."

There was another pause in which the sisters—the cousins—did not look at each other: one of their many forms of complicity, and involuntary by now, Dr. Potter perceived.

Louisa then pointed the way back, by saying, slightly impatient: "It isn't her 'boy', mother—it's her grand-boy, if you like. Maybe his mother named him. Or is she dead?"

"No, no, not at all. The young man specifically mentions her—explains, in fact, that he handles her affairs for her—with his grandmother, I presume—because she is at present resident in Italy. I would judge," he said delicately, "from the dissimilarity in name, that his mother has remarried. He refers to her as the 'countess' something—I'm afraid the name itself escapes me."

"Well, it will be in the letter you'll send us," said Louisa. "You will send it, won't you?"

There were limits even for Louisa. Millie said quickly, "Of course he will, Lou—Mr. Leach never forgets anything we ask him."

Mr. Leach said he tried not to; and it being clear by now that copies of his correspondence with Chicago were well hammered into his head, Louisa abandoned him.

The increasing melancholy of Dr. Potter must have come to his aunt's attention, then, for she turned to him.

"Don't you think it'll be nice to see Uncle John's boy, dear?" she asked, like a conciliation. (Poor Polly, about to lose his little house.)

"Yes," he said; and made an effort. "You ought to dig out your old photographs to show him."

Bullseye. Relieved at once of his aunt's attention (she seemed again about to leave the table) he found it had only exchanged it for Millicent's. She spoke with affectionate teasing; it seemed genuine.

"Polly's seeing it as a big chore," she said. "He always gets stuck with the men visitors."

"No, I'd like to see him," he said, stubborn. "Maybe he's a throwback to Grandfather Onderdonk—who knows?"

"I wish he had sent a picture!" said Aunt Cora. "But I suppose he thought it might be forward."

Now Louisa was examining her cousin.

"You are going to help with him, aren't you, Polly?" she demanded.

"Gladly, if I'm here, Lou."

"Oh, he'll come long before you have to go away, dear. Don't you think so?" his aunt appealed to Mr. Leach.

Louisa still wasn't satisfied. She said, under the elders' talk: "What do you mean? You're not leaving early this year, are you?"

"I haven't got any definite plans, Lou."

She stared, and then said: "I'll walk over to the farm with you, after lunch."

"All right."

Millie, bringing in coffee, caught his eye. He looked away, but she said firmly: "Polly? Come help me a minute."

Out of the room she put her hand on his arm. He saw that her easy manner to him at luncheon had been genuine, and their estrangement was mysteriously over.

"Go on," she said, "you don't have to stand any more of this. I'll say I asked you to go somewhere."

"Nonsense. I'm not suffering."

But she continued to smile at him, all olive branch; and he muttered: "I only want to get Cressa. She probably imagines she's missing a real party."

"Then go ahead, dear."

"Lou wants to walk over with me."

"Lou wants to tease secrets out of you," she said, indulgent. "Go on."

"Well. I'll take the car, and bring Cressa back to say hello."

"Yes, do that. Just put in an appearance, and then you can really ditch us. I imagine old Peachy will stay forever." All over; all mended. Back to where they were.

Yet as he drove away he felt nothing—no relief, nor any irritation. It was as though some vital part of him were so engrossed that it had no attention left for small occurrences. Either that, or the weather was due to break on MacDonald's hay—and without ill will, he hoped it was the latter.

CHAPTER ELEVEN

The first rapid return to normalcy, which had startled Dr. Potter at the time, went right on without slackening. The hay was cut, the linen mended, and Hall and home farm run on their usual routines—but in some total vacuity that made him increasingly uneasy. When he noticed Cressa becoming affected by it too, he saw that his feelings had cause.

From being a person of enormous busyness, racing through crowded days, she was dwindling to a little girl with nothing to do, and a tendency to cling to him. Even that didn't work; for while they could quite happily have idled their time away together anywhere else, they had here a sense of being fugitives. Of ducking obligation. For Cressa's new idleness did not come from being unwanted on the estate. It came from being too much wanted, by all of them. Clutched at.

Even MacDonald, to keep her, would leave what he was doing and offer special treats—would bring the old horse out and walk him round and round, holding Cressa on his back and looking up at her with steady attention. ("D'you like that, lassie? D'you like that, now?" And Cressa, desperately polite: "Oh, yes ... thank you, MacDonald ..." Dr. Potter, coming on this scene, thought it one of the saddest he had ever seen.)

From being a privileged observer in this little world, that had ticked so busily of itself, his daughter had become more like a mainspring. It was too much to ask of her, and she felt that it was.

To Vinnie, one morning, he said: "All that business I was worried about—the first days, and the funerals—turned out very well, actually. But it's this backwash, or whatever it is, I don't like. I think I'll take her away for a while."

"What do they do?" said Vinnie, interested.

"Well, nothing, specially. Just a general impression they'd like to sit holding her in their laps all day."

"Not *Millie?*"

"No ... I thought we might go to the Hoffmanns' for a while—you remember him, in Humanities. Her people live out on the Island, and they make a big thing every year of how we must come and stay, so I thought we might do it. They've got a great big place, and there are other kids. You used to like them both," he said, when she didn't answer. "Don't you remember?"

"Yes, I remember."

"Well," he said, "what about it, then?"

She said, "I hate to think of you both just wandering around like that, Paul. Just because you can't stay there."

"Of course we could stay here—and we're not wandering! This is a side trip."

"Besides, they probably think I'm subhuman. The Hoffmanns."

"If you think that, you don't remember them at all, Vinnie."

She didn't answer. He sighed, and said: "Well, think it over, and call me back pretty soon, will you?"

"No, that's silly," she said quickly. "No, wait … I don't want you hanging around in that drugstore—"

"I'm not in the drugstore, it's all right."

"You mean you're sitting there in the *hall?* The way sound goes up those *stairs?*"

"Vinnie, I'm not plotting anything! Listen, think it over, and call me."

"No—Paul, I was thinking about this anyway, and it's a much better plan than you and Cressa wandering around visiting people, when we could all go to Mexico instead! There—I mean it, we really could. I've saved everything you send for *months*, and Aunt Millicent's dividend checks, and there's plenty! And I can take a whole month off because I could come back with ideas, and I didn't take any vacation at all yet because I thought … I was going to suggest it before, and then I was afraid you'd think I was trying to do them out of having Cressa there, or that I didn't want her to go. But if you're just going someplace *anyway*," she said, breathless, "why not Mexico?"

It was their old dream, back in the days of Vinnie's growing need for some escape, and liveliness, and color. He had shared it, out of some need of his own. Out of impossibility it had turned into a joke (Oh, sure—as soon as we get to Mexico) and then to silence. And now here it was revived, bigger and realer than ever, like some old movie blown up and wildly colored and blaring with sound. The Potters' trip to Mexico!

He didn't know he was angry until he began to speak—and even then, not quite why.

"I see," he said. "Well, that's quite a surprise, Vinnie. So we get to Mexico after all, do we?"

"Well," she said, warned by his voice, "we could—if you want to."

"Well, I don't think I do," he said pleasantly. "The price seems a little high—two years of separation for a jolly month in Mexico. Besides, do you think it's decent? Are we supposed to have separate rooms, or what?"

She was entirely still. He knew exactly how she looked. He was hurting her, hurting himself, and had to stop.

"I think we'd better just go and see the Hoffmanns," he said. "I'll write to you when we leave, and when we get back. Goodbye, Vinnie."

There was no sound of her receiver going down, although his descending hand was slow, and the hall was very quiet.

That night after Cressa had gone to bed he wrote Vinnie what he meant to be a more adult answer.

"There is no use in our trying these part-time arrangements, Vinnie. If we are essentially apart, then brief meetings are only going to confuse and sadden us. This is true for you as well as me, however you imagine the trip would be. Because what you have in mind is only a part of something that used to exist, and would be meaningless without the rest."

After a time, dissatisfied, he added: "Unless you want this trip to be a beginning. But since you speak of going back to your job, I did not understand that you meant that."

He sat a long time over the paper, but wrote no more. He was not going to hold out any lures: the tentative offers from Toronto, and the Coast—either offering more money, more rank, and a large and cosmopolitan center in which Vinnie could find a place for her own work if she still liked. No; if she came back it must be to him. It was himself, mainly, that she had left; he understood that, if she did not.

Later still, he went out roaming along the still and private dark roads of the estate. There was a quarter-moon and clear starlight—the weather held, as of course it would if MacDonald said so; and he carried his flashlight unused at his side. He made obliquely for Lake Millicent, as they always did on night walks, and found his cousin Millicent already there.

She had been in the water and was now wrapped in long toweling, sitting at the end of the dock and dangling her feet in the water. Her long hair was down and gave her, in that colorless dark air, the look of some medieval lady. Boethius' Lady, perhaps.

"You look capable of saying something wise, Millie," he said, settling beside her. "Why don't you? We could use it."

But all she said was: "Are you really going away?" He began, not comfortably, to explain about the Hoffmanns; she broke in before he got very far.

"I wish you would stay while this boy is here. He's coming quite soon, I feel sure, and he can't mean to stay very long. Couldn't you put your visit off till he's gone?"

"I suppose so, Millie. But why? He isn't coming to make any trouble—if he meant to do that, he would keep all the communicating between lawyers. It's a very good sign that he wants to come, you know. Excessively amiable, if anything."

"I don't want his excessive amiability," she said, not smiling. "I don't want him to come at all. Why should he? What can some strange boy want with us—an old woman, and two middle-aged spinsters! Why does he want to come? What does he expect?"

"Probably nothing. At that age people are just full of general curiosity—and the energy to satisfy it. Or maybe his grandmother is the curious one, and is sending him."

"She has no right to be curious, she gave up that right a long time ago! And *he* has no right to come here and inspect us, either—as if we were a zoo! Vanishing Onderdonks," she said bitterly. "Come see them while they last."

He was reminded of Louisa, at the zoo, innocently thinking that "the camels look rather like us." But it was no time for old family jokes.

He said bluntly, "He has every right to come here, Millie. Half the place belongs to him—or to his mother."

"No one disputes that. Let them have it. Although it's perfectly absurd," she said more quietly, "that some idiotic woman in Italy gets half of all we have, and you nothing." She turned to him then, almost herself again. "But I want you to know that Lou and I are both making wills in your favor. At least we can do that. Mr. Leach has taken the instructions back with him, if he doesn't lose them on the way. It probably won't mean much to you, Polly, since we keep our useless lives so long, but it will to Cressa. And to Lou and me," she said touching his hand. "It will still be some sort of bond between the three of us, when everything else is gone."

He looked at her in astonishment; but she clearly meant this, and drew comfort from it.

"Well, that's a very nice gesture, Millie," he said; and cleared his throat. "Let's not take it too seriously, though. Both you and Lou may very well marry, now. There's no reason why you shouldn't have children, for that matter."

Inattentive to his words, but looking at him still, she made no reply. Then he felt a little shudder go through her body, and she withdrew her hand.

"Let's start back. Unless you want a swim?"

He didn't. On the grass, she slid her long feet into their old moccasins and then, taking his arm, paced down the road beside him. The long toweling-cape moved round her as she moved; her loose hair drifted; she seemed almost serene.

"I can see, in a way, why my father left this whole tangle alone," she said. "Legalities are a very special kind of confusion, aren't they? Imagine a way of looking at us where you don't belong at all, and this woman in Italy does! Not to mention her energetic little boy."

"Are you beginning to regret this?"

"Regret?" She took a while to answer. "No. I think regret implies some choice, some wrong choice. I've never felt we had choices, Polly, any of us. Not even you, dear—not even the famous medical school disaster! Given who we were, and what we were, the things that happen to us seem to me inevitable. Even Pete," she said, regarding him steadily, "is probably inevitable, at a particular stage of decay."

"I think what you are expressing is masked regret, just the same," he said stubbornly. "And I think you had better take your own advice to Lou, and be sure what you're giving up before you go ahead anymore."

She only smiled at him—impervious to this sort of advice. But quieter, at least, for having spoken out. And there was no one else to whom she could speak in this way, not even Lou.

They parted where their roads diverged, and she said no more to him about staying for young John's visit—apparently taking for granted that he would stay. He, who meant to leave all the same, said nothing either.

But as it turned out, he was there. Their new cousin arrived the next morning. In a Thunderbird, said Pete, who had been asked to stop by and tell Dr. Potter on his way to the garage.

"You better get up there, Doc," he said. "They're going to need you; this is some high-powered boy, I seen his kind before."

He looked as if he would like to stay himself—watchful from the background, in the interests of his garage. Dr. Potter said briefly that he would come when he could.

"Want a ride up? I can hang around a little while."

"No. Thanks. Go on, Pete."

But when Pete had gone, he hurried—or told Cressa about the new arrival, which came to the same thing, since she gave him no peace until they were on their way up to the Hall. A week ago she would have gone by herself; but now, when they came in sight of the advertised Thunderbird, she pushed her hand into his. The way Vinnie used to do, when they came visiting here.

He said, as he had said then, "We won't stay long"; but she looked blankly at him—a little as her mother might have done; and he gave her hand a squeeze as they went in.

CHAPTER TWELVE

John O. Watson (the "O." *was* for Onderdonk) had the true family "camel" look—tall, remote and sandy. Aunt Cora, in a daze of joy, declared him to be the image of his grandfather. Nothing in the cousins' memory or in the family photographs bore this out, but John said his grandmother had noticed some likeness, and seemed content to have it confirmed.

He was a very serious young man. No undergraduate in Dr. Potter's experience could approach those dancing school manners (he said most of his schooling had been in Europe) or the profound and serious innocence underlying them. He was a ready conversationalist, and had the equally ready smile of good social training: his large white teeth looked as if the orthodontic bands had just come off. Cressa fell in love with him instantly. Her father could see that the Hoffmanns were out of the question as long as John O. Watson remained.

How long this would be was left unsettled. Aunt Cora was ready to keep him forever; and now that he was here, Millie seemed to accept him quietly enough—even with some amusement. Whatever contemptuous and scornful young relative she had imagined, he was no relative to John O. Lou, of course, wouldn't care one way or the other, so long as Millie didn't.

On the whole, Dr. Potter felt considerable relief—and some interest, too. He had seldom met anyone so minutely explicit, yet within the bounds of good manners; for John O. Watson clearly conceived his first duty to be the clearing up of the family misunderstanding. He managed to explain his grandmother's behavior to them without in any way diminishing her personality—an admirable one, to her grandson. It would seem that the second (or third?) Mrs. Onderdonk had continued to live as though her marriage had endured, never considering remarriage and devoting her life to her child and grandchild, and the management of their affairs. She was still, said John O., very active in this way. But being a woman of strong and lasting feelings, she had not been able to bear reminders of the failed marriage and had allowed her own connection with the family to lapse. Entirely without bitterness, however, said John O.—the family name was kept, and he and his mother were entirely free to do as they liked about the connection. (The former Mrs. Watson didn't seem to come into the explanation very much.) His grandmother had even gone to Rhodes and given her husband a proper funeral when he died, as perhaps Aunt Cora didn't know. (What about the incumbent Mrs. O.? said the cousins' glances to each other. Nothing, obviously. Paid off, if poor, or swept into the sea.)

Aunt Cora hadn't known this; and forgave any amount of silence to hear of Johnny's nice funeral. She wished so much that Uncle Humphrey might have known, too ... and that John O. could have come a little sooner ...

"You know how it happened, of course, dear. Just leaning to poke the frog, the way he used to do, and that treacherous knee ..."

John O. wished he had come sooner, too. He had always, he went on presently, set the year of his majority as the time in which he would like to visit his Onderdonk connections. But he had come of age only that June, and it had been a rather busy summer ... He came to his first dead stop, noticeably. (A girl, said the cousins' looks. Good. Won't stay so long.)

Recovering, John O. apologized again for his sudden arrival—but his aunt's letter had been so warm, and he had felt sure she would excuse his just jumping in the car and taking off, since he happened to be rather near anyway ...

She did, she did.

Cressa was leaning very heavily on the new cousin's shoulder, passionately examining, it seemed, his left ear; she had already been dislodged twice by her father.

Dr. Potter felt that all this was enough, for a while, and got up.

"Well, let's go round a little, if Aunt Cora can spare you," he said. "Or do you want to come, auntie?"

She hesitated, wanting, she said, to show Long Acre to John herself. Not wanting to get too tired, and miss the rest of this lovely day ... There were family signals, which John O. was as quick to notice as any of the family, and discreetly backed. Perhaps just a quick look round, now, while his aunt rested?

"Well, be sure to go to MacDonald first, then," said Aunt Cora. "I know he'll be waiting to see you."

The two men went off in the Thunderbird, with Cressa, who made a rather oppressive third. John O. had hit on "Sir" for Dr. Potter, as appropriate to any relationship, and Dr. Potter was tiring of it.

"You had better say 'Paul,' John, he said, whizzing over the familiar roads at an unfamiliar angle. "We're not really cousins, but that won't save you, here. I am the son of your great-aunt Millicent's husband, in case you are wondering where all these Potters come from."

"Not at all, s—Paul, and thanks very much," said John O., earnestly. "I'm awfully glad you're here now—I expect you know the place inside out. You practically grew up here, didn't you?"

"Not very practically, no," said Dr. Potter—overruled by Cressa's instant, indignant: "Daddy, you did! You *lived* here, when you were a little boy!"

"Yes, I know, Cressa," said John O., "and there can't be many nicer places for growing up in. I hope you'll do a lot of your growing up here."

"Turn up here, John—here!" she cried, since her father seemed to have forgotten; and the Thunderbird in an easy swerve slid up to the home farm and stopped.

MacDonald, who must have been hovering just inside the door, came instantly and massively into view; Aunt Cora had warned him, of course.

Aunt Cora was affected by many things, and her tearful, exciting welcome of Johnny's boy had not seemed out of her proportion. But the effect of him on MacDonald was thunderous. It produced a MacDonald whom Dr. Potter barely recognized—standing there clutching his own great red hands as if he did not know what to do with them and staring with as much reverence as if the young man in front of him wore a halo. (More, since his bare-bones Scots religion did not hold with any popery.)

"This is MacDonald, John," said Dr. Potter, "who ran the place under your great-grandfather, and still does. And here is John Onderdonk's grandson, MacDonald—John Watson."

They both knew, already, although they heard him out; and the young man was obviously determined to get one of those great hands and wring it. He succeeded; he said warmly that he had looked forward to this for many years, that it was a great pleasure to meet MacDonald at last. MacDonald looked as if he were receiving blows upon the head instead of words.

"Muster John ... Muster John ... welcome home, sir," he stammered, the prepared words falling out first. And then: "Ye knew about us, lad? Ye knew of us all the while?"

"Of course I did, MacDonald."

"*Then why did ye no' coom?*"

There was no need for Dr. Potter to intervene. John O. was pleasantly explaining how he had lived abroad a great deal, and in Chicago with his grandmother, but that it had always been his intention to come when he took control of his own affairs—as he had now done. Cressa had clearly never heard anything so grand as this statement, and listened soundless. MacDonald showed much the same reaction.

"Aye," he mumbled. "Aye. Ye meant to coom all the while, then?"

"Of course."

"I never knew of it," said MacDonald simply, and regained his dignity. "Wull, now you're here, Muster John, and that's enough. You'll find all in good order," he said, "like your great-grandfather left it, and meant it to be."

John O. said he was sure of that, and MacDonald began to show signs of total recovery.

"You'll want to go round, and I'm ready to take you," he said. "No doubt you'll want to begin with your own house. I've sent the men down to open it up, you won't mind if it's a bit musty at the first—you'll find it in good repair generally speaking, though there's things I'd like to go over with you."

"I think not now, MacDonald," Dr. Potter interrupted firmly. "Mrs. Onderdonk is going to take us over later, after lunch. You wouldn't like a fast swim, would you, John?"

He was a quick boy at the signals, John O. Otherwise it was quite probable they wouldn't have got away. MacDonald, lowering, was already turning to say, "Now, Paul—what do you want to rush Muster John round like some visitor for?"—when John O. stopped this by getting a hand again. A real tour later, he said, but for the moment just a quick look round, and it was splendid to know MacDonald at last—really splendid.

"When will you come?" said MacDonald, defeated but dogged.

As soon as he could, said John O., he would send word ahead. They got back in the Thunderbird with no more trouble and drove off, free.

"Neatly done," said Dr. Potter, rather warily. "None of us even attempts to handle MacDonald anymore."

"He's really splendid, isn't he? Just as I imagined him."

"When?" said Cressa. "When did you imagine MacDonald, John? And why does he call you 'Mr. John' and daddy just 'Paul'?"

"He hasn't known me so long," said John O. without any hesitation. Dr. Potter began to realize he had better get his summer-fuzzed wits into working order, and fast.

"I'd like very much to see your place, Paul," John O. went on, as they sped along. "I understand you've written most of your book there—is that right? We have it at school, you know, and it's used a lot."

"And we could change into our swimsuits!" said Cressa. "You can wear one of daddy's!"

Partly from the low car's rapidity, perhaps, Dr. Potter began to have the short-breathed feeling of one who is not going to catch up until the pace changes. His wariness increased; he began to bide his time, leaving the amenities to his daughter.

But when she, with new modesty, had shut herself into the bathroom to change, he came out to a silence he still wasn't prepared for. John O. was looking respectfully at the books. He didn't think it was too early for a small drink, and accepted one gladly.

Then he raised his glass.

"To a very important day," he said. "To me, at least."

"To us all, John."

"I can't tell you what it means, to find such a welcome here. It was the one thing I couldn't know—and to tell the truth, I guess I've been putting off finding out."

"Yes, I understand. Of course you would know all about the place, I see that now. No doubt the bank has been reporting to you regularly all these years. I'm afraid we're not very practical people around here, John. You'll have to give us time to catch up."

"All the time in the world," he said warmly.

Dr. Potter got up and went into the bedroom. His daughter was softly calling to him.

"Please do my hair!" she said anxiously. He saw that she had been trying, without success.

He looked at her a moment.

"I'll tell you what, Cressa," he said. "I think you had better run up to the Hall and get it done right—and also ask if they would like to come to the lake with us. We mustn't be rude," he said, to her opening lips. "Now run ahead—we'll pick you up there. Go out the other door, then John won't see you till you are fixed."

That decided it. Dr. Potter came back and sat down to his drink again.

He said, "I'm also beginning to understand that you and your grandmother have been extremely forbearing all these years. After all, a considerable sum must be lying around here, half of it yours—and I don't see that you can have received anything from it at all."

"We haven't felt that way, sir," said John O., for some reason slightly embarrassed. "I think my grandmother has always felt that the estate made a good long-term investment, if nothing else. But mainly I—we both know that something is being preserved here that—no amount of financial return could replace."

He was really turning pink.

"How do you mean, John?" said Dr. Potter, determined to know the worst.

"Well, I think you would have to know a little more about us to understand what I mean ... Actually, I'm hoping we can all—that pretty soon we'll all feel we know each other well enough to talk over everything we haven't had a chance to talk over, all these years."

"Yes," said Dr. Potter. "Well, your aunt is already totally receptive, John, and I'm sure your cousins will be. I don't mean that they are any less glad to see you, but at the moment they're almost totally bound up in the prospect of having a decent income for the first time in their lives. They've had a pretty thin time of it here, I don't know whether you knew that or not."

But of course he did; and the embarrassment of that secret knowledge was very apparent.

"My grandmother has always admired the way Uncle Humphrey stuck it out here," he said. "I guess you must think it strange that she didn't ever offer—some kind of help," he went on, turning pinker. "But it wouldn't have been easy, you know, with—with things the way they were. And because my grandmother has so much, uh, dignity herself, she's naturally very careful not to offend other people's pride. Uh, dignity."

"And a very sound feeling. Poor people's dignity often turns to sheer pride, I'm afraid."

"Yes," said John O. "I mean, I suppose it does."

He was beginning to look uncertain, for the first time, which was the most Dr. Potter had hoped for at the moment. Warned, and offering counter-warning, he felt that anything more would have to wait.

"Well, come on," he said. "Let's pick up our passengers and go swim in your great-grandmother's lake."

He meant this as a lighter end to their more serious exchange; but John O. didn't receive it lightly. His uncertainty disappeared, and his look of beginning doubt. This actual, ancestral lake was no doubt more real to him still than the possible problems of cousins, and more important. Dr. Potter thought it might do him good to get into it at last, and find out about those icy springs. Which, of course, might not bother him in the least.

CHAPTER THIRTEEN

It was hard to tell just when John O. became an enemy to Millicent. In spite of her first seeming acceptance, she might never have considered him as anything else. But she allowed him the time to declare himself, if he would.

They saw little of each other that first day. Millie didn't come to swim with them because of luncheon preparations, and she was in and out of the room too much during that meal (Louisa being in New York again) to take much part in the talk. Afterwards there was the clearing away and washing up, so she didn't come down to Long Acre with the rest of them. She could perfectly well have left the work till later, even if Jenny couldn't come; but Dr. Potter saw that she did not mean to, and persuaded his aunt to let her have her way. Aunt Cora was quite vexed with her, she said.

She had some reason. Millie, drudging away always, never looked or seemed the drudge as she did on that first day. Did she want to make it clear right away what her life was like? What it was that she did not mean to endure any longer, whatever John O. Watson meant by coming here? It seemed a more petty approach than Dr. Potter would have expected from her; and yet ... when they returned, she was polishing silver in a soiled apron with a strand of hair hanging over her pale face.

"Really, Millie!" said Aunt Cora, unhappily. She meant, We do our drudging *privately*, dear.

It was all wasted, too. Wary of his cousin, Dr. Potter had turned John O. over to MacDonald on the way back—and that wouldn't break up quickly. Besides, however much truth there was to Millie's pantomiming, he felt out of sympathy with his cousin just then. There had been something very touching about John O.'s introduction to Long Acre, and its effect upon him.

That goblin-mansion of their childhood, occupying the high heart of the estate, had somehow come to life for the first time in this visit. They had all seen it open and airing before, of course, and made the tour of the swathed and sheeted rooms, and sneaked in for goose-pimply games. But none of them had considered it as a real home, past or future, or had any tender feelings for it: not even Aunt Cora, who had echoed her husband's helpless dislike for his father, and consequent distaste for his home.

But John O., innocent of personalities, dreamed only in terms of generations. "My great-grandfather's house," he said, standing in the main hall.

"And your grandfather's, dear, for many years," Aunt Cora reminded him. "He grew up here, he and your Uncle Humphrey. And your Aunt Millicent."

The idea seemed more—and of more importance—than their descendant could grasp. He stood staring round as if this were all he could cope with, for one day, until Cressa grew restless.

"There's *lots* more, John," she said finally. "Don't you want to see it?"

He did; and let his aunt slowly, explicitly, begin to take him round. There was something very nice indeed about his reception of these really unappetizing rooms, in endless series. Too enclosed, too cluttered—with something at once heavy and mean in their narrow-windowed, heavily paneled and columned style, they offered no possible aesthetic joy to a contemporary eye and John O. pretended none. But neither did he show anything of disappointment or contempt. He might have been meeting the ancestors themselves, such gentleness and respect—and deep interest—did he show for every dreary detail.

"My grandmother always remembered this house," he said. "I think her life might have been very different if—if she had been able to spend it here."

"Oh, *all* our lives, dear!" Aunt Cora cried. "I've wished so often—your uncle could have told you how often I've wished that she were here!"

John O. said later, "This will probably seem very strange to you, Aunt Cora, but we have never really had a home."

"Oh, how can that be, dear?" she said, as upset as though he had confessed to sleeping in alleys.

(How indeed, thought Dr. Potter.)

"Well, my other great-grandparents built, of course, but in the city—and Chicago grew pretty rapidly, you know. By the time my grandmother came back," he said, delicate, "with my mother, the neighborhood had gone down too much for her to live in. She didn't feel she wanted a house while—while she was alone, so she took an apartment. And we've always lived in apartments, ever since. We still do."

"You mean the house is *quite* unfit to live in? Still?"

"It isn't even there," he said. "Hasn't been for years. There's an office building there now."

(Which you no doubt own, you sad case, you, thought Dr. Potter. He was still on Millie's side.)

"But surely when your mother grew up and married ..." said Aunt Cora; and grew delicate in her turn.

John O., looking stolid, said that his mother had had several houses (several husbands, translated Dr. Potter), but mostly in Europe. He had always thought of his grandmother's apartment as their real home.

"It's a very pleasant apartment," he admitted, pushing in a few stops, "and we've always had the same summer place, up at Bar Harbor—we're very fond of that, and mean to keep it. But for someone who values continuity, and tradition, the way my grandmother does, a place like this would have meant so much."

"Do you think it's too late for her to come here?" Aunt Cora suggested timidly. She was avoiding Dr. Potter's eye. He didn't care; he wasn't trying to catch hers.

"Oh, I think so, yes," said John O. "I doubt if she'd even visit, now. You know how people get past the time when things are possible to them, Aunt Cora. Even things they want."

"I do indeed," she agreed; and Dr. Potter looked at John O. with a new interest. Perhaps it was then that he began to waver.

But his point of transfer, he thought later, came when they had finished a first tour of the house and were pacing slowly round it, at John O.'s suggestion.

"I'm probably going to shock you now," he said suddenly, "but do you know what I can't help seeing when I look at this place? One story," he said, firm. "Just as it is, outwardly, except for doors and windows, of course. And with a big overhang roof. That interior could be really marvelous, with the same outline and different room arrangement—and then it would be an entirely practical place to live in for—for these times. And it would still," he said, "be Long Acre."

They all stood and looked at the great stone heap—John O. with his vision, Aunt Cora bewildered but trying, Cressa in some happy dream of destruction, no doubt. And Dr. Potter, with no possible architectural opinion, looked at the house and thought of the young man. No sentimentalist, after all. Nor grandmother's errand boy. A kind of reverent realist, then ...?

He cleared his throat; said, rather grumpily, "Probably cost more than a new house."

"About as much, I'd guess," John O. agreed. "But quite aside from everything else, that stone's worth it. They don't quarry like that anymore."

"In certain lights, it's very beautiful," Aunt Cora agreed. So far as she was concerned, it was clear, John O. could do as he liked. She didn't even like to remind him that other permission was necessary. What she said, finally, was: "Why don't you talk it over with MacDonald, dear? Before you really set your heart on it, you know."

"With MacDonald, auntie? But why?"

"Well, you know, the trustees set great store by what MacDonald says," she answered in a low voice; and a wave of color came up in her face.

More surprising, to Dr. Potter, was the answering slow blush of John O. He took time in answering—even placed an arm about her shoulders, before he spoke.

"But Aunt Cora—we are two-thirds of the trustees. Didn't you know that? Your family and—ours."

"Oh, yes, I know that your uncle ... But he didn't care to argue with the bank, you know. The bank," she repeated, in anxious warning.

"The bank is only there to help us, auntie. They're amenable to anything within reason, I promise you. And of course, the estate wouldn't be asked to bear any of the expense of this."

"Oh, yes, I see," said Aunt Cora. "But—I would just mention it to MacDonald first, John. I couldn't bear for you to be disappointed," she burst out, and then hurried away ahead of them.

Obviously she did not see—perhaps never would. Dr. Potter rather hoped not. He wasn't enjoying his own enlightenment. All these years of careful government, the excellent farm equipment, the prompt repairs, the inexplicable long tenderness to Long Acre ... these were not MacDonald's doing, nor the awful Bank's. In default of Uncle Humphrey's voice, which he refused to raise—or even admit that he possessed— they had lived all these years by the word of an old lady in Chicago. Who was holding the place for her own child.

Well. At least she had allowed Uncle Humphrey his fishpond.

Walking side by side with an equally quiet John O., Dr. Potter said without looking at him: "It's your cousin Millicent you'll have to settle these things with, you know. Not Aunt Cora."

"Yes, of course. I don't want to rush anything, though," he murmured. "And I would like to talk to you about it first, Paul. I want to go about it right."

What was the right way to go about the impossible?

"Don't waste time on me, John," he said, in sudden impatience. "Surely you understand none of it's up to me. And you must have known when you came here that you and your cousins want different things."

"But I'm not at all sure we do! Surely they don't want to leave the place? It's a matter of necessity with them, isn't it? And if that necessity didn't exist any longer ..."

"Your cousins aren't very likely objects of charity, John. No matter how well disguised."

"Lord, no! Paul, you must understand I wouldn't dream of a thing like that!"

There was no time for more, since they came then to the Onderdonk car with Aunt Cora sitting patiently in it. Less patiently, Cressa inhabited the Thunderbird. Dr. Potter climbed in the older car and apologized for his daughter—an unnecessary gesture.

"But she's going to the Farm with John—didn't you say she could, dear?"

She waved to them as they shot by (while Dr. Potter was still coaxing the older car to life). "Oh, what a happiness, to have young people here again! Isn't it, dear?"

She had apparently forgotten that he himself was not a contemporary of hers—appealed to him as if to another elder, to appreciate his successors. Well, he could; one of them was his child. But if he were Millie, or Lou, he was afraid he would be less content to have himself, his wishes and needs, so quickly set aside in favor of the bright new ones. To become forever "the reserves".

"Aunt Cora," he said. "Don't tell Millie about this Long Acre business, will you? After all, it's up to John to settle it with her. Let him do it."

"To settle it? Whatever do you mean, Polly?"

"I mean that Millie will have to agree," he said bluntly. "As I understand it, she is the new trustee."

"*Millie* is—? Oh, I think you must be mistaken, dear. And in any case," she said, "what difference does it make? If MacDonald and the bank are—"

"Listen, auntie—just let John tell her about it. As a matter of courtesy to him, if nothing else. Will you?"

There came, then, the rare voice of Aunt Cora offended.

"I don't think, Polly, I need to be reminded to be courteous!"

He had fixed that fine. No doubt she would have gone straight in and tackled Millie before she took her hat off, if the drudge-act hadn't been in operation. But that stopped her.

She was more distressed by her daughter's appearance than by anything he had said. Not because, he thought, her beautiful Millicent could look like that, but because she could allow herself to be seen looking like that.

"Millie," she said, struck to the heart. "*Really ...*"

The long eyes, rising, went past Aunt Cora and found Dr. Potter in the background. He said nothing; he was out of sympathy with her now. Of course she saw that. And of course it made no difference. Whatever was between them was so deep, so old, so tough, that the moment's sympathy or lack of it made no difference at all.

She said with equal indifference for them both: "Where is our new cousin?" And when she was told, went without comment back to her polishing. Dr. Potter left them at that point—Aunt Cora reproaching, Millie listening calmly. Passing time, he suspected, until her enemy should reappear. He had no doubt anymore about what she felt—was only surprised at his own naiveté in expecting her to feel anything else.

CHAPTER FOURTEEN

Directly after dinner that evening Dr. Potter took his child—his excuse—and left the Hall for his own place. He didn't intend to come back.

Dinner, rather late because MacDonald had hung on to his prize once he got it, had gone off in entire amity. Neither John O. nor his aunt mentioned any plan for Long Acre; the conversation fell into reminiscences and stayed there. And Cressa's chatter helped. So although Millie was almost constantly at table (Aunt Cora had insisted on Jenny tonight), nothing awkward happened. Dr. Potter could even see John O. falling under his cousin's quiet spell, trying to evoke that lovely small smile of hers, and triumphant when he got it.

She doesn't like you, you ass, he thought with despair. She hates your guts! Go home, Chicagoan, go home ...

But John O. felt himself to be at home. No matter how modest, he was young—he couldn't be blamed for relaxing and expanding under the double encouragement of his aunt and MacDonald, who had spent the whole day handing him the place on a platter. At most, Millicent must seem to offer only reserve, to a stranger's eye. No opposition—just the reserve you might expect from a woman of quiet temperament who led such a quiet life. Perhaps she would continue to show herself in the same way all evening, with the three of them—Aunt Cora, John O. and herself—sitting in the night shadows of the tulip tree. Dr. Potter didn't care to guess about it; neither did he intend to remain and see.

Yet alone in his own house he found no relief. Cressa was worn out from her lively day and fell asleep almost at once, so he might have gone back if he had wanted to. Quite soon, he reached the point where he almost did want to—just to be sure of what was happening, rather than to sit here wondering. Yet he did not go. Whether he liked it or not, whether he intended it or not, he would join that group—if he joined it at all—as Millie's ally. She would feel that he did. He was not going to add weight to whatever she meant to do.

But the pull was surprisingly strong.

Lying on his study couch, unable to read or sleep, he realized just how out of sympathy with Millie he was. As well as she did, he thought he understood the 'inevitability' of her life, and the long, secret defense of herself she had been forced to make. But all at once he was tired of it. There must have been other chances before this one, for her to yield a little, to fall in with some offered, genial plan that wasn't her own, but might have been better than the loneliness she had. She never yielded.

Whatever tactful juggling this boy had in mind, so that the Onderdonk ladies would end up with an income and their home as well, he was doomed to fail. To fail, or to fight—Dr. Potter couldn't yet guess which. All he could guess at was the slow disillusionment ahead for John O.

Watson, as he came to realize that his desire to pump new money, new blood into the Onderdonk Estate was being unconditionally refused. And himself with it.

Small sounds at the windscreen beside him drew Dr. Potter's attention outward for a moment. He listened the sounds came increasing and unmistakable: rain. MacDonald's weather was over.

And that group around the fishpond would have to break up now. He shut his window gratefully, went in to shut Cressa's and then made the rounds. Before he finished the rain was coming down hard and steady, drumming on every part of the little house. They would be having a nightcap up at the Hall now, preparing to separate for the night, since Millie wouldn't lose this chance the weather had given her. The boy—John O.—would be off Dr. Potter's mind for the rest of the night; he could forget about him until tomorrow.

Relaxing (and the tension had been considerable, he realized when it left him), Dr. Potter lay down again with a fresh drink and listened to the rain. He liked the sound for its own sake, too, because of the accumulated happy memories of rainy days within this room. Vinnie had loved them too. Because no one would expect them anywhere else on the estate, or would intrude upon them here. She said the house really seemed their own, on rainy days ...

The glass dipped in his hand. He set it down and turned off the light; and almost before his empty hand returned to place he fell asleep.

The hard crash of thunder woke him.

Or so he thought at first, lying dazed with the last reverberation in his ears. Then some other sound made him think "Cressa ..." and he was struggling up, groping for slippers, when he saw the woman in his door.

It was she who had made the sound. She made it again. He reached out for the lamp switch.

The sudden light made no difference to Jenny. She stood there clutching what looked like a man's coat around her—wet and windblown, limp hair plastered on cheeks and forehead. And bare feet.

He got up at once and came towards her.

"What is it, Jenny? What's wrong?"

"Oh, Mr. Paul—excuse me coming in," she said, a dreary whisper. "But you wouldn't hear—I tried."

"It's all right, Jenny. What is it?"

"Oh, it's father, please come back with me ... please come ..."

She began to cry, without any noise. He took her hands. "Your father's ill? Did you call Dr. Kennedy?"

"Oh, I don't know what's wrong with him," she wept. "He sits there like a dead man, he doesn't say a word—she'll kill him, I know she will! She's like a crazy woman, Mr. Paul—please come and make her go away—"

He stood still a moment, feeling some anonymous hard pulse in their clasping hands. Then he said: "Listen Jenny—you stay here. In case

Cressa wakes up. Go in the bathroom and dry off, wear my dressing gown. Here. And Jenny," he waited till she looked at him, and added, emphatic: "Tell her your father's not well and I'll be right back. Nothing else. Do you understand?"

"Yes, Mr. Paul, be careful—you don't know what she's like, she's a mad woman, Mr. Paul—she's a mad woman!"

"Be quiet! Stop it," he said; and waited until she did. "Don't go in unless she wakes up, and tell her I'll be right back if she does."

The kitchen clock said only quarter to twelve. He pulled his raincoat over pajamas as he went through; and head ducked, ran out to the Ford and dived in the open door, slamming it behind him. The headlights burned on a tangle of rain, the engine was running. As he put it in gear a great blare of light lit up the whole clearing; the following crack of thunder was immediate.

He drove hard, ducking past great tossing branches that bore down at him. But nothing was down yet, to block his way. He kept the accelerator down, a wary eye out for fallen or falling branches—the narrow road was littered with slippery leaves; and then he struck one branch that was large enough to jolt the car. Another cracked against the roof as it fell. He didn't pause.

At the T of the main road, between Hall and home farm, a dark car slashed out of the night at him. It was almost impossible not to ram it. Swinging his wheel—hanging on to it, pumping his brakes for dear life, he felt that black juggernaut rush by. It was gone like a dream by the time he got control.

He sat a moment, just breathing. Then he restarted the motor and went on.

The farmhouse door stood open to the rain. Light came out. He went in and shut the door behind him, stood looking round the long empty room.

He said with idiot sternness: "MacDonald."

Some stir of movement came from beyond the open bedroom door. He went into the low, clean room, with its tidy bed. MacDonald stood beside it. He looked up at Dr. Potter and said, as if in some agreement:

"Aye, Paul. She's no' here anymore."

It was impossible to know which woman he meant. Dr. Potter didn't stop to wonder. What absorbed him was the welted old face that stared at him so sadly, the torn shirt bloody from torn flesh beneath. The closed and welted eye.

He went round and tipped the lampshade.

"Let me see that eye," he said.

MacDonald stood like the old farm horse under hands.

Indifferent alike to his wound and its care. The other eye, steady upon Dr. Potter, seemed drained of life.

"I heard poor Jenny sneakin' out to you," he said. "It's no matter."

She had whipped him. Some hard and supple thong—and a raging force—had ripped and cut this flesh. Incongruous and dumbfounding, the question stuck in his mind: but where had she got hold of such a thing? They had not had riding horses for years, nor proper habits ever.

In the kitchen, carefully removing the shirt, he saw that MacDonald's great hairy forearms and hands were not marked. He had not made any defense of himself.

The eyeball was not damaged.

Dr. Potter went upstairs and raided Pete and Jenny's bathroom. When he came back the old man stood by the sink as he had left him. God, how old he did look! Ageless, eternal MacDonald, sunk almost to senility in one hour.

Working with wincing care, although MacDonald never winced, Dr. Potter muttered between his set teeth: "To sit and smile at that boy, and then come and do this to you ... *Why did you let her?*"

"The boy ..."

It was a whisper, a sigh: a sound such as he had not thought the lungs of MacDonald could produce.

"He's nothing to us," said MacDonald's low voice then. "She's right about that, lad. He's not for us. It's too late for all that now."

"*Why did you let her?*"

He expected, and got, no answer. But before he had done with his careful daubing and examining, the flesh he was working on removed itself from his reach. Slowly, one hand closing over the torn shirt to take it with him, MacDonald was walking out of the room.

To Dr. Potter's startled objection, MacDonald said with absent gloom: "You'll say nothing of this to Pete, mind."

His bedroom door closed as the kitchen door pushed open.

Dr. Potter had not heard the car, between rain-sounds and his own concentration. He was standing there with cottonwool in one hand still, in no way prepared for a lively and curious Pete. Who was also, it would appear, fairly high.

He turned away and began cleaning up.

"Hey, Doc!" said Pete, and came up behind him. "What's going on? Who's hurt?"

"Your father-in-law had a little accident. He's gone to bed now, leave him alone."

"What do you mean, an accident? What kind of accident? And where's Jen?"

"If you'd stay home nights, you'd know these things for yourself," said Dr. Potter in a burst of irritation. "Here—these go back in your bathroom."

Pete accepted the bottles and cottonwool, but his sharp glance was still for the bloody waste.

"*You* try spending a few evenings round here, boy," he said, but absently. "No fooling, what is it? What happened?"

"Your wife will no doubt tell you all about it ... she's at my place, with my daughter. Bring me down your aspirin, will you?"

He turned his back again, intercepting one last flicker of interest as

Pete discovered his muddy feet. But the reminder of Jenny had done its work: there was no doubt she would tell him far more than anything he could get out of 'Doc'. He went upstairs and came back fast.

"Here you are—how many you want?"

"The bottle. Just wait here a minute."

He went into the closed bedroom and found MacDonald, as he expected, sitting on the edge of his lonely bed. He watched Dr. Potter shake out three pills and recap the bottle.

"Where are your pajamas?" said Dr. Potter sternly.

Incredibly, something like mute amusement seemed to peep from the old man's eye. But his silence was less that of stubbornness than of the lack of any capacity to respond. Dr. Potter began to open drawers. Then a mild voice said behind him:

"Go on, now, Paul. Bring Jenny home, poor lass."

"Pajamas," said Dr. Potter. "Damn it!" He opened another drawer. A familiar huge hand came gentle on his arm.

"Aye, lad—I'll do as you say. The three wee pills and my nightshirt. Go along now. And thank ye, Paul."

Pete was jigging round in the living room, waiting for him to come out.

"Come on," he said, after one abortive effort to see past Dr. Potter's shoulder. "I'll take you down."

"You will not. You're too drunk to drive me, whatever your wife likes to put up with. Make yourself some coffee so you can take in the whole story," he added grimly, and picked his coat up. "Is the road still clear?"

"As a bell," said Pete, who had no doubt found it so.

For some reason, mildly enraging to Dr. Potter, nothing he said to Pete ever set off that hair-trigger temper. Pete had apparently settled long ago to regard him as some kind of 'character'. He had never found this more annoying than now; and he went out without another word.

The farm Ford slid on leaves, pushed by rain and wind, on the way back. There were other and heavier branches down, too—a couple of them big enough to go around. He thought, I'll have to drive Jenny back, keep the car till morning. Wonder if Cressa slept ...?

These were surface thoughts; he clung to them, searched for more. Underneath lay so dark a rage he did not dare to examine it until he was alone, with nothing more required of him that night. His cousin's image was blacked out by it. He did not think of her at all.

CHAPTER FIFTEEN

The last of the storm muttered and flickered as he drove into his clearing. But the wind-tangled rain still came down, and he slid through mud again on his way to the back door.

Jenny opened it to him. He came just inside, and said briefly: "Hand me a cloth, Jenny. Anything. That towel."

He threw off his coat, and then leaned to do what he could about his feet. She still hadn't spoken.

"Did Cressa sleep?"

"Oh, all the time. I looked to make sure—she slept all the time. Mr. Paul—"

"Your father's in bed, and your husband's home," he said, straightening. "Let me get some shoes on, and I'll take you back—it's bad driving."

"Jenny whispered then, "Is she gone?" and he looked at her.

"Yes."

He struggled with the flicker of anger that came up in him—a nudging from beneath, of the lid he had clamped down on what was there, and had nothing to do with Jenny.

In a flat voice, he managed to say: "Get your coat, Jenny. I'll take you home."

"I don't know what to do, Mr. Paul. I'm afraid. I'm afraid."

He stood without answering, because he found he could not say: Don't be afraid. There's nothing to be afraid of.

"What shall I do?" she said, whispering still. "No one listens to me. They never do—Pete won't, nor my dad ..."

"I will, Jenny. Come and talk to me when you're worried. And don't ... don't be afraid. I'm sure nothing like this will happen again. It never has before, as you know. Now get your coat, and I'll take you back."

She went and got her coat, slow to go and to return. Head down, her hands thrust into the pockets of the man's coat, she came and stood by him again.

"Ready?" he asked, to rouse her.

She looked up into his face.

"There's harm in her," she said. "There's harm in her now."

"She harms herself most, Jenny."

But she was shaking her head, drawing a package of some sort from her pocket and pressing it on him.

"You keep these," she said. "I'll tell Pete you have them—I don't care what he says. I don't want them in the house anymore. They're her letters," she said, urging him to take them.

He took them.

The package was more than an inch thick. It was wrapped in some clear plastic that showed the contents, but only as folded paper—soiled and creased paper, folded upon whatever words it might contain. His hand's reluctance made the little pile of papers seem heavy as lead; he could scarcely force his voice out.

"Letters ... to Pete?"

"She's never written a word to Pete," said Jenny, bitter. Her fear seemed to be leaving her with the letters. "That's the only reason we took them, Mr. Paul. In case she tried later to go back on what she promised. But he's never seen her like you and I have. He doesn't know. I won't have him to keep them anymore. I don't care what he says, I don't care!"

Her whimpering breath was loud in the silent, rain-tapped kitchen, She stood looking up at him, doglike, stubborn.

"I won't have them anymore."

Of all that was in his mind, he chose presently to say: "Nor will I, Jenny. I'll give them back to her, of course." Instantly she was panic-struck.

"But you can't, Mr. Paul! She doesn't even know about them—and if she sees them again then she'll know where they came from, she'll know it was me," wailed Jenny, and began to cry again. And sank down away from him, into the nearest chair.

So he was going to have to know. All about this, too.

He pulled up another chair, and sat close beside her.

"All right, Jenny. You had better tell me about it, then. What are the letters, and where did you get them?"

"Oh, I didn't, I didn't! I never touched them till he made me keep them, Mr. Paul," she wept. "I didn't even know about them before—I swear I didn't! It was just something mother had in her hand when I found her, I didn't hardly notice them at all—it was Pete took them and opened them up and read them! And then he made me hide them, all the time—I have to keep them on me all the time, Mr. Paul, and I can't stand it anymore—I can't!"

In her mother's hand, when Jenny found her. Dead; prone; halfway to the door.

Where had Mrs. MacDonald been going with these letters, with the last of her life? To whom? Or to what secret place of hiding—or what destruction?

There was no more, really, that he needed to ask. The knowledge had been in him all the time, a part of his whole knowledge of them all. Unexamined and refused, like so much of that knowledge.

"From abroad," he said aloud. "From Scotland. When they sent her away."

"I guess so," said Jenny, without much interest to spare for such details. "Oh, but you won't—"

"No. I won't. I wouldn't dream of giving these back to her, Jenny," he said, and got up. "Not after all these years."

In the study, kneeling by the cold fireplace, he shook the old letters out on the bed of ashes, separated them so that they would burn. Jenny came and knelt beside him as he struck the match. She made no gesture to stop him. At the edge of his vision he was aware of her hands, working with excitement upon her coat.

"I'll tell him you did it, you burned them," she muttered eagerly. "I'll say they fell out and you took them and burned them up and I couldn't stop you!"

He didn't reply. The letters were not burning well, folded as they were. He began to open and crumple them one by one. Jenny's hand came out, eager to help, and he put it back. Now the familiar tall slopes of writing could be seen—words, individual phrases started up at him:

"MacDonald, you are not ..." He deliberately blurred his vision.

MacDonald, you are not ...

But he was, of course. The only splendid, powerful male her world had shown her. And more than that, the whole heart of what was hers and must, somehow, be claimed.

Of course, MacDonald.

And equally certain, the thin and reserved woman in MacDonald's home. Who had the power to put an end to what she disapproved of. The riding horses, suddenly sold. When he came home from school one summer they were gone. They had all understood without quite understanding that Mrs. MacDonald's disapproval lay behind that; but only Millie would have known why. Millie, reduced to foot, no longer able to race proud and urgent about her land after her lover.

Had she loved him, ever?

There was no one to turn to now with such a question. Except Jenny, crouching there beside him with her eyes wide to the flames. The letters were going fast, now. In another moment they would be gone.

It was time. After nearly twenty years, it was time.

The loss of her horses had not stopped her. The letters told him that— the letters, and the long exile from which they had come ... to fall into Mrs. MacDonald's hands. Perhaps, he thought, to be placed there by MacDonald himself: an acknowledged sinner, who meant to sin no more. Who had agreed to send Millie away and keep her away—the cold wet winter long, in Scotland. Millie's trip abroad. So thriftily suggested by Mrs. MacDonald.

He must have made some sound, aloud, for Jenny turned to him. The excitement of the flames had roused a desire for speech in her, too.

"It was always my dad I was afraid would find them on me," she said. "It was him I was most afraid of. Even when I heard her come in tonight, I wasn't afraid, Mr. Paul. Not of her. He always made her do what he said before."

"Never mind, Jenny. Come on; let's go."

But she didn't stir. Neither, to his faint surprise, did he.

"When I heard her start screaming at him like that, I thought he would stop her—he did before," said Jenny, unbelieving still. "Why, I could hear her as plain as plain, clear up the stairs—an old cheat, she called him! She did, Mr. Paul, and worse. An old devil, if you want to know. An old cheating, lying devil! There! And never one word could I hear out of my dad, even when she started that crazy laughing, like the other time. And telling him he was nothing but an old man now—a useless old man with nothing and nobody in the world but—but me and Pete," said Jenny, flushing. "And I wouldn't like to repeat the way she talked about us."

"No."

"Then she was hitting him, Mr. Paul! I could hear it, clear up the stairs! Hitting and hitting him, and not a sound out of my dad," said Jenny, trembling now with nervous excitement, clutching at his arm.

"Mr. Paul, it was like the end of the world to me, I thought he must be a dead man to sit there like that—I didn't know what to do! Do you know what I did?" she demanded. "I went out my window and over the kitchen roof—I did! And dropped to the ground! The keys were in the Ford, or I'd have run down here in my bare feet—that's how scared I was!"

"Yes," he said, a dreamy monosyllable.

Shivering, but alert now, Jenny needed no words from anyone else. Only the chance—in safety—to spill out her own.

"Mr. Paul, I'll tell you something nobody knows in this world but me. And Pete, of course. About when she came back from Scotland that time ..."

"No," he said. "No."

Or perhaps he didn't say it. Jenny gave no sign of hearing.

"I was up over their heads that time too—up in the hayloft. I was only a little girl, Mr. Paul, but I never forgot a word of it, and I never told a soul until after I was a married woman! I don't know what she said to him at the beginning, because they were talking low and I wasn't listening. But she started that same kind of crazy laughing, like tonight, and it scared me then, too. And she said she hated him, Mr. Paul—she said, I hate you, and I loathe you, and I despise you, MacDonald! I never forgot that," said Jenny, solemn, "and I never will as long as I live. And she hit him that time, too."

"Jenny—"

"But just the once! Only the one slap, Mr. Paul—and then not another sound! I don't know how it was my dad stopped her that time, but he did."

Frozen together, with her arm caught in the great hand of MacDonald. Caught and held.

"All he said to her was That's enough, Millie. That's enough, he said, and it was, too. She ran away! And then to sit there tonight and let her go on and on like that—do you wonder it scared me out of my senses?" she said. "When he stopped her so *easy* before?"

He got up then, and Jenny scrambled up with him.

"I know he's a lot older now," she said, "but he didn't seem so awfully old, before. Not that old."

She followed him out to the kitchen, through the door he held for her. Gave him an uneasy glance as she passed. "You won't tell, Mr. Paul?"

"I won't tell."

Pete's yellow car came into the clearing just as they reached the Ford. Jenny seemed to fall behind Dr. Potter when she saw it, babbling something, all her terrors renewed.

He ignored her and started forward, with a sudden pleasurable awareness of every part of his own big body.

Pete stuck his head out into the rain, winced, and said crossly: "What the hell's going on down here, anyway? Jen! Get over here!" Then he cocked his head to see up into Dr. Potter's face looming over him.

"What's going on, Pete," said Dr. Potter, "is that I've been burning up those letters you took from your mother-in-law's body."

Half-drunk, rained on, with his neck literally sticking out, Pete received this warily.

"Yeah?" he said.

"Yeah. Get out. I'll tell you more about it."

The hard eyes stared upward a moment longer. Then the head went in. Jenny, timidly fumbling the other side, disappeared into the car with one sharp yelp, over her husband's muttered: "... in here, you cow!" Then the door handle ripped itself from Dr. Potter's grasp, backward. He yanked his foot from the tire's path just in time.

At the edge of the clearing the yellow car jolted to a stop and Pete stuck his head out again.

"Some hot piece, wasn't she, Doc?" he yelled.

Then—backwards—they shot off again. One long wail came from Jenny, but not the expected crash. Somehow, and audibly, they reached the road and roared away out of hearing.

CHAPTER SIXTEEN

About three that morning, with the rain softened to a patter and the wind down, Dr. Potter made a fire and a pot of coffee.

With this acknowledgment to himself—that he was not going to sleep at all that night—he began to feel his deep tiredness, like a relief. And presently, with the fire, with his coffee, to relax into sorrow without anger.

It was not that he stopped thinking. At no time, it seemed to him, had he achieved anything so dignified as thought. But the stark and painful images stopped springing up in his mind—the real and the imagined—and in that respite he could feel himself return to some kind of humanity, and inner order. And could feel himself alone again: a man sitting by a fire, with his small daughter asleep nearby. He was glad of the solitude, the minimum identity.

The first bird call roused him some time later from what was probably just stupor, and he went out in the kitchen and opened his door, looking out on the sodden and storm-littered clearing in first light. He was glad to see it. As if he had been away a long while. And in a random gesture of return, of greeting, he opened the last of the vin rosé and stood drinking it quietly at the open door, while light and bird calls increased around him.

After that, he must have gone back and fallen asleep in his chair, since that was where Cressa came upon him.

Much later, Louisa drove into the clearing, while he and Cressa were still coping with their after-breakfast chores. It was a little after nine, which meant that she must have left New York around seven-thirty; and this wasn't her regular day to come. But she wasn't, of course, aware of having received any urgent summons.

"Oh, mother called me up yesterday afternoon—all about this cousin," she said, in answer to his question. "So I thought I'd come up and see." "You got an early start." "I woke up early," she said simply.

Lou, if anyone, could have made him believe in extrasensory perception. Sometimes there seemed no other way to account for her.

She was hungry, and wanted breakfast here before going on up to the Hall, so he started more eggs for her. Out in the clearing, beside her little Hillman, the farm Ford waited to be taken home. It was the only tangible reminder of the night; he found himself glancing out at it from time to time.

Later, from the study, he heard Louisa asking his daughter: "Why is the Ford here, Cressa?"

"Because MacDonald hurt himself last night, and daddy had to go help him. And it was raining hard, so he drove back. Do you want to go with us and see MacDonald when we take it back?"

"I want to go see the boy, first."

"He isn't a *boy*, Aunt Lou—he's bigger than you!"

"Is he really?" said Lou, interested. It was true that not many men were.

Afterwards she asked him: "What happened to MacDonald?"

Cressa was out of earshot. He made sure of it, before saying: Millie horsewhipped him.

Then of course he didn't say it.

But the incredible thing was the way that she let her own question, and his lack of a reply, slide into limbo. She was already putting away the book she had taken from him last time and running an eye over the others. Perhaps that hesitant glance round of his had warned her in some way, or his expression. Yet she was not just being discreet. If he should say it to her now—*Millie whipped him*—she would be completely disoriented. "What?" she would say. Or even: "Who?"

The silence between them extended. He could not tell whether she was aware of it too; but it began to be more than he could bear.

"Well, I'm going along now, Lou," he said. "I want to see how MacDonald is, and then we're going up to the lake."

"You won't be able to swim after that storm," she pointed out, still reading. Lake Millicent always took a little while to clear. He passed over her reminder, as she had passed over the reference to MacDonald.

But as they left, as if to some twinge of doubt, Louisa asked: "When are you coming to the Hall? They'll ask me."

"I don't know."

Cressa seemed to find it an odd answer, though she didn't say anything, for a wonder. Maybe Louisa found it odd too—she did come out and watch them drive off.

The estate workmen, day-men and crofters too, were busy on the roads this morning, clearing away the debris of the storm and checking for any branches that might yet fall. This was an automatic duty after any heavy storm, and Dr. Potter still expected to find MacDonald at the farm rather than directing it. But only Jenny was there, and she was evasive and sullen. Pete had evidently given her a hard time.

"I don't know where my dad is," she said, as if they were callers she didn't know or trust. "Or when he'll be back."

"Well, how is he? How's that eye?"

"I don't know. He didn't say."

Walking away, Cressa said in some bewilderment: "Is she angry because he hurt himself, daddy? It isn't our fault, is it?"

"No, Cressa, it isn't our fault."

She said presently, "I wish we had kept the Ford. It would be nice to go to the drugstore and call mother." He laughed, and gave her hand a squeeze.

"Oh, I think we might do even better than that. How would you like to go down to New York and see her?"

"You too?"

"All right. We'll have a little fling. Just for fun."

That restored her cheerfulness completely—so he was committed to it. As, he admitted, he wanted to be. Something about the vin rosé in the early stillness, after that awful night, had put the notion into his head. He hadn't meant to do anything about it, though.

They never reached the lake. A couple of local boys, employed here for the summer vacation, were working on this road; apparently they were special friends of his daughter, or else she was glad of any young, uncomplicated companionship. The four of them ended up spending most of the morning on one tree, with a high, heavy, dangling branch which ordinarily should have been reported to MacDonald and left alone. Of the four, only Dr. Potter had any sense of wrongdoing, at their exciting game. He came almost to hope for the ominous appearance of the estate wagon, the authoritative roar to "Come down out of that, ye young leekies!"

It didn't happen. The young ones had a dangerous and pleasant morning, undisturbed. It was almost as if MacDonald were already gone.

At lunchtime, dragging Cressa home, he stopped where the road branched between his own place and the Hall. Where Millie had nearly run him down last night. Now, he had at least to stop by and say to his aunt that they were going.

Cressa was perfectly willing; she wanted in any case to see John O. Watson. He did not. Nevertheless, finding the drive longer than he had ever known it to be, he walked up with his daughter to the house which had contained most of his early life, and the women who had formed it.

The grounds were still disheveled from the storm; and with just that one layer of disorder round it the erratic old stone mansion already looked semi-abandoned. It was built in the style—last-century, mad-baron—which one associates with abandonment and decay; and he perceived that only the timeless and well-kept beauty of the grounds gave it what dignity it had. Surely, he thought, coming slowly towards it, John O. must see it to some extent as it really was?

Or perhaps he secretly hoped to reduce this one, too, to a one-story-with-overhang. ("It's still the Hall. My great aunt and cousins still live there.")

Unaccountably, his spirits rose a little. They came into a silent house, where no one answered his voice; and as if it were any day, he went on back to the big, orderly kitchen. No one was there, either. He began to make orange juice for Cressa, who was thirsty, and they were still at this ordinary employment when the family car came by the window, containing his aunt, John O. Watson, and Louisa at the wheel. They came in the back way, his aunt and John O. still discussing some feature of Long Acre—it seemed they had spent the morning there. Louisa shooed them all out of the kitchen, so that she might get lunch ready. No one mentioned Millie, and he did not ask.

CHAPTER SEVENTEEN

"It's really too bad of Jenny not to come," said Aunt Cora, complaining. "I'm afraid she is quite a different girl without her mother. I wish you had at least met Mrs. MacDonald, John—she was a woman of very great character."

They were at luncheon, to which Millie had not come down. She had, said her mother, one of her migraine headaches, poor child. Louisa was not skillful at handling things alone, but she would not let John O. help, or Cressa. Her older cousin did not offer, although he was still, rather gloomily, present. Louisa had just dropped and broken a plate, which had called her mother's attention to the fact that things weren't going very well.

John O. looked tactful, supposing them to be on the edge (as they were) of the entire subject of lack of help and money.

"What do you think is wrong with MacDonald?" he said. "He certainly didn't have much to say this morning, did he—and he looks as if he'd fallen into his thresher."

Louisa, re-entering, gave an abrupt laugh, and then ignored the subject. Dr. Potter cleared his throat, which made the others look at him.

"He was probably drunk, John. I'm afraid he also wenches. In the unfortunate absence of Mrs. MacDonald."

"*Polly*," said his aunt. He turned to her gravely.

"I'm sorry, but we do know, auntie. You wouldn't believe how many years your children have known about MacDonald."

"But you make it sound so much worse than it is, dear!"

"No," he said. "I don't think so."

"Besides, I know he would never forget himself now, just when John has come, and he's so happy about that. I know he would not, Polly—

and I think it's just as John says, he must have hurt himself on a machine."

"Fallen into his thresher," Louisa muttered, swallowing another choke of laughter. Cressa looked at her seriously.

"But that would *kill* him, Aunt Lou!"

"It's a joke, honey," said John O. "Not a very nice one—I shouldn't have made it."

"No, you shouldn't, John," she agreed.

Dr. Potter, thus recalled to nice-mindedness, ate the rest of his lunch in deep silence. When Louisa rose to crash into action again he said to his daughter: "I think Aunt Lou might let you help now, Cressa. No, do let her, Lou. In fact, she can wash the dishes—I'm sure you have other things to do, with Millie indisposed."

"Listen, don't the men get to turn a hand around here?" said John O., embarrassed. "I'm a good—"

"No, never," said Dr. Potter firmly. "Except peerless MacDonald, who works, drinks and wenches for all of us. Excuse me, auntie," he said, to his aunt's startled expression. "I'm speaking figuratively, of course."

"Yes, dear ...?"

"And if John will tolerate a little more figurative speaking, I would like to take him away for a while. Perhaps we could use the library, if you don't mind."

"No, dear—but wouldn't you be cooler out by the fishpond? There's shade now."

"I think the library," said Dr. Potter, whose private intention regarding the fishpond was never to go near it again. He did not understand nor intend to investigate his aunt's placid, almost pious, urging of it upon them.

"John?" he said, putting up his napkin.

"Certainly, sir," said John, unnerved to this old form of address. Aunt Cora understood that they wished to get up, and sighed herself to her feet. Clearly she did not like to lose John even for a while.

She said wistfully, "I believe there are some very nice books—Polly will show you. Louisa could tell you all about them."

"Louisa has her work to do," said Dr. Potter austerely. His aunt looked mortified, but could not deny it: all the beds, still; and she had no intention of leaving her good dishes to Louisa or Cressa.

"It really is too bad of Jenny," she sighed again.

In the library, John O. had enough confidence left from other encounters to grin faintly at Dr. Potter as he shut the door.

"What's up?" he asked. "Is it really MacDonald?"

"MacDonald will do to start with," Dr. Potter agreed. "Sit down, John. I'll open the windows. Take off your jacket."

He took off his own, and pulled a chair nearer the entering breeze.

"They keep the windows shut because of the dust. You've no idea what a job it is to take down and dust an entire library—we had to do it once a year regularly, the girls and I. It took about a week ... but then

Lou read most of the time. I hadn't thought of it, but I suppose Millie does it alone now."

He fell silent, looking out at the familiar stretch of lawn, until John O.'s tentative young voice said:

"This help problem is really something, I can see. Surely there must be a way—"

"Well, that's something else again," said Dr. Potter. "Now, to get back to MacDonald. I don't know whether it's occurred to you that he's not a young man at all."

"Well, I know that great-grandfather Onderdonk brought him—"

"Yes," said Dr. Potter. "He's well past seventy. With his wife, he might have been good for another five or ten years—at least to supervise. But he's been surprisingly hard hit by her death, and I doubt now if he'll last the year—at least, without turning odd, and undoing a lot of what he's done here."

"Well, that poses a problem, certainly."

John O.'s expression was sympathetic, but wary. Dr. Potter suddenly smiled at him.

"MacDonald has set the pattern here," he went on quietly. "He should have trained a successor, but he never has. He won't now. I doubt if he could. And I don't believe it's a pattern anyone else, even someone trained to estate management, could come in and carry on. Or would care to, frankly. No one else could handle those crofters of his, for one thing."

"I suppose they would have to go back," said John O. thoughtfully, as of some unwise purchase. "It's a pity, but I see your point."

"Do you, John?"

"Yes, I think so. You're trying to tell me—I think—that the present way of life here," he said with care, "will have to change a lot, and lose a lot of its flavor when it does. I'm not glad about it, believe me. But I— I've allowed for that, already."

"Have you," said Dr. Potter. "Then what is it that attracts you here, John? The land itself, the fact that your great-grandfather bought and settled it? Even though you would have to turn round and resettle it for present-day living?"

The eyes on his were puzzled by now.

"Well, I didn't have too much change in mind, you know. I mean, certainly nothing that my—that the family would object to, I hope."

"John, no one here would object if you put up hot dog stands and a roller-rink," said Dr. Potter simply. "I expect that's what I'm really trying to make you understand. There's nothing here anymore at all but the land itself, for whatever that means. I suppose we were a family once," he said. "In a queer sort of way. Two families—the Onderdonks, and the MacDonalds. But the two people who kept those families going, more or less, have just died. And to those of us who are left, this is the year of our freedom. We have none of us been free before."

He spoke with deliberation. What he was saying was becoming too personal to himself for those earnest, guarded young eyes to go on witnessing. Yet he wanted to finish, and he got up and stood at the window so that he might continue.

"You see how strange it's been, to have you come here in the very moment before we dissolve, so to speak, and see us and believe in us as something we aren't. We haven't quite known what to do, without hurting you. We understand long-term dreaming very well, John—it's about all we do understand, I think—and we respect yours. But we don't see any reality in it, and we don't know how to tell you. That's what I'm trying to do now."

John O. gave a sudden, uncomfortable laugh.

"Surely you're not saying that you're all on the point of whizzing out of here, Paul? Why, Aunt Cora—"

"Aunt Cora is a special case," said Dr. Potter firmly. "She has a rare talent for living in the exact moment, as it seems to be. I don't believe we've ever had a project or a plan she didn't fall in with, while it was hot. And she has never embarrassed anyone by bringing a dead mouse back indoors, bless her. As for the rest of us," he said, "Louisa and I are already gone. We have come back when we could because we were needed. But that need ends when Millie goes ... and she's free to go now, after a great many years when she didn't have that freedom. Or the hope of it."

"It's just fantastic," said John O., on a long breath. He got up too. "I simply can't believe you all want to walk out on a place that's bred in your bones, you might say—that's been your whole life! Why, it's something most people would give their eyeteeth for, a background like this. A real home!"

"Only the dreamers, John. And there are fewer of us than you think. Besides," he said, becoming restless, "any place you can't leave becomes, quite simply, a prison. No matter how pleasant. And there are very few people, not old, who won't choose to walk out when the prison door opens."

Young John was already recovering from his shock—which hadn't, Dr. Potter saw, gone very deep, and it occurred to him that John was well used to dealing with the crochets and depressions of the elderly. He was already getting the patient, skeptical expression he must use with his grandmother ... and the underlying stubbornness of the young-who-know-better. No doubt they did seem old to him. In comparison, no doubt they were.

"All right," said John O., and drew another long breath. "I get the picture now, Paul, and I'm really very, very grateful to you for bringing yourself to explain it. I know it must be hard, and I know I must have seemed like a prize ass, not noticing a thing!"

"Certainly not. We're all experienced dissemblers, we've had to be. And as I say, we respect dreams, here. Even when we can't go along with them."

"All right," said John O. again. "So it's been a dream—and the real

Onderdonk Estate has been more like a prison all these years. But you can't stand there and tell me you don't love this place, deep down inside. Really love it, I mean."

"Oh, I think I could ... But let's agree that a great deal of emotion has been expended here," he said quickly, to those young brows coming down with increased stubbornness, "and attaches to the place itself. The real residue of that experience is in ourselves, of course, but the place can be—often is—a stimulus to recall it. But that sort of stimulus wears off rather soon. Weakens; falls into habit. And isn't particularly healthy anyway."

"Well," said John O., "I'm not going to argue about that, Paul. Next thing you'll be telling me I'm too young to know." He grinned. "Maybe I am. But I'm not too young to have noticed one thing—and that is, that people who can't wait to get out of something, or some place, often wish they could go back when it's too late. I don't want that to happen here. Not if I can prevent it."

There was no doubt he spoke from deep feeling. Something about the mother? Whatever the chasm was, slowly opening to view, Dr. Potter decided to leap it before it got any wider.

He said bluntly, "That's not an important possibility to those who desperately want out. And in this case, John, 'out' is synonymous with 'over.' What my cousins want is quite literally their lives instead of their land."

"Well, but damn it! they don't have to choose! Listen," said John O., and sat down again. "Here's what I'm trying to get up the nerve to propose to Cousin Millicent—and I don't know why I never seem to get there, I just can't make it when I'm with her. But it's perfectly simple. My God, I agree they should have the freedom to move around, if they want to, or else know they can live here without all this damn slaving they have to do. No wonder they're sick of it! But if they could realize the entire value of their share—*more* than they would probably get from a real dispersal—and still see the estate intact, their home, theirs whether they want to come or go—well," said John O., flushed, "it can be done that way, I promise you."

"I don't doubt it in the least."

"In fact, as I say, they'll get *more* than breakup value. We'll count all appreciation, every possible accrual. There'll be *no* tax loss—and we can reinvest those damn funds to bring in three times what they get now. And in addition to that, if they want to come back, they'll come back to a place that's running right. That's alive!" said John O. vigorously. "That people can really live in, and—and bring up their families. Now this can be done, Paul. If you want to sit down with me right now and let me—"

"No," said Dr. Potter. He cleared his throat. "This sort of thing you must take up with your cousins, you know."

"Yes, I know. But I thought maybe if you—if I could—Hell, I can *talk* to you," said John O. "I was thinking maybe I could explain it to you, and you could pass it on. Maybe we could get started that way."

"I don't think it would help, really, John."

He was forcing down, behind these minimal responses, the vision of Millie hearing John O.'s dream. Of the estate that would be running right, and 'alive', and most of all, *still here*. Always here, whether she came back or stayed away. Indifferent to her presence or her absence just as it always had been. And irrevocably gone from her control.

He understood her need then, in seeing how it might be defeated. The hot dog stands, the roller rink, the rows of development houses would be balm to her heart compared to a view of little Watsons splashing healthily in a renewed Lake Millicent, Long Acre lived in (as a one-story with overhang). What she wanted, quite simply, was to end it—the final act of thwarted possession. Had thought herself, perhaps, bending over its quiet corpse—and here came all the bustle of revival! One side, madam, I'm a doctor. Plenty of hope yet, every possible accrual. And *no* tax loss.

"John," he said.

It came out almost a groan. He cleared his throat again. Some part of his dismay had touched the other. He was looking a little lost ... but not much.

"You think they might resent it, don't you? As if I were pushing in—taking over. Is that what it sounds like?"

"Yes, a little. Not in itself," he managed to go on. "What you want is probably quite practical—benevolent, even. I know you mean it to be. But it's what *you* want, John. It's brand new," he said sadly, "and everything here is pretty old."

"What I've seen looks sound, though. Excepting poor old MacDonald," said John O., with a faint smile.

"Well, the oldness is what attracts you, I know. But it has a life of its own, and a strong one—more complex than it seems."

What would alter that unalterable young look? To know of 'poor old MacDonald' beside his wife's empty bed, slashed, bleeding, utterly defeated? Or of Mrs. MacDonald dead on her bedroom floor, with the old letters clutched in her hand? To see how Millicent's beautiful head might look, gone skull-like and silently screaming, as on that night in the kitchen? Or a view of Uncle Humphrey head down in the waters of his pretty toy?

Behind him, the attentive silence continued. John O. knew when to wait, at least.

"If it is only the land—the property—you want," said Dr. Potter slowly, "perhaps you will be able to arrange to have it. I don't know. But you mustn't count on any of the old life—the people—that went with it. I think it's time one of us said this to you ... so that you can decide how much difference, if any, that would make to your plans. I don't know you well enough to be able to guess." Some impulse of mercy moved him to add, "Your great-grandfather, of course, started with much less."

He heard John O. stir—but only a little.

"In any case, this is between you and your cousins," he went on more firmly, "and you will have to settle it with them. Forget about the rest of us—your aunt, me, MacDonald. Decide what you really want, and then talk it over with Millicent. Soon, John. Get it out in the open. Do the best you can, whether you feel it goes well or not. It isn't easy for any of us to talk to Millie about some things."

He looked round then and met, with slight shock, the speculative eye of a strange young man. As though he really had been talking to himself.

The strange young man said, with quick courtesy, "Well, I'll certainly think this over carefully, Paul. And thanks very, very much."

"Yes," he said.

Almost absently, he left the library then, and went back through the house to the kitchen.

His aunt, at the sink, started guiltily—then relaxed as she realized he was alone.

"I'm almost finished, dear—I thought you would keep him a little longer ...? You haven't left him all alone, have you?"

"John is fine," he said, absent still. He stood watching his daughter, carefully drying silverware but primarily, he thought, waiting for his return. Somehow he had been quite sure she would not be upstairs with either of her courtesy-aunts.

It was time to leave.

Cressa said, an echo to his thoughts: "When are we going, daddy?"

"Now. We'll just have time to get some things together and catch the three-ten. I'll call you from New York about coming back, auntie."

About not coming back, said his mind—an effortless adjustment.

His aunt looked at him then, with concern, but only partial attention. "Oh—you're ...? I'd forgotten you were going," she excused herself. (He hadn't mentioned it before.) "Is it—will you be long, dear? Is everything all right?" (She meant Vinnie.)

"Fine," he said. "Just a jaunt."

He spoke with no attempt at jauntiness. It didn't matter. Too long, too easily reassured, Aunt Cora turned back to her hasty, furtive kitchen work, her thoughts clearly with their deserted guest. He gently pushed Cressa ahead of him towards the door.

"Goodbye, Aunt Cora," said her small voice, unprompted.

"Oh! Goodbye, dear," she said, trying to rally. "Have a lovely time, sweetheart—and come back soon, we'll miss you ..." But almost immediately, under her breath, they could hear her add: "Really *so* inconsiderate of Jenny ..."

CHAPTER EIGHTEEN

Exhausted and very sad, Dr. Potter dealt with the mechanics of going on holiday. Remembered to call the station taxi from the Hall; got Cressa's case and his own packed full of presumably useful things;

remembered to take a blank check, and all the money he could find in pockets and drawers. Got them on the train.

All he forgot was to warn Vinnie they were coming—the chore which lay heaviest on his mind.

It didn't really matter—they could call from the station; they could go directly to the apartment (to which he always carried the key she had sent him) and call from there. Or they could just 'surprise her with dinner all ready'—Cressa's warmly urged plan.

By default, it seemed that this was what they would do. It was too awkward to hunt up the telephone in Grand Central, with Cressa and luggage trailing; then a little too brassy to call up from the apartment itself, once they got there. Besides, he was upset to find there was no doorman at all—just a vestibule of the sort most attractive to thugs, and a buzzer system that absolutely invited disaster.

He was tired enough to feel this a kind of last straw. It wasn't that Vinnie had deceived him—she hadn't. But surely she understood why he kept sending every cent he could send, over her protests and disbelief in where he got it (raises, royalties, lecture fees—mostly apocryphal). Or perhaps, he suddenly thought, she did not understand at all. The terrors that haunted him, for those two butterfly creatures of his alone in this city, probably never occurred to her; and his pleas for large, young doormen and elevator operators, his nagging 'hope' that they took taxis instead of wandering subway corridors, simply amused her. In any case, she apparently had just been sticking the money in the bank, and feeling quite virtuous about doing so. He sighed and sat down, first automatically removing Cressa's crayons from the couch. Oddly enough, in this pleasant room where almost nothing, individually, was familiar to him, he felt at last able to relax. Or rather, unable *not* to relax. His indefatigable daughter, keyed up to surprise, saw him begin to slump, and pounced. They had to *market*—they had to make a list and market, and *hurry*, because it was getting *late* ...

He admitted it, not moving. The truth was, of course, that any room Vinnie made (with her daughter's help) would look familiar to him. The glowing colors she loved so well, the clutter of 'prizes' they both dragged home incessantly and kept forever. The sketches, the books, the swatches of material that would probably never be made into anything, the paperweights and little statuettes, even the Christmas card too charming to throw away, still thumbtacked up. And colored postcards, and records where they would get damaged sooner or later, and one little ice skate with its white boot, fallen behind the radiator. They knew no seasons, these two—life itself was the season, and it never ended; and everything was useful and delightful ...

"What do you need to make *potato salad*, daddy?" his daughter was imploring, at his ear; and he had to open his eyes to answer.

"... Potatoes ... No," he said. "Too late to make it, we'll buy it ..."

He watched her solemnly printing, felt his eyelids sink—and murmured quickly: "Cold boiled ham. Rolls. Olives and pickles."

"And frozen éclairs!"

"Certainly ..."

Coffee. He had better make some now, rather a lot. A cup or two would get him going again, and they could ice the rest for dinner ... Vinnie always had good coffee, and a good pot to make it in. What was more, he knew exactly where each would be—could see the clean pot sitting at the back of the stove, just as it always did when not in use, and the round coffee tin on its special shelf in the refrigerator ...

He could smell the fragrance of it.

That was real.

For a long moment he simply accepted the fact that real coffee fragrance was reaching him, where he lay supine and alone in a shadowed room. An edge of light and a smother of little noises drew his attention, then; and with the first slow turning of his head he woke completely—appalled.

Vinnie was home. No doubt of it. They were out there in the kitchen now, getting the 'surprise' dinner. She had come in and found him lumpishly asleep and Cressa at loose ends, and that was her surprise. Oh, lord.

Very shy, groping to reorder his appearance, he got up and went creaking across the room. Pushed the door open. Much light—and two identical quick looks, serious and lively.

"Oh, daddy, you're too soon," Cressa cried—and her mother, equally absorbed, corrected her. "No, because he hasn't washed. Now there'll just be time."

Not angry, of course. Bustling, and pleased—pleased to have a reason for bustling. But a little wary? (He remembered that miserable, stiff note about Mexico.) The apology he made her was for that, really.

"Well, Vinnie," he said. "This wasn't exactly the surprise we planned for you. I seem to have botched that."

She said nonsense, it was the best possible surprise just as it was, and would he please wash now? And the wariness was gone. Gone and forgotten.

After dinner, in the last of the light, the three of them went for a walk in the little park near Vinnie's apartment—promenading sedately past the Mayor's house, along the river's edge; watching the lights come on and glow in the colorless evening air. They were all three inclined to quietness, after a burst of talking. And Cressa was tired by now. Vinnie too, of course—after all, she had worked all day in summer heat, and then come home to prepare and serve an impromptu dinner party. But it was the custom somehow to regard Vinnie's activities as a kind of play—so far as he could see, only because she was cheerful about them— while those who solemnly did much less, and less well, were considered to be more solid citizens.

He took her arm, entwining their arms, and saw from the corner of his eye her delighted upward glance.

But she also took courage to say what was in her mind.

"I bet you're here because Millie's not speaking to you. It wasn't something Cressa did, was it?"

He grinned.

"You lose your bet. We are *au mieux* with all concerned."

She was glad to hear it, she said ... and increasingly curious, although she did not say that. Feeling more glances coming his way, he looked down at her.

"But things are very wrong up there, Vinnie," he added soberly.

"What—more than usual?"

Then she was vexed at herself. Why? Had he used to take offence so easily? But when the surface was still unbroken, the pretense still going strong ... his own pretense, of course, as well as the family's ...

They were coming back through the park again, very slowly. Cressa seemed to have a good acquaintance among the promenading dogs and their owners, and had stopped to throw something for the entertainment of a large schnauzer, illegally off his leash. Dr. Potter frowned.

"Is that dog safe, Vinnie? He's as tall as she is."

"Oh, heavens, yes—they do this every night. We might as well sit down and wait, actually," she said.

They sat down, parental, on the nearest bench. Vinnie still kept discreetly quiet. She did not expect to be told any more about the family; there was his answer. He was ashamed; and would have given anything to be speaking openly to her, by now, of all that was on his mind. But how should he begin? He could not find where to begin. Any incident he settled on led backward, and then still backward, and then in a curious circular way became part of its beginning, without any break of entry. It was like following a long fence—or a wall that had no opening. You were either inside, or out. And if one of you were in and the other out, did you go on walking side by side with the wall between you forever?

"Vinnie—" he said: an explosive sound, which startled her. He said angrily then, "I'm trying to think how to get into this damn tangle, to tell you about it. Or if it's worth telling—!"

"Oh, Paul, you don't have to," she said.

She looked embarrassed now. No doubt he was scowling ferociously. He tried to straighten his look—and then she did take alarm.

"Please, Paul! Please don't worry about it." She said, an earnest plunge, "I'm really not jealous of Millie, dear—I never was, whatever people say."

That astounded him into quietness.

He said presently, "But I never thought you were. Why should you be? And what," he said, ominous, "do people say?"

She had courage, Vinnie, and suddenly used it.

"Why, that you always loved her best," she said, almost impatient. "What else?"

"That isn't true, Vinnie."

"Of course it isn't. She wouldn't—the idea of her wouldn't be hanging round your neck like a dead cat all the time, if you did. That's not the way you feel about people you love!" Nervous tears sprang into her eyes; before he could speak she rushed on: "And that's what I do resent, if you want to know—and I resent it about all of them, not just Millie! Millie the most, though," she added, honest. "Because she hangs on hardest."

She took his handkerchief, like a quick squirrel, and turned her back. He heard her say, "*Damn* ..." and blow her nose. He put his arm along the back of the seat, the hand coming down upon her shoulder.

The minute he touched her, her muffled voice broke out again.

"And that's all nonsense about Millie practically bringing you and Lou up, too—just nonsense! As silly as saying you're in love with her. Millie's no more like a mother to you than I am. Or poor Lou. And she's *not* the strongest, Paul—she's much more needy than either of you, she always was!"

Needy. The word distracted him a little, with pleasure in its exactness.

"I know it," he said. "You're right—a lot of what you're saying is perfectly true, and don't cry. Please. Turn round." When she did, he took the handkerchief and gently tidied her. She said, not looking it, that she was sorry; and he said mildly: "Why? Don't be. It's true Millie is the neediest—and that's a very good word for it. But don't be fooled by that, Vinnie. The strong are needy, and their needs are strong. Ordinary people can get by on ordinary requirements, but strength needs a lot of feeding. Millie's tragedy has been that there wasn't any food. I see we're promoting her," he observed, "from a dead cat to a kind of hippopotamus ..."

"With you and Lou shoveling in the hay," she agreed; and they were both smiling, a little; and left it like that.

But they were still just touching hands over the wall. Presently Vinnie would realize it too.

She didn't seem to, on the walk home in tranquil summer dark. From streetlight to streetlight, her face turning from Cressa to himself showed no return of doubt at all—none, even, when Cressa decided to give up her twin bed to her father and sleep out on the couch.

"Because it's just right for me, and it's too little for you," she explained.

He said, dry, "It wasn't this afternoon."

"But that was a nap! Besides, I like to sleep out in the living room, and I can do it when Marie stays, so why can't I when it's daddy? He counts more than Marie."

"Who's Marie?" he said, helpless. It was all he could think of to say. Vinnie hadn't said anything; her expression was discreet, preoccupied. There was no doubt in it, though.

"Oh, at the office. Sometimes we bring work home and keep it up till all hours. She's very nice, Cressa loves having her."

A little nervousness was in her voice now, and her look. She was talking to be talking.

"As a matter of fact," he said falsely (he had forgotten to do it), "I've made a hotel reservation. No intention of turning things upside down for you in the middle of your work week, of course. Especially when we're just passing through, so to speak."

It didn't help to have Cressa standing down there with her mouth open.

"But why are we just passing through? You said—"

"Let daddy decide, Cressa," her mother said, unlocking the door. She added, over her shoulder, "Come up and get your bag, anyway, Paul."

If he stayed, he thought suddenly, maybe they could talk at last—get through that damned wall in familiar, conjugal darkness, talking away the night, as they had done before. Only now there was so much more to say, and the need to say it and be answered was so much greater. And they were not, after all, hot young lovers who couldn't be trusted behind a closed door. Old married people of ten years' standing—good lord, what was he running away from? It was just himself and Vinnie, who needed desperately to have a little privacy—to come to some understanding, if they could.

At the top of the stairs, breathless with more than climbing, he said to Vinnie: "It would be nice, to be able to talk awhile. If you're not too tired." Watching still for the first sign of that doubt she must feel, since the wall was there, and strong enough to have driven her away once.

But he couldn't see a sign, a memory of it. Not then, in her discreet agreement, nor during any of the succeeding (of course) bustle, to rearrange bedding and belongings and toys and towels and whatnot. During all this, his brief self-deception ended. Naturally, now that he had committed them both. That door, which would close, was the most ominous object he had ever seen in his life; his own revealed pajamas froze him completely; and he could not begin to remember what it was he thought he should say.

Nevertheless, shut in at last (cornered, in fact, by the farthest window), he stood looking down into darkness and said, numb: "We've got to talk about this, Vinnie. We've got to."

There was only silence. Then, turning, he did at last see what he had known must be there—the terrible, big-eyed doubt, that cut him to the heart, so that without any more doubt or hesitation he went back and took her in his arms, to make it go away.

CHAPTER NINETEEN

Of course they talked too. Babbled, he said, would be more like it— after he, in instant capitulation, told her all about the Coast and Canadian offers, the new life with no more summers on the estate, while she eagerly claimed that there was nothing she wanted more in the world than to be right back in Indiana where they had been so happy, where she must have been out of her mind to think they had no real life of their own, and it was her fault entirely that she hadn't enjoyed the summers on that beautiful estate—she didn't know what had got into her, but it wouldn't anymore.

"Don't remember things wrong, Vinnie," he said, uneasy for her. "They weren't good summers, and it wasn't your fault."

"Yes, it was—you'll see. Things will be all right now, I can—"

"As a matter of fact," he broke in, inching for room in the tiny bed, "there won't be any more summers there anyway. We won't be near enough, and there'll probably be no estate to go to—Millie wants to break it up now."

"Can she?" Vinnie sounded surprised.

"Probably. Or else sell out to this new broom cousin. Either way the whole problem ends for us, Vinnie. It's not a problem you should ever have had in the first place. That was my fault."

"But I didn't have it—you did! And I was no help at *all*. I just kept resenting it, and wanting to go home. Or to Mexico! Oh, Paul, I'm so ashamed." He was peering at her, in beginning concern, when she fiercely added: "And I *hate* the way they keep calling you 'Polly'—as if you were a—a *pet!*"

He began to chuckle, and then silently to laugh—shaking the little bed and Vinnie too. Who muttered, "It's not funny"; but put her arms tighter round him and began savagely on his ear with her teeth, to make him stop.

He stopped.

Even after ten years he was simple enough, in the morning, to be surprised by the flood of activity that day brought. For himself, he was perfectly willing just to hang around the strange, familiar rooms, consuming coffee, half-listening to the birdhouse chatter and rush he had missed for so very long. But he understood, gradually and reluctantly, that this was the day on which a new life began—in earnest. First there was Vinnie on the telephone—apparently to a succession of people, and warmly voluble to each. This was Giving Notice; it lasted nearly an hour. And even then, as she explained afterwards, she would still have to go in for a while. But not today, of course. Because there was so much to do.

Cautiously amenable, he didn't inquire what. Time enough for that when he had to put shoes on; and experience suggested this would not be soon. They were just getting up steam now. Sure enough, the shoes didn't appear until late afternoon when they were all hungry and went out to eat, grandly, in a restaurant. By then he had assisted his daughter in the sorting and mending of all her possessions, reviewed and passed judgment on Vinnie's entire wardrobe (with special attention to what would be suitable for the West Coast and/or Canada) and agreed that the Mexico money had better go towards a station wagon to move their absolute indispensables with them.

"That way, we could afford a trip too," Vinnie said. "We could go up to Maine, or somewhere! Couldn't we?"

"Why not Canada?" he suggested. "Look the place over, if you like. Hell, we can go on out to the Coast afterwards, if we feel like it!"

Euphoria was catching; he had forgotten how much so.

By the evening of the third day real achievement had begun to quiet them (and real fatigue). The station wagon was bought—snatched, rather: a long, shiny black object parked almost directly under the apartment windows. A lot of time was spent in jockeying for such space, since Cressa liked to keep an eye on her new car.

She was at the window that evening, thoughtfully arranged upon her elbows in the last of the day's light. She could still observe, however, that the car looked rather dusty from up here.

"We'll dust it first thing tomorrow," said her father, reading. She murmured something else, which he did not hear. He had put his paper down, caught by some tone of Vinnie's, who had gone to answer the telephone. Another moment, and he got up and went out to her, in the little hall.

She was watching for him, with the slightly glazed look of strained attention; and said to cue him: "I really am so sorry, Aunt Cora. He's perfectly all right, we all are, he—we just forgot. I'm afraid it's all my fault ..."

At that point he took the receiver from her.

"Aunt Cora?" he said, more abruptly than he had meant to. "What's wrong?"

He got a long silence for that, of course ... he could see her bewildered expression, so far away, in the big and empty hall; and seeing it, his mind made its old effortless adjustment to compassion.

"I forgot to call you, didn't I?" he said. "Sorry, auntie. How are you all?"

"Why, we're all right, dear," his aunt said, faintly at first, but quickly reverting to normal. "Missing you, of course, and the baby. And it's so nice to hear dear Vinnie's voice again! You don't think she might like to come up for a little visit, do you? I mean, now that we have got someone her own age, for company?"

Since Vinnie was thirty-four and John O. Watson barely twenty-one, it took him a minute to make the connection. Then he laughed; he couldn't help it.

"How is John O.?" he said. "Still planning?"

"Well, he's gone to get his grandmother," she said. "Isn't that nice? But he'll be back very soon, even if she won't come, and I really think she will when she knows how much we're longing to see her. Don't you?"

That was rhetorical. He asked, "How's Millie?" and she said eagerly: "Oh, much better. It's just those migraines, you know—you just have to wait for them to pass. But she's quite all right now. You didn't," said Aunt Cora, delicate, "imagine it had anything to do with you, did you, dear?"

"No. I knew it hadn't."

"That's right. We know our Millie, don't we? Oh, and Louisa is here, she's taken a week to stay—so we could be quite a nice little party if you and Vinnie and the baby came. Do you think you might?"

"Well, we'll see," he said, incapable still of direct refusal. And slightly exasperated with himself, he added: "MacDonald's all right again, I suppose?"

"MacDonald? Oh. Oh, yes, I think so—but you know, we hardly see them anymore, Polly. It's so queer! Just Pete, bringing the—Oh, I'm supposed to tell you he wants to talk to you. He wanted me to give him your telephone number there, but I put him off, of course, and he said would I ask you to call him at the garage. He's such a *funny* boy."

"What does he want?"

"He didn't say, just that it was 'important'. Don't worry about it, dear— he probably just wants to sell you some dreadful old car. And I really don't feel we need go out of our way to oblige them, these days, when he and Jenny are behaving so peculiarly to us. And MacDonald too, MacDonald too. I know they've had a great loss, and all that—but after all, so have we," said his aunt, and began—disconcertingly—to cry.

He came back to the living room sobered, and met Vinnie's anxious glance.

"Nothing new," he said to it. "Just the same old thing."

"Are you—are we going up?"

"No," he said.

His unfinished paper didn't invite him. He looked down at it a moment, and then went over and picked his daughter off the window sill.

"Come on," he said, "say goodnight to it, and let's go to bed. Big day tomorrow."

They had settled by now to put Cressa into one of the twin beds and move her out when they retired—a semi-magical process which she enjoyed thoroughly, and which made bedtime practically painless. When he came out and closed the bedroom door, some half hour later, he saw that Vinnie was waiting for him—thinking, as he had himself thought, that he wanted to talk things over with her.

Yet he stood there, in a kind of surprise, finding that he had nothing much to say.

What was there to say? Things were wrong, in his old home—very wrong. As Vinnie said, they always had been. The only difference was that now he knew more about it. But the knowledge didn't change anything. At most he could still be, if he still wanted to, the person who stood by to pick up the pieces when the next explosion came; that was all he had ever been, wasn't it?

Polly, indeed.

Vinnie's small voice said, "Maybe you'd feel better if you just ran up there, alone, for a day? I wouldn't mind, really."

He sat down on the arm of her chair. Leaned and kissed her.

"What for?" he said. "Vinnie, I see I'm not capable of the instant reform I thought I was. But it isn't going to hurt you and Cressa any more, I promise you that. Maybe you can just think of it as my old wound, say, that throbs when the wind is in the east?"

But she wouldn't answer his smile.

"Oh, Paul … it's so *sad*, isn't it?"

It was.

Later that night, when Vinnie was in her bath and he had gone in to move Cressa, the telephone rang again. He got there fast; it was almost as though he had been waiting for it. But the rough, furtive voice wasn't what he had expected.

"Doc?" it said. "Is that you, Doc?"

"This is Pete, I suppose."

"That's right. Listen, Doc, when are you coming back here?"

An instant irritation, almost a rage, rose up in him.

"What do you care?" he said, cold. "And where did you get this number, anyway?"

There was a pause; then the hushed voice again, conciliatory.

"Now keep your shirt on, Doc," it said. "I don't bother you for nothing, do I. Did I ever?"

This time the pause was his. Reluctantly, at last, he broke it.

"Well, what is it?" he said; and could tell from the change in Pete's voice what change there had been in his own.

"Trouble," said Pete, prompt. Almost triumphant. "What else? And I think it's bad trouble this time. You better get up here fast, Doc—you get that midnight train, and I'll come and meet you. There won't be a soul around the station that time of night. How about it?"

"Certainly not," said Dr. Potter. "What's the matter with you? What are you talking about?"

"I'll tell you what I'm talking about when you get here," said Pete, dogged. "And you better come. It's you or the police, I'm telling you."

"Then you'd better call the police," said Dr. Potter.

Far away, perhaps with his eyes on the closed door of MacDonald's room, Pete could be heard unselfconsciously breathing. When he spoke again, his voice had become almost conversational.

"Now, this fellow didn't leave by any train, Doc," he said. "That I'll guarantee you. And he didn't leave in that Thunderbird because I know where that Thunderbird is, and it's hid good. What do you think of that?"

"I think you're drunk."

"And all his bags and stuff is in it. And another thing—you know that hypo thing of yours isn't where you keep it. And I know you don't take it along on no short trips. How about that?"

"You keep the hell out of my house," he said—words, like a pole to cling to. A greased pole.

"Yeah, well, I'm not the one that took it, and you know that. So you get that train, Doc, and I'll be down and meet you. With the Ford—you'll see it, and I'll be in it."

"Rot in it, then," said Dr. Potter, and hung up.

He knew where the Thunderbird was. Not for one sick, shaking moment did he doubt that it was there, bags and all. He could see it—it stood like a real memory in the shadows of that part of his mind, that lumberyard, which held all he knew, and would not know, and now would have to know at last.

A cry made him look up, and Vinnie stood staring at him, clutching her robe to her.

"Oh, my God, Paul—what is it?"

She ran to him, and he held on to her.

"Oh, darling—what is it? Is somebody dead?"

"Yes," he said, then. "Yes, I think so."

"You *think* so! What do you mean? Who was it?" she said, leaning back, bewildered. "*And who are you calling now?*"

"The police. State Police, I think. Yes, that'll be it."

He had the illusion of perfect clarity, so strong that his shaking stopped and he began to act—yet so wild an illusion that Vinnie put her hand over his without any hesitation at all.

"Darling, you don't know what you're doing yet," she said. "Come and sit down a minute—please!"

Then, somehow, he was sitting down, and his head fell forward into some supported blackness, and then that went by too. He could straighten up, put his head back, look into Vinnie's face.

That oriented him.

"It was Pete, Jenny's husband," he said. "Remember him?"

"Yes. Yes! What did he say?"

"He implied very strongly," said Dr. Potter, "that Millie has done away with her new cousin."

"You mean he's found his *body?*"

"Probably. And what he wants, of course, is for me to come up and help him conceal all the evidence, so that Millicent will not lose her inheritance, because she has promised to buy him a garage when she gets it."

"Oh, Paul," said Vinnie, after a pause. "What do you really mean?"

"Just that," he said.

There was a strangely idle period, in which Vinnie began to tremble, very strongly, and he drew her down into his lap.

"What can we do?" she whispered. "What can we do?"

"I don't know. It needs thinking about."

But for the moment he was not thinking. He was holding on to Vinnie, and his mind had been as though blown apart, and that was all.

She said presently, still whispering, "Couldn't we call up Millie?"

"To ask her if it's true?" he said gravely. She put her head down again.

After a while he sighed, and murmured: "Could you make us some coffee?"

"Yes," she said; and crawled off his lap, going like a slow child sent away, into the kitchen. He got up too and went quietly into the bedroom where Cressa still slept, and by the light of the open door found what he would need and quietly dressed.

When he came back Vinnie handed him his cup, and looked directly into his eyes.

"Are you going to help him hide it?"

"No. Oh, no. We're past those days, Vinnie."

"I'm afraid," she said. But he shook his head.

"That time's past too," he said.

When he was out of the house and alone, he realized what she had meant: that she was afraid for him. He was sorry he had not made her a better answer, and looked up and gestured to her, at the window, as reassuringly as he could.

But it was such a simple, clean way to be afraid, he could almost envy her that simplicity.

CHAPTER TWENTY

He could not think what she might have used in that hypodermic. All the way across Manhattan, guiding the still-unfamiliar car, his thoughts fretted and held to this useless wonder. Had she got hold of something, somehow, from Dr. Kennedy?

He turned into the highway, and into another wonder. How far would Dr. Kennedy go, for Millie? How far had he, in fact, already gone? For in the light of the truth about MacDonald, many of Millie's strange, unresolved relationships with men had become less strange to him. All Millie's sad suitors, who never quite succeeded or clearly failed—the men whom she would not marry, and yet needed and kept, for her allies, her supports, her *people*. In that unpeopled world where she lived ...

But he didn't need to put on that damned act by the fishpond, thought Dr. Potter, in one flash of bitterness. Who was it for—me, or himself?

It didn't matter. The time when it did matter had gone by, rather: he saw it, briefly, like a halcyon time lost forever and lying far behind them: the days when it was still not too late.

What should he have said or done? Where had he failed, in not forcing them to bear away from this direction ... this destination, where they now were. His thoughts went scrambling and groping in a hopeless hunt—picked up and threw down a hundred irrelevancies, couldn't begin to find the one, large, clear thing he needed. All those tentative and *polite* attempts to talk to people! To MacDonald, to Dr. Kennedy, to Aunt Cora. To John O. What a waste—a stupid, imbecile waste, all of it ... It was Millie herself he ought somehow to have reached.

They understood each other without words, they three. That was the tradition. The myth. How long had he known it wasn't true? That wordless linkage belonged to three children; and it was on the level of childish needs and perceptions that they had gone on using it and holding to it. Whatever part of each had grown up had grown up silent. As adults, they had no means of communication at all.

He and Millie—and Lou?—had said nothing to each other for nearly twenty years. Nothing that belonged to the real present. It seemed to him that they hadn't even tried. Perhaps they hadn't dared.

He was rushing through darkness now, far from the city. The mechanics of the car and the road no longer troubled him; and at one point, roused to a bewildered attention (horrified to find his cheeks wet), he found he had no idea where he was. But it didn't matter; he was somewhere on the road home. There was a part of him that wouldn't let him turn off it if he tried.

Nevertheless he settled grimly to pull himself together. What he had to realize—or else turn round and go back—was that he was coming as a stranger to intrude on desperate strangers. Compared to the women waiting somewhere on those dark acres, even Pete might be called a friend.

He put the accelerator down, and swept on.

When at last he turned up the familiar road—with its ugly gateposts and empty gatehouse—the dashboard clock told him it was only a little past midnight. He knew exactly where he was going, and made no detours. First, he had to know.

Past the dark gap that led to his own little house, past the Hall turnoff (with its standard lamp glowing weakly among leaves) and then straight and fast, down the stretch that led to the home farm and the lake. But he was not going that far. Halfway, he slowed and turned up the old, unlighted driveway to Long Acre.

It was a long driveway, but potholed and no longer planted to please. The house itself was not visible until the last turning, and then it leapt in view—enormous, menacing, totally dark. He drove round it to the back and stopped by the great carriage house—switched off his motor, and got out.

The silence that surrounded him was entire—the darkness engulfing. He hesitated, then reached in the car and turned off his headlights—their concentrated blaze was more hindrance than help. Instead, waiting a moment to receive vision, he added to it the milder gleam of a flashlight and walked up to the big doors. They were locked, as always. The whole carriage house was supposedly strongly locked, because of the several "antique" carriages, and the sleigh, and some of MacDonald's implements kept here too. (Was that what had brought Pete? No; nothing so legitimate, he felt sure.) But a smaller side door would yield entry to one who knew how. The estate children knew how.

Inside, picking his way through cluttered passages, he came back to the main, echoing vault of space and found there, at his light's first sweeping search, the Thunderbird. There had been no attempt to hide it beyond driving it inside and resetting the bolts on the doors. It contained exactly what Pete had said; no more.

Dr. Potter unfastened the bolts and set back the catch on the Yale lock. Then he went out into the night again and pushed the door roughly to.

Oddly enough, this immediate confirmation lessened his certainty. He felt a new confusion, and his heart beating more heavily, as though after all he had kept some hope of being wrong. He no longer felt sure of what he had to do; and for a moment or so did nothing—just stood there shining his foolish light upon the ground.

Hearing sound, he raised it. His cousin Louisa was standing like some forest creature at the edge of its rays.

He said dully, "Lou ..." and she began to come forward, an uncertain and slow approach. She had on jeans and pajama top, and her hair was wild.

She said, with extreme doubt, "Was that you? That car?" Then, looking past him: "The door isn't shut ..." He put the light off, abruptly.

"Where's that boy, Lou? Where is he?"

"Away," she said. "He's coming back."

They were a child's meaningless words, said like a lesson, with no attempt to convince. He turned and walked away, the torch hanging in darkness from his hand. He heard her go over to the carriage house doors and begin fumbling with them; but he made no attempt to interfere, and was soon out of earshot.

He had reached the house and was rounding it, following the dark walls, when he heard her coming after him. The slow, awkward run that meant Lou—that meant wait, and let her catch up.

When she came near enough to see him standing there, she stopped dead.

"Polly ...?"

He didn't answer. Her voice became almost timid.

"Polly, where are you going? Is that your car over there?"

A harsh voice that was his own spoke out then.

"Is Millie home? Do you *know* that she's home?"

"Yes. Of course."

She began again that slow, doubtful approach to him. "Why? Did you think she was here? She isn't."

She was close enough now so that he could reach out and grasp her arm—the solid, bony wrist around which his fingers would not close. It remained passive in his grasp.

"You go back and stay with her," he said. "Stay with her, and tell her to stay there. I'll come over as soon as I can, and I want you both there."

She said nothing; and he added: "Tell Millie that if she doesn't wait there for me—if you both aren't there when I come, I'm going to leave. And I won't be back. How did you get here?"

He heard her sigh. He felt her pulse, very slow, under his fingers.

"The woods path," she murmured. "John made them clear it."

"Go ahead, then. I'll come."

He dropped her wrist and turned away. She no longer followed him.

He was up on the terrace, down the row of French windows to the one with the loose rod—had worked this up, and was inside the house, before he became aware of Long Acre itself. Then the sense of place shut down on him, like the enclosed and stuffy darkness indoors. Only this was a sense of place divorced from time, and from any sense of his present personality. He was no longer himself entering a house, but a living consciousness whom the great mausoleum of Long Acre enclosed: a small spark of life in so much deadness: defying the dare, going alone into Long Acre at night.

It was very strong while it lasted, but it didn't last. A child's terror was little—comfortable, really—compared to what the grown mind could encompass. In only a few seconds his years and his despair came back to him, and he switched on his lamp and went out into the hall, indifferent to the shadows round him.

She had made no secret—to them—of where enemies should go. The game was serious; no one real was ever shut up there, even "to see how it would feel". And in the years when the game was serious, they had not had the power to shut anyone up—so that no faint glimmer of impossibility had ever lightened the darkness of that absolute threat. It remained completely awful, until the years buried it. Or seemed to.

Dr. Potter heard him shouting as he came down the last steps.

He broke into sweat, and began to run—to shout in answer, idiotically, for only one short passage lay between him and the wine-cave door. Then his bobbing light caught the hands frantically outstretched to him, and he reached out too—was seized and painfully held against the iron grille-work by one hand, and in his own abrupt silence heard the boy's ragged, sobbing breath.

"All right, John," he said. "All right ... *Are* you all right?" He shone his light through and then, embarrassed, withdrew it. "All right," he said again, foolishly. "Hang on—I'll have you out in a minute."

But John O. did hang on, literally, as if unable to let that flesh-and-blood hand go—even after, in shaky attempts at laughing, he began to apologize.

"... *Christ*, what a nightmare! I couldn't believe—I heard, I thought I heard ..."

"Yes, I know."

A new padlock, and a strong one.

"... you begin to feel your damned ears and eyes are on *stalks*, and nothing's real ..."

"I know ... Let loose, will you, John? I want to see—" But the first loosening was followed by a convulsive new grip, and the deeply embarrassed young voice managed to say: "Oh, hell—shake hands a minute longer, Paul ... it's damn fine ..." Then he made himself let go. "How about a—cigarette ..."

"Here. And matches. Don't light up for a minute." The frantic hand had been ice-cold. He moved away a little, throwing his light round, giving John time. "I haven't got a key ... What we need is something to give it a good whack ..."

The voice behind him went high again.

"Paul! Don't go away!"

"No. I'm here."

He came back and stood touching the grille, the light between them. A tire iron out of the car would do it, as soon as the boy was calm enough to leave. That wasn't yet. He said as matter-of-factly as he could, "What's it been—the whole three days?"

"Three nights. Two days. My God, Paul—when I think how I sat there and listened to you and didn't—"

"I wasn't warning you about anything like this. It wouldn't have occurred to me. Have you had any kind of drugs—hypo?"

"I don't think so. Unless it was in the water, but I don't think so."

"You had water? Food?"

In a harder voice, which Dr. Potter was relieved to hear, John O. said briefly: "Oh, the apartment was furnished when I moved in. There were half a dozen wine bottles—of water—on the racks, and a box of bread and cheese. And a pisspot. What more could a guy ask?" Dr. Potter said nothing. He went on: "The hell of it is, Paul, I still can't think of her as crazy. She knew what she was doing, every move. My God, she was cool!"

"And how did you come to move in?" Dr. Potter asked, barely audible.

"I walked in," said John O. bitterly. "To see if the rare old port was still okay. That rare old port I've been drinking ever since Jesus, even after she shut and locked the door I still didn't get it! You should have seen me standing here, all polite and dumb. 'Cousin Millicent ?' he says. 'Cousin Millicent?'"

"Yes," said Dr. Potter. "Did she answer?"

"Certainly she answered. What do you think she is—a barbarian?" He drew a sudden, audible breath. "Hunt up your weapon now, Paul. I'm all right. Only—don't be too long, huh?"

"What did Millie say to you, John?"

But with resurgent confidence, John O. was getting restless. "Oh, just that she thought I ought to spend more time here before I made up my mind. Get to know more about the family. What else? Listen, let's get me out of here and then hash it over, all right?"

"All right. I'm going up to the car for a tire iron, about five minutes. Keep the flashlight, I don't need it."

"Hell, no—you take it. I don't want you falling down and busting a leg now!"

"I won't. Think about being out. What are you going to do, when you are?"

John O. became very still.

"Does my getting out ... depend on the answer?" he asked finally. "No."

He had reached the stairs, when John O. flung after him: "Well, think about it, Paul! What would you do—that wouldn't make a public ass out of you?"

And then, fainter with distance, the young voice exploded after him: "God—I wish she was a man!"

Dr. Potter kept climbing, steadily following his light. His first rush of relief had drained away entirely; not an echo of that—or, indeed, of any emotion—remained in him. He was just a man going a long way in darkness, to get a tire iron. What lay outside that specific darkness he didn't yet try to see.

He finished the second flight of stairs, and pushed at the house door. When it didn't yield, he leaned his forehead against it, and became still.

Through the door, very doubtfully, Louisa's voice said: "Polly?" He didn't answer.

"Polly ...? Are you alone?"

"Yes."

He heard the key turn, and straightened a little. When the opening was large enough he passed through. His cousin stood close, a big shadow; he felt her trembling.

"I was afraid you'd let him out ..."

"Why? Isn't his sentence up yet?"

"Oh, wait—!"

He was ploughing ahead, mechanical and dour, but she caught hold of his arm—a considerable drag. He raised the light in a movement of pure exasperation, and saw that her face was almost unrecognizable—streaked and blotched with tears.

"Lou, what the hell are you doing here?" he burst out. "Go do what I told you! Go home!"

"Polly, I can't, I—"

She made one helpless gesture against the light, then no other. She was clearly almost at the end of her capacity—out of her element too long, he thought, and savagely desired a book to be thrust into her hands—to leave her there with it, and the flashlight, until he came back.

Instead he seized her wrist again.

"Come on. Stay with me, then."

She stumbled after him through the dark and sheeted rooms, out into open night. He stopped there and took a breath, of his own element.

"Did you know he was down there all the time?" Anger was beginning to stir in him, a welcome return, and she heard that.

"Please listen, Polly—please don't let him out yet—!"

"Oh, come on," he said, and started forward again. But she would not move with him. Nor could he budge her.

They stood linked, opposed, a moment longer. He saw that the stranger he had surmised was here, was Lou—and another stood in his place and was himself. He found nothing to break their strangers' silence.

It was Lou who spoke at last, very low.

"Vinnie gave you that car. You're going away with her ..."

She freed her wrist in one turn and left him, breaking into her awkward, loping run, going across the terrace and then the lawn, towards the woods path to the Hall.

He went around to his car and got the tire iron. When he came back the French window stood as he had left it. He went in, back through the ghost rooms, to the doorway to the cellars. That key he took; and with the iron struck at the bolt until it was useless; and went on down.

CHAPTER TWENTY-ONE

Where do you want to go?" Dr. Potter asked, as he followed John O. out on to the terrace.

He got no reply for a moment. The young man's flow of rather nervous volubility broke off as he stepped out of doors; and when Dr. Potter joined him he was just standing and looking round.

"You know," he said, "It's odd, but Millicent has really given me rather a tremendous experience without meaning to. I mean, I feel that I've at least had a glimpse of ... myself, and ... others that I might have gone all my life without even approaching."

Dr. Potter made no reply. He was past the age for this sort of emotional see-sawing; and besides he suspected young John of beginning to ego-soothe. For which, God knew, he couldn't be blamed.

"I think an awful lot of really necessary experience is of a kind that you wouldn't voluntarily undergo. Don't you?"

Dr. Potter began to feel his own silence as lumpish. He growled out, "Unless you just want to get the hell away from here, you can stop in and use my place. Your things seem to be all right, in your car."

John O. laughed.

"You mean you're standing to windward of me? All right," he said. "I would like to clean up. And then"—with care—"I think I will go and pay a little call on my handsome cousin."

They started round the house, John O. in no apparent haste, Dr. Potter keeping step with him.

"You wouldn't believe the evolutions of mental revenge I've gone through in just three nights and two days," said John O., pacing. "At first, naturally, I was going to throw the book at her—and the hell with the newspapers. Then I got a little more cunning, and played round with lunacy commitments. Aunt Cora would be a sitting duck, there. Then around the second night it occurred to me that a very pretty retaliation would be, simply, to go ahead and jive the place up. But really. Make it into a sort of country club. A good, long, determined effort to cheer poor cousin Millicent up. Who wouldn't have a red cent to get away, of course. You wouldn't believe how I enjoyed building that one." He looked sidewise. "Are you shocked?"

"Not by you, John."

They came to the carriage house, and the big doors were locked again. Dr. Potter sighed, and started round. Behind him John O.'s voice was quieter.

"Of course, at the back of my mind, there was always—was I going to get out at all? I guess that was why I hung on to the idea of how sane cousin Millicent was. I had to."

He waited, and then started to follow through the coachmen's door. Dr. Potter reached back and stopped him.

"Go round front. By the big doors. I'll open them."

John O. seemed not to understand, or to have heard.

"What do you think, Paul?"

"About what?"

His voice cracked, but John O. didn't notice.

"About what—she meant. To do."

With great control, Dr. Potter said evenly: "That is something you will have to take up with Millicent. Go round, John."

After a moment, John O. said, "All right," and turned away. Dr. Potter shut the door and put his back against it. Then he shot his torch beam out in what, before, had been a random sweep of light.

It was still there.

How had he missed it, the first time through?

He went over and knelt down, saying "Pete" without reason, or much sound. Those eyes held no more capacity for response. In a frenzy, then, as if his hands could trap and recover what so recently was there, he moved and felt and even shook the sprawling body. Then all at once he abandoned that, and stood up.

John O. had begun to pound on the big door. "Hoy—Paul! Paul!"

The pounding stopped, quite soon; he would be coming round here again.

Fast, stumbling in darkness—the torch had fallen somewhere—Dr. Potter got to the carriage doors and found the lock. It had simply been re-sprung; the bolts were open, and the door itself swung back while he was unprepared, so that he half-fell with it. John O. came back in time to catch at him.

"I thought you busted that leg for sure. You all right?"

"Yes."

"Sure? You seem—"

"Now there's your car," he began, with a terrible loudness; and then couldn't go on.

John O. came closer to him.

"Hey, what is it?" he said—and then, gentler, perhaps with some satisfaction, he made his discovery. "Why, you're just about out, fellow! Come here and sit down a minute—"

Dr. Potter said, "I'm all right. Go on."

"Sure," said John O., not moving. "Sure, Paul. Except that what you've got is a very fine case of delayed reaction, you know that? Now just hold it a minute," he said. Dr. Potter held it. "Lord, I'm sorry! I never thought ... You've been so damn calm, I just took it for granted that you were all right. But I can see this must be worse for you than for me, in a lot of ways. I mean, I suppose they're really your responsibility—or you'd feel they were, somehow?"

"Oh, shut up," said Dr. Potter. He had begun, beyond hope of hiding the fact, to shake. "Go on. Will you?"

"Sure," said John O. "Sure."

He moved, with maddening slowness, towards his car. Time—

quantities of it—went by, before the sleek car began slowly to back past him. It paused.

"Listen, Paul—why don't you ride down with me, and then—"

"You get the hell out of here," said Dr. Potter. "Now."

He stolidly watched—almost could see, John O.'s slow grin.

"Brother, you're a hard case. All right." The car slid backwards again. "I'll meet you at the Hall in half an hour. Tell 'em hello for me."

Eventually, he left. Silence succeeded him, and the renewed dark.

"Lou!" said Dr. Potter suddenly.

He pushed the door wider—struck it back, hard—and went into the great vault. They used to come here and yell, once, long ago. He yelled now: "*Lou!*" and "LOU!" and the vault poured it back on him—a solitary man's voice, yelling.

He turned and went out, striking whatever he passed, striking hard, striking the big door again, last, and leaving it wide behind him.

He was into the woods path before he remembered the new car and went back for it.

The Hall was in total darkness. He used his key and went in the front door, turned on the light, and ran up the wide staircase. A small lamp burned quietly in the upper hall, and by its light he kept on going, until light was lost down there behind him.

Her door was open; all those high windows gathered enough glow, even in moonless air, to show him the ordered, octagonal emptiness of her room. But he went round, whirling chairs to face him, senselessly throwing pillows to the floor—and out again. And down.

She was halfway up the lower staircase and stopped when she saw him. Her long hair was down and she wore a raincoat belted over her nightgown; he had interrupted her in some hurry, or excitement, of which she meant to tell him nothing.

"Where's Lou?" he demanded, from the top of the stairs. She didn't answer, and he came down, savage and quiet.

"She's killed someone else," he said, into her still face. "For you. Do you know that? Do you even care?"

She said steadily, "You're the one who doesn't know or care—anything about us. You don't belong here anymore, Polly. Any more than that boy. Both of you had better go."

He stopped her forcibly when she made to go past him—an indignity that made her long eyes blaze.

"Listen, you madwoman," he said between his teeth, "this private party of yours is over—try to understand that! It isn't MacDonald or Dr. Kennedy I've got to call this time, it's the police—and if you've got any love or mercy for your sister at all, you won't let them come here and find her wandering round with a—a hammer in her hand, or whatever the hell she hit him with! *Where is she?* By God, Millie," he said—and his hands upon her told her what he meant, her closing eyes acknowledged and understood—"you tell me where Lou is, or I'll—"

She could not, of course, have spoken at all then. And when, in terror at himself, he roughly let her go, she still made no sound or motion. But her eyes gleamed at him steadily.

"You *are* mad, Millie," he muttered, not even to be heard. But she heard; and with one sideways glance of total contempt, defining his total defeat, she went past him and on up the stairs.

He went down.

It was between Lou and himself, then, where he would find her. Where he would *know* to go and find her. It was not Millie but his own boy's mind that would tell him where to find his cousin now.

But his memory said nothing. Every place he thought of seemed equally probable—and there were so many of them, so many. He stood, listless, by the telephone which was dead. He felt a faint surprise that Millie should have stooped to so trivial, so conventional a dodge and knew that the old line between Lou and himself was dead too.

Because the Lou he sought had no counterpart in their past with the exhausted, terrified woman who roamed the estate now, or cowered in some corner of it. Nor was he much kin to the boy he had been. Exigency had changed them; only where Millie was concerned did the old certainties remain, because Millie herself never changed, nor acknowledged any part of them which did.

Listless still, in some fatigue of horror, he got in the new car and started for the farm. It was all the same. He would have had to go there anyway, to tell Jenny—and MacDonald—before the police arrived. To wait with them. Halfway, in sudden illumination, he realized how much Millie had wanted to get past him and go upstairs. That was all their encounter had meant to her—obstruction. But why? Lou wasn't up there ... was she?

Then light flicked at him again—real light, at the corner of his attention, and he stopped the car. The windows. The great, high, octagon of windows where nothing would hide from her view what was still obscure at ground level: the fire in the carriage house. A fire well along now, or he would not be able to see it from this road.

He had a moment of total indecision. Because of Lou. But if Lou were there, it was already too late—and she wasn't. She wasn't, she couldn't be—no more than Millie herself. There was no *reason* to destroy Lou. Only Pete.

He put his hand on the horn of the new car and left it there—blaring wildly all the rest of that ride. The farm door flung open as he came up to it, and he leaned shouting into Jenny's face: "The carriage house at Long Acre—it's on fire!"

Well trained, she was at the telephone by the time he got in the house. MacDonald emerged from his bedroom, dragging on pants.

"How far along, boy?"

"Going hard. Give me the key, and I'll—"

"It's no' lockit. Jenny, the crofts too. Hurry, lass."

They had their own mounted chemical tank, in one of the out-buildings. It was not meant for great conflagrations; but it was something to begin with. He had backed the Ford to receive its shaft by the time MacDonald came out, and together they wheeled the tank into place.

"That damn' Pete," MacDonald grunted, "never round when he's needed. Where would a married man be this time of night if he's not home? —tell me that."

The yellow car was nowhere here that Dr. Potter could see, nor had he noticed it near Long Acre. But when they came racing up to the great house, all illumined now, it showed plain enough—run up against the bushes, where a deeper dark had been.

MacDonald saw it too, with a hard grunt.

"So it's his doing," he said; and Dr. Potter answered then: "He was in the harness room, dead, before the fire began. I saw him there."

In the stopped car, as if they had only come to watch, MacDonald turned and looked at him a long time. "Where's Millie?" he asked at last.

"Safe at home. It's Lou I can't find."

They still did not get out. There was, in truth, little the two of them and their tank could do now; but it was not in MacDonald's nature to accept that.

He began to back the car.

"Those walls will be down," he observed. "All's lost in there, Paul—it's the trees in back we must look to now."

The mild wind favored the house, but acres of woodland and field lay in the other direction, summer-dry. It was there, as the others arrived (crofters with shovels and spades; the volunteer fire companies of the district) that the real fight began. The carriage house itself was, as MacDonald had said, lost; its walls were of stone, but the entire inner framework and partitioning was ablaze and the stone itself not safe to go near, under so much pressure of heat. Yet close in, where the trees made their approach—as if determined to yield not one of these without battle—MacDonald fought alone.

No one joined him, nor did any of the organized line interfere with his choice. His great, vigorous figure was visible ahead of them from time to time, but no one shouted to it. At the first sag of stone Dr. Potter heard one scream somewhere behind him, from a man's throat—then several hoarse cries, as the wall monstrously buckled and seemed almost to explode. But among these men who knew him so well belief was slow—incredulity most strong, in his being a part of that disaster. They could not believe in the failure of the long legend that had been MacDonald.

Nor could Dr. Potter. What he saw, and at last knew that he saw, was the terrible success of a man who no longer wanted to survive.

CHAPTER TWENTY-TWO

"If you are waiting to see Millie," said Dr. Kennedy's tired old voice, "you can go up for a minute now."

In morning light, in the unbroken quiet of the Hall, Dr. Potter looked up as he might have done to a genuine apparition—and with no more impulse to reply.

"I know you're tired, and it's a long way," the doctor went on wearily, "but I think you had better go. She is feeling very much alone, Paul."

He moved MacDonald's bottle of sour mash whisky towards himself as he spoke—an undoubtedly human action, which stirred Dr. Potter to reply.

"She intelligently ... assesses the facts," he said clearly.

Dr. Kennedy looked at him, and sat down.

"What is it?" he said then. "Do you blame her, for Lou?"

Dr. Potter said "Excuse me," and took the bottle back. As an afterthought he added, "Yes."

"Then you will agree. She blames herself."

Dr. Potter acknowledged this in polite silence, as if it were an interesting statistic on Triobriand Islanders.

"She feels that she should have brought Lou back here with her by force, if necessary. It seems that Louisa was very much afraid of meeting you. And Mr. Watson. She had a healthy sense of guilt, you know—that girl. Something poor Millie would not be able to achieve."

Dr. Potter, head down, made no comment once more.

But some movement of his hands must have betrayed those still unstupefied areas of his mind, which the old man continued to address.

"That makes it impossible for her to understand why Louisa should ever have gone back inside the carriage house, you see. To Millie, it's not conceivable that Lou should have been unable to give up that evidence of her own guilt, and watch it be destroyed—even though she had helped to set the fire that would destroy it. Or if you find that fanciful," said Dr. Kennedy simply, "perhaps she was only afraid he might not really be dead. She certainly hadn't meant him to die. I understand she only struck him once, with her torch, when she came on him suddenly."

It was a long time since Dr. Potter had put his hands over his ears. He didn't now, although the impulse was there. Instead he straightened up and looked Dr. Kennedy in the face. The old man seemed relieved to see him.

"Can't you go up, Paul? Only for a minute."

"I will kill her if I do," said Dr. Potter distinctly. "Don't you understand that? You seem to be clear about everything else."

He pulled himself to his feet, and leaned on his hoisting arms to stare down into the anxious face below.

"Does Millie always confide in you this way, Dr. Kennedy?" he asked. "What did she say to you after her father died? And what was the purpose of that song and dance out by the fishpond? *Did you have to do that?*"

His voice broke; and Dr. Kennedy reached out a hand to him.

"Sit down, Paul—sit down," he said, pulling at his sleeve. He watched anxiously until Dr. Potter, discovering he had no choice, obeyed; then he took his hand back, with a deep sigh.

"You had better go ahead and talk to the police," he said. "As long as this passes for three fire deaths, you will never be able to forgive Millie. Or yourself, I don't know. I don't really know about these things," he said humbly.

He allowed Dr. Potter his silence then, and this extended—perhaps each of them thinking, with equal longing, of the police still helpfully stationed in their grounds, where the diminished fire was not yet entirely defeated. John O. was somewhere there now, where it ate its slow way along—a young man revived by uncomplicated action, and gladly leaving the Hall and its inmates to Dr. Potter.

"Or perhaps you feel you cannot, because of your aunt," said Dr. Kennedy after a time. "And poor Jenny, of course."—Speaking of them together since they were together, two utterly crushed survivors, of about equal capacity to understand what had happened to them.

Dr. Potter said honestly, "No, it isn't that."

"Then what, Paul?"

"I don't know, Dr. Kennedy. All I have in my mind is Lou, the last time I saw her. You didn't see her then, you don't know. Why was she at Long Acre at all? Why did she *have* to be there? Why wasn't Millie guarding her own hell-brew," he said, savage then, "instead of leaving poor Lou to do it?"

"Don't imagine that she did," said Dr. Kennedy at once. "Don't make things worse for yourself, my boy. No," he went on, "it's the same business we spoke of before, you know. Millie had no idea of keeping watch over that unfortunate young man. He was safely shut up, he deserved to be shut up, and he would stay shut up until she got ready to let him out— that was Millie's view of it. But Louisa was terrified by what her sister had done. She couldn't keep away from the place. I saw her yesterday, and I know what her condition was."

"And did you also know why?"

"No, Paul."

He said presently: "You asked me about the night your uncle died. I've wanted to talk to you about that. I want to tell you now that I still feel there is no evidence at all that his death was anything but the accident it seemed to be."

"Did you ever look for any?"

"I looked," said Dr. Kennedy, "where I felt most certain of finding my answer. I saw both Millie and Lou, at once."

With an awakening pity, Dr. Potter listened to the old man—who spoke so certainly, and so uncertainly touched at his glass, his cuffs, his own hands, while he spoke.

"Of course we know," he said, "that there was that curious ... blunt streak in Louisa. She had disliked—perhaps she had more than disliked her father, for many years, and she felt quite justly that he stood very much in Millie's way."

"A point I had just driven home to her, the night Uncle Humphrey died."

"Yes," said Dr. Kennedy. "We have to think of all these things. I believe I have done so. And I still feel that the actual deed, no matter how impulsive, would have left an obvious mark on her. Obvious to me, at any rate. There was none. None."

What use was it, to say any more now? It was all so far in the past. So buried there.

"Louisa," said Dr. Kennedy, going doggedly on, "had a very strong and healthy instinct in her, you know. Towards normalcy, I suppose you might call it. She knew from the first, as my poor Millie never did, that she could find nothing in her home that wasn't warped. Nor could she leave it, as you were able to do when you went away to school. So she turned to books, and they made a little island of ... understanding; intelligent understanding, for her to stand on while she grew. And as soon as that little island provided a—a bridge to the mainland, she took that. In her own patient way, Louisa was working her way into the wide world, you know. And she belonged there."

Listening (with his heart, maybe, more than with his reason) Dr. Potter felt no impulse to disagree.

He said gently, "You loved Lou."

"Very much, Paul. And so did you. And Louisa loved us in return, she was very capable of it." He said, a little slower, "Not so much as she loved her sister, of course."

"No."

"I watched Louisa, when she went away. I wanted to see what change the world would make in her. I had great hopes for her, you know. But in one way she was not as lucky as you, Paul. She was not ... an obviously attractive girl, I suppose. And she was so shy. Well, however it was," he said, "no one seemed to come along who wanted that love she had to give. And so it stayed with Millie."

"You mean Millie kept it, don't you?"

The sudden bitterness surprised them both, breaking out again. Dr. Kennedy looked at him with some sternness.

"I think you could be more generous than you are, Paul. She didn't keep yours."

"Didn't she?"

"No; and if you don't know it, I do. So did Millie. Millie hasn't been in your heart for a long time, my boy—only on your conscience. I admit she clung rather hard to that ... but can you blame her for it?"

"I blame her only for Lou. Only for Lou. And not just last night," he

said, getting up. "But for all those years ... those *years*, of loading Lou
up with her own desperations and urgencies ... As if Lou really were
some poor camel," he burst out, "who would just stand there and take
the load without any idea of defending herself. As long as she could."

He stood at the window, looking blindly out. Not moving, even when
at last he heard the old doctor getting up behind him.

"Yes," he said, like a sigh. "There's truth in that too, of course."

He went out of the room. Dr. Potter let him go.

Then, from the doorway, he spoke again.

"Oh, Paul ... stay on a while, will you? Until I can send someone up."

"Yes, of course," said Dr. Potter then; and came out of his corner. He
accompanied the old doctor out into the hall. "I'll go up," he said.

"You needn't. She'll be asleep now."

He put his black bag on the hall table and opened it.

"I must give you back your syringe," he murmured.

When it was in his hand, Dr. Potter could say: "Millie had it, then?"

"Yes."

"Who was it for? And what was she going to use?"

"Oh, air," said the old man. "Just air ... for herself. She read somewhere
an air bubble would stop the heart, if you could get it in the right
passage."

"Oh, God. She didn't—?"

"No, no, of course not. She'd made a complete mess of it, and of course
I wouldn't help her."

He turned round then, his bag refastened and hanging at his side—a
matter-of-fact old man with tears running down his face.

"You don't think I would let her fumble her life away like that, do
you?" he asked. "Our beautiful Millie ...?"

He stood at the screen door a moment, wanting to find the catch; and
then found it, and went out of the house.

THE END

Made in the USA
Middletown, DE
01 April 2024